Jasmine
NIGHTS

Jasmine NIGHTS

S. P. SOMTOW

ASIA BOOKS

Published and Distributed by
Asia Books Co. Ltd.,
5 Sukhumvit Road Soi 61,
PO Box 40,
Bangkok 10110,
Thailand.
Tel: (66) 0-2714-0740 ext. 3202–4
Fax: (66) 0-2714-2799
E-mail: information@asiabooks.com
Website: asiabooks.com <http://www.asiabooks.com>

First edition published by Hamish Hamilton, 1994
Second edition published by Penguin Books, 1995
Third edition published by Asia Books Co. Ltd., 2001

Typeset by COMSET Limited Partnership
Printed by Darnsutha Press Ltd.

ISBN 974-8303-53-5

*This novel is affectionately dedicated to
my four grandparents:*

*K. Thow and Prapaipis Subhavanich
Phra Phibul Aisawan and Sobha Sucharitkul*

and to the memory of my great-aunts:

*Phra Sucharit Suda and
Somdej Phranangiao Indrashakti Sachi, late Queen of Siam*

Contents

Dramatis Personae

Justin's Household

Sornsunthorn, known to his family as "Little Frog" and to himself as "Justin", a twelve-year-old Thai boy.

Homer, a chameleon.

Ning-nong, Nit-nit and *Noi-noi*, his three aunts, often referred to by Justin as the "three Fates"; he also calls them *khun aah*, an honorific title meaning "younger sibling of my father."

Justin's great-grandmother, often referred to as *khunying*, a minor title of nobility.

Vit, his uncle, a gynaecologist (also a *khun aah*).

Samlee, a maid, later Vit's concubine.

Kaew, a maid.

Piak, the gardener's son.

Piak's father, the gardener.

Piglet, Justin's great-uncle, the family patriarch (often referred to as Justin's grandfather owing to the difference in Thai kinship terms).

Piglet's wives and *concubines*.

Justin's parents, who are usually somewhere else.

Justin's Friends

Virgil O'Fleary, the boy next door.
Renée, Virgil's mother.
Jessica, his sister.
Dr. Richardson, the family doctor, a rake.
Griselda, his daughter.
Piet van Helsing, an Afrikaner.
Wilbur Andrews, an American.

Justin's School

Mrs. Vajravajah, a teacher.
Miss Cicciolini, a science teacher.
Father Regenstrom, a Catholic priest and musician.
Dr. York, the headmaster.

Da stieg ein Baum. O reine Übersteigung!
O Orpheus singt! O hoher Baum im Ohr!
Und alles schwieg. Doch selbst in der Verschweigung
ging neuer Anfang, Wink und Wandlung vor.

Rainer Maria Rilke

1

Death of a Chameleon

It is January of the year 1963 and I am a creature of two worlds. In one of these worlds I am a child. The world is circumscribed by high stucco walls topped with broken glass. By day the sun streams down and the mangoes glisten in the orchard behind the blue Gothic mansion with its faux Corinthian columns, the house of my three grandmothers and of our familial patriarch. Evenings, the jasmine bushes bloom, and the night air sweats the choking sensuality of their fragrance. Three other houses stand on the estate: my bachelor uncle's, uncompromisingly Californian in its split-level ranch style and adobe brick walls; the wooden house of my three maiden aunts, whom I call the three Fates, with its pointed eaves, backing out on to a pavilion above the pond, where I live among intimate strangers; and last, the ruined house, which is the entrance to my other world.

In my other world I am not a child. I am what I choose to be. I speak the language of the wind. I have synthesized this world out of images in history books and story books and books of poetry and from half-remembered scenes of England. It is cool in this world. A balustrade can be a stepladder to Olympus where I stand and look into the eyes of Zeus, who bears a remarkable resemblance to Finlay Currie, the white-maned St. Peter from *Quo Vadis*. A marble foyer draped with cobwebs is the Roman Senate, and from behind the arras I can hear Hamlet whispering to his mother, and Clytemnestra pleading with Orestes for her life. There is a room with as many books as there are stars. There is an attic where I have fought the Trojan War a thousand times over, fine-tuning the outcome with my fellow Olympians. There are more rooms in the ruined house than I have ever counted. There are tapestries and busts of forgotten people, and cobras that slither through century-old piles of laundry.

I have lived inside the walled universe for almost three years. Travel in and out of the universe is accomplished by means of a silver-green Studebaker driven by a man in a khaki uniform, whose name I have still not learned. I am an alien here. I sweat like a pig all the time. I forget to bathe. I have never uttered a word of the language; my tongue will not form the words, even though over the years I have begun to grasp their meaning. My numerous relations do not know I understand them, and they address me in a stilted Victorian English, which I refer to as "*eaughing*", since it so frequently makes use of the phoneme "*eaugh*". Some of the servants have begun to realize I am not deaf; they regard my refusal to speak Thai as an eccentricity, one of the many inscrutabilities of the privileged. They call me Master Little Frog. My secret name is Justin.

I have not seen my parents in three years. There is a photograph of them beside my bed. They are standing in front of a snowbank. It is England, or perhaps Canada. They are waving to me. It is a smudgy photograph, taken with a Kodak Brownie from the steps of a Caravelle jet plane. The frame is exquisite—black lacquer inlaid with Vietnamese mother-of-pearl, with an intagliate rendition of our family crest, a design of mating *nagas*. I am not entirely sure what has caused me to be separated from them or why I have been shipped to the walled universe. Sometimes I think I am to blame. Sometimes I think they are on a secret mission in Russia, spying on an atom bomb plant under the guise of mink-farming Siberian peasants. Sometimes I think they have gone to Mars, where they are doing reconnaissance work for the American president. I have written a poem, over two hundred stanzas long and still unfinished, in which I enumerate all the places where they might be; I keep the poem inside a box of blue marble whose lid is a three-dimensional reproduction of Botticelli's *Venus*. One of the three Fates brought it back from Italy last summer. The marble box is my most precious possession, along with a portable Hermes typewriter that once belonged to Rupert Murdoch.

Here's a slide:

A closeup of a set of false teeth, floating in a glass of water on a shelf next to the bathroom sink. They belong to Samlee, my nanny, my secret beloved. Samlee sleeps on a straw mat at the foot of my bed. Before she goes to sleep she sits and fans me with a bamboo fan, and she tells me stories about disembodied heads that crawl along the garden paths at night, dragging their slimy guts behind them. She does not know how frightened I am because she does not think I understand.

The beauty of this nanny is not easy to describe. She is not quite sane, and she is middle-aged, and I have seen her sleepwalk into the garden sometimes and stand in the moonlight unkempt and half-clad, her visage white as death from the perfumed powder with which she paints her face each night. On such occasions she mutters to herself in a dialect I cannot understand. Perhaps it is because she has left her teeth behind.

The glass of water is empty all day long. But in the small hours, as she snores, her betel nut breath mingling with the jasmine that wafts in through the wire mosquito netting of the windows and the disquieting odour, a little like *nam pla*, that arises from her cotton *panung* somewhere to the south of her silver belt-chain . . . in the small hours when I creep into the bathroom for my late-night date with Homer or Euripides, I often look up from the *Harvard Classics* and see the false teeth glimmering in the half-light. The bathroom is also the residence of my pet chameleon. The Homer is bound in a red so bright he cannot quite accomplish the transformation. I let him run up and down my leg while I accomplish the ostensible purpose of my visit to the bathroom. A *tukae* barks in the distance.

My chameleon, too, is Homer, though he's too stupid to know his own name. I pick him up and drop him on a twig in the terrarium. Banana leaves brush against the bathroom window. I don't dare open the window to get a banana because I'm afraid of letting in the mosquitoes.

I tiptoe to bed and wrap myself around my side pillow. I close my eyes. The false teeth dance in my head. They chatter. The walls of Troy are crumbling.

They are crumbling in the ruined house. I have wound a silk curtain around my skinny shoulders, and I rage up and down the stairs. I am the fire sweeping through King Priam's palace. I am the wooden horse ramming the Cyclopean walls. I run down corridors, brandishing the plastic sword I received from my father Zeus.

I'm in the temple where Priam prays with his withered arms embracing the altar. The Greeks are charging. Their bronze boots smash against the flagstones. A sword flashes. The king's head flies through the air. What sacrilege! What gross impiety! I am the flame that follows the head as it rolls downhill, the furious flame, the eater of cities. Homer, on my shoulder, holds on for dear life.

But now the fire is out of control. I do not know where I am. I have turned a corner, opened a door that has always been locked before. I freeze. Troy fades. I am not alone.

This room is not like the others. An electric fan stands in one corner, swivelling from side to side, dragging the cobwebs with it. Silk curtains are tightly drawn, permitting no light save that of a naked bulb that sways a little. There is a low table surrounded by triangular cushions, and on the table are a mortar and pestle and a silver *phaan* piled with leaves and betel nuts. There is an enormous leather armchair in the room. It rocks. It faces away from me. Poking up from behind the chair's high back is a tuft of silvery hair.

There is someone there. The light bulb sways. My shadow sways. The cobwebs sway in the wind from the electric fan.

I have seen *Psycho* fifteen times. I have visited the fruit cellar of the Bates house in my dreams. I know what is to be found in leather armchairs in abandoned houses. I feel my heart stop beating.

Will the armchair suddenly whip round to reveal the mummified corpse of Norman Bates' mother? I step back. My Homeric drapery slides to the floor.

"Who is there?" The chair has not moved. The voice is as ancient and gravely as the stones of Troy. It speaks in Thai. "Come on, who is it?"

Before I can stop myself, I say, "It's me, Norman."

The tuft of silver hair shifts. The chair rocks. The room is black and white. Black and white. I have seen *Psycho* fifteen times but I have never seen it quite this close before. I step back, slam the door, run down the corridor, stand at the top of the stairs breathing in spasms and clutching my breast with my eyes squeezed tight shut.

When I open my eyes again there's colour. The floor of the foyer is pink marble. The weeds in the cracks are a ferocious shade of green. A celadon vase, taller than me, leans against the wall, which is luridly wallpapered with red and gold leaf. I blink a couple of times to make sure I've left the Hitchcockian universe far behind.

It was a fantasy, I tell myself. I put Homer on the lip of the vase and wait to see if he will turn the cold blue-green of the worn glaze.

Another slide:

The first day of the funeral. I do not know whose funeral it is. Every car on the estate has been commandeered for our convoy. It is an important funeral, because Aunt Ning-nong, the eldest of the three Fates, has personally supervised my bath, squatting on the toilet seat and barking out directions to Samlee as she applies the sponge. I never remove my underwear when I am being bathed by women, but when the moment comes for Samlee to hand me the sponge so that I can take care of my aubergine (as she coyly calls it) my aunt does not avert her eyes as does Samlee, thrusting the sponge at me and casting her gaze down at the floor as she kneels beside the tub, a pose that is not dissimilar to the picture of the nymph Europa about to be ravished by Zeus in the form of a bull in *Every Child's Picture Book of Greek Mythology*, whose every colour plate I have committed to memory; but I digress since I was actually talking of my aunt, who stares fixedly at me as I attempt to stuff the sponge down my underwear and take a few half-hearted swipes. . . .

Yes indeed, it is an important funeral. We will be in and out of it for seven days. A new suit has been ordered for me from the tailor, a white suit with long trousers that will chafe my ankles all week long and a black armband. I wear black patent leather shoes.

I share the front seat of the Studebaker with Samlee and the nameless driver. We move sedately through the gates, crossing the *klong* by way of a creaky bridge, threading our way through the labyrinth of *sois* toward the funeral site, some temple. My three aunts are in the back seat; despite being dressed in mourning, each has managed a dazzling display of décolletage.

Ning-nong stares out the window at a water buffalo. Their facial similarity does not escape me. I sit glumly between the two servants, my hand in my pocket and Homer in my hand.

Nit-nit, the number two, says, "Well, this has certainly cast a pall on the New Year. By the time it's all right to throw a party, no one will be doing the mashed potato any more."

"You never could do it anyway," says Noi-noi, the youngest. "You always step on everyone's feet."

"At least it's not the Madison," Nit-nit muses.

"Yes," says Ning-nong, whose thirty-one years give her pronouncements an unassailable authority, "you really made a fool of yourself at the American ambassador's Christmas party."

"You're all so boring," I say, "with your dances. I wish you'd left me at home."

"*Eaugh!*" the three of them exclaim in uncanny unison. Ning-nong adds, "Show some respect, Little Frog. It's not every day someone as important as"—at this point she mumbles the name and titles of the deceased, which go on for some time—"passes away."

"Yes, but why are we going for seven days?"

"Because, my recalcitrant nephew, the Visoksakuls are going for *six* days, and if we don't go for *seven*, people won't realize that we are more closely related to the dearly departed, even though it is only through the female line. . . ."

"But we're just going to be sitting around listening to a bunch of monks chanting for hours and *hours*. . . ."

"Oh, nonsense, Little Frog. The food'll be good."

The food is astoundingly good. On the first day of the funeral I never get anywhere near the place of honour, or the golden cone in which the body of whomever-it-was has been encased. We are ushered directly to a banquet-in-progress.

We proceed to a vast canvas pavilion that has been erected in a meadow inside the temple compound. The dinner tables are so long that one cannot see to the end of them. The repast is a twenty-course *toh chiin*, so our showing up *in medias res* is unlikely to leave us hungry by the end of the evening. As we arrive they are just bringing on the suckling pigs, thirty or forty of them, on silver platters, each one with electric lights in its eyes. If there is any chanting of mantras going on, it is somewhere in the distance, submerged in the gossiping of relatives; I am only subliminally aware that this is a sacred place. There are children running around everywhere. I resist the temptation to join them. I am afraid that when challenged I will not be able to speak.

I take the first vacant seat and find myself surrounded by the inhabitants of our family estate; it is as if I have never left the house. At the head of the table sits the patriarch of our family, my honoured grandfather, or, strictly speaking, great-uncle, who is only spoken of in whispers. To his left is Vit, my bachelor uncle, who was recently sent down from Cambridge but has managed to set up a gynaecological clinic on Sathorn Road. Opposite him are my three grandmothers (I should say one grandmother and two great-aunts, the one a sister of the patriarch, the other a number three wife going on two) who are methodically dissecting one of the suckling pigs.

The three Fates have not deigned to sit at the table; they are milling around, protesting about their diets, and Nit-nit is botching the twist. Where is Samlee? I wonder. But I know she may not enter this pavilion; there is another pavilion, conveniently out of sight but within summoning range, for the various attendants, chauffeurs and spear-carriers.

Uncle Vit expounds learnedly on the wonders of the female anatomy, and everyone at the table is spellbound. He is the only person not wearing one of these tailor-made white suits; on the other hand, he is a doctor, practically a holy man; his cowlick, five-o'clock shadow and horn-rimmed spectacles are the sigils of his sanctitude. I find him immensely boring, and I cannot follow his Thai, because he rarely utters a word that contains fewer than seven syllables.

I sit in silence for a while. I can be a very solemn child sometimes. Although I have no emotional connection with the deceased, I do not feel that levity is called for. After all, I reflect, the funeral of Hector was a grave affair, taking up the entire last book of the *Iliad*. Trying to disguise my greed behind the appearance of fastidiousness, I toy with my ivory chopsticks for about five minutes before allowing them to plummet toward the pig like a pair of Cruise missiles.

I stop short barely in time. Homer is resting on the suckling pig's back, nestled between two squares of crispy skin. For once, he has taken on the exact coloration of his environment. Furtively, I look for a way of directing my chameleon unobtrusively into my pocket. He starts to climb up my chopstick. All you can see is a head, because his torso has blended chimerically with the pig.

"My goodness," says one of the grandmothers, glancing my way, "isn't that a *jingjok*?"

"It most certainly is not!" I say. "That's Homer, my pet chameleon—"but I have no chance to finish because Homer has scampered off the edge of the tablecloth. Quickly I duck under the table.

It is another world. It is dark. White fumes curl up from a dozen dishes where coils of anti-mosquito incense smoulder. Here and there, an aluminium spittoon punctuates the row of legs—stately shapely columns that terminate in black stilettos. Grass peers through holes in the straw mats. A scrawny temple dog scratches and waits for alms. Where is Homer? There, there . . . weaving in and out of the forest of legs . . . I crouch down on all fours. I cup my hands over where I think he'll leap. I don't call his name. Chameleons never listen.

He's resting beside a shoe, about a size eight, shiny and black. A spiked crocodile-skin heel nuzzles the size eight. I creep closer. I almost have him. I hold my breath. Don't move, don't move.

Then, abruptly, there is music—a jangling heterophony of xylophones and gongs and wailing oboes. The size eight begins to tap in time to the music. It's going to descend on Homer. It's going to crush him. I make a grab. His tail comes away in my hand. His torso has been impaled on the crocodile spike. Before my grief can register, the leg has swung and hurled my chameleon into a spittoon.

I fly after it. My hand reaches into the spittoon and clasps the body of my chameleon. Homer expires. My hand touches something else, something hard and clanky. The smoke clears a little, and I see what it is. I recognize it at once, for it is achingly familiar to me from my long nights of immersion in the ancient classics. It is a set of dentures.

It is *the* set of dentures—for have I not memorized every rill, every ridge, every cusp and molar? I clutch the dentures and the dead lizard to my bosom. A feeling of utter desolation steals over me. My stomach is tying itself in knots, and I am on the verge of tears. I have never felt so alone.

At that moment, my sense of smell tells me Samlee is near. It's that heady smell of jasmine and *nam pla* that issues nightly from her nether garments. How is it that my true love has come to me here, in this secret world walled off by lace-trimmed tablecloths? I look up, and there she is. She is on her knees, and her arms are clasped firmly around the legs of Uncle Vit, whose trousers have somehow fallen about his ankles. Samlee, elder goddess of my secret pantheon, has her eyes closed and bobs her head up and down, and her lips are tightly wrapped around my uncle's gnarled and rampant aubergine.

An unholy terror seizes me. Fifteen viewings of *Psycho* have not prepared me for so outlandish a ritual. I am a castaway in an alien kingdom, my only friend in two pieces in my clenched fists. I cannot breathe. The mosquito incense chokes me. I'm drowning in the humid air. Desperate, I claw my way out between the legs of one of my grandmothers. For a second, glasses tinkle, lights dazzle, conversations buzz. My uncle is still holding forth on the virtues of gynaecology. Does he not know that my nanny has bewitched him, that she's sucking the life force from him like a *phii krasue*, a spirit of the night?

I duck through a canvas flap, and suddenly I am in a curtained-off inner pavilion. Women in black dresses sit on the mats in various poses of reverence. There is a single chair in the room, and on it sits a woman ancient and skeletal. A tuft of silver-white hair adorns her head. I know that hair. I look around. This is not black-and-white. This is not a movie.

I'm standing there with my dead chameleon in my hands. Oh God, I start to cry. It is the most appalling moment of my life. So far.

The ancient woman speaks. "Norman Bates, is it not?"

"I—I—"

"Come now. Come to me. You don't have to crawl if you don't want to. Are you surprised that I, too, withered as I am, have seen *Psycho*? Ah, but I was a spry eighty-nine when it came out. I could still get to the cinema." She coughs and then commands, with an imperious wave, "Betel nut *woay!*"

A servant scurries up to her with a tray.

"Come closer, Little Frog. You're the one who refuses to speak Thai, is it not?" She does not say "*Thai*" but "*bhasa khon*"—the language of human beings. "Ah, but you wince when I call you Little Frog. By what name do you call yourself?"

"Justin."

She cackles like the Wicked Witch of the West. "Justin! Now I've heard everything." She has switched to English. I become bolder. I approach her on my hands and knees, for it seems to be the custom. She wipes away my tears with a fold of her silken handkerchief. "Now tell your great-grandmother why you are crying."

"Homer is dead."

"Delicious! My, my, what a refined sensibility you have, my dear! But don't you think three thousand years is a long time still to be in mourning?"

I start to laugh. "No, no, Great-grandmother! I mean my pet chameleon." And I show her Homer's gory remnants. Seeing him like this sets me weeping again. "And furthermore, I've found out that my nanny is a *phii krasue*."

"A very tragic day indeed," she says with due solemnity. "But you must bring his body over to the ruined house, next time you come, and you and I will have a proper cremation. Otherwise his spirit will wander the earth, unable to be reborn into the cycle of karma."

"Oh, Great-grandmother, you *do* understand." I'm still weeping, but they are tears of pleasure as well as bereavement.

She spits her betel into a Ming spittoon. She takes my face between her palms, smoother than calfskin, and she says, "Little Frog, Little Frog . . . you must *give* a little more. You are so unbending. Here you are, twelve years old, and you do not even know your own name! And you have only one year left. One year to find out who you are." She picks at the gold threads in her *jongkabaen*.

"What do you mean, Great-grandmother?"

"You mean they haven't told you yet? That you're being sent to Eton when you turn thirteen?"

"Eton?"—I have heard of Eton. Eton is in my other world. The cold world. England. The place of the Olympians and the Norse Gods and the ancient Romans. My geography, you will note, is much of a piece with my perception of time. Suddenly I can feel the wind and the snow. I shiver.

"Now listen to me, my child. Contrary to what you may have led yourself to believe, you are not English. I know you are a creature

11

of two worlds"—I gasped at the millennial sagacity of one so able to divine these secret truths about me—"but the path you must take lies between them. Think of your chameleon. Perhaps his death is a sign. Perhaps it is you who must absorb his spirit now, my child, you who must learn to change your colour as you change your habitat . . . without changing the colour of your soul. If you don't learn this, I promise you that you will spend the rest of your life adrift, clinging to planks, without ever catching sight of land."

"So how is it, Great-grandmother, that you know so much? I don't think I've ever even met you before, and yet . . ."

"Well, Little Frog," she says, "we do have the same taste in movies." And, plucking the betel nut pestle from the tray, she begins to stab at the air and shriek "*Wheet! wheet! wheet!*" I begin laughing, and soon I'm bawling again, but this time it is sheer joy.

Another slide:

I'm dozing off in the Studebaker on the ride home. I hear the three Fates whispering.

"So, Samlee, you're being transferred to the brick house then?"

"So what is it you've done to attract the attention of the *khun phuchai*? You're not even pretty."

"Oh, but she has talents."

"Oh, shut up! That's nasty."

A slide:

I wake up in the night. She is sitting on the bed. She is idly rubbing my back, not knowing that I'm awake. She mumbles toothlessly to herself and to me: "Oh, Master Little Frog . . . oh, Samlee's angel . . . how I'm going to miss you . . . oh, it's terrible to be born into this world a lowly *khiikhaa* like me . . . oh, you can't know . . . life is suffering."

I open one eye. I quickly shut it again before she can see me. A single still after-image lingers behind sealed eyelids.

In the moonlight, in the jasmine-scented breeze, my beloved nanny weeps.

2

Downward into Limbo

Slides, slides, slides!

When you are twelve years old, life is not a movie that unreels relentlessly toward its dénouement, but a slide show: a compendium of perpetually frozen images, smells, sounds. The slides can be shuffled on the carousel, and you can linger on a favourite vista as long as you like, and you can fast forward through traumas and disappointments or go back and savour one picture over and over. But for each of us there is a definite moment when we realize that the non-linear has become linear; that the left brain has commanded the right to tone down its poetic blandishments; that time is huffing and puffing as it leaves the platform to turn to the south like the choo-choo train to Penang.

To some, this definite moment is an awakening, a call to adulthood. But it is also true that it is in this moment of a human life that reality begins and fantasy becomes mere fantasy.

That is why I am telling the story of the coming of that moment as though it were a sequence of slides. For though the train is ever accelerating (it is one of those Einsteinian trains, you see, and our metaphor is something in the nature of a thought-experiment) the slides are never lost. The frozen images are always there, if only we have the courage to look back, and the heart.

May I have the next slide?

I go to sleep in mourning; when I wake up I am not quite sure I am awake. I feel as though a ten-ton safe has landed on my chest, as happens so frequently in cartoons. My eyelids are jammed shut, and I try to force them open but I'm pushing against walls of darkness. I wonder if it is death. I wonder if I shall soon see Homer, my beloved chameleon, harp in claw, scudding above me on a cumulus cloud over the Elysian Fields. I try to imagine death, and I can only feel this monstrous thing crushing down on me, pushing up scream after scream from my abdomen, scream after scream that dies on my welded lips.

And then it's gone.

I open my eyes. The Chinese silk blanket is in a bundle at the foot of the bed. My side pillow is on the floor. Samlee is looking down at me as she dusts the marble box that contains my unfinished poem. It is morning, but already we are drenched in sunlight.

Samlee frowns. I say, "I felt—I can't describe it—a terrible *thing* squatting on my chest—"

She doesn't understand my English, and yet she knows exactly what has been troubling me. "Master Little Frog," she says, "you have been afflicted by a *phii am*. It's an imp that pins you to the bed. It feels like you're being squashed by an elephant." This is a perfectly matter-of-fact explanation to her, and she moves from dusting the box to polishing the lacquer frame of my parents' photograph. "I saw the *phii am* come down in the middle of the night. You'll soon be needing an exorcist, I expect."

I laugh as I spring out of bed. I love to hear about different kinds of *phii*. I jump up and down while I'm putting on my shirt. Yesterday—the funeral—the death of the chameleon—my accidental discovery of Samlee's propensity for witchcraft—those horrors belong to yesterday. I still believe in the plasticity of truth.

"Brush your teeth," Samlee cautions, never looking up from her cleaning.

I run into the bathroom. Homer is still in two pieces in the terrarium where I left him last night. The glass that nightly receives the dentures of my beloved is gone from its shelf. I remember the eyes of the old woman, sunken yet still full of laughter. Truth is not so plastic this morning.

I brush my teeth grimly. It is not something I do gladly at the best of times, but today I do it with the gritted determination of a medieval flagellant. I finish my ablutions and stalk off to breakfast. I am so full of rage that I don't even look at Samlee. She has no right to leave me.

Breakfast today is presided over by all three of the Fates. They are eating *khao tom* while I, Englishman manqué, wolf down my bacon and eggs in proud isolation at the far end of the *sala* that overlooks the pond. dragonflies buzz among the lotuses. My aunts are dressed in the regulation black, as befits their ostensible mourning, but they are cackling and carrying on at 78 rpm, paying little heed to me except for the occasional chiding from Aunt Ning-nong when I don't wipe my mouth or when I drop my fork on to the floorboards.

"Careful, Little Frog! You know very well this pavilion's a hundred years old—"

"And brought over piece by piece from Ayuthaya," I say. I've heard this before. What does a century-old piece of wood matter when my friends have been torn from me and my loved ones have turned out to be predatory supernatural creatures? I wash down my bacon with a swig of *nam manao*. The tart lime and the sugar and the salt combine to soften my insouciance.

The gardener brings in the battery-operated phonograph from the pantry. I roll my eyes. My aunts are twitching and twiddling their thumbs, and I have a feeling we are in for another morning of the latest dances. When the gardener's boy enters the *sala* too, glancing around uneasily as he removes his flip-flops and prepares to profane the pavilion with his shirtless torso and his muddy *phakomaah*, I realize that this will be a more elaborate operation than usual, and when the gardener and his boy stand facing each other, grasping the opposite ends of a bamboo pole, and Nit-nit gingerly puts a forty-five on the record player and the strains of Chubby Checker's "Limbo Rock" fill the air, I realize that we will be in for a spectacle indeed.

Ning-nong is the most businesslike of the three. She bends back and passes under the pole with robot-like precision. Noi-noi's efforts are rather tentative. But Nit-nit rams the pole and slithers on the polished teak floor, and before she knows it, her legs have slid between the railings and her designer mourning clothes are soaked.

Noi-noi shrugs. "Par for the course," Ning-nong says. The gardener and his boy lower the bar.

This time Nit-nit tries very, very hard. But the gardener's boy—who doesn't come up to the house often enough to have learned the art of maintaining the pokerfaced serenity of servitude—becomes so convulsed with laughter that he lets the pole shoot up at a forty-five degree angle, and it smashes against one of the hundred-year-old support posts.

"*Eaugh!*" scream the three Fates.

Appalled, the gardener has dropped his end and prostrated himself at the feet of the eldest Fate. "Piak's just a boy," he says, placing his folded palms between her knees and haunching his buttocks high into the air. "He didn't mean anything. He's just nervous in front of all the *khun phuyings*." Noticing me, he adds, "And the *khun nuu*, too," and then he crawls toward me as though I might be able to order a stay of execution.

This makes me nervous. The gardener's boy is nowhere to be seen. In his haste, he has left his flip-flops behind. I hate the title of *khun nuu*. It's bad enough being known as Little Frog, but Mr. Mouse just doesn't cut the mustard.

"Limbo Rock" continues to fill the morning air with its jaunty, pseudo-Caribbean rhythms. Nobody is dancing.

"*Eaugh*, Little Frog," Noi-noi says—for all the parties in the pavilion have now turned expectantly to me, hoping that I'll come up with a solution—"what *are* we going to do?"

I clear my throat, arrange my knife and fork on my empty plate, and stand up. "My honoured aunts," I say, "the problem is one of human frailty. You, Aunt Nit-nit, can't help making people laugh, and Piak, bumpkin that he is, can't help laughing. We're in the modern age now. Time to replace men with machines. Time to eliminate human error by creating an entirely mechanical limbo rock device." This little speech is a paraphrase of something I've just read in an Isaac Asimov novel. Homer is God, but he has only written two books; the next best thing is science fiction.

Noi-noi loves it when I am pompous. She giggles, Nit-nit looks nervous, and Ning-nong assumes a self-righteous aspect. "You're right, Little Frog," says my eldest aunt. "We haven't time to train the servants to do this right—Father says we can stop mourning after three more weeks, and if we have the party any later than that, we shan't have any friends left! We're just going to have to go down to the bamboo factory and—have a limbo thing built, you know, with notches. Nit-nit, see to it, will you?"

In addition to being considered the clumsy one, my portly aunt also suffers the middle sister's onus of being the one who actually has to get things done. "I'll take Little Frog with me," she says. "For company."

"And to protect you from the lascivious advances of those bamboo cutters, doubtless," Noi-noi adds. As the most beautiful of the three, she is also the cruellest.

It seems that I will not have time this morning for my usual journey into the world of fantasy. It is just as well. Since discovering that the ruined house is not quite uninhabited, I have been a little afraid of going back. I do not quite feel ready yet to face my great-grandmother; I fear she knows too much about me.

The bamboo place is one of those open-fronted shops somewhere in Yawaraj. I don't get out of the car. I just watch with the window rolled down while Aunt Nit-nit attempts to explain what she wants to an elderly *thaokae*, whose fingers never leave his abacus as he listens open-mouthed to her description. She gesticulates. She prances up and down the dusty pavement. At length, she goes the whole hog and, arms on her hips, bends backward as far as she can and hops awkwardly over to the *thaokae's* desk.

The *thaokae* wears no shirt, and his shrivelled breast heaves up and down as he laughs.

A pair of street children has come out to watch. A dog howls. In the store next door, two society ladies who have been bargaining over sandals crane their slender necks like a pair of giraffes.

I decide I'd better come to the rescue.

I get out of the car, borrow a pencil from the old man, and take a scrap of paper from his ledger. The shop is piled high with bamboo. In the back, an army of children is working with assembly-line precision, cutting bamboo into precise lengths and stacking it up in cords. Bamboo smells good and clean. There is sawdust everywhere.

I draw two tall poles on stands, with a row of notches going down each; then I draw a narrow pole going across and resting in a pair of notches.

"Oh," says the *thaokae*. "It's for 'Limbo Rock.'"

Nit-nit looks murderously at me. I shrug. "I'll kill you, Little Frog," she says. She sounds like she means business.

Her tone changes completely when we are going back down Sukhumvit toward the estate. "Why do they call it limbo, anyway?" she sighs.

"It's sort of a dead baby place, isn't it?" I say. "Limbo, I mean."

"Yes . . . a place where dead babies go when they haven't been baptized." Like every well-bred woman in her circle, Nit-nit is a graduate of Mater Dei; of course we are Buddhists, but ten years among Ursulines cannot fail to leave its mark on a girl, especially one rendered sensitive by her middle position and her tendency to fat. "They're perfectly happy, but you know, they're cut off from God . . . yet they can't yearn for God because they can never understand what it is they're missing. . . ."

Suddenly I realize that this is more than a theoretical discussion. In fact, my aunt has worked herself up into a highly emotional state. I am so confused that—even though we have just passed a *roti* vendor coming out of a side alley, wheeling a cart laden with mouth-watering dough cakes oozing with sugar and condensed milk—I forget to insist on stopping for one.

"Are you all right, Aunt Nit-nit?"

She's dabbing at her eyes with a handkerchief. I am sure she is not grieving for the dear departed, whose name I have still not found out for all that we're due for another round of funeralizing tonight. "No, no, Little Frog—it's I who am in limbo! I who yearn for the unattainable, I whose every yearning is unnameable.

"I'm sure I don't know what you mean," I say crossly, for the missed opportunity of the *roti* is starting to dawn on me as the vendor disappears toward the mouth of the *soi* followed by a dozen squalling street urchins.

"Look, Little Frog. I can't trust the others, but you're just a child, and you're my nephew so you have to do as I say."

This is the kind of remark that generally presages the demand that I perform some onerous and useless task. Nevertheless, it is not my place to argue. Sullenly, I listen.

"There's someone I have to meet next Saturday. I mean . . . you know . . . someone . . . male."

The possibility of blackmail occurs to me.

"I want you to ask me to take you to a movie on Saturday. Be really insistent and public about it. I'll keep refusing, but eventually I'll sigh and say yes."

Bingo! I am to be the dueña for my lovesick aunt! "Very well," I say, "but I get to pick the movie."

"Oh, all right."

"And"—I have to speak quickly because we are nearing the gates of the estate—"it'll cost you fifty baht, all in advance." It is an outrageous sum, but I sense a certain desperation in my aunt. I wonder whether the traffic will bear so astronomical a bribe.

"Twenty-five now and twenty-five on completion of the deal," she says. "I'm no fool."

"Done." She must be in love indeed to part with fifty baht with only a half-hearted attempt at bargaining. I will never fall in love again, I tell myself, and I resolve to forget the faithless Samlee. I wonder what it will be like to lie in bed without hearing her shallow breathing, without tasting her fragrance in the night air.

The gates swing open. Aunt Nit-nit won't look into my eyes. I think that the chauffeur understands more than he lets on.

3

Funeral Rites

By the time I return to my room, the mortal remains of my chameleon have begun to reek. I must cremate him soon. Homer can have no lying-in-state, no golden cones, no wreaths. His funeral shroud will be the Sunday edition of the *Bangkok Post*, which has a picture of Jacqueline Kennedy on the front page. Homer will have a divine consort on his journey to the West.

As part of my contract with Aunt Nit-nit, I have managed to secure a leave of absence from this evening's festivities. At about two in the afternoon, as per our bargain, I begin to complain of a headache, and Nit-nit pulls out the thermometer that we have earlier secreted in her purse. We have agreed on a temperature of one hundred degrees Fahrenheit—higher would be to precipitate the summoning of the terrifying Dr. Richardson—and I am sent off to bed with a glass of soothing hot *nam manao*.

I lie in bed, tossing and turning now and then so that the maid, Kaew, who has been assigned to fan away my fever, will not think I am faking. All signs of Samlee have vanished from my room. No longer do I see the rolled-up mat at the bottom of the closet, and the pile of neatly folded *panungs* next to my shoes. The maid Kaew is a poor substitute. She is barely older than I am, and I am sure there are things she would rather be doing than being my unwitting accomplice in the creation of an alibi for the evening's proceedings. Kaew is a dour girl. I can barely understand her when she babbles on; she speaks in the lilting accent of the North. But when she begins to sing a soft lullaby to me, I can see she is not really dour at all. The hands that clasp the handle of the fan are calloused beyond her years. I wish I could talk to her. The words almost form themselves on my lips. But still they won't come out. Why can't I bring myself to speak these words, my own mother tongue? Am I afraid I will forget the other words, the windswept words of ancient poets, the words of the other kingdom?

"Samlee," I whisper. Names are the same in every language. To say a name surely does not betray my loyalty to English.

"She has gone to the brick house," Kaew says, breaking off her song in mid-syllable, "and when she comes back, she won't be a servant any more."

This frightens me. I mean that the idea that one could change one's state, metamorphose from servant to master, is a concept that seems to make no sense within the boundaries of this pocket universe. More than ever I am convinced that my ex-beloved is some kind of sorceress. Haven't I seen her stalking through the mango orchard in the middle of the night, muttering to herself? Didn't I see her working her spells on Uncle Vit right in the middle of the funeral banquet, making his aubergine bloat up like a zeppelin? And this morning, didn't she tell me she had seen a *phii am* with her own eyes, coming down from the ceiling to squat on my chest and crush me half to death?

For a moment I think I really *am* going to come down with a fever. But at that moment music comes flooding in through the window. It's a Dee Dee Sharpe record, and I can also hear Aunt Nitnit's thudding rendition of the mashed potatoes. The aunts are out in the *sala*, practising for their party again. Their bare feet are pounding the teak-wood floor in a bizarre arrhythmic counterpoint to the song. It is a relief when the record ends and they turn to the watusi. I am sure they must look pretty stupid, waving those imaginary spears in the air, but at least they are no longer stamping their feet on the off-off-off-way-off-beats. Why do they even practise? The party is three months away, and most of my aunts' friends have barely mastered the cha-cha-cha, let alone anything recent. I hope that 1963 will not have too many new dances; perhaps they will finally settle on something sensible and simple, like the twist. Even I can do that.

We hear a crash followed by a resounding "*Eaugh!*" Kaew looks at the floor so I won't see her giggling; her sense of decorum is clearly more developed than that of Piak, the gardener's boy. I really do feel for my aunt; she has not always been this accident-prone. It must be something to do with having a secret lover. I am already fond of the secret lover because he has brought me fifty baht as well as a choice of movie. I've already decided which it is to be. It's a toss-up, actually. I want to see *Barabbas*, but I understand that *The Three Stooges Meet Hercules* isn't bad either.

After a while, I hear the funeral convoy revving up. Soon I shall be free. I have not forgotten that it was my great-grandmother who told me that Homer must receive the proper last rites in order for him to be able to complete his karmic cycle. But I am intimidated by the idea of seeing her again. I am still a little disillusioned by the discovery that the ruined house is not mine alone . . . that she has perhaps always lived there . . . that she has perhaps occasionally spied on me as I stood on a chair, flailing around in an ersatz toga, declaiming half-remembered speeches from Shakespeare . . . I admit I am afraid because I know she has divined my innermost secrets . . . and because she knows *Psycho* as well as I do. That is the worst thing of all, to discover that all these wondrous things you thought were yours alone are special to someone else.

In short, although it is my great-grandmother's idea, my plan is to carry out the funeral rites in secret, before she has a chance to find out. I am very jealous of my last moments with Homer, and I don't feel like sharing.

It is all going to work out perfectly, I tell myself. After all, my great-grandmother will be at the *other* funeral. . . .

It is now about five o'clock. Kaew has dozed off. I don't blame her. Sunlight is streaming into my room. I slip out of bed and put on the tailor-made suit I was to have worn to the funeral of my mighty but anonymous relative. I make sure the black armband is on straight, and then I spend several minutes Brylcreeming out my cowlicks. In fact, I start to snip off a stray strand of hair, then remember just in time that it is Wednesday.

To cut one's hair on a Wednesday, as Samlee has repeatedly told me, is very, very, very bad luck.

I go into the bathroom where Homer's body and tail have now been laid out on top of Jackie Kennedy's face. I have cut out a diamond-shaped piece of the newspaper with the photograph in the middle. The entire ensemble rests on the toilet seat. Now I fold up the newspaper and tuck in the edges to form a kind of envelope. I stick the putrefying Homer in my pocket and go out into the living room.

To my surprise, Piak, the gardener's boy, is waiting for me at the entrance to the shoe-removing room. He's on one knee, looking quite contrite about the slapstick *faux pas* in the teak pavilion. He has a cone-shaped lacquerware box in one hand and a toy boat in the other.

"The *khunying* sent me, Master Little Frog," he says.

He has a note from my great-grandmother that he fishes out of his *phakomaah*. I take it from him.

My dear Little Frog, it says, *I have contrived to stay away from that boring old funeral this evening by faking a bout of rheumatism. I hear you are sick, too, so I can only conclude that you and I are of a similar mind. I am sending you a funerary urn and a gilded boat to send your beloved friend into the next world. Meet me in the mango orchard at six p.m. Eat properly beforehand, and be absolutely certain that you have been to the toilet in advance. There's nothing more tiresome than an incontinent high priest.*

The boat: It's old. I turn it over in my hands. It's very light—balsa wood perhaps—but it doesn't seem to have been made from a kit.

It has shields painted down its sides. Its prow bears the face of a dragon. Perhaps we shall have a Viking funeral for my chameleon.

On second thought, I decide that I am not wearing the right clothes for this event. The funeral of my great and anonymous ancestor is taking place in the world of white suits and black armbands, but the venue of my friend's last rites will be the secret universe, the country of my fantasies. I run back into my room and throw the good clothes in a heap on the floor. Then I pull off the bedspread and wrap it around myself in the manner of a Roman toga. I scoop out a handful of leaves from the terrarium Homer once inhabited and fashion them into a makeshift wreath. I stuff the *Harvard Classics* edition of the *Iliad* down my toga, in case I need inspiration for the peroration.

My great-grandmother is waiting at the place where the path forks out toward the mango grove. She is in a wheelchair. She is alone. There is no indication of how she has managed to reach this place unaided. The sun is setting behind the trees, and I can see the wall behind the trees, dark against the lurid glare, its shards of broken glass glinting here and there as though to ward off thieves, abductors and molesters. My great-grandmother, too, is a silhouette, her silver hair haloed in the crimson light. She stretches out her arms to me. She is no longer threatening. I am angry at myself for thinking of her as the mother of Norman Bates. Awkwardly, with the boat under one arm and the lacquer cone stuffed in a fold of the bedspread along with Homer chameleon and Homer *Iliad*, I fall to my knees and pay my respects into her lap, my folded palms falling into place on the silken cushion that she keeps on her lap specifically for such obeisance.

"Thank you for the boat, Great-grandmother, and the funerary urn, too."

"For an Englishman, you *kraab* very prettily, Little Frog," she says and nudges me upright, laughing. "Now you must push me down the pathway toward a secret spot that will always remain sacred to

you. Don't go too fast now—I'm ninety-four years old, not a tod-
dler in a shopping cart."

I grasp the handle of the chair and begin wheeling her toward
the trees. The heat has abated a little, and the air is dripping with
the scent of ripe mangoes. "Great-grandmother—" I know it is rude
of me, but I cannot help myself. "Great-grandmother, I've lived here
for almost three years. I've been playing in the ruined house for a
year now. I've gone from room to room and taken every book in
the library down from its shelf . . . so how is it that I only met you
yesterday? Where have you been hiding?" Surprising myself with
my own passion, I say, "You could have told me you were there.
There were times when—when I needed someone—someone like
you."

"Thun Hua," says my great-grandmother affectionately, "you
really must stop orating. When was the last time you had a conversation with another child?"

"Well, I spoke to Piak just now."

"I said a conversation. Or, better yet, a fight." We have reached
the grove. It is suddenly much darker. My great-grandmother removes a bottle of mosquito repellent from somewhere in the
recesses of her wheelchair and dabs herself with it; then she hands
the bottle to me. The path forks, and I select the left, at random.

"I can't help it if there's no school." The Scola Britannica in Tung
Mahamek has been closed down for almost a year because it does
not have a licence from the Ministry of Education. They are nego-
tiating with the Ministry of Foreign Affairs for a new kind of licence
that will allow them to continue teaching according to the British
syllabus. This sudden isolation from other children may be what
has caused me to start on my inward odyssey. An experiment with
a Thai-speaking school proved disastrous; it lasted precisely two
days.

"You must find some friends your own age," my great-grandmother says. "It's true that you and I can talk about the classics
together, but an old woman cannot climb trees or swim naked in
the *klong*."

"And nor can I," I say uneasily, hoping she'll change the subject.

We have reached a spot along the wall. The smell of incense wafts toward me, and I know that someone is praying at the spirit house that stands near the gates of the estate. I hear the croak of the *ueng-aang* and the stridulation of the grasshoppers and the steady sawing of mosquitoes.

"Did you bring kindling wood? And matches?" my great-grandmother says.

"I'm not allowed to have matches. Aunt Ning-nong says I will burn down the house. It's all wood, you know."

"It's good that I've come supplied, then, Little Frog." She takes out a bundle of wood and a box of matches from the place the insect repellent is stashed. She also has three joss-sticks.

I find a place beneath the shadiest of the mango trees. I build a pyre from the sticks. Lovingly I place the chameleon inside the lacquer box and the box on the wooden boat. I love the way the boat feels, impossibly light, poised for a Viking raid. For a moment I don't want to burn it. The sticks won't catch fire, and I try dousing them with mosquito repellent, which works very well. The pyre blazes up. I stand there, watching the flames creep up toward the balsa and the lacquer. I start to weep.

"Great-grandmother—" I whisper.

"You must be alone with him now. Perhaps you will see his spirit flying away. Perhaps you will be able to catch his soul before he flies, and he will come to be inside you forever. There is much he could teach you."

My great-grandmother claps her hands. Out of nowhere, the gardener appears. She waves to him. He takes her wheelchair and begins to push her back toward the ruined house.

He has obviously been watching the whole time, just out of sight. Suddenly I am furious. Shall I ever escape this prison, this simulacrum of paradise? My great-grandmother has watched me for a year without revealing herself . . . and she, too, is watched . . . and I . . . my most private moments spied upon, dissected, analysed, laughed over! Cautiously I look around. I wipe my eyes on a fold of my toga. I would not dishonour my dead friend with an un-seemly exhibition of grief. It must be grave, sober and full of propriety.

I take out the Homer and look for an appropriate passage to read aloud. The flames rise almost all the way up to the sheltering branches of the mango tree. I put Homer down for a moment, light the three joss-sticks and close my eyes to pray, although I do not know to whom.

And then I hear a trickle of water. I open my eyes. It is stream-ing down from the mango tree on to the pyre. Suddenly I realize that someone is urinating down on the mortal remains of my pet chameleon. Who dares to profane the sacred mysteries?

I hear laughter. It is dark. Something moves up in the mango tree.

"Great-grandmother!" I shriek.

Nothing. I think of all the ghosts and spirits Samlee has told me of. Then I think of little Homer, pierced to the heart by the spike of a lady's high-heel, and I'm not afraid of any evil spirits. I rush at the tree and start shaking it.

More laughter, high-pitched, mischievous.

This is not to be tolerated! I have clambered halfway up the trunk before I remember that I don't know how to climb trees. I pummel the moist wood with my fists. I grab the branch and shove it back and forth. The laughter becomes more strident. I shake and shake and shake, and suddenly there is a thump, and the miscre-ant has landed on the ground, rubbing his buttocks and looking at me with amused derision.

Up in the tree, someone else giggles.

4

The Treehouse
on Top of the World

At first I can only see his eyes. He is standing in front of the funeral pyre, blocking my view of my chameleon's ascent into the celestial realm. His eyes are wide, white and ferocious. The giggling from overhead continues softly. I begin to make him out. He is as black as the night around us. He wears only a pair of cut-off jeans. He seems about my age, but he is taller, he is wiry, he is lithe, his skin glistens like a ripe mango. I have never seen a Negro before. I am sure that is what he is. I am afraid of him. My knowledge of Negroes is confined to the films I have seen, where they are always wild men of the forest, imploring Tarzan for aid, or sleek, oiled Nubian gladiators propounding noble sentiments in mid-Atlantic accents. They are exotic creatures, reeking of ancient times, barbaric splendour, jungle savagery. In books, Negroes tend to say things like, "Is our rude fare too meagre for you?" as our hero squats on the woven rushes, contemplating the shrunken heads in the garland around the chieftain's neck. I shrink-back against the tree-trunk.

To my amazement, he speaks to me in perfect Thai: "You idiot! What were you doing, trying to burn down our treehouse?" Then he shouts up into the mango tree: Piak! Come down from there! We've got ourselves an enemy! Tie him up, and we'll piss on his face."

Piak leaps down from the tree. He becomes confused when he sees me. He doesn't know whether to abase himself before me or whether to obey the wild stranger.

My mind is racing. Although this creature speaks Thai, he surely cannot be one. I know, in a theoretical kind of way, that his race exists. Mostly they live in America. I resolve to see if he speaks English.

"Now look here," I say, appearing much bolder than I am, for in truth my bladder is almost bursting from terror, "this happens to be my house, and you are a trespasser. If I do not have immediate satisfaction, I shall be forced to summon aid."

"Holy Moley," he says in English, "now I heard everything—a dink that talk like a English lord. My daddy's gone die laughin' when I tell him."

"You talk pretty strangely yourself."

"I is from Georgia."

"Oh," I say. Anxious to prove that I am no idiot, I add, "Georgia, Georgia—that's in Russia, isn't it?"

"Don't you be calling me no commie, dink," he says. "Or you gone be sorry."

"I beg your pardon?"

"I ain't no commie. My daddy he a military advisor."

"Your daddy he a military advisor."

"Don't you be making fun of the way I talk."

"Making fun? Hardly! I love the way you talk . . . I mean, how can I express my joy at what I'm hearing, the exotic music of it, the poetry? Oh, God, it sends my fantasies racing through antique lands and sunken continents, through temples buried in the rainforest, through vast savannahs where the wildebeest roam. "I think it's . . . beautiful!"

He laughs. Then, stepping back, he looks at my handiwork, the flames blazing once more despite his attempts to douse them. "Look at that boat. It a crying shame burnin' up a good boat like that. It worth a good fi' dollars."

"Homer was worth at least five dollars," I say ruefully.

"Homer?"

"My pet chameleon."

"Oh . . . oh . . . pet chameleon. I understands." He holds out his hand. "You was having yourself a Viking funeral. I didn't mean no harm. But . . . you shouldn't of lit you fire under this tree. This tree special."

"Special? But this is our mango orchard," I say, "and this is our estate. What gives you the right to decide which trees are special and which ones aren't?"

"You wants to know?"

"Yes, of course." The pyre is blazing now. "I've a right to know."

If I don't sound confident of my rights, it's because in my mind the mango grove has transmuted into an endless rainforest. Monkeys chitter and tigers growl and macaws screech. I could swing away on a vine, perhaps, but some of the vines could be boa constrictors. Meanwhile, the ferocious cannibal king continues to regale me with the mellifluous poetry common to barbarian races. Were I better prepared, I would threaten to bring down the wrath of the gods. There would be a sudden eclipse of the sun, and in a trice I would be an object of worship to half a million naked savages. But I know the eclipse ploy will not work. It doesn't work at night.

"'I've a right to know,'" he says, mimicking the way I talk. "I ain't never heard nuthin' like it! I's just sitting up in my treehouse with my friends, mindin' my own business, when along comes a dink which talk like a English butler and wear a bed sheet wrapped around he shoulders and tells me he having a Viking funeral for he pet chameleon."

"You've got a treehouse on my estate?" I say, realizing that there are now five houses within the walled universe.

Piak says to him—half whispers out of fright, although he doesn't think I can understand Thai—"That's the *khun nuu* I was telling you about. This whole place belongs to his family. You'd better get me out of this, brother, or my father will get the sack."

"We'll see about that," says the barbarian king, drawing himself up and looking down at me with chieftainly *hauteur*. I have not thought to bring the sacred plastic sword of Zeus, nor have I had the presence of mind to carry some modern weapon on my person, such as a water-pistol filled with *Phantom of the Opera*-type acid. My enemy assails me now with a string of Thai, the like of which I never heard. I can only assume that these are the vulgar words that a *phudii* like me is not allowed to hear, let alone use. I can tell from the expression of Piak, who appears to expect to be struck down by a thunderbolt at any minute, that what assaults my ears must be language of the loathsomest ilk. After a while, however, the Negro boy seems to realize that his abuse is not evoking the appropriate response. "Don't you understand no Thai at all?" he asks me.

"Well," I say, "I understand quite a lot . . . but I must confess that I have no idea what you're talking about."

"I is casting aspersions," he says grandly, "upon the sexual inexcretions of you momma, and, in addition, I is accusing you of having homer-sexual proclivities." He waits for me to react adversely, but I am unable to construe his utterances.

It is clear that this boy is far more worldly than myself. I am in awe of his poise, his self-confidence and his vocabulary. As my great-grandmother has astutely pointed out, I have not really conversed with another boy in some months. I have no idea how to behave in the presence of other children. I would like to be his friend, but I suspect I have already lost too much ground. On the other hand—if he is capable of making a companion of the servile Piak, why not me, the scion of the lord of the estate?

Behind us, my chameleon burns. His soul is descending into the land of Yama, where he will wait to be reborn into the cycle of karma. There's a lot of smoke. Piak begins to cough. I am coughing too. The flames are swelling now. These are not the mythic flames that have engulfed Troy many times over in my mind. I have never seen flames like these. The smell of charred chameleon is not unlike that of the barbecued chicken you can buy at the boxing stadium. My great-grandmother has filled the funeral barge with incense. It's a heady smell and we're all choking on it.

It takes me a few seconds to come to the conclusion that the flames are raging out of control. I scream.

"You fool!" says the boy from Georgia, looking askance as I point and back away. "We got to put it out."

"How? How?" I am wailing. I wish my great-grandmother would come back, but I am sure she is well out of screaming range by now.

My captors turn their backs on me and begin to urinate noisily on to the flames. Suddenly I realize that my bladder is about to burst from terror.

"Don't you be standing around while *we* puts out the fire you started! Get on over here and start peeing!"

I stop waiting around. I scoot over to stand next to the two boys and whip it out just in time, for the floodgates burst. With my efforts added to theirs, we manage to put out the flames. A few tendrils of smoke curl up where once the soul of Homer blazed. The smell of ammonia hangs in the air, and I notice with annoyance that my mosquito repellent has started to wear off. I start to slap myself. A mosquito squishes in the palm of my hand, oozing blood. The other boys are slapping too. We are all slapping and laughing. It is too absurd. While the grownups are away at the temple playing at grief, it seems to me that, here in the mango orchard, it is we children who are experiencing the cosmic verities—life, death, eternity.

"Can we go to the treehouse now?" I ask.

"Yes. But first I want you to know that it be my treehouse and in my treehouse there ain't no servants and there ain't no masters. When you in my treehouse, you in America, you hear?" He turns and translates this to Piak while I nod my agreement. "All right, start climbing," he tells me.

"I don't know how," I say.

"Jeepers, is you a boy or a girl? Piak, help him." The gardener's boy kneels beside the tree-trunk and lets me get on his shoulders. I grab hold of the branch above and manage to swing my eighty-eight-pound carcass up into a fork of the tree. I find a foothold and then another. There will be many Everests in my future, but this is the first. I look down in wonder at the spectacle below—the smouldering pyre, the trunks of the trees, the footpaths winding their way toward the main driveway lined with jasmine and *phuttachaat* bushes.

"Hurry up!" I am being prodded. My toga keeps snagging on twigs. It occurs to me that my robes of office are probably not the best attire for the average jungle adventure. I crawl up the branch until I see the treehouse. It is miraculous! Oh, it is a hideous thing slapped together from soap boxes, corrugated iron sheets and cardboard, but to me it is as if we had scaled Parnassus and reached the Temple of Apollo. A trapdoor slides and I am able to push myself up into the first of many rooms. The other boys climb in beside me, and Piak ceremoniously turns on the light. There is, I am astonished to find, an electric cable leading out of the window. There are cushions, a nude poster of Marilyn Monroe, and even a toaster. It is the toaster—a labour-saving device—that gives the impression that we've really arrived in America.

Piak no longer acts like a servant. I don't mind. It seems natural here. I look up and see that there are wooden steps nailed into the trunk, leading up to higher chambers.

"Does my great-grandmother know about this place?"

"Oh, the old woman? Sure she do. She a fine lady. Sometime in the evening she come out and watch us play."

I feel a twinge of envy, because these boys have had the benefit of my great-grandmother's wisdom far longer than I. It occurs to me that she has probably engineered this whole meeting. Hasn't she just been telling me that I don't talk to other children enough? I become sullen for a moment. Then I remember my manners and I say, "But we haven't been properly introduced. My name is Sornsunthorn, but you may call me Justin."

"Justin! A fine name you done chose for yourself, Little Frog," he says, laughing. "And I am Virgil Achilles O'Fleary, but you may call me Virgil."

Another twinge. What right does he have to so grand a name, redolent with ancient history, while I must put up with the sobriquet of Little Frog? I become even more sulky. Virgil doesn't notice because he and Piak are busy lighting some coils of mosquito incense.

"Want to see more?" says Virgil.

I nod. He shimmies up the trunk to the next level and I follow. From here I can see that one end of the treehouse rests on the wall of the estate. A ladder leads downward from the second level out into someone else's lawn. So that is how Virgil has been able to get in and out. It is chilling to me that there is a means of egress from this universe other than the Studebaker through the front gates. We are not as sealed off from the outside as I had thought.

"Come on, come on," Virgil says urgently. "You ain't seen the observation tower yet."

We climb. And now we're on top of the world. A skull and crossbones flutters in the night wind. The observation tower is the tiniest of the treehouse chambers, little more than a platform on which three children can barely squat. Its roof is a piece of siding lashed to the topmost branches with ropes. Mangoes dangle. My chameleon's pyre seems infinitely far away. There is a wooden chest with old clothes and chocolate bars—a veritable pirates' treasure.

I can see beyond the walls in every direction. I see things I have never seen before. I see that the pond on which the wooden house abuts flows underneath the wall to join up with a *klong* that runs all the way along one side of the estate and out toward an expanse of paddy fields. Two boats are moored beside the *klong*, which turns a right angle at the backyard of Virgil's house—which is really a cottage on the grounds of an estate not unlike ours, with a separate driveway to an unpaved alley. There are other ways into our estate, too: behind the brick house there's a little gateway to where the two boats are moored.

There is also a telescope. "Sometimes I come here in the middle of the night," says Virgil, "and I look at the moons of Jupiter and the canals of Mars. Lord, it a sight to see." He hands me part of a mushy Mars bar and I gulp it down.

But I am not looking at the stars. I train the telescope on the brick house. A light is on in an upstairs bedroom. I see Samlee. She appears to be arguing with someone. There is nothing at all servant-like about her stance or her demeanour. She is completely naked. I cannot see whom she is arguing with, but there is a lot of passion. I am stunned. I have been trying to imagine Samlee in the nude for some weeks, and each time my daydreams have been interrupted by a bizarre stiffening of my aubergine; yet so startling is the reality that this strange reaction does not occur. In any case, I have barely a second in which to glimpse the swaying of her pomelo-like breasts before she begins putting on her clothes. A vase flies through the air and lands somewhere out of sight. The light goes out.

Within ten seconds, the fully dressed Samlee is outside the house and slamming the gate shut behind her. In the moonlight I can see her quite clearly as she marches purposefully toward one of the boats, gets in, and begins rowing down the *klong*.

I drop the telescope. "Jeeze, Justin," says Virgil, "you see a ghost?"

"As a matter of fact," I say, "I have."

I go on to tell my new friend, who explains some of it to Piak, that Samlee is a supernatural creature who used to be my nanny—that she seems to have cast some kind of spell over my Uncle Vit. I talk about her habit of standing, gibbering, in the full moon. My flesh crawls. What is happening over at the brick house and why has Samlee gone rowing off into the night?

"Only one way to find out," says Virgil.

Piak grins. "Let's follow her," he says in Thai. "My father's already gone to bed. He'll never miss me. There's another boat."

"Follow her?" I say, dismayed. "Without permission?"

"Oh, don't you be such a fraidy-cat," says Virgil. His enthusiasm and his confidence rebuke me. He is a real boy and I am just a wraith. I know I am being drawn ineluctably into his universe. That's why I'm so afraid.

"I can't go out on the canal wearing nothing but a bed sheet," I say at last. It is a perfectly logical objection. But I see that Piak already has the answer. He's pulled a pair of dirty cut-offs out of the treasure chest and has thrown them into my arms. Then they're scrambling down the footholds toward the ladder that leads to the world outside the walls.

5

Crossing the Styx

The *klong* that leads away from my family estate will have many names. We pause for a moment to collect the many images of this canal from their positions in time. One day it will be the Rubicon, the river of no return. One day it will be Alph, the sacred river, from the opium fantasies of Coleridge. It will be Oceanus, the river that surrounds the world, and the Ganges, washing the ashes of the dead toward the place of their rebirth. I will name this *klong* all the great rivers of myth and history, and yet later there will be no *klong* at all, not even a trickle to mark the stream that carried my first love away from my home. There will be a shopping plaza, a five-storeyed mall, a hotel, a McDonald's, a Pizza Hut, a condominium-in-progress. Sometimes the waters that fertilize our fantasies run dry; sometimes they are glaciers that flow but an inch a year down from the Himavant of remembrance. I have compared this story to a slide show, but to see this *klong* for what it is, one must extend the metaphor. One must take the myriad slides that show this *klong* and bunch them up together and hold them to the light and know that a moment can be many moments.

This is a digression, because the moment that I see Samlee slip into the boat and begin to row toward the paddy fields west of

Sukhumvit, this moment when I stand in the observation tower of the treehouse, trying to tie down the too-wide borrowed cut-offs, seeing the first cracks appear in the crystal spheres of the perfectly hierarchical universe I have hitherto inhabited, is a moment of truth and pain to me.

As I follow my new friends down the ladder into a backyard that is not my own, as we crawl, like Red Indians after buffalo, toward the empty boat still moored beside the missing one, I think no metaphysical thoughts. The excitement is almost unbearable. I have never before felt the sharp grass scrape bare skin, or tasted canal mud in my nostrils. It is only after we clamber on to the boat that I begin to seek out mythic analogues for the adventure. The *klong* is the River Styx and we are crossing into the land of the dead. When Piak seizes the oars and Virgil stands at the prow, I realize that Piak is Charon the ferryman and Virgil is Virgil, who will be my guide as we descend into the dark places . . . and Samlee, of course, is Beatrice, the unattainable, gliding toward the pungent paddies. Turning, I see the other side of the back wall of our estate for the first time. The side that faces the *klong* is as dilapidated as the inside side is well maintained, cracked and caked with soot and mud.

"Row faster, Piak," says Virgil in Thai. "She's slipping out of sight."

"Why is he the only one rowing?" I ask. "I thought you said no more servants."

"In the treehouse, we in America," he says. "We on the *klong* now." But he is obviously not very comfortable with my accusation, and doesn't speak to me for five minutes. It occurs to me that perhaps we are not so unalike after all. He too is of two worlds.

The boat moves toward a bend in the canal. To my left are walled estates. Sometimes I can glimpse the upper balconies of their mansions over the tops of the walls. The moon is full and I can see all three of us rippling in the *klong*, dark-eyed, solemn. To my right are stilted houses whose stairways stretch into the dark water. Women in sarongs wash their clothes by moonlight. A mother bathes her child from an enormous jar of rainwater. A television set leans against the railings of a veranda, and faintly, behind the ever present buzzing of mosquitoes, I can hear the music from the closing credits of *The Outer Limits*. We pass under a wooden bridge. We are gaining on Samlee. At Virgil's urging we crouch down. She will only see the tops of our heads, three pairs of eyes glittering in the night.

"Keep down! Keep down!"

But I have to look. We are within a few feet of Samlee's boat. There are other boats on the *klong* too—one laden with coconuts comes between us, and for a moment I lose sight of her. As it passes out of sight, lacing the air with the scent of coconut milk, I am suddenly thrust so close to her I can see the tears forming at the corners of her eyes and furrowing down through the pancake makeup.

"Maybe you right, Little Frog, maybe she *be* possessed. She sure do look possessed. She face it white as death."

"Do you really think so?" I say. Because to me it seems that Samlee has become less and less terrifying. She is rowing with great agitation. She's weeping, she seems terrified herself, and I can see her lips moving, as though whispering some mantra to keep away demons.

"Well," says Virgil, "I ain't never seen no *phii krasue* myself"—although we are speaking English the phrase *phii krasue* makes Piak almost drop an oar into the water—"but I know there a lot of weird shit here."

Then I'm separated from her again as a small flotilla comes through. A portable phonograph plays jangling Chinese opera music and a girl in a silken costume is removing her makeup in front of a mirror by the light of a paper lantern. Her hair is done up in turrets and stuck with golden pins, making my Aunt Ningnong's bouffant look positively simple.

"Where are they coming from?" I say.

"There be a opera playing up at the temple fair, a couple miles up the *klong*," Virgil says. "It probably not bad if you can understand Chinese."

Another bend in the canal: a lone pagoda stands in an empty field. A clothesline connects the pagoda to a tree. A pair of jeans is flapping in the breeze. A gibbon, tethered to the tree, bares its teeth at us. I think about Homer. If I had tied him up more often he might never have been killed by a thoughtlessly placed stiletto heel. I wonder whether he would have relished being still alive, tied to a twig in the terrarium in my bathroom. Samlee puts down the oars to pay homage to a Brahma shrine at the water's edge. The god sits many-armed, bronze glimmering by flickering candlelight. Piak prays too, and even Virgil performs a perfunctory *wai*, but I, true to my secret gods, am too stubborn to acknowledge the powers that rule this land, these waters.

The *klong* grows narrower as we pass under another bridge, creaking, half-rotted. The water smells dank. Coke bottles lie among heaps of decaying fruit, old newspapers, cardboard boxes. The houses that line the *klong* are not houses at all but shanties, lean-tos patched together from aluminium siding and planks and whisky boxes. There is ugliness, but I still see Samlee in her boat with the moonlight on her face, siren-like in her peculiar beauty. The air is foul and close but the music of the night is still seductive in its cross-rhythms of frog and *ueng-aang*, wind and water.

She looks round. We duck. She pulls around to a landing. Stilts rear up from the silt. There is no rubbish around this house. Orchids hang from teakwood baskets. There are several boats tied to the dock. About a dozen pairs of flip-flops are scattered on the steps up to the veranda. Light wavers in the doorway. Four or five people are sitting on the steps. Their palms are folded in prayer. I smell incense.

Samlee staggers up the stairs, her sandals flying off and piling up on the bottom step. She elbows past the suppliants and disappears into the doorway. I hear music coming from somewhere in the distance. It is a Del Shannon song.

"What kind of a place is this?" I whisper as we creep out of the boat. Nobody seems to notice us as we remove our shoes and scramble up the steps. They are like robots. There is magic in this place, dark magic. I can feel it. We squat down on the top steps, the three of us, and nobody sees us.

"Where did she go?" I say.

"Inside," says Virgil.

Although the door is open we cannot see very clearly. There is a lot of smoke. Shadowy figures sit cross-legged on the floor. Now and then one crawls to a different spot.

"What kind of place is this?" I say.

"It a kind of a voodoo place," Virgil says. "A magic man he live here and sell all kind of spells and love potions."

A chill comes over me. But I want to see more. I have to see what's inside, even though I'm so frightened that I can feel the hairs rippling on my arms. I get up and start to inch my way around to the side of the building.

"What you doing?" Virgil whispers.

"Maybe there's a window or something. Or a back door."

Hugging the wall, I make my way to the back of the house. There is another entrance. I look round and don't see the other boys, but it's too late to turn back. I slip in through the back door. A passageway leads to a large room. I'm crouching behind a vinyl sofa. The room is full of fumes.

Samlee is facing me! She doesn't see me because my face is shrouded in smoke. She is on her knees in front of whoever is seated on the sofa. All I can see is a few wisps of hair. Samlee is crying out, "*Ajarn, ajarn,* you must help me . . . I don't know where to turn . . . I've been sent away from my Little Master and forced to abase myself. . . ."

A withered brown hand reaches out to her. She unbuckles the silver belt that holds up her *panung*. With one hand she holds the cloth tight round her waist, while with the other she places the belt in the wizened hand. It beckons. A young boy sneaks up with a tray. The belt drops. The boy backs away into the shadows.

"It's all I have in the world," Samlee says. "All my life I've worn all my riches around my waist. I've been saving my wages since I was a little girl and every three months I buy another silver link for this belt. But you can have it all if you'll help me. Oh, please, *ajarn*, I only have one chance."

And now the *ajarn* speaks. His voice is like the voice of an old *ueng-aang*, deep and buzzing. He says, "What happens between a man and a woman is a mystery. You ask me to look in the dark places."

I hardly dare to breathe. Dark places! Has Samlee not spoken to me a thousand times of ghosts and demons and she-monsters and spirits of the sea? And is this not the darkest place I have ever experienced, this house of sorcery on the far shore of the Styx?

The old man claps his hands. Suddenly there is no one in the room but him and Samlee and me, concealed behind the couch. The front door creaks shut. He has sent them all away because the next ritual is a secret one.

"Now we are alone," says the old man. But I swear that he knows I am here. Surely he can hear the beating of my heart. But I lean forward, trusting the shadows to hide me from Samlee's gaze.

"Now," says the shaman, "you must reach into your dark places and fetch me a fetish to bend this man to your will." He reaches out. Gently he pries her hand free of her *panung*, finger by finger. It falls to the floor and now I can almost taste her odour, more overwhelming than the incense. And for the very first time I see how a woman is fashioned and what makes her different from a man.

The shaman lifts up his hands and passes them over her face, and her eyes close. She is in a trance. Her hands seem to move independently. They rove all over her body. She caresses herself. She strokes her own thighs and her own breasts. "Yes, my daughter," says the magician. "Deeper now. Darker. Further into yourself."

She moans. Her left hand plunges into the thicket between her legs and plucks out something. She hands it to him. Delicately, he picks it out of her palm with a pair of tweezers.

"I think this will do very nicely," says the old man. She pulls her *panung* back up and sits on her knees, swaying, her eyes still closed, rocking to a secret music.

I lean forward a little more. He's holding something between his thumb and forefinger. It is a human hair. I lean all the way over. The hair has a faint odour of *nam pla*. They do not seem to notice me.

The old man turns.

I am looking straight into his eyes. They are slitty, topaz-coloured, faceted. They have no pupils. His face is all ridges, and it gleams with gold paint. He cannot be human.

Someone touches my shoulder.

Before I can stop myself a scream tears from my throat. But Samlee does not move. It is as though she cannot hear me. I have to get through to her, to draw her out of her dark ensorcellement. I scream and scream and scream, heedless of the magician's dead eyes as they bore into my own.

6

Love Potion No. 9

A hand clamps down over my mouth and I am dragged back behind the vinyl sofa. "Master Little Frog," Piak says, "you'll wake them up!" and Virgil, who has pinned my arms so I won't jump up, whispers, "Didn't they never teach you to keep you mouth shut when you in the presence of black magic?"

"But—but—" My voice has become little more than a squawk. "Didn't you see his face? He's a— he's a—"

"Look again." Virgil lifts up my head and pushes it up over the back of the couch once more, and I realize that the magician's monstrous face is only a mask. The mask is painted with gold and crowned with the headdress of a *ruesii*. The mask does not fit over the face but rises slightly above it, so that the magician seems to have two heads, one on top of the other, one human, one supernatural. His human face is not much different from the *thaokae* in the bamboo shop, wrinkled and weathered.

"Oh, a mask," I say, thinking myself suddenly very stupid to have screamed.

"But what a mask! When the man be putting on that mask," Virgil tells me, "he putting himself into a trance. When he take it off, then he become just a plain old dink and don't have no magic powers."

I keep watching. I can see the front door up ahead, and, behind a cloud of incense, one or two pairs of eyes. The nanny and the mage don't seem to notice us. They haven't even heard my screams. In fact, they seem to be a little out of phase with us somehow. It is as though I am sitting at the intersection of two universes whose physical laws are not wholly congruent.

Samlee is still kneeling with her eyes closed, rocking slowly to a music I cannot hear. The shaman is kneading a lump of clay in one hand, and now he begins to murmur a string of incantations. He holds the strand of Samlee's pubic hair in his other hand between his thumb and forefinger and twirls it this way and that. Then he suddenly brings his two hands together, squishes the hair into the clay and begins to mould it into a crude figurine. As he squeezes the clay he whispers, "*Kamadeva, Kamadeva, Kamadeva.*"

On shelves behind us there are several rows of these clay figures. There are also dozens of vials of fluids in fluorescent colours: yellow, pink, blue and green. There is also—and this reminds me achingly of my dead friend Homer—a rack on which ten dried lizards, ranked longest to shortest, hang by their tails. A mortar and pestle rests beside a rhinoceros horn. On the top shelf are images of strange deities with many arms and animal heads, garlanded with strands of jasmine.

"I come here all the time," Piak says. "He's a very powerful wizard who has a day job as a janitor in a Brahmin temple. He's only a janitor because he's come down to earth to learn the meaning of humility. My father sends me to buy love potions. They work for a day or two, but after the girl finds out he is only a gardener she usually dumps him." This is the longest speech I've ever heard Piak make, and it is dawning on me that there is a lot more to him than just running around delivering messages and holding up limbo poles.

"Love potions don't work," Virgil says to him in Thai, and then to me he adds, "You people too damn superstitious."

"What do you mean, 'you people'? What about you people with your cannibals and your voodoo? You sit around worshipping King Kong, for God's sake! You strangle your wives, too," I add learnedly, for I have recently read an annotated edition of *Othello* that was lying around the ruined house.

At which Virgil begins to laugh with such gusto that Piak glances nervously at the mage and his client, who still do not seem to see or hear us. I don't understand why he thinks this is so funny. I hate it when I get the feeling that there are some jokes that cannot be understood from reading books. He laughs, and I wriggle free from his grasp and crawl around to the front of the couch, confident now that the mage and my beloved Samlee will not return to earth for a little while longer.

The room is packed with fascinating objects—figures of carved ivory, bundles of foul-smelling herbs, candles of every size and colour, the skull of some exotic small mammal, a marmoset or shrew.

The *ajarn* speaks again. This time he has a piping voice like a small child's. "Take the amulet," he says to Samlee. "You know what to do." He hands it to her.

"She gone wake up!" Virgil whispers urgently, and I scurry back behind the couch. And indeed Samlee is stirring. Her eyelashes begin to flutter. The mage puts his hands up to the mask. He is going to lift it off his head. I know that as soon as the mask is off the trance will be broken, and the shaman and the nanny will be back from the Twilight Zone.

We don't dare stay any longer. We dash through the back passage and emerge on the veranda. We run around to the front and sprint down the stairs to where the boat is still moored, and we set off down the *klong* again, but the moon has either set or concealed itself behind a cloud, and Piak rows the boat through darkness, dense with the scents of sewage and jungle-flowers.

I squeeze my eyes tight shut. Not two hours since the cremation of my pet chameleon I have harrowed hell with him, I have braved the Styx, I have faced the dark gods of chaos. I have also, in my haste, left behind one of my flip-flops. The comparison with Cinderella springs inevitably to mind. I am shivering with terror. To go back for the flip-flop is unthinkable, and yet—they are a very special pair, with leather thongs, which the three Fates purchased for me in a shop next to the Fontana Trevi, in Rome. There are no other flip-flops like them. They are as unique as the dentures of my ex-beloved, and what if the shaman shows up at the gates of the estate, brandishing the sandal and refusing to leave until we've all tried it on?

It dawns upon me that I am in trouble. The loss of a flip-flop is surely not as dire as the loss of my beloved nanny and my faithful chameleon, yet the loss looms large in the litany of spankable offences. While adults cannot comprehend the importance of a chameleon's friendship, they do attach immense value to footgear. Perhaps it is because they are incapable of abstract thought.

"Where are we?" I say at last, opening my eyes. It seems we have been drifting half the night, though probably only about ten minutes have passed since the epiphanic moment.

It is very dark still, but Virgil has a candle and is cupping the flame in one hand. The shadows dance across his face. "We didn't bring any candles, did we?" I say.

"Piak bought 'em cheap," he says.

I am not sure what he means, but—my eyes becoming used to the darkness—I see that there is a small stash of familiar-looking objects piled up near the front of the boat. My eyes widen as I realize that the two boys may have been engaging in criminal activities.

"Five-finger discount," Virgil says proudly.

I crawl over to the front of the boat. There are three or four little bottles and some candles. I know that the boys know better than to steal anything sacred, like a figurine; magical statues have a will of their own, and can be quite impish in their revenge.

"Why?" I say.

Piak understands "Why?" and answers in Thai, "This is my father's favourite kind. He says it makes his thing stand up for hours at a stretch."

I'm not quite sure what a "thing" is, but I am beginning to suspect that it all has to do with the mysterious workings of the aubergine.

"Anyway, they are nine baht apiece." He hands me one and I look at it curiously in the candlelight. Its label bears only the Thai numeral ๙. The liquid has the colour and consistency of Pepto-Bismol.

At that point, Virgil begins singing a fifties song called "Love Potion Number 9". He sings very well. He stands at the prow, waving and pointing his arms in a series of extravagant yet disciplined gestures, which I will later come to associate with Motown music. He makes Piak laugh and, to my amazement, Piak joins in in broken English. So do I, although my English is far too *eaughing* for me to be able to get into the spirit of a pop song.

This is my last slide-image of the night:

The three of us, improbable companions, are slowly drifting down the *klong* in a pitch-black night. The moon and the stars are obscured by clouds. We are singing at the top of our lungs, our young voices shrilling over the amorous clamouring of the frogs, crickets, mosquitoes, toads, *ueng-aangs*, dragonflies and *tukaes*. We are screeching our war-cry as the dragon-prow ship ploughs through the rocky fjord, laden with booty from Vinland's barbarous shores. We have pillaged, we have plundered, we have raped—whatever *that* means.

Piak the Pirate! Virgil the Victorious! Justin the Invincible! Amid such spectacle, it is easy to put aside my uneasiness over the coming troubles. Tomorrow will be time enough for me to deal with any problems that may arise from my not being in bed at the correct hour, and from the prized Italian sandal having vanished into thin air. Tomorrow, I tell myself; and in childhood, the distance between tonight and tomorrow is eternity.

Obviously the three Fates will have to be turned against one another. Ning-nong, the most severe, will have to be softened by the imprecations of Nit-nit, over whom I already have the power of blackmail.

The opportunity arises over breakfast. To my amazement, no one has the slightest suspicion that I have come back from the wildest adventure of my life. The limbo rock device has been delivered, and two of the Fates are running around supervising its installation in the ballroom of the big house. Only Nit-nit and I are in the *sala*, eating our separate breakfasts and looking nervously past each other.

The portable phonograph is playing The Four Seasons' "Big Girls Don't Cry", but it has little effect on Aunt Nit-nit, whose eyes are decidedly puffy. I decide that it is probably a good time to press my advantage.

"Aunt Nit-nit," I say, "about the movie on Saturday.

"*Eaugh*, don't bother me, Little Frog; can't you see I'm agonizing?" She dabs her eyes with a tissue she has removed from her Christian Dior handbag.

"But Aunt Nit-nit . . . we really need to decide on a game plan."

Aunt Nit-nit is very distracted. Her tremulous lip is disfigured by a smear of *khao tom*, and a piece of tear-soaked tissue is floating in the bowl among the little pieces of shrimp, ginger and garlic.

"Come now, Aunt Nit-nit dear. . . ." I start singing along with the record, "Big girls don't cry."

She laughs. "*Eaugh*, it's nice of you to try to comfort me, my dear, dear nephew," she says, and attempts to thrust her bulky arms around me from across the table. As she does so, however, the handbag falls over on its side, and I suddenly see, glimmering within its depths, a small vial containing a viscous fluid with the telltale tint of Pepto-Bismol.

"Good heavens, Aunt!" I say sweetly, knowing suddenly that I will not be getting into trouble for a long, long time, "isn't that the infamous nine-baht love potion from the sorcerer who lives down the *klong*?"

She looks at me in horror. She has been caught, as they say in America, with her hand in the cookie jar. She's wondering, doubtless, how I could possibly know the going price of *yaah saneh* in the Bangkapi market. "Oh, don't worry, Auntie," I say, attempting to retain my look of simultaneous innocence and superiority, "I shan't breathe a word. Of course, you realize I'll be bringing a friend to the Saturday movie."

Wringing her hands, Aunt Nit-nit says, "The plot's thick enough as it is, Little Frog—don't be ridiculous." But I know I am going to win this one.

At that moment, however, the two other Fates come running on to the pavilion.

"Come and look! It's scandalous! It's appalling!" Aunt Ning-nong is saying. In one hand she carries the left half of my pair of sandals, and my heart sinks. "It's outrageous! Right in front of our very noses!" They are both pointing straight at me.

"I didn't mean to—" I begin, but Nit-nit has turned to stare in the direction of their pointing, and I realize that they are actually pointing past me, past the other side of the pond, past the bushes, where the driveway of the brick house can be seen.

A Mercedes-Benz convertible has pulled up—Uncle Vit's car. Uncle Vit springs out and opens the door of the passenger seat—and I suddenly see what has caused my aunts to react with such horror.

A woman steps out of the car. She has a Cleopatra hairdo. She has shocking pink lipstick and rouged cheeks, above which she sports a pair of gilt-edged dark glasses. She wears a floral sundress and one of those hats popularized by Jacqueline Kennedy. Her high-heels are giving her trouble, and she doesn't quite know what to do with her Gucci clutch, but Uncle Vit is beaming.

"*Eaugh!*" the three Fates say in unison.

I am speechless. For if I had not seen her only a few short hours ago, swaying to the spell of a sorcerer, I would never have recognized this society lady as the once-beloved Samlee, former nanny and handmaiden to my unhappy self.

7

Metamorphoses

The glimpse of Samlee in her new incarnation is tantalizingly brief. She removes her sunglasses to reveal a painterly confluence of mascara, eyeliner and eyeshadow. She turns, catches sight of the horrified Fates, and enters the brick house, pausing only to remove her stilettos and place them on the shoe rack. Although she has taken on many of the attributes traditionally associated with beauty, to me she has become less beautiful. She has betrayed me. She is no longer the night-creature in the orchard with the sublimely odoriferous *panung*, but a denizen of *their* world, unyielding and unapproachable.

I turn my back. I return to the breakfast table. My three aunts march grimly about, each professing to be more scandalized than the last. Distractedly, I start to eat, oblivious to the beauty of the morning, the dance of the dragonflies above the lotus blooms, the sunlight glimmering through the 7-Up bottle green of the pond, the waxed teak smell of the pavilion floor. I don't even know what I am eating. It is only when I am halfway down the bowl that I realize that it is Aunt Nit-nit's *khao tom*.

"*Eaugh*, look at Little Frog," Aunt Noi-noi says, and I suddenly become aware of her standing over me, "I didn't know he knew how to eat that!"

"The Little British Lord is going native at last," says Ning-nong. "About time, if I say so myself. Three years of bacon and eggs for breakfast . . . just isn't *natural*."

Being discussed in the third person is unnerving. I try to concentrate on the food, only to find, to my horror, that it's not half bad. The shrimp have a firm, yet juicy texture. The little green oniony thingies add a thousand points of piquancy to the colloidal consistency of the rice gruel. The discovery that eating this food isn't going to kill me is almost as epiphanic as my recent confrontations with death, rebirth and transfiguration.

I realize all at once that my great-grandmother has been right. I am going to have to honour the spirit of my dead chameleon Homer by becoming more like him.

"I daresay my diet could use a few changes, revered aunts," I say.

But they have ceased to notice me. Aunt Nit-nit has started up the phonograph again, and once more it is playing "Big Girls Don't Cry", and she is kneeling at the railing of the *sala*, gazing soulfully into the water's mirror stillness.

"Whatever is the matter with you, Nit-nit?" Ning-nong says, and she and Noi-noi take their places at the breakfast table.

"Leave me alone!" Nit-nit says.

"It's just her period," says Noi-noi, "and we've something far more interesting to talk about. You know what I mean."

"Yes! What's to be done about it?"

"One thing's certain," says Noi-noi, "I'm simply going to have to change my hair. One can't have the same hairdo as the servants."

"Whatever are we going to *call* her? I'm afraid that 'Ee Samlee' is probably out of the question, but it's too galling to refer to her as 'Phii Samlee', assuming she is our *phii*. She must be pretty old, though naturally those coarse peasant girls do age a lot more quickly than we do, without our supplies of Pond's Angel Face . . ."

"*Eaugh*, Phii Ning-nong, don't be ridiculous. Nobody's saying we've got to have her at the dinner table! Provided she stays over at the brick house, we really don't have to call her anything at all."

It is abundantly clear to me that Samlee's transformation has had a disrupting effect on our little Utopia. I, too, am planning a transformation, but it is obvious that my change must be gradual. Otherwise I know I shall end up like Homer, with a spiked heel through the heart.

To affect this metamorphosis, my first step must be to master the Thai language. I am going to practise it in secret; I don't plan to utter one word of it until my conquest is complete. To this end, I say to Aunt Ning-nong: "Samlee's been transferred to the other house, and I'm frightened to sleep by myself."

Nit-nit looks up from the pond and says, "Oh, my sisters, how could we have neglected our poor Little Frog so! All we are worried about is how the maid's elevation is going to make us look, but the child must be quite devastated without his nanny to tuck him in at night."

"Quite so, quite so," Ning-nong says, sighing. "We'll assign Kaew to baby-sit the young master and—"

"I wouldn't do that if I were you," Nit-nit says. "She's a pretty young thing, and, well, he's getting old enough to notice . . ."

What a stroke of luck! They are going to do everything my way, without my having to ask!

The three Fates look at each other. There is a moment of gathering tension. Noi-noi is barely able to suppress a chuckle, while Ning-nong forces her face into a mask of severity.

"What about Piak?" I say innocently. "He could sleep on the floor in my room, and I don't think he has any other duties." It is from him that I intend to learn my own language, for only from him can I acquire a working repertoire of choice swearwords and nasty epithets.

"And who is Piak?" says Ning-nong, even more bewildered.

"The gardener's boy."

It doesn't really surprise me that Aunt Ning-nong hasn't bothered to learn the names of all the servants. "He's about the same age as I am, and Great-grandmother told me to seek out other children as companions, or I'd become an old man before my time."

"She's right, you know," says Nit-nit. "A boy can't sit around in a toga reading books all day long. It's unnatural. Boys are supposed to . . . well, play cricket, or something."

"I know so little of boys," Ning-nong says and sighs again.

"Enough of this nonsense!" says Noi-noi. "Just give him what he wants. Meanwhile, I'm going to go and get my hair changed. Come along, Little Frog. There's a bookshop near the beauty parlour. I don't want you cooped up here all day, brooding about the loss of your nanny."

"Yes, yes," says Ning-nong. "Go and fetch your flip-flops, my child."

"I'm afraid I was forced to bury them," I say. The lies come thick and fast as I take advantage of the three Fates' confusion to manufacture a quick explanation for the disappearance of the one and the mud-soaked condition of the other. "You see, one of them was . . . um . . . chewed up by one of the alley dogs, and I . . . well, the other one's bound to have rabies germs all over it, and I didn't want someone with an open sore on his foot accidentally stepping on it."

Incredibly, Ning-nong swallows the whole story and sends a maid up to her room to fetch me a fresh pair of leather sandals, purchased, like the defunct pair, in Rome. "Take better care of these, Little Frog," she admonishes. "You're lucky I happened to buy an extra pair." This is a peculiar quirk of the eldest Fate; she is a steadfast advocate of redundancy.

I am a little peeved at having to accompany Aunt Noi-noi to the beauty parlour, especially since I have been hoping to slip away to the treehouse this morning. I know that Virgil will be there, watching the skies with his telescope and planning his next escapade. Still, going to the bookshop is not a bad idea, and when, on our way to the hotel arcade where Noi-noi's favourite salon is located, my aunt begins to question me about Nit-nit's obsessions, I realize that this is a golden opportunity to gather more material for blackmail.

We are stuck in traffic for about half an hour at the railway tracks where Sukhumvit becomes Ploenchit. The policeman whose job it is to regulate the traffic light appears to have fallen asleep, and a bevy of angry motorists, leaving their cars parked in the middle of the road, have converged on his booth to prod him awake. Children with sponges have swabbed our windscreen and are thrusting garlands of jasmine in our faces, while a water buffalo is licking the hood ornament of our Studebaker.

These familiar sights do not interest me. I'm thinking about Virgil. Perhaps we will ride up the *klong* again tonight. It is hot, even though the air conditioning is blasting, because the sun streams mercilessly through the glass and heats up the leather seats. In my daydream we're drifting on the water and Homer is perched on my shoulder again; his feet are cold as ice, for he has been in the land of the dead.

I rarely converse with Aunt Noi-noi, since she generally has only two topics of discourse: her own beauty, and the beastliness of the universe.

So she jolts me out of my reverie by asking me: "She's got a secret lover, hasn't she?"

"Who, Aunt Noi-noi?"

She tosses her head back prettily and says, "Why, Phii Nit-nit, of course. I saw the way she manipulated you into demanding a trip to the cinema next Saturday!"

"I really don't know what you mean." For fifty baht, I can surely keep my mouth shut for a few days. "I do want to go to the movies on Saturday."

"You know as well as I do that Nit-nit is no fun at the movies. She talks all the way through them. Besides, she hates epics and horror and science fiction, which are the only films you like. Obviously, she has an ulterior motive in agreeing to take you. Didn't you see her this morning? She moped, she sniffled, she brooded. These are the signs of being in love. I said at breakfast that it was her period, but that was only so she wouldn't suspect I might be on to something!"

What was all this talk of periods? I wondered what sort of a period she had relegated her sister to. If she was referring to Nit-nit's dinosaur-like rage, she undoubtedly meant the late Cretaceous. Or was it something more recent, like the Age of Anxiety?

"So who is it, Little Frog?"

"But Aunt Noi-noi—" I began.

"No buts! I *must* know whom she's seeing. If you promise to spy for me, I'll buy you any book you want at the bookshop. If you don't, I have a certain muddy sandal in my possession. . . ."

I have not escaped unscathed after all. The wrath of the Fates could still descend upon me at any moment. "I'm afraid you've out-manoeuvred me, Aunt Noi-noi."

Just then we arrive at the Erawan Hotel arcade. Noi-noi pauses to pay her respects to the shrine of the Four-faced Brahma. The bookshop by the beauty parlour, catering as it does to tourists, carries a large stock of English-language books. It is a dingy place with freezing air conditioning and tinted windows, its shelves packed so closely there is barely room to squeeze between them. It is a literary jungle presided over by a salesman who is himself engrossed in the year's best seller, *Happiness is a Warm Puppy*.

Noi-noi takes my hand and steers me inside. I know she doesn't want to spend much time there, so I march straight to my favourite section, the Penguin Classics, which happen to be right next to the rack of DC comics, of which *Legion of Super-Heroes* is my favourite. Since I am a fast reader, I rarely buy comics, for they can be read in the five minutes that it takes to flip the pages. Instead, I peruse the shelf of little black paperbacks. The names on their spines are words I have never heard pronounced. I don't think I will ever hear them uttered. Nobody ever looks at this shelf but me. It exists for me alone. What names they are: Xenophon, Procopius, Pseudo-Eratosthenes, *Prior and Posterior Analytics* . . .

And speaking of posterior analytics, here's a book at the end of the row that I yearn for. Its cover shows an ancient painting of a nude and decidedly steatopygous woman with her arms out-stretched, disporting herself in a sacred laurel grove. The book is

Ovid's *Metamorphoses*, and I can't think of anything more appo-
site. I need a new epic poem to read, Homer and Virgil having
become dog-eared and familiar, and there is a certain family resemblance between the Bacchanalian cover girl and my once-loved
nanny, whom I have seen dance half-naked in the moonlight
amongst the mango trees. It is a similarity that pains my heart,
especially when I read on the cover that this is a poem about trans-
formations . . . women turning into cattle . . . gods into golden
showers . . . the dead into the living.

"Well?" says Noi-noi. "I can't wait around all day, young man."

"This is the book I want," I say, displaying the Ovid triumphantly.

Noi-noi demurs. "Naked women! What will you try next?"

"But you said I could have any book I wanted."

"I'm not as easy to manipulate as my lovesick elder sister. That
is obviously a dirty book. Ning-nong would never forgive me for
buying you something like that. What about this one?" She holds
up a book that has a picture of an innocent-looking little girl with
dark glasses. It is called *Lolita*. "This one seems harmless." Noi-noi
is by no means the most perceptive of the three Fates. When I look
indecisive for a moment, she thrusts a twenty-baht note at me and
says, "Oh, enough of this nonsense. Buy what you wish. I'll meet
you at the beauty salon."

She stalks away. Unfortunately, the Ovid costs thirty baht, and
I have not had the presence of mind to bring the extra money from
blackmailing Aunt Nit-nit. I start to take it back to the Penguin
Classics rack. But as I'm replacing the book between Plato's *Republic*
and Apuleius's *Golden Ass*, I suddenly realize that I am the only
customer in the shop, and that the proprietor still has his nose
firmly buried in Snoopy. I think back to last night. The darkness.
The mating calls of the frogs. The mosquitoes in their pinprick
multitudes. The lively odour of the river. The dead eyes of the shaman's mask. Love Potion No. 9. *The five-finger discount.*

I peer over the bookrack and see that the salesman has dozed off. My heart is beating fast. I cannot help what I do next. It is so easy, and the thrill is indescribable.

***

In the salon, my aunt is sitting beneath one of those mosque-like hair-drying devices, reading a copy of *Life*. On the cover, Elizabeth Taylor and Richard Burton are depicted. *Cleopatra* is coming out soon, hence the popularity of the hairstyle. Aunt Noi-noi went into the device with Egyptian hair, but the machine is a diabolical sort of chrysalis from which she will emerge transformed. There is a whole row of such devices, and under each one sits a woman; most are reading, but one is eating a bowl of noodles while simultaneously slurping *oliang* from a plastic bag filled with shaved ice.

I sit down on an armchair in a corner. Manicurists and hairstylists are working feverishly. The smell of perming lotion permeates the air. Fitfully I attempt the book, but I am too excited to concentrate. I know now that I can be like the other boys. Virgil and Piak have liberated me. I, too, shall climb trees and swim naked in the *klong*. I, too, shall soon say nasty words whose meaning I am only now starting to guess at. I, too, shall indulge in a life of kleptomania and heroic excess. My hands are trembling as I clutch the book in my lap. Over and over I relive that heady rush of adrenalin I felt when I held the Ovid in my hands and *knew* I was going to steal it.

Presently, Aunt Noi-noi's chrysalid headgear is whisked away. I gasp. Truly we have both undergone a metamorphosis. For she has gained a bouffant, and I have lost my innocence.

8

Guess Who's Coming to Lunch

It is several days later. I have tried to shut Samlee out of my mind. I know now that she is employed as a receptionist at Uncle Vit's gynaecological clinic, and she departs and returns with my uncle in his Mercedes convertible. It is the opinion of the three Fates that Uncle Vit's fixation will not last and that at some stage she will be demoted back to her servile status.

By day I play in the ruined house. I have not seen my great-grandmother since the funeral of my chameleon, but there is a rumour in the servants' quarters that she has gone away to hospital. Sometimes I am worried, but no one ever speaks of it, and it is easier not to think about it.

I play alone, jealous of my territory, unwilling as yet to let Virgil share my private fantasies. By night I take Thai lessons from the gardener's son; the lessons are a secret. I have already learned words I have never heard from the lips of my three aunts.

Now it is Saturday and the day of Aunt Nit-nit's love-tryst. I have persuaded her that my new friend will be no trouble. He is the boy next door, I've told her, and an American. The plan is simple: at the movie of our choice, we will sit in the darkened theatre while my aunt slips away to join her paramour for an hour of stolen passion. This, at least, is what Aunt Nit-nit calls it. She is an avid reader of *True Confessions*, and I—in my constant search for reading matter—have perused a few issues myself, and have a general notion of what "stolen passion" means—something best enjoyed in a Maidenform bra.

I have decided—and Virgil has concurred, after an afternoon scrutinizing the listings in the *Bangkok Post*—that the film will be *Spartacus*. We've both seen it before—I've seen it four times—but it has been held over for thirteen weeks and I suspect it may be departing soon. *Spartacus* seems to have special meaning for Virgil, for the mention of it stirs him to a fervent cry of "All *right!*" It's a film with a lot of spectacle and rousing battle scenes, but it also has a few mushy *longueurs*, during which I may be able to sneak out and spy on Aunt Nit-nit. If the information is juicy enough, I should be able to exact quite a price from Aunt Noi-noi. Or I may just keep it all to myself.

Virgil is to be introduced to the three Fates at lunch, which, today, we take in the formal dining room of the wooden house, a place of high ceilings and intricately carved mouldings. I fetch him from the treehouse—he is stunningly dressed, in pinstriped shorts, long-sleeved purple shirt, and black velvet bowtie—and lead him triumphantly down the walkway and into the shoe-removing room. Virgil acquits himself well, gracefully removing his shoes before entering the dining room and not once pointing his feet at anybody. He is twice the Thai I am.

The three Fates are seated at the teak-and-glass-topped table in descending order of age, left to right. They are all, of course, still in mourning for my anonymous relative. Their black dresses are all a-spangle with lace flowers, rhinestones and sequins. They are gossiping as we approach, but their chatter falls silent when they see us. Piak, in a brand new uniform, is pouring iced tea—since he is now spending his nights in the house, it has been decided that he should be trained in the fine art of serving lunch. The portable phonograph has been moved to the side buffet, and we hear Neil Sedaka crooning in the background.

Virgil stands in the doorway, a dashing figure—the magnificent jungle king whom I, intrepid pith-helmeted hunter, have captured and brought to the benefits of civilization. He's beautiful and untamed. Oh God, I'm proud of him and proud to have been seduced by him into a life of crime.

I fully expect them to be impressed with my new friend. What I don't expect is for the three of them to "*Eaugh!*" in startled unison.

It dawns on me that they cannot have expected Virgil to be a Negro. For a few minutes, they look straight through him, studiously pretending that he isn't there. Ning-nong says to Nit-nit, in Thai, "My word! I've never seen one up close before. Do you think he'll bite?"

To which Noi-noi adds: "They strangle their wives, don't they?" thus showing that she is not entirely devoid of culture, for at least she has read *Othello*.

Virgil stares at the floor. I am so embarrassed that I contemplate suicide. I'm furious, too. This is a side of the three Fates I have never encountered before. I decide to go through with the proceedings despite them. I flash a grim smile and say, "Aunts, this is Virgil O'Fleary, our next door neighbour from America."

Virgil says, in flawless Thai, "I'm so delighted to have met you, my three Khun Aahs."

My aunts do a triple double-take. In the space of about two seconds they analyse what they have heard, come to the conclusion that they cannot possibly have heard it, and wrench their faces back to their previous vacuous expressions. Virgil and I remain standing.

"O'Fleary," Aunt Ning-nong says at last. "That's an Irish name, isn't it?"

Virgil loses his temper. "The only Irish that's in me was the overseer which done raped my great-grandma and eight months later he done whupped my granddaddy right out of her belly and left her bleedin' to death in the middle of the cotton field. She was only fourteen years old and one year shy of the 'mancipation proclamation. No ma'am, I ain't Irish, I is Yo-ru-ba and I is *black*!"

For some moments there is silence in the dining room save for the dulcet strains of Neil Sedaka. My aunts appear to have turned to stone. In our pocket universe we are not accustomed to such passion, such pain, such rage. They are foreign to us, so foreign, in fact, that my aunts refuse to acknowledge their existence. In fact, the next thing Aunt Ning-nong says is, "Well, well, well. I suppose we'd better have lunch now." I am appalled. Sullenly I sit down, and Virgil sits beside me.

Kaew comes in bearing a tray. Lunch consists of *khao chae*, rice flavoured with jasmine floating in a basin of water and crushed ice, served with shredded, sugary beef jerky and tiny lumps of shrimp paste. It is a meal that has taken the combined efforts of three kitchen staff members about three hours to prepare. In Virgil's honour, he and I are served hamburgers and black-and-white shakes. Virgil eyes the Thai food jealously. Nobody says a word for about ten minutes.

"So," Noi-noi says finally, "what film are you children going to see?" She stares fixedly at me so I won't forget that I have promised to spy on her sister.

"*Spartacus*," I mutter between mouthfuls of ground beef.

Virgil turns to ask Kaew for another glass of water. Surely it cannot have escaped my aunts' notice by now that he has understood all their disparaging remarks.

"And who are your parents, young man?" Ning-nong inquires of my friend. "What do they do for a living?"

"My father a military advisor. He a air force colonel. He in Saigon now. My mother she a anthropologist. She be studying Siamese culture for her dissertation."

The three Fates raise their eyebrows. The meal continues.

At last, the plates are cleared away. Virgil clears his throat and says to Aunt Ning-nong, "If you don't mind, ma'am, I'd like to use the bathroom. That is, if I *allowed* to use the same bathroom as you folks."

His irony is lost on my aunts. It is lost on me, too. It is only later that I will come to understand the bitterness beneath his breezy confidence. He gets up, carefully pushes in his chair, and leaves me to face the wrath of the Fates.

"How could you! How could you! How simply could you!" Aunt Ning-nong begins.

"How could I what?"

"You know very well what I mean! Bringing that . . . savage creature, that *monkey*, into this house."

"Don't be preposterous, Aunt Ning-nong," I say. "You heard him say that his father's a colonel and his mother's a scholar. He's obviously well brought up. He's an American, for God's sake, and Americans are practically civilized."

"They most certainly are not! They haven't even got a king."

"Actually," Noi-noi says, "he's really rather attractive, don't you think? I wonder if it comes off in the wash."

"He's not an animal, you know," I say. "He's my friend. Furthermore, he's a friend of Great-grandmother's, too."

"My dear Little Frog, much as we respect our honoured grandmother, she can hardly be considered anything other than a senile old bag," says Noi-noi, teasing at her brand-new bouffant with a steel comb.

Only Nit-nit has contributed nothing to this parade of prejudice. I wonder what is going through her mind. She sits there, chewing on a stick of beef jerky, mulling things over I suppose. But when Virgil returns from the lavatory it is she who takes on the role of conciliator.

"Virgil," she says softly, "forgive my sisters. They are easily frightened by new things. They have never seen someone like you before. They cannot quite believe what they see. To them, you are as mythical a beast as the unicorn or the harpy."

"I sees that," says Virgil.

"They will not do it again." She leans forward and touches Virgil lightly on the cheek, then turns and scowls at her sisters as if to say, "Look here, you silly girls, it doesn't rub off."

I am profoundly grateful to Aunt Nit-nit for trying to smooth things over. I decide that I will always be loyal to her, and I'll never reveal the identity of her secret lover to Noi-noi, even if she bribes me or rakes me with her fingernails. It is now too that I understand that my three aunts are afraid, deathly afraid, of anything outside the confines of their walled Eden. I put my hand on Virgil's shoulder and try to convey all this without words, but perhaps it is too late.

"I think we should be on our way to the cinema now," Aunt Nit-nit says at last. She wipes her mouth, takes both us boys by the hand, and drags us out of the room toward the foyer and the waiting Studebaker.

We are in a movie theatre in Wang Burapha. What a theatre! A soaring palace with balconies and boxes and cathedral ceilings frescoed with mythological scenes. I hear the breathing of thousands upon thousands in the dark as our usherette points us to our seats with her flashlight. Refreshment vendors scurry up and down the aisles, laden with rare viands—Smarties, Mars bars and *buoi khems*. At Nit-nit's insistence, we have obtained twenty-baht seats at the back of the first balcony, centre aisle, near the exit, so she can slip away quickly. I haven't told Virgil about her planned escapade.

Nit-nit summons a passing vendor and buys more sweets than a human being could possibly consume in two hours without vomiting, and drops the entire pile on our laps. She is becoming more and more distracted, glancing down every five seconds at her luminous Cartier, fussing with her purse. Virgil doesn't speak because his mouth is full.

Aunt Nit-nit frets her way through the commercials and only perks up when a trailer for *Cleopatra* comes on.

At last the curtain rises. The screen image stretches and curves out so that we seem to be completely surrounded by the film, and the rousing score by Alex North fills the auditorium. It is the overture. We've got a good seven or eight minutes before the film begins.

I pop a handful of Smarties into my mouth and then I realize that Aunt Nit-nit has already disappeared. She hasn't even bothered to wait for the opening credits.

9

Dr. Frankenstein

The mountains. The slaves. The centurions trudging uphill, wielding their whips. The chains that clank in the streaming sun. Kirk Douglas, slick with sweat, hamstringing a guard with his teeth, while heroic music pounds us. Peter Ustinov, simultaneously dainty and corpulent, surveys the spectacle under the shade of a ridiculous parasol. Oh God, I love this film and so does Virgil; he's reciting every line of the dialogue under his breath, pausing only to stuff himself with Smarties.

I am being ineluctably drawn into the drama, and yet I am also wondering where Aunt Nit-nit has gone, and whom her secret admirer could be. I know that the longer I stay the harder it will be to tear myself away. Virgil has no idea of the intrigue that has brought us here today. I will slip away, silently, silently, slither along the aisle like a *phii krasue* in the night. Quickly, before Aunt Nit-nit vanishes into thin air.

I'm standing in the aisle now. Peter Ustinov gestures languorously as he selects Kirk Douglas to be trained in the art of combat. Virgil stares straight ahead. But then, as I turn my back on the screen, I hear him murmur, "Bring us back some more candy, Justin."

"Sure," I whisper. I leave him to his fantasies.

I pass through murky velvet into brilliant daylight. The foyer of the theatre has been temporarily redecorated in the style of a Roman temple, with Ionic columns and plaster busts of Laurence Olivier and fake marble cupids fluttering over the concession stalls with their candy and their glass cases full of pickled guavas; the sun streams down past god-like cut-outs of Kirk Douglas and Jean Simmons, three storeys high; from behind me thunders the epic score. Where is Aunt Nit-nit? There is no one in the foyer save for the women in the concession booths and a man sipping a soft drink on a marble bench, a white-haired man whose back is turned to me, who seems to be staring anxiously ahead, waiting for someone. He is wearing a Hawaiian shirt, and I can see the back of his neck, red and leathery. He is a Caucasian.

Could this be the man? Surely not. He cranes his neck in the direction of the theatre, and I catch a glimpse of his face. Quickly I duck into the shadow of the monstrous two-dimensional Kirk Douglas. That face . . . I have seen that face before.

Leering over me as I lie feverish and twisting. Gleefully brandishing a hypodermic syringe. Cackling as he expounds, in intimate detail, the reproductive cycle of the streptococcus.

Dr. Richardson!

Hunched down, terrified of discovery, I peep over the top of Kirk's sandal. I cannot risk being seen.

At that moment, Aunt Nit-nit emerges from the women's lavatory, jowls a-tremble, glancing furtively behind her, glancing left and right, glancing everywhere but at the place where Dr. Richardson awaits. Her lipstick is redder than usual, her mascara bolder. She sort of works her way over to the bench while the good doctor studiously sips his soda. Neither of them looks at the other. At length, she sits down on one end of the bench, gazing fixedly to the west, while Dr. Richardson stares with equal concentration toward the east.

They speak—in opposite directions—each one taking turns. I do not understand how one can hold a conversation in this manner, yet they seem to manage. My aunt protests; Dr. Richardson cajoles. My aunt weeps. Dr. Richardson consoles; my aunt laughs. Dr. Richardson assumes a sombre aspect and proffers a mentholated Benson & Hedges cigarette. I have never seen her smoke, but she seems quite proficient.

I desperately want to watch some more, but my body clock tells me that Kirk Douglas, Woody Strode, et al., are about to do battle for the amusement of Roman patricians in the private arena of the obsequious Peter Ustinov. It is a gladiatorial combat not to be missed, for not only does it contain a fair amount of bloodshed, but there are also friendships betrayed, lustful glances exchanged, and skulduggeries spawned. Aunt Nit-nit and Dr. Richardson, though they are present in the flesh, cannot quite compete with the passion of Kirk Douglas and Jean Simmons, for, far from rolling about in the meadows of the foothills of Vesuvius, they are not even looking at each other!

In any case, I promised to bring Virgil more candy, and he might grow suspicious, so I start to back away toward the staircase that leads to the balcony. I have no money for sweets, but my newly acquired skill at the five-finger discount allows me to pocket several tubes of Smarties as I make my way up the stairs.

The scene of gladiatorial combat is stunning. I note that Virgil doesn't seem to have moved since I left him. As I slip into the seat beside him, he holds out a clammy hand for Smarties. Laurence Olivier jabs a poignard into a recalcitrant fighter who has dared to try to storm the spectators' gallery, and the audience gasps. I am torn between wanting to watch the next scene and finding out what my aunt and the doctor are up to now.

After a while I can't stand it any more. Like Dr. Frankenstein, I have to know more. I get up again.

This time, Virgil murmurs: "You got a bladder like a sieve, Justin."

I pour more Smarties into his hand.

"You gone miss the whole damn movie."

"I can't help it, Virgil—I've got to go. You know how it is—too many milk shakes. Asians can't metabolize cow's milk very well, you know," I say, repeating one of Dr. Richardson's lectures verbatim, "that's why it gives us diarrhoea."

"No more biology lessons! Just don't be doing it in your pants!"

I am just in time to see the star-crossed lovers leave the foyer and venture into the street. They are still not looking at each other. They do not seem about to walk in the same direction, and yet there is a certain purposefulness in the way they both veer to the left. Dr. Richardson pauses to buy a bag of pickled guavas; my aunt pauses to look in the window of an antique shop at such an angle that she can see Dr. Richardson's reflection shimmering over a row of Ming spittoons. Presently, Dr. Richardson crosses the street, dextrously weaving in and out of the screeching traffic, while Aunt Nit-nit, puffing furiously on her cigarette, works her way slowly toward the corner without ever seeming to heed him. It is a *pas de deux* of studied indifference, and both of them seem well versed in its steps. Indeed, for a woman who cannot essay the mashed potatoes or the limbo rock without falling flat on her face, Aunt Nit-nit is performing this dance with surprising grace. There is something of *Fantasia* about it all, though. I mean that segment with the elephants lumbering through the "Dance of the Hours", or perhaps it's the part with the dinosaurs dining on one another to the strains of Stravinsky.

A little farther down the street, there is an open-air noodle stand nestled in the shadow of the Central department store. Its roof is a blue tarpaulin attached at one end to a tree, at another to a pole, and at the back to a crude bamboo scaffolding. In front, a vendor is juggling three or four bowls of *kuaitiao*, seasoning one, chopping meat into another, ladling broth into a third. The air swims with heat, moisture and petrol fumes.

My aunt has not seen me. There are too many people, and I am quick to duck behind parked cars and telephone poles.

The two of them sit down at adjacent tables. They order food from a girl who shrieks out their order to the juggling chef, and their bowls of soup appear almost at once: Aunt Nit-nit's a noodle-less *kaolao*, Dr. Richardson's a crimson *yentafo* that reeks of vinegar and spice. I am almost close enough to touch them now. I wish I could hear what they are saying to each other, these two strange lovers who never look at each other as they sit, grimly sipping their soup. I take cover behind the tree from whose branches hangs the tarpaulin shielding them from the sun. I can't hear what they're saying, but I see that Aunt Nit-nit has taken advantage of Dr. Richardson's distraction to remove the *ajarn's* nine-baht love potion from her purse and is even now dumping its contents into his *yentafo*. Oh, to know what they are saying to each other, this pair of flightless lovebirds—my aunt who waddles like a turkey, my doctor who cranes like an ostrich!

Spartacus is quite forgotten. In any case—if I have judged the timing correctly—we have reached the moment when Tony Curtis, an improbable boy bard, "sings" to the congregation of escaped slaves that ennui-inducing poem about purple mountains and crimson shadows or something—a moment which seems to go on for ever, with Kirk and Jean hugging and kissing and carrying on about how they're going to have a baby and so on and so forth—a part of the film entirely devoid of spectacle, gore or martial music.

Here, on the other hand, music is blaring from a radio. It's the opening theme from *Ben Hur*, which shortly segues into an episode of one of the daily radio soap operas. It's hard to eavesdrop above the din. If I could only inch my way just a little bit closer. . . .

If only I could get up on that branch below the tarpaulin that so conveniently overhangs the space between their two tables. . . .

It has only been a week since I first learned to climb trees. But of course, I am now an expert. *A little learning is a dangerous thing.*

The treehouse in the mango orchard is surely far more daunting than this tree that sprouts up from the crowded pavement. But the treehouse is in a secret place; this tree is very public. Nevertheless, no one is paying much attention to me. I am just eighty-eight pounds of boy, slim as a sliver of shadow. The trunk is exposed but the rest of the tree is so dense with foliage that I can easily camouflage myself or, flitting among the leaves, be mistaken for someone's pet gibbon. I close my eyes, take a deep swallow—and it's as though I've teleported up to the branch. I'm crawling along the bough now, breathing in sap and ants, and presently I find myself right between the two of them, precariously perched a couple of feet above their heads.

They don't say anything for perhaps five minutes. I am stretched out along the limb, my toes curled around and locked to keep from falling. I don't know what kind of tree this is but it's making me itch. Sap oozes on to my fingers. Where the bark has bitten me, the rheum seeps into the sore and the burning makes me want to scratch. It is unbearable. Furthermore, the *kuaitiao* broth smells so good I'm afraid I may drool into Dr. Richardson's aphrodisiac-spiked *yentafo*.

Just when the itching, the mouth-watering and the balancing have become intolerable, Dr. Richardson speaks, and I become too absorbed to think of my discomfort.

"You know," he is telling Aunt Nit-nit, all the while avoiding her gaze, "I'm afraid this can't go on. The wife, you know. Bit of a nuisance, but, well, I say, yes, what."

"Bit of a nuisance!" Aunt Nit-nit replies. "After a year of clandestine assignations, you want to destroy my life to stave off a 'bit of a nuisance'! Don't you know that you've ruined me—that I shall never love again?"

"Come, come, old thing, what, what. We've had some jolly times, but, well, I say, what, what, what."

Dr. Richardson out-*eaughs* my three aunts. His mode of utterance redefines the very concept of *eaughing*. But I don't have time to be impressed. Dr. Richardson is making me quite, quite angry, because I really am rather fond of Aunt Nit-nit, who was the only one to spring to the defence of Virgil at lunch, and who, after all, is paying me fifty baht for an alibi. For fifty baht, I think, she deserves at least a few honeyed words, not this laconic "what, what, what".

And the good doctor had "ruined" her! Perhaps she had allowed him to use her in his experiments—perhaps, even now, a strain of mutant streptococci was taking over her entire body and would soon transform her into a giant bacterium!

"And besides," she adds sulkily, "I've missed my period again."

"Oh, I say, what."

"I'm not going to have my brother Vit do it! I'd feel safer using a coat-hanger."

This conversation is taking a decidedly baroque turn. I am now convinced that scientific experiments are involved. So Dr. Richardson is a modern-day Frankenstein after all, as I've always suspected! I lean forward a little more, rubbing my body against the branch to quell the itch.

"And what am I to say to you next time you make a house call? Knowing how many times I feigned an attack of strep throat just so you could satisfy your lust?"

So it *is* the demon streptococci! I'm furious at Dr. Richardson, but the idea of Aunt Nit-nit turning into a fifty-foot woman or a giant cockroach does have its appeal.

"And I can tell," Aunt Nit-nit continues, "that you're still in lust, even if you're no longer in love. That's why I've reserved a room for us at your favourite sleazy hotel."

Dr. Richardson raises an eyebrow. "Oh, I say, what, what." He drains the last drops of the *yentafo* broth and adds, "Well, you know, I suppose, well, all of a sudden, I am in the mood, ra-*ther*." Clearly the love potion is starting to kick in.

"Oh, don't worry, there's plenty of time. My nephew is watching one of those beastly Roman epics—it won't be over for at least another hour and a half."

It is at that moment that I discover that I'm not quite as good at climbing trees as I thought. The urge to scratch overpowers me. I shift. I lose my balance. I swing my arms out wildly and manage to seize hold of my aunt's hair. She screams. I come tumbling down, and find myself ignominiously squatting between the doctor and my aunt, an upturned bowl of noodles on my head.

"A spy!" Dr. Richardson whispers and turns accusingly to my aunt. I can hardly see them, because my eyes are smarting from the pickled chillies.

Somehow I have to salvage the situation. Aunt Nit-nit is in danger. If I don't talk fast, I'm going to be in even worse danger. "I'll save you!" I squeak. "Don't let him touch you again!" And then, venting the full force of my childish wrath on Dr. Richardson, I start pummelling him with my fists.

"I won't let you turn her into a giant cockroach!" I scream. "Quick, Aunt Nit-nit, run, before he lures you back into his laboratory!"

10

Love's Labours Lost

To my amazement, Aunt Nit-nit does not seem too pleased at my display of chivalry. Rather than praising me for rescuing her from a fate worse than death, she braces herself to release a penetrating shriek. In mid-scream, however, she changes her mind, and what actually escapes her throat is a practically soundless, strangulated *eaugh*. Dr. Richardson, on the other hand, seems more bemused than horrified.

"Oh, I say," says Dr. Richardson. "Ra-*ther*."

Aunt Nit-nit sits down again. An aluminium soup spoon clatters to the floor. With excruciating slowness, the noodle bowl slides off my head and shatters on the pavement. Three or four mangy dogs converge upon it, and the rest of the scene is accompanied by a chorus of canine slurps, yelps and growls. I study my aunt's face and try to fathom the emotions at war within her. There is a trace of amusement in her demeanour at first, but it is rapidly being replaced by an insensate rage. Indeed, I have never seen her this furious before.

"I'll pay back the twenty-five baht advance," I tell her. "With interest, if you like."

She fumes.

At last, Dr. Richardson simply cannot help himself. He starts to laugh. His laughter becomes a hearty guffawing, and when I look around I see that the other customers at the noodle stand are steadfastly looking away, politely shielding their mirth behind purses, beer bottles or newspapers.

"What a splendid lad!" Dr. Richardson says, and claps me on the back with such force that I am propelled across the grease-slicked pavement and find myself all tangled up in one of those metal folding chairs. "He thought I was going to use you for my experiments, what, what. Streptococci! Oh, I say."

"When we get home," Nit-nit says, "you are going to take the longest, most thorough, most skin-scraping bath of your life. You reek of pickled peppers and *nam pla prik*."

Her words strike terror. No longer is she one of the Fates—she has been transmogrified into one of the Furies, who can only be appeased with human blood.

"Oh, let the boy be," Dr. Richardson says. "As a matter of fact . . ." Suddenly he has a twinkle in his eye and a kindliness I have never seen, perhaps due to the fact that he has realized that I now know his identity and could conceivably ruin everything by blabbing to the wrong person. "How would you like to see my laboratory with your own eyes, what, what? I've got several new mutant streptococci and . . ."

Suddenly he no longer resembles Dr. Frankenstein. He is more like one of those imposing, all-knowing scientist-heroes who populate the novels of Isaac Asimov, all of which I have read countless times.

"In fact," he says, dropping his voice to a dramatic whisper, "I'll even let you chain your aunt to the lightning rod yourself!" He starts to whistle the eerie theremin theme from the opening credits of *The Outer Limits*, and I realize that there is some common ground between us after all. "Oh, you must be burning all over. Those trees itch like the very devil. Used to climb them meself, when I was a lad, what, what." He fishes a tube of ointment out of his pocket and hands it to me.

I get up and try to clean off some of the mess by dousing myself with ice-cold tea. At length, the good doctor pulls twenty-five baht from his wallet and hands it to me. "I say, here's the rest of your bounty money," he says, "and now you'd best get back to *Spartacus* so your aunt and I can get on with . . . ahem . . . our little business."

Aunt Nit-nit hasn't said a word. She is baffled by the conversation between me and the doctor. I am not surprised at her confusion, since my reading of science fiction books as well as DC comics has shown me conclusively that scientific discourse is confined to the male of the species. In science fiction, women only make coffee, wring their hands, or sigh admiringly and uncomprehendingly at the abstruse utterances of their beaux. I am honoured that Dr. Richardson has seen fit to invite me into his lab. Obviously he respects my intellect.

"Don't worry, Aunt Nit-nit. I will never betray you," I tell her with the utmost gravity as I pluck the last pieces of noodle from my shirt. "Even though Aunt Noi-noi offered to buy me any book I wanted if I would reveal the identity of your lover."

A look of sudden alarm crosses Dr. Richardson's face. But it is quickly suppressed. For a moment I wonder if he has more secrets to be discovered. But surely there have been enough secrets for one day.

Aunt Nit-nit smiles faintly. Although she is not the most beautiful of my aunts, she does have the most appealing smile. One can see, behind her rotundity of visage, the fragility of Noi-noi and the strength of Ning-nong, and there is also a serenity in her that the other two do not possess.

"My beloved nephew," she says in Thai, "how I wish your parents were here to see how well you are growing up. Oh, to think that you would think of trying to rescue me, trapped as I am in a prison of my own making!"

I think she knows I understand her. She can see through me more easily than her sisters, but I do not really mind that she knows. She turns to Dr. Richardson and continues in English, "Yes, for old times' sake. The sleazy room, the half-truths told to your poor wife.

Next time we meet we will just be acquaintances. And about my period . . . I lied."

They get up and walk away. They do not avoid each other this time. They walk side by side, almost touching. Why is it that the three Fates always speak of periods? I conclude that women have a broader view of history than men, that they are more aware of their place in the grand totality of time. Ruefully I watch my aunt and my doctor disappear into the crowd. Are they estranged now, or are they closer than they were before—or both?

And then there is the mention of my parents. I am reminded of my uncompleted epic poem, hidden in the Botticelli box, and I think cold thoughts. I think of snow and secret missions.

I am dismayed to discover that I have missed most of *Spartacus*. They are already crucifying everyone by the time I arrive back in my seat, and Peter Ustinov has already been lashed and undergone his change of heart. As I slide in beside my abandoned friend, I notice that he does not seem to have moved; although the sweets have long since been consumed, he continues to stare at the screen with rapt attention.

It is the final scene of the movie. Jean Simmons has been released from slavery, and she is being driven out of Rome, her baby in her arms, past the thousands of slaves who have been crucified along the Appian Way. The revolt is crushed, slavery will not end for another two thousand years, and Kirk Douglas, his cleft-chinned visage clenched in an expression of marmoreal pathos, looks down at his beloved from his cross. I realize from having devoured countless books about the Romans that this is an inaccurate crucifixion. When thousands were to be crucified, the Romans did not use the Jesus-style display crosses, but strung up their criminals at street level, so that passers-by could look right into their faces as they rotted away . . . oh, yes, they rotted, as it were, on the hoof, since they didn't use nails except on very special occasions, preferring instead the slow asphyxiation, the body sagging, caving in on itself, crushing the lungs. Oh, yes, I know my ancient tortures all by heart, for there is an excellent book by Daniel P. Mannix on the subject.

Jean Simmons holds the baby up for the dying Spartacus to see. "He's free," she whispers. "He's *free!*"

There are tears in her eyes. And suddenly, as I cast a sidelong glance at my new friend, I see that he, too, is weeping. Openly, copiously, without shame. And his lips are moving softly, mouthing the words of the script: *free, free.* Truly Virgil is an impassioned creature. I think back to his outburst at the lunch table, and I realize what this film really means to him. I realize that he is thinking of his great-grandmother and the overseer and the awful circumstances of his grandfather's birth; I realize that his great-grandmother, raped at thirteen, dead at fourteen, is as real to him as my own great-grandmother is to me, although he has never met her, has heard of her only through the tales passed down through the generations, down through a hundred years. I do not yet quite know what rape is, except that it's something Vikings do when they go on raids, something that goes with fire and the sword, but I know that it is some kind of violent disruption of the cycle of birth and death.

Oh, God, I envy him his oft-told tales. I do not have a past. I don't know where my parents are. All I have are some vague memories and an epic poem that I'm writing out of my own imagination. My own great-grandmother is still living; she is not a shadow of a remembrance like the young black girl on a plantation in Georgia. Yet I did not even know of her existence until a week or so ago. She is a fount of wisdom, yet I have been denied that wisdom until now. Oh, why did I not have her to turn to in the three years that have gone by? I feel a pang of guilt at not having thought of her in the last few days. I wonder what has happened to her. I wonder if she has been taken to the hospital to die. Virgil is more faithful to his great-grandmother than I am. Did he not rise to defend her honour when the Fates impugned it, even at the risk of spoiling their lunch?

Virgil is a child of a country less than two hundred years old, yet his life is rooted in tradition. I, a creature of a far more ancient culture, have nothing; I manufacture my own past.

These thoughts flit through my mind as I watch the scene. For some reason I cannot get involved in the plight of poor old Spartacus. Surely I have not become jaded by spectacle! No, no. It is only that so much has happened in the last few days. The tragicomic chain of events that began with the death of my chameleon is leading inexorably toward the unravelling of the threads painstakingly spun by the three Fates. I am overwhelmed with the wonder of life as I sit there, soaked in noodle broth and fish sauce, dreaming of the past and the future.

In the days to come, the other two Fates begin to accept Virgil, if not an equal, then at least a necessary evil. The seven-day funeral of my anonymous ancestor has finally drawn to a close, and the Fates' discovery that Virgil is a great expert at the dance crazes of 1963 has enticed them to admit that he is, at any rate, a fit companion for my wayward self.

Mornings he comes over for breakfast. No longer do I demand bacon and eggs, for under his influence I have become a connoisseur of the foods of my own country—I no longer balk at rice gruel, though I am not yet daring enough to spice my food with whole chillies the way Virgil does. Over breakfast there is the obligatory dance class, and the three sisters line up and go through their steps as Virgil gently urges them on in Thai. Piak, our servitor in the presence of the Fates, giggles with us when their backs are turned. Aunt Nit-nit, of course, is still sick with love. I have promised her I shall become quite ill next week to provide her with fresh bait for luring the good doctor back to the house.

Afternoons we play in the treehouse. We spy on the goings-on through the windows of the brick house. Samlee is hardly ever to be seen now, since she accompanies Uncle Vit to the clinic every day. There is a gaping wound in my existence that my newfound friends cannot quite heal.

Nights I add to my repertoire of obscene expressions. I dream of going on another nocturnal foray down the *klong*, but there doesn't seem to be any good reason for it yet.

Then, one day, up in the treehouse, as we munch on the exotic peanut butter and jelly sandwiches that Virgil has brought over from his house, my friend says to me: "It ain't fair. Every day, I come over here, I be in you territory, I be eating you food and dancing with you aunts. It about time you come over to the other side of the wall. It about time you my guest for a change."

"Is our rude fare too meagre for you?" I ask him in my best imitation of an H. Rider Haggard African king.

Virgil laughs. "No, it don't be too meagre a-tall. But I want you to come over to where us poor folks lives. I want you to sleep over at my place and meet my mother and my sister Jessica."

I have never spent the night under any roof other than my own. Oh, now and then a hotel, but always with some relative well within screaming distance. Yet they are planning to send me away, thousands of miles away, to a school in the cold and secret country.

"Well, ain't you glad I asked you?" says Virgil. "My mother she anxious to meet you. After all, you people owns the house we renting. It a good thing for her that you and me friends."

11

Another Country

It is another week before I venture to accept Virgil's invitation. For one thing, I have had to become very ill one day in order to facilitate the summoning of Dr. Richardson, and my imaginary illness is followed by an imaginary convalescence of two days. Dr. Richardson's visit is, in fact, accomplished in haste. Surely, I think as I lie in bed being fanned by the faithful Kaew, surely there cannot have been time enough to do whatever it is that adults do that is so important as to make them devise all these convoluted plans to do this thing, whatever it is, for which I have no name.

Dr. Richardson is so distracted that he doesn't seem to remember that he promised me a tour of his laboratory. In fact, he doesn't even seem to realize that I am pretending to be sick in order to please Aunt Nit-nit. In fact, he actually gives me an injection in the buttocks, which lends, I think, a little too much verisimilitude to our drama.

Thirty minutes. It hardly seems worth the agony. And since, of course, I am lying in bed, I cannot eavesdrop on the two of them as they converse in the pavilion over the pond.

After half an hour Dr. Richardson pokes his head into my bedroom. He seems chagrined. "Keep taking the pills, old chap," he says, and then departs. I hear, diminuendoing into the distance, a long and continuous "what, what, what", like the rattle of a repeating rifle.

It dawns on me that the injection was no accident. It is retribution. The good doctor has not been pleased with me. Somehow I have interfered with his love life. I have become, along with his wife, "a bit of a nuisance".

In my depression, I open the Botticelli box and gaze at the epic poem I have been composing about my parents' absence.

O Muses! the poem begins, for there is nothing nobler than an apostrophizing opening:

> O Muses! sing of my parents' absence inexplicable,
> Which hath cast a blight upon my wretched soul;
> Sing of my sorrow, for the Fates are fickle,
> And furthermore, I'm only twelve years old.

As I stare at these lines, penned in a state of lambent passion, it occurs to me for the first time that I'm not much of a poet. I know of rhyming what a colour-blind person knows of colour, and as for prosody, I am blessed with two left feet. Inspiration does not, it seems, automatically give birth to technique.

It is a chilling realization. To know at twelve years old that one is incapable of attaining one's ambitions! Ah, hubris! Unlucky in love, ungifted by the Muse, and stabbed in the rear by the dart of Dr. Richardson's revenge, I am the world's most miserable creature.

It is probably time to embark on a new career. A nuclear physicist, perhaps. International espionage has its attractions, though I'm not quite sure how one goes about getting such jobs.

And there is always suicide, which holds an aura of romance, though it does have a certain finality.

On the appointed day, I walk over to the O'Flearys' house, my overnight appurtenances carried in a little BOAC flight bag by Piak, who observes proper protocol by lagging a seemly two feet behind me. In my hands is the pilfered Ovid. In my heart trepidation.

The O'Flearys have no servants. The door is flung open by a buxom black woman who greets me effusively. "Justin, honey," she says to me, and plants a kiss on my forehead, "Virgil has told me so much about you. Why, you're just about the smartest kid he's ever met. You write poetry, I hear. You must give us a recital."

This is the first stunning discovery of the day. Virgil's mother does not talk like her son. Her speech has another kind of lilt to it, and is innocent of Virgil's unusual grammatical constructions. The difference becomes even more obvious when Virgil bounds down the stairs, shouting, "Well, it about time! I just about done give up on you."

"Now, Virgil," says his mother. She turns to me and shrugs. I do not know why she is shrugging, so I just shrug along with her. Perhaps it is some arcane Yoruba ritual of greeting. Since Virgil's passionate announcement to my aunts that he is Yoruba, I have looked "Yoruba" up in the dusty encyclopaedia in the ruined house. It appears to have something to do with Nigeria, which confuses me still further. I know that Virgil is from Georgia, and that it's not the Georgia that's in the Soviet Union. Or is it? If I can be a creature of two worlds, surely my friend can be one of three continents.

"Come on upstairs, Justin," Virgil says, "I'm gone show you my room."

Then the second astonishing thing happens: Mrs. O'Fleary turns to her son and addresses him in the language with which I have become familiar in the last few weeks: "I told you a million times, honey, don't you be talking like you daddy in front of just ever'body. People they don't follow what you saying, and—" Turning to me, she adds, switching dialects in mid-thought, "I don't want to forbid him to speak Black English, of course—I want him to be proud of who he is—but you know, I do try to encourage him to practise the prestige dialect in his interactions with the world outside our cultural microcosm—you know what I mean, I'm sure, Justin." She chuckles, and I feel that I am being made privy to some complex joke, were I but able to comprehend its convolutions.

"That easy for you to say, Momma," says Virgil, "cause you a cultural anthropologist."

It occurs to me that I have been so busy being astonished that I haven't really begun to take in the immense spectacle of this, the living room of an alien family. It doesn't surprise me to see Mrs. O'Fleary wearing a pair of shoes, nor that I have not taken my own off. I remember that from England. It doesn't surprise me that Piak has cast aside his servile stance and is now brazenly standing right beside me; we have a tacit agreement now that he need behave like a servant only when my relatives are present. But the décor, the décor . . . it is as though the set of *Leave It to Beaver* had been transplanted to Bangkok and painted in lurid colours. The floral couches are huge and plump, so that one could well lose oneself in them. There is a shaggy pink wall-to-wall carpet that makes me wonder why people don't want to take their shoes off and wiggle their toes. A kind of shrine, with military portraits, topped with a photograph of a smiling President Kennedy, stands against one wall. Opposite it, next to the staircase, is an incongruous tableau: a leering wooden African mask, a couple of drums, an assegai and an ebony statue of a monstrously fat, nude woman. My gaze lingers on the mask, with its empty eyes, and I think of the shaman beside the *klong*; I stare at the thick shaft of the assegai, with its stranded pennon wrapped around a deadly spike—I cannot tell whether the brown stain on the spear-tip is rust or blood.

So amazing is this spectacle that I fail to observe that my friend Virgil isn't wearing any clothes. Not until he speaks to me again, awakening me from my reverie, do I notice that he is wet, dripping and clenching a towel under one arm.

"You stay here, Justin," says Virgil, "while I finishes my shower. Momma she fix you something to eat."

I am dismayed to discover that Virgil is larger than me in every respect. I don't know why I should feel so dismayed, but my little aubergine shrinks in shame to see my friend's endowment so shamelessly displayed. Confusion floods me. Why is this thing so important? I don't even know what it's for. Well, not exactly.

Virgil rushes back up the stairs, leaving me alone with Mrs. O'Fleary, for Piak, after dumping my things on a chair, has unceremoniously departed.

"Oh Justin, honey," she says, "Virgil is so, ah, undisciplined sometimes. Maybe you can teach him some manners."

She directs me to one of the sofas. I am pleased that she is addressing me by my secret name. She is a handsome, full-figured woman, and she wears a voluminous batik robe, which she fills almost to bursting. As she sits down, she makes an enormous dent in the upholstery, which curls on either side of her. I sit, too—on the neighbouring couch, for there is something a little forbidding about her amplitude—and see that there is a plate of chocolate chip cookies on the coffee table, alongside a pitcher of milk and some glasses.

"Do try one, darlin'," she says to me, "I made them myself."

I bite into one. The sweetness dazes me. I am transported. I gobble up the entire cookie, heedless of decorum.

Mrs. O'Fleary chuckles. "My husband tells me that my cookies send him straight into insulin shock."

"Um, thank you so much, Mrs. O'Fleary."

"Won't you call me Renée?"

I become even more confused. Is nothing sacred in this topsyturvy house? Is there no hierarchy at all, that children can casually call adults by their Christian names without dire reprisal? All is chaos here. I do not know whether this is Asia, America, or darkest Africa. In my despair, I stuff another cookie into my mouth.

It is at that moment, with the cookie crumbs cramming my throat and Mrs. O'Fleary discoursing learnedly whilst pouring me a glass of milk, that I hear, for the first time, the voice of an angel, a voice that will propel me through the mysteries of manhood; a voice that will be present at the moment when I complete my metamorphosis and emerge from the chrysalis of childhood. It is the voice of a girl, and it is singing to me from an inner room, accompanied by throbbing piano chords. I do not know what language she is singing in. It is a silvery, high-pitched voice. A young voice, a voice whose seeming innocence conceals a subtle sensuality.

At first, I am sure that this is some kind of private visitation from the gods. Mrs. O'Fleary, after all, does not seem visibly touched by any angelic manifestation. She finishes pouring the milk and holds it out to me in her cushiony hands. I do not take the milk. I just sit there, mesmerized by the sound. The melody is a continuous stream, an arc of sound, soaring up until it teasingly touches an impossibly high note and comes plummeting down to rest.

At last, the song ends. But the final chord still hovers in the air, and I feel a yawning emptiness within me. I realize that Mrs. O'Fleary has been talking to me. I have no idea what to reply.

"Delicious," I say. I down the entire glass of milk. I forget that I hate milk. I'm not supposed to drink it because, according to Dr. Richardson, people in this part of the world lack the enzyme necessary to digest it. As a result, I will spend the entire evening farting. This will deal a fatal blow to my attempts to project unassailable *savoir-faire*.

I compound the error by wiping off my milk-moustache on my sleeve.

At that moment the owner of that voice enters the living room. She is preceded by a gaunt, bespectacled Catholic priest, who carries a sheaf of music books under his arm and whose hair is a wild mass of white.

"Jessica's doing very well with the Schubert, Mrs. O'Fleary," he says in a German accent, "I do think her performance on Tuesday will be most fetching, *nicht wahr*?"

"Well, Father Regenstrom," says Mrs. O'Fleary, "I'm glad you could take the time to come and play through her songs with her."

"Ah, but what is life without *Lieder*?"

That, I think to myself, is probably how Jupiter felt when he transformed himself into a swan, an episode that I have just been reading in my Ovid. And that is what I'm thinking now as I gaze at Jessica O'Fleary, who has become, in an instant, Samlee's replacement, the dusky angel of my passion. Nay, let us not say replacement. Let us say rather that, having seen only imperfect copies of womanhood in my life, I am now gazing in adoration at the Platonic ideal of woman.

Jessica smiles at me. She is a year or two older than Virgil. She is tall and wiry like her brother, and she is very dark, with narrow, almost Caucasian nose and lips. She is wearing a white halter-top that hugs her shallow breasts, and a pair of faded jeans with tattered holes that are windows to the firm flesh beneath. Her hair is woven into beaded strands, and in her ears are hoops of gold.

Mrs. O'Fleary offers the priest some cookies. I continue to stare at Jessica as though I've never seen a woman before.

"*Und wer ist dieses Dreikäsehoch?*" Father Regenstrom says, patting me on the head. His cookie crumbles into my hair.

"Oh," says Mrs. O'Fleary, "that's Justin, the boy next door."

"Pleased to meet you, my son," says Father Regenstrom. He strokes my hair. I feel somewhat put out. Surely he should know that the head is the seat of the soul, not to be profaned by a stranger.

"Justin," says Jessica. Even without singing, there is music in her voice.

There is a moment of unbearable tension. I realize we are alone together, for her mother is seeing the priest out. What does one say when one encounters a messenger of the divine? Jessica reaches out to touch me on the cheek. A shudder thrills through my entire body.

Then she turns and goes up the stairs just as Virgil comes dashing down, dressed and full of boyish energy.

"I see you done met my sister Jessica," he says.

"Y-y-yes."

"What do you think?"

It comes blurting out all at once: "I think she's absolutely splendid! I want to see more of her!"

"Oh, you will," he says. "You gone see a lot more of her. *A lot.* Tonight."

He winks at me salaciously, leaving me to wonder what new adventures have been planned for me by this wayward and eccentric family.

12

Orpheus in the Underworld

Dinner at the O'Fleary household is a chaotic affair, and utterly devoid of *eaughing*. I do not enjoy dinner that much, for the gas has already begun to build up from the glass of milk. The repast consists of exotic delicacies—Cajun fried catfish, barbecued ribs and so on—and I am forced to admit that even the wildest concoctions of the three Fates' kitchen are not as bizarre as these. It does not help that Virgil continually teases me during dinner by asking me whether their rude fare is too meagre for me.

"It's very good, thank you," I say in my most priggish voice. The propinquity of the beauteous Jessica, seated right across the dinner table, smiling, laughing, now and then giggling daintily, does not make it any easier for me to eat, especially since I am endeavouring to restrain myself from farting.

"Do try the black-eyed peas," Mrs. O'Fleary says.

I cannot get used to being served by the mistress of the house. I keep looking around warily, wondering whether the servants are going to pop up from behind the buffet or the grandfather clock.

The black-eyed peas roll around on my plate.

"So, darlin'," says Mrs. O'Fleary—I cannot quite bring myself to think of her as Renée—"you're going to Eton next year?"

How could she know this? I have never mentioned it to Virgil. It is one of my secrets.

She sees my dismay, for she adds, "The old lady, the *khunying*, told me about it. Oh, you are such a lucky boy . . . I've been there, and I've seen the spires of College Chapel from the ramparts of Windsor Castle . . . oh, you are fortunate . . . though maybe you'll be lonely at first."

"I don't even know whether I'm really going," I tell her. "There's an entrance exam to pass, you know, and I haven't been to school in months."

"I ain't goin' to no school," says Virgil, "even if it open up again."

"We've been making do," says Mrs. O'Fleary, "and Father Regenstrom has been kind enough to come and help with our Jessica's music lessons. Do have some root beer, Justin honey."

I try it. It tastes like carbonated pepper.

"It real special root beer," says Virgil. "We gets it from the PX."

"What was the name of that song?" I ask, not quite daring to pose the question to Jessica directly.

"It be called '*An die Musik*,'" she says, "which mean 'To Music'. It's German." Her voice itself is music. I can't help staring at her, can't help looking in every direction that her eyes dart. She starts to translate the words of the song: "'Oh, music,' it say, 'you beautiful art; when the dark and terrible time come, you done magicked me away to a better kingdom, far away . . . "It kind of corny," she adds, "but the tune is pretty."

What profound, poetic sentiments! Surely I have found my muse. Surely this is she who is destined to become my lifelong inspiration. She, not the faithless Samlee, is to be my Beatrice.

At that moment, I realize that there is a playful but insistent pressure against my toes. It is too much to hope for, but my dark nymph is actually rubbing her foot against mine. A feeling of intense pleasure permeates my feet and begins to spread upward, warming my calves, my thighs, my—

So overcome am I with passion that I can no longer control myself, and a cacophonous fart tears from my sphincter, drowning the fragrance of Cajun herbs and spices in a cloud of methane. It is an appalling instance of bad timing. I am so embarrassed that I feel like vanishing under the table.

What am I to do? All hope of having my solecism ignored evaporates when I realize that Virgil is laughing uproariously, Jessica is giggling, and even the motherly Renée cannot suppress a chuckle.

To top it all, I start to cry.

The rest of the evening does not turn out so badly. We watch *The Outer Limits*. They have the radio tuned to the FM station with the English-language soundtrack, so that I can actually hear what the real actors sound like. At home, out of consideration for the servants, we are forced to watch American television in a dubiously dubbed form. Then we sit around playing Monopoly.

I do not concentrate very hard on the Monopoly, or even on *The Outer Limits*, although it is one of my favourite episodes, *Demon with a Glass Hand*. I am too busy gazing at Jessica in a kind of religious ecstasy. Mrs. O'Fleary hovers in the background, occasionally bringing out more cookies. I have managed to keep my flatulence more or less under control; it is like a distant machine gun rather than a nuclear explosion.

In fact, it is an evening of quiet domesticity, the one thing which I cannot seem to have in my estate with its four mansions, its arbours, its hidden rooms, its jasmine bushes, its labyrinthine love trysts. There is only one thing our two worlds have in common: on both sides of the wall, activities are invariably accompanied by the strains of Dee Dee Sharp, the Four Seasons, and Dion. It is music that unites us as Virgil carries the portable phonograph from the dining room to the living room and finally upstairs to the bedroom.

Virgil's bedroom is not at all like mine. The floor is a no-man's land, strewn with Lego, toy cars, plastic soldiers of every epoch, bits of wire and metal, slabs of balsa wood for model building, and dirty clothes. This, I reflect, is how it is to have no servants! America must be a squalid country, for I see now that toys and clothes cannot put themselves away. Filling half the room is an enormous bed. It seems to be the size of my entire bedroom. Virgil leaps on to the bed and begins to roll around, and I see that the bed possesses a strange fluidity; like the ocean, it has billowing waves. A waterbed, he tells me. Gingerly, I test the current with a finger. Then I lie down. It is like sinking into the infinite sea.

An enormous window overlooks the *klong*. An air conditioning unit is thrumming away, and the chill is strange, for through the window one can still see the palm trees, hazy in the tropic air. The moon is full and one can see all the way to the bend in the canal that snakes toward the shaman's dwelling-place.

Beyond the massive bed is a walk-in closet that connects directly to Jessica's room. I can hear her humming to herself, but I cannot see her. I wonder whether I shall see her again tonight, or whether Virgil was merely tantalizing me with veiled promises of forbidden pleasures.

Presently—we are lying down on this massive bed-lake, watching the moonlit *klong*—Mrs. O'Fleary comes in to kiss her son goodnight.

"Story time, Momma," he says. She dims the lights.

She sits on the edge of the bed, which now inclines sharply in her direction, like a mountain stream. She says, "Maybe you and Justin would like to spend the night talking . . . maybe you don't want your momma to be in your way."

"Oh, no, please, Mrs. O'Fleary," I say, for to be honest I am slightly dreading the fulfilment of my secret desires, "do tell us a story."

"What about?"

"Something about Great-grandma," says Virgil. "Tell the story about how Great-great-uncle Orpie harrowed hell."

"All right," she says softly. When she begins to talk again, I see that Jessica has crept into the closet and is leaning against a pile of clothes, listening raptly. Mrs. O'Fleary tells us her story in a dream-like voice, and her speech shifts into the language of her children.

"Your great-granddaddy, O'Fleary, he done your great-grand-momma a grievous wrong. He had the power to whup her, but there won't no call to whup her until her baby come screamin' out of her body and she lie dead upon the ground. And your Great-great-uncle Orpie, he powerful angry about it and he say, 'I'm gone get you back out of the ground, Arcola Jones, even I has to wrestle old Marse Death to fetch you.'

"This Orpie a powerful wizard. When he sung out he magic incantations, why, he set the very stones to weepin' and carryin' on. When he play his magic banjer, the tall grass part to make a pathway for he walk. He could close he eyes and send he soul right 'crosst the big blue sea till he reach Mother Africa herself, and he knew all the Old Gods by they nicknames. And he says, 'I'm a-gone send my soul flying to the Old Country, and I'm a tell the King of the Dead to give me back this woman what was still too young to die. It just too blame unfair to snatch her into the darkness, and she just fourteen year old.'

"And so Orpie he close he eyes and send his soul a-flying over the ocean. And he reach the place which is now Nigeria, where there a mighty king name Shangó who rule the land for a thousand years. Shangó, he hung himself on a tree and come back again to rule the dead and the living. He a man, and he a god too, all in one.

"But Orpie show no fear, and he cry out in front of the king throne, 'Give me back my sister.' But the king he say no. 'What's dead stays dead,' he say.

"Then Orpie he done sung and sung until the rocks and the trees they weeping so hard they make a moat around the king palace. So the king say, 'Here, take the girl back with you to Georgia.' And Orpie see your great-grandmomma standing in front of him, and all her scars be healed, she slim and tall and beautiful as the day before your great-granddaddy done violated her body and her soul.

"And the King Shangó he say, 'Don't you look back at her until the time you reach Georgia, else you gone lose her again and this time it be permanent.'

"And Uncle Orpie he say, 'Take my hand and come with me out of this dark hell, cause I'm a-carry you home again.'

"She put her hand in he hand, and her hand it warm, like a living person. And they begin a-walkin' to America "crosst the great water. And Orpie he thinking, look to the future, don't look back Arcola face. But presently, when they in the middle of the sea, Arcola say, 'Orpie, Orpie, I don't want to go back to the country of the living. There be pain in that country. My wounds they gone bleed again. My sores they gone fester.'

"Orpie say, 'Don't you want see your baby, honey? And don't you know that your baby he gone grow up free, because we all 'mancipated now?'

"But Arcola she say, 'Arcola afraid. The earth she soft and warm and Arcola craves to stay in her final restin' place. No, no, don't you take me toward freedom. Arcola never had no freedom, never wanted no freedom. Freedom a scary thing.'

"And soon they quarrelling, the two of them, and time they reach sight of America country, and the hills of Georgia rising up from the edge of the big blue sea, Arcola too afraid to go on. She snatch her hand away and make Uncle Orpie turn back to look at she face.

"And she cry out: 'Oh, sweet Jesus, I see O'Fleary standing at the far shore. Oh, Orpie, don't make me go to him.'

"At first he see her the way she be in the kingdom of Shangó . . . beautiful, with her ebony skin unscarred by the whip, and her eyes shining like two stars. But when he reach out to grab her hand again her hand it cold, cold as ice, and he see the wounds burst open on her flesh, and he see the eyes go dead as glass, and she sink down into the depths of the great sea. And Uncle Orpie he take his banjer and he play and play, but the waves done swallow her up for ever, and she never wash to shore.

"So when he come home to Georgia, Uncle Orpie he take your granddaddy in he arms and he say, 'Sweet chile, I want you to take O'Fleary's name, and I want you to bear it with pride and with defiance. Take unto yourself the name and title of that wicked man. Because I want you to know that you is free, now and for evermore, ay-men. Because you ain't never gone fear no overseer's name so much you'd sooner stay in the valley of death than stand out in the bright warm sunlight. You ain't never gone be afraid to call the darkness he own name.' And he kiss the child and bring it into he house and rear it as he own. And that was one hundred years ago.

"And that how your granddaddy come to be called O'Fleary. And this a true story, because I heard it from your daddy's momma, who heard it from her father, who heard it from he uncle, your Great-great-uncle Orpie hisself."

"Well," says Mrs. O'Fleary at last, switching dialects as easily as putting on a fresh pair of sandals, "I hope you liked the story, Justin, and that one day you'll tell it to your children's children."

We are lying down on the bed whose surface is the sea. Mrs. O'Fleary's story has been so vivid, so tragic.

"It's Orpheus and Eurydice!" I exclaim. "I just read it in my Ovid. Orpheus went down to the underworld to bring back Eurydice from the dead. His singing made the stones weep . . . the king of the underworld told him never to look back at her. . . ."

"Ah, you clever child," she says, "you have divined my secret. What good is family history," and she strokes my forehead, "without a thorough lacing of cultural anthropology? All stories are the same story."

I know it is the truth. Uncle Orpie was Orpheus, the past is continually reborn. I too, even I, stand at one end of an immense chain of being whose links are the myths we share.

Virgil is snoring.

"He can never last all the way to the end of one of my stories," she says, chuckling. And kisses me on the cheek, and leaves me, leaves the door ajar, leaves a pale triangle of light over the edge of the woolly carpet.

The full moon shines over us. I glance over at the closet, and I see a pair of eyes. Jessica has been there the whole time. And now she rises from her hiding place and steps toward me, into the patch of yellow light. She smiles and her teeth glisten in the moonlight.

I think of Samlee, standing in the mango orchard in the selfsame light, dappling the whiteface smothered on her. . . .

Oh, Jessica, I think to myself. Is it you who are to be my Muse? Is it you who will lift me up from the slough of poetic despond, from the quagmire of my sub-literate maunderings, to the true fulfilment of my artistic destiny? Are you, in truth, a messenger of the gods?

Or not?

But Jessica is beyond philosophy. She simply stands there, framed in the closet doorway, and behind her I seem to see the underworld itself. I see the Africa of King Shangó. I see the cavern-labyrinth of Pluto and Proserpina, King and Queen of the Dead. Perhaps we are about to re-enact the myth. But you and I, Jessica and Justin, I think, we have reversed our roles: It is you, Eurydice, whose voice can cause the stones to weep, while I, the poetaster, am struck dumb.

13

The Mysteries of Sex

My meditation on the nature of poesy is short-lived. As Jessica approaches me, a hand grabs my wrist. "Uh-uh-uh!" says Virgil, and, whipping round, I realize that he has been shamming sleep the whole time. Now both are looking at me with a kind of half-laugh in their eyes.

"You startled me," I say.

"No shit," says Virgil. "You like her, don't you?"

"Yes," I say. I sense this is no time for dishonesty.

"Look at the moon," Virgil says. "The moon full, you a stranger in a strange land, and now it time for a initiation ceremony."

Terror seizes me. These O'Flearys are surely insane! I have been lured into this gingerbread house only to be popped into the oven! "What is the matter with you people?" I say.

"I know, I know," Virgil says, "we strangle our wives."

He winks at Jessica, who lets out a full-throated laugh. He must already have told her about my *faux pas* in the matter of *Othello*. My embarrassment is an exquisite torment. Jessica sits down beside me. Not all women smell alike. There is no *nam pla* odour wafting from the nether regions of her nightdress, but instead a faint aroma of jasmine.

"Okay, sister," Virgil says, "let's commence the torture."

He reaches over to the portable phonograph, which lies on the floor beside the waterbed, and puts on a record. It is "Sugar Shack" by Jimmy Gilmer and the Fireballs.

"Oh, Virgil, you gone wake up Momma," says Jessica reprovingly.

"No way. She sleep like a log." But he turns down the volume.

He then proceeds to lock his arm around my neck so that I can't move my head, and then, with his free hand, with a flamboyant flourish, yanks down my shorts. I don't know what to do. Perhaps I ought to scream, but what if Mrs. O'Fleary comes in and sees me like this? I struggle, but Virgil's grip tightens as he flings my underpants across the room, exposing me to the wistful gaze of Jessica, who is even now doing a kind of dance as she slowly, oh, so slowly, begins to shrug away her nightdress.

Oh, could I but convey the sensual nuances of that dance, the confusion that clouds my senses, the undulation of those slender hips, the quivering of those breasts, which in the moonlight glisten like mangoes, their soft skin sheened with succulent sap . . . no amount of willpower can prevent the stiffening of my wayward aubergine. I know now why her body carries a whiff of jasmine. A garland of Jasmine circles her waist, and from the garland depends a single rose that conceals the cleft between her thighs.

As Jessica approaches, the air-conditioning no longer cools me. I am sweating. Virgil is laughing. "Leastways you ain't no homersexual," he says.

At length, Jessica sits down beside me. My bewilderment is complete. She giggles softly. Her voice seems to belong with the chattering of the insects and the hum of the air conditioner.

"You're choking me," I manage to say.

"Well, promise you won't struggle," says my implacable tormentor.

I try to nod my head but Virgil's arm is cutting off my breathing. "Yes . . . I promise . . ." I whimper.

He lets go. "Lay back and enjoy you initiation," says Virgil. "Relax, Justin. It only a game we likes to play."

So saying, he reaches under the bed and produces an enormous can of Crisco.

"Good heavens!" I say. "What on earth is that for?"

They do not speak to me. They only plunge their hands into the lard and begin rubbing them up and down against my flesh. The feeling is indescribable. It is awe-inspiring. We exchange no more words, but pass the can of Crisco around, and we each take turns scooping out the glop and slathering it upon our bodies. In the moonlight, we take on an ethereal glow, as though we were wearing the very moonbeams themselves. Their hands caress me. I stare into Jessica's eyes. Her fingers dance across my chest, dart down toward a region of my body that seems ready to burst with something alien, mighty and unnameable.

"What is this game called?" I whisper.

"It called sex," says Virgil in mantra-like tones.

"Yes," says the beautiful Jessica, pouting as she gazes past me at the light over the *klong*. "It called sex."

"But what do we do now?" I say. This is not the first time I have heard the word 'sex', but surely there is a little more to it than a generous application of lard to the epidermis.

"What do we do now?" Virgil cries. "Why, we wrestle, of course!"

With one hand he reaches over to restart the record. Then, all at once, we're wrestling, which means that the three of us are climbing over one another, rolling around on the capacious waterbed, and I'm getting seasick from the slow waves that ripple across the bed, and Jessica and I and Virgil become all weirdly entangled and slick and sweaty, and at the back of the mind there's always this nagging thought that surely this isn't exactly what it's all about . . . and then, at the moment when "Sugar Shack" dies away one more time and Virgil leans across to put on another single, then, in a moment when Jessica and I are sort of in each other's arms, and I think—I'm not sure because I daren't look down—that her breasts are sliding back and forth against my neck—she has me pinned to the headboard, and the moonlight is full on her face, and her kinky ringlets are sparkling like the jewels on a tiara—yes, in that moment when Virgil is preoccupied, and she and I are almost alone together—I am suddenly possessed by the overpowering feeling that something has got to be inserted into something. This epiphany hits me with the force of a divine vision. But what must be inserted into what?

An image flashes into my mind: Uncle Vit . . . Samlee squatting beneath the funeral dinner table . . . the corpse of my pet chameleon . . . surely, surely what was transpiring was no witchcraft, no demoniacal ensorcellement. But my engorged aubergine is nowhere near the mouth of my beloved—surely some other opening must exist . . . but where?

I become desperate. Seizing my beloved with every last ounce of my strength, I thrust her down upon the billowing waves. I tear at the jasmine circlet around her waist. Blind instinct leads me on. I am maddened by this nameless emotion. I hardly see the object of my desire. I plunge headlong I know not where, knowing only that I must extinguish my flaming passion within some cave, some tunnel, some ravening reticule.

Before this consummation can be achieved, however, Virgil emerges from fiddling with the phonograph. He tears me away from Jessica, wagging a finger in my face. "Don't you ever do that!" he says. "That against the rules of the game. That nasty."

"But—but—"

"You ruining the game," he says. "And furthermore, if you was to actually do that, why, Jessica she *have* to have a baby."

"Oh, I see," I say. I don't see in the least.

I slump back against the headboard. Jessica does not seem upset at all. In fact, when she is sure Virgil is not looking, she winks at me, looks at her brother, and rolls her eyes as if to say, Justin, you and I can have secrets too, and *he* doesn't have to share them.

We wrestle a while longer, but only in a desultory fashion. My passion is spent. I suspect theirs is too. Jessica slips away, and I sink into a kind of sleep.

Perhaps it is not sleep at all. I seem to be floating on the infinite sea. The waterbed has become contiguous with the waters of the ocean that surrounds the cosmos. I am probably dreaming, I tell myself, for I do not remember falling asleep in this snow white tunic, nor can I recall ever having this four-stringed lyre cradled in my arms, nor indeed can I recollect ever having studied the instrument, though chord after chord cascades from my skilful fingertips. The vehicle I am travelling in is not the Studebaker of my day-to-day forays, but a sort of giant swan, whose wings stir up the waves to a fine froth. The air tastes salty on my lips. A high wind is blowing and the sunlight is streaming down, and the sky is so blue that this is surely the Ægean Sea or some other mythic place.

Who am I? Whither am I bound? I have no memory of having come here. But after racking my brains and strumming a few more chords, I reach the inescapable conclusion that I must indeed be one of those bards—Orpheus, perhaps, or even the great Homer himself. Well, probably not Homer, because I don't seem to be blind.

Well, if I am Orpheus in this dream—if dream it be—I tell myself that I must be on some kind of quest. In fact, I am probably journeying to the realm of Death in order to rescue my dead beloved. Surely not Jessica. It is someone else. Someone out of the past.

And where exactly is the kingdom of the dead? For some reason we seem to be headed toward Africa. In the distance I see a curving, many-furrowed shore. As my swan nears land, dozens of longboats come pouring out of some inlet, each one occupied by dusky, bare-breasted native women, who are singing and throwing garlands of jasmine at me, trying to ring the swan's neck in a sort of aquatic quoits game. This part seems to be more Tahitian than African.

The swan is towed toward shore. Drums are pounding and men with plumed headdresses and assegais are dancing, kicking up a whirlwind of sand. I pluck a few notes, and I walk toward the beach upon a cushion of surf. On the beach, there is a choir of *apsaras*, winged women with heavenly voices, who are being conducted by Father Regenstrom. A dozen choirboys in blue cassocks, white surplices and red sneakers are swinging censers, while in the distance, against the backdrop of the deep green jungle, a Greek temple stands, its Ionic columns topped by a frieze of the three Fates, my aunts, sitting in solemn judgment over the world's destiny.

"Ahem," I say, "excuse me, does anyone know where I can find Yama, the king of the underworld?"

All at once, the wind drops. The choir's celestial warblings gurgle to a halt. The sound of the surf is stilled. I can hear my own heart beating. I cry out: "I'm looking for the God of Death! You have someone who belongs to me, and I want her back!"

The crowd parts. I am standing at the beginning of a yellow brick road that leads straight into the jungle's heart. How then shall I journey toward the throne of Shangó? What magic can I use? The only magic is in my hands and on my lips.

"Take me to your Lieder," I say. Or is it Leda? My swan looks soulfully into my eyes.

I pluck my lyre.

At the sound of the first note, the wind starts up again. The choir launches into a soaring rendition of Schubert's "*An die Musik*". The waves batter the sand with a sound like a woman's impassioned breathing. The wind lifts me up and carries me along the road, the road that detaches itself from the bonds of the sublunary and arcs upward to the clouds. I play. The notes dance around my fingers, little lightning-jags of gold.

Once more I seem to be riding the swan. It skims above the yellow brick road like a noiseless hovercraft. The road threads through the lowest cloudbanks and carries me to a realm of dazzling sunlight. My hair streams in the warm wind. Here and there are *apsaras* perched on clouds, each one performing on a *ranaat* or *phin*, and the air is filled with the percussive tinkling of their music. As I rise above the world, I see below me the elephant's head profile of Thailand. I see Africa pulsing like a giant heart. I see Greece with its Parnassian temples and beyond Greece, England; a few patches of green, a steeple here and there, all draped in impenetrable fog. I even see the shoreline of America.

At last I see the pointed eaves of a pavilion, girt with golden *nagas*, the rooftop tiled with dragon scales. The three Fates, my three aunts, sit at the gates, spinning the thread of fate. My swan flies over them and comes to rest in the throne room of the death god.

I step from the swan-chariot. All around me is a sea of prostrate backs. There are *yakshas* with bejewelled headdresses, rich women in minks and ermines, doctors in lab coats, servants in *panungs* or *phakomaahs*, all performing the *kraab* of reverence. None dares look up at the distant throne. I do not dare look either. Awkwardly I get down on my knees, my hands in the *phnom mue* position, to pay my respects.

"Well, well, well," says a familiar voice to me across the vast distance of the pavilion. "If it isn't Norman Bates!"

Jolted, I look up. The consort of the King of the Dead, sitting in a wheelchair beside the golden throne, is none other than my great-grandmother, looking no different from the last time I saw her, just before she disappeared into the shadows on the night of my chameleon's funeral.

And as for the King of the Dead himself—he has grown a little, and the weight of the seven-tiered crown does seem to bother him somewhat, but I have no difficulty in recognizing him. He is Homer, my pet chameleon, cremated in two pieces but now miraculously reincarnated in one—Homer, who in my dream has become enthroned as the God of Death himself.

"I'm so glad you could come to see us," Homer says. How similar his voice sounds to my own! We could almost be twins.

"I'm glad, too," I say.

"I've got a lot to talk to you about," Homer says, and he beckons me toward the throne with a gnarled, golden claw.

14

Justin's Dream

The clarity of the air, the immediacy of the smells and colours are such that I cannot quite believe I am dreaming. Rather, I tell myself, I have broken through to some *Twilight Zone*-like parallel universe in which I am about to learn about truth.

So I approach the throne of my erstwhile friend with humility and reverence. I place my folded palms at his feet.

"You've certainly become very elevated," I say.

Homer says, "So have you . . . riding around on swans and strumming on lyres . . . and you didn't even have to die first."

"Actually, I'm not entirely sure *why* I'm here," I say. "I'm looking for someone, but I'm not quite sure who."

"Pull up a cloud."

I gather up some swirls of the fog, moulding them into a makeshift cushion, and ease myself into the lotus position. My buttocks disappear into the cottony softness of the cloud, which floats a foot or two above the straw matting of the pavilion floor.

My pet chameleon claps his claws. "Perhaps you'd care for a bite to eat?" he says. "I don't mean to be churlish."

A silver *phaan* materializes miraculously between us. It contains some betel nut-chewing paraphernalia and a couple of pomegranates.

"No pomegranates please," I say. Pomegranates in the underworld are invariably a trap.

Homer sighs. "Can't say I didn't try," he says.

My great-grandmother looks on. There is an unearthly serenity about her, although the wind whips at her white hair. "Great-grandmother," I ask her, "why is it that you are here, in the realm of the spirits? Why do you appear to me as Persephone, the Queen of the Dead, even though I know very well that you are still alive?" Surely, I think, she didn't fall for the old pomegranate trick!

"Thun Hua," she says, bending down to toy with my hair, "I'm not entirely dead, nor am I quite alive. My soul is caught between worlds. That is why I am able to come to you in this dream."

I know that my great-grandmother has gone away to the hospital. Seeing her here, seated on her wheelchair in this golden pavilion atop the clouds, I am forced to face what I have suppressed for so many weeks.

"I'm sorry I haven't been thinking about you," I say. "I've been selfish . . . I was preoccupied with my friends, with my aunts' intrigues, with Dr. Richardson's streptococci . . . I just haven't been concentrating on what's important."

How much time is there left? Beneath my sorrow is a residue of anger. Why won't anyone say what's wrong with my great-grandmother or *if* there's something wrong so that my only source of information isn't the rumours coming from the servants' quarters?

"It's all right," says my great-grandmother. "You must let go, little by little, of the earthly things that bind your soul. Only then can you be free of the cycle of karma."

"I don't want you to die!" I scream in a sudden outburst of emotion. I turn round, and see the throng look up at me in consternation, whispering amongst themselves, scandalized that I dare raise my voice in the house of Yama. Perhaps it is my great-grandmother who is the object of my quest. Perhaps it is she whom I must bring back to the land of the living.

She only smiles an enigmatic smile.

"And how is your chameleonizing these days, Little Frog?" my chameleon asks me. "Have you been working hard to emulate my ability to change colour?"

"I don't know," I say. "I've been preoccupied."

"Yes, You've had many adventures," says Homer. "I've been following them. This Virgil fellow is very interesting, though hardly an adequate replacement for myself."

"He is a far better chameleon than I am," I say. "He speaks perfect Thai; he can get along with Piak as well as with the three Fates. He's got an engaging personality, whereas I am pretty damn charmless."

"Well, at least you admit it, Little Frog," Homer says. "And yet there is something you can teach him. You see, you and he are on converging paths of enlightenment. Virgil speaks the language of the heart, yet he obstinately refuses to learn the language of the external world. You, on the other hand, have spent the past few years of your life completely absorbed in the language of the intellect, and you have only recently begun even to acknowledge the existence of the other language, with its dark and dangerous music. You are opposites, and opposites attract. Now you are seduced by his wildness, his boyishness, and follow where he leads, but a time will come when he will enter your terrain, and it will be up to you to guide him."

By now I am heartily wishing that old Homer had never learned how to talk. How I loved him when he was just sitting around in that tank, changing colour and munching on assorted insects! How often, when he was alive, have I wished he could talk, have I envisaged endless Platonic dialogues between us! How little did I imagine that he would end up pontificating polysyllabically from an Elysian cloudbank!

"Oh, Homer," I say, "what a philosopher you have become."

"Sure you won't have any food?"

"Quite sure."

My great-grandmother says, "Come and see us again sometime, Little Frog." It is clear that I am being dismissed. The fog rolls over us, and the pavilion and its denizens are rapidly blurring, fading into the wind stream. "Your swan awaits," she says. The strains of

Schubert, interlaced with the tinkling heterophony of the celestial *piphaat* ensemble, wash over us. The light swirls, fractures, explodes into kaleidoscopic symmetries around us. "Goodbye for now, my child. I shan't always be on hand, but you can always reach me if you learn the language of the heart."

At that moment dozens of questions come popping into my head. I try to get them all out as quickly as I can, even though the death-god and his consort are fast dissipating into cacophonies of colour. "But Great-grandmother! Homer! There's so much you haven't told me! Earlier tonight something happened to me, something big and wonderful and absolutely terrifying ... something Virgil and Jessica called 'sex'—and then they said something about having to have a baby! What was all that about?"

I can no longer see my great-grandmother or my pet chameleon. But in the bright air I hear a voice. It seems to belong to Homer, but it is also a plaintive echo of my own: "Sex and death are the two great mysteries of life. As a poet, it will be your job to explain them. I don't know anything about the human condition. How can I? I'm a god. I just work here."

All at once I am riding the swan-chariot once more, speeding through the skies like a jet plane. I'm soaring. I'm plummeting. I'm rocketing up into space, and I do a quick figure-eight around the rings of Saturn. I buzz the spires of Eton College Chapel. I thumb my nose at the Statue of Liberty, who has become the beauteous Jessica, draped in a bed sheet, towering over the waterbed of her brother. I glimpse Samlee, leaving my uncle's convertible, stumbling into the gynaecological clinic in her awkward high-heels. My mind is awhirl with wild new thoughts. I am losing control of the swan. It honks. It is metamorphosing into a goose. No, an ugly duckling. No, no, no! I'm falling, the ride has become an accelerating swan dive, the abyss yawns wide beneath me—

I'm falling ... I'm falling
falling
falling.

It is daylight when I awaken. I'm in the same room I fell asleep in—the scattered clothes and Lego, the stylus of the phonograph clicking ceaselessly on the turntable. There is no one else here. The air conditioning is off and the window is open, letting in the moist breeze and the smells of *klong*, mango and banana. It takes me a few moments to remember where I am. Gingerly I climb out of the billowing waterbed and fish some fresh clothes out of the BOAC bag.

I make my way downstairs, where breakfast seems to be in progress. It is not an organized breakfast. Jessica is already doing her vocal exercises in the den. Mrs. O'Fleary can be seen through the kitchen door, tossing flapjacks. Virgil is seated at the dining room table with a mound of pancakes swimming in syrup.

"Tried to have yourself some jelly roll last night, didn't you?" he says, with a lascivious wink.

"I'm not at all sure what you mean," I say, "but I'd love to have some pancakes now."

"My sister like you a lot," he says.

I am anxious for him to expand upon this tidbit of information, but his mother comes in at that precise moment, bearing a gargantuan platter of food. It is my initiation into the American breakfast, which appears to be roughly the same as the English, except that it is all drenched in a sea of maple syrup.

"I had a really strange dream last night, Virgil," I begin, when Mrs. O'Fleary has departed once more.

"Weren't no dream," Virgil says. "Was real."

I am not, of course, referring to the communal massage and lard anointing, but to its aftermath—my visit to the kingdom of the dead. I see now that to discuss this vision is no use. There are roads that must be travelled alone. I must solve these riddles by myself.

Jessica's voice! But I find I am no longer trembling uncontrollably at its sweetness. I have a much more reasoned appreciation of its qualities now, after last night's encounters. I think I shall enjoy my friendship with this new Muse far more than my anguished relationship with Samlee.

Suddenly there's a pounding at the front door. I hear the door being opened and someone running inside. It is Piak. He charges into the dining room with his sandals on. He's out of breath.

"Master Little Frog," he says, "you've got to come home right now! The Studebaker's waiting to take you to the hospital . . . it's the *khunying*. . . ."

"The *khunying*?" All at once my dream returns to me, vivid and foreboding. I remember my great-grandmother fading into the mist and her last words to me: *I shan't always be on hand, but you can always reach me if you learn the language of the heart.*

"Great-grandmother!" I cry out. I do not weep. This is too big for weeping. Numbly I follow Piak back to the house, leaving the O'Flearys behind without a word of farewell. The three Fates stand grimly in front of the Studebaker, and the driver lets me into the front passenger seat, and soon we are barrelling down the *soi* at breakneck speed.

15

The Hospital

The sense of foreboding that took root in my mind when I first saw the three Fates grimly waiting my entry into the Studebaker becomes worse as we get nearer and nearer to the hospital. I sit in the front seat, glumly reflecting on the precognitive accuracy of last night's dream. My moment of interrupted ecstasy with Jessica is all but forgotten.

We drive in silence until the hospital is in sight. But there is a lot going on that is unspoken. I know it. The air is heavy with the three Fates' maleficent humours—oppressive, like thunderclouds before a monsoon shower.

Only when we actually drive into the hospital's parking lot does the storm break. It is Ning-nong who speaks first. "There's really no need to subject Little Frog to this rigmarole," she says. "What can she say to him that she can't say to us, for goodness' sake?"

"Well," says Nit-nit, "she is the titular elder. She can do anything she damn well pleases."

"Oh, shut up," says Noi-noi.

"How dare you tell me to shut up?" says Ning-nong. "Are you forgetting I'm your older sister?"

"Shut up!" says Nit-nit.

"Shut up!" Ning-nong screams.

"What on earth are you screaming for?" Nit-nit says. "And besides, we oughtn't to be talking in front of him as though he weren't there."

"Why not?" says Noi-noi. "He doesn't understand a word we're saying anyway, the little shit."

"He most certainly does," says Nit-nit.

"Shut up!" Ning-nong screams.

"No, *you* shut up!" Nit-nit screams back.

Noi-noi screams herself. I don't look back, but I get the distinct impression that the three Fates are pinching each other and pulling at each other's hair. The driver is enjoying all this immensely. When he thinks no one is looking, his studiously impassive demeanour breaks into a smile, quickly suppressed. I decide it is better to pretend to have understood nothing—I don't want to blow my cover just yet—and I stare steadfastly into my Ovid, which I have had the presence of mind to bring along.

I'm not really reading; my mind is in too much turbulence for that. I'm just skimming through the pages. In the Ovid, women are wildly turning into bulls, trees, bears and flowers, but this is no more fantastical than what is transpiring in the car, for the three Fates have surely been transformed into harpies this morning.

As the car stops and the doors are opened for us, however, the sisters abruptly regain their composure. They step out of the Studebaker one by one, each more dignified than the last.

"Well, come along, Little Frog," Ning-nong says to me in English. "There's no time to dawdle, you know."

We enter the building. A nurse has obviously been awaiting us. She jumps up from the reception desk and escorts us down corridors, up in elevators, and through a maze of twisting passageways. There is an unnerving odour of strange chemicals. The three Fates show unwonted nervousness. I lag behind, peering into half-opened doorways marked "Pathology" or "Radiology" and other assorted 'ologies', wondering what they mean.

At length we reach my great-grandmother's two-room suite. The inner room is curtained off. In the anteroom, the entire clan seems to have gathered. Most, like my aunts, are dressed in mourning for that anonymous old relative of a month ago. The patriarch, my great-uncle, reclines in the only armchair. Uncle Vit paces back and forth. Samlee, the only woman not in mourning, sits uncomfortably on the floor. There are a number of relatives I don't recognize. They too are squatting on the carpet. I can tell they are my relatives because they look something like my aunts.

The room is spartan. To one side there is an enormous cart, draped with linen, on which rest surgical implements and reagent bottles. The place is not unlike the lair of the *ajarn* with its love potions, idols and votive objects. There is a sense of spirits lurking everywhere—behind cabinets, under the armchair, in the rows of brown glass bottles. People die here. I feel a chill. The hairs on my arms are starting to stand on end.

To my astonishment, my entrance seems to provoke something of a stir. Everyone starts talking—softly, as though they don't want me to know I am the subject of their conversation. A servant crawls around with a tray full of glasses of iced rose water, one of which I take but do not drink.

Everyone seems to be waiting for something to happen. The tension is almost unbearable. I lean against the wall, racked with guilt, wondering whether last night's dream-confrontation means that my great-grandmother is already beyond all help. I have never seen a dead person, only my pet chameleon; the prospect fills me with dread. Why won't anyone talk to me? Why does everyone seem to resent my presence?

At last, the curtain to the holy of holies is whisked aside. Silence falls abruptly. Dr. Richardson is standing beside the doorway, flanked by masked nurses wielding hypodermic syringes. He seems unnaturally tall, out of proportion to all my relatives. Aunt Nit-nit gasps, and Aunt Noi-noi stares steadfastly at the floor.

"She's ready, what," says Dr. Richardson. "Not too long, you understand. She's got to have plenty of rest."

Nobody moves.

I realize that everyone is looking straight at me.

"Well, go on, then," Ning-nong says, giving me a little push toward the skeletal doctor, "you're the one she asked to see . . . she won't deign to talk to the likes of us."

A firm hand—Dr. Richardson's—propels me into the inner sanctum. The good doctor then withdraws, abandoning me in the room, dimly lit, unwindowed, its air thick with the odour of bodily humours and strange medicines.

My great-grandmother is lying in the hospital bed. She is propped up against a triangular silk pillow; a bowl of betel nut rests by her bedside. She is attached to a battery of equipment—flashing oscilloscopes, dangling bottles of fluid, electrodes that lead to black boxes that occasionally go *ping*. She does not look well. Her hair stands on end, like the Bride of Frankenstein, and her face is a skull-mask. Her eyes are open, but they seem to be staring straight ahead. The scariest thing of all is the smell. It is pervasive. It is sickly, like the smell of plucked jasmine petals rotting in the sun. I know it is the smell of death.

I am not sure what to do. *Waiing* doesn't seem quite right somehow. I am not even sure if she can perceive my presence.

Then I hear her voice. "Come closer," she says. "Come right up to the bed." It is a raspy whisper. "Closer, I tell you."

I creep forward.

"Oh, don't be so silly, Little Frog. I'm not a corpse yet."

I hasten to obey. I'm standing right next to her now. She grips my arm and pulls my face down close to hers.

"I didn't mean to imply that you were, Great-grandmother. A corpse, I mean. Are you all right?"

"Listen to me. Listen carefully. Speaking is a great effort, you know. I've had a stroke or something. Today's the first day I've been lucid in a week, they tell me. Now, Little Frog, peek over at the curtain and tell me if anyone is listening."

I turn and look. "Coast seems clear, Great-grandmother."

"Good, good."

"I dreamed about you last night, Great-grandmother. In my dream, you were already . . . already. . . ." I cannot bring myself to say it. I feel ashamed to weep, because it is unseemly to mourn one's elders before their actual passing.

"You dreamed, did you?"

"Yes.

"So tell me . . . were they pleasant? My surroundings, I mean. *Apsaras* plucking on harps, floating around on clouds? Or was it dark and fiery and full of the groans of the damned?"

"Oh, no Great-grandmother . . . it was pleasant. Very pleasant."

"Good. Good." She closes her eyes. "I assumed, of course, that the next life would be easier for me than this one, but occasionally one has one's doubts."

I can't stand it any longer. "Tell me it's not true, Great-grandmother!"

She sighed. "Those creatures out there—they're vultures, all of them. They think I've got money stashed away. They want to know if they're mentioned in the will. That's why they're so annoyed that I said you were the only one I was willing to talk to!"

"The will?" I said.

"Yes, yes, yes. The joke's on them though—I'm too tough to die that easily! In fact, I've made a promise to myself that I won't go on to my next incarnation until a certain crucial event has occurred."

"And what event might that be, Great-grandmother?"

"That is for me to know, my child."

It seems to me that I can delay my great-grandmother's death— if only I can find out what event it is I must prevent. Enigmas and conundrums! I wonder whether her mind is wandering or whether she is in fact more sane and more clear-sighted than all the rest of my madcap family. I know there is a special bond between us, one that the others envy and resent; it is because she and I both stand at the gateway, I of my life, she of her death, and we both know that it is a revolving door.

"Now listen to me, Norman Bates! I want you to go over to the door and summon the others now. Run along."

"Yes, Great-grandmother."

I go back to the other room. A hush falls as soon as I am seen. "Um," I say, "she wants to see you now."

Everyone rises and troops into the inner chamber. Everyone, that is, except for Aunt Noi-noi, who swoops into the armchair just vacated by the patriarch, pulls out a mirror, and begins teasing at her bouffant with a manic intensity.

I hear my great-grandmother's voice: "Now listen to me, all of you! I'm not quite dead yet, I'm afraid. But you're all dressed in mourning. I know, I know, it's for Khun Phra Whatsisname, not for me. Still, it's depressing to look at, and I want it to stop. Now see here, Piglet—"

The patriarch of our family jumps to attention. "Yes, Khun Mae?" he says in a humble voice I have never heard him use before. The scene is amazing. I have never heard my great-uncle addressed by his baby-name before. It never even occurred to me that he *had* a baby-name, though of course everyone does; Piglet, indeed! Even Little Frog is less embarrassing. . . .

"How long a mourning period did you decree for the family?" says my great-grandmother.

"Three months . . . ah, weeks," says my great-uncle. "To be honest, I'm not sure any more."

"It will stop right now," says Great-grandmother. "I want a little colour round here, do you hear? I don't want to see any more black. And as for that limbo rock party that you three sisters were planning to put on. . . ."

Ning-nong starts at being directly addressed by so august a figure. "Yes, Khun Yaah?" she says in the same tone of humility.

"I want you to put on that party as soon as you possibly can. By the Four-faced Brahma, I'm going to do the limbo rock before I croak . . . even if they have to shove me under the pole on a stretcher!"

A hubbub breaks out at this pronouncement. Some of my relatives are now quite convinced that Great-grandmother has gone stark staring bonkers. Others are praising her stoutness of heart. I am disheartened by the spectacle of so many relatives hovering over her, analysing her, speculating about her motives. I decide to withdraw to the waiting room.

Aunt Noi-noi is still there, still fiddling with her hair, gazing into a little hand-mirror, the picture of narcissism. Dr. Richardson, too, is there, standing with his back to her. For some reason their being alone together unnerves me. I well remember what happened the last time the good doctor was alone with one of my aunts. I decide that I should observe them. There is no tree or arras nearby, however. The best hiding place seems to be the cart, whose lower shelf is completely concealed by linen drapery.

I whisper to the spirit of my pet chameleon: "Homer, Homer, lend me your powers of camouflage." I think he hears me. I crouch down on all fours. It is relatively simple for me to dart over to the cart and insinuate myself behind the draperies. I am discomfited, however, to discover that I am sharing the cramped shelf with a large jar that appears to contain a human brain, bobbing up and down in a formaldehyde bouillabaisse. There is also a stack of Petri dishes.

I manage to manoeuvre closer to them by reaching out and punting the cart across the linoleum. Luckily, the wheels do not squeak.

"I've got a pain," Noi-noi says at last. "Would you mind looking at it?" It seems to me that she is saying this awfully loudly. Obviously she intends the relatives in the other room to hear her.

"Oh, a pain, eh? What sort of a pain?"

"Oh, I daren't say," says Noi-noi. "It's a matter of some delicacy."

"Well, why don't you come along to my surgery, what, what, what."

They start to walk away. My eyes, peering through a flap of the linen, are just about level with their calves. They stand at the doorway, and when I crane my neck I see Dr. Richardson glance furtively from left to right.

"Not so close," Noi-noi says urgently. "I wouldn't want anyone to get the wrong idea. Everyone knows that all you *farangs* are sex-crazed maniacs."

At the mention of the mysterious word sex, whose meaning I have barely begun to grasp since my adventures of the previous night, my heart beats faster. Could it be that the indefatigable Dr. Richardson, having tired of the faithful but rotund Nit-nit, has now turned his attentions to the self-involved but ravishing Noi-noi? They are about to disappear down the corridor, and I fear I may never uncover the truth. But, in the nick of time, Dr. Richardson remembers something and comes back into the antechamber.

"My streptococci," he says. "I may as well take them back to the office while I'm at it."

I huddle beside the bottled brain and pray that the doctor won't notice the extra weight as he begins to wheel the cart down the corridor.

16

Streptococci
and Dinosaurs

I am holding on to the bottled brain for dear life as the cart lurches along, bumping over thresholds, swerving to avoid patients being rushed to surgery, hydroplaning across wet linoleum. Dr. Richardson, unaware of the human cargo that has stowed away among his Petri dishes, trundles me along at top speed. Aunt Noi-noi is hurrying along beside me, fashionably knock-kneed, her high-heels skittering.

Fearing discovery, I stop peeping through the linen. It is just as well, for at that point we take a particularly dangerous curve at high velocity, and I hear a door slam shut. The cart clangs as it hits the wall. The brain sloshes back and forth. We come to a halt.

A Rolex-adorned arm slides in beside me and removes a pile of Petri dishes. It misses my face by half an inch. I try not to breathe.

"I say, hang on a minute, will you, Noi-noi, while I put these away?" I hear Dr. Richardson's footsteps go off somewhere. Emboldened, I look out once more through the parted drape. It is, indeed, the laboratory to which Dr. Richardson once promised he would take me! Row upon row of gleaming flasks, test tubes and reagent bottles line the shelves. There is a worktable in the middle of the room; on this table is an array of retorts, Bunsen burners, coils of glass tubing with bubbling neon-green and purple fluids, all interconnected in a crazy kinetic sculpture. Noxious fumes billow up from one seething mixture. It is hard for me to suppress my coughing. On the wall are medical charts. One shows the garishly coloured viscera of a baby; another appears to be our friend the streptococcus, enlarged a billion-fold, with all its parts scrupulously labelled.

Incongruously, a framed photograph of a blonde girl leans against a rack of test tubes. Her face is classically proportioned, save for her mouth, which is a kind of paean to the orthodontist's art—a symphony in metal, strands and bolts and knobs and wing-tips, precariously held together by a couple of rubber bands.

My Aunt Noi-noi, awaiting the return of Dr. Frankenstein, picks up the picture and scrutinizes it. She handles it between thumb and forefinger, as though afraid it will contaminate her. She looks around warily. She is clearly afraid of being discovered. What could be going on? I hear Dr. Richardson approaching once more, and Aunt Noi-noi quickly puts the photo down. She knocks over the test tubes in the process. Luckily, they are empty.

"So, my dear," says Dr. Richardson, "why don't you tell me where the pain is, what?"

"Everywhere!" says Aunt Noi-noi. But she does not appear to be in pain. In fact, she begins to giggle uncontrollably.

"Let's have a look, then, shall we?"

To my astonishment, my aunt begins to disrobe. She unzips her dress of mourning and lets it drop to the floor. Like a Maidenform girl, she stands in bra and panties amid the glittering panoply of scientific apparatus. She looks every bit as splendid without her clothing as one might expect. The image is marred only by the fact that she has removed a mirror from her purse and, pursing her lips, begins redoing her lipstick.

Dr. Richardson begins to caress Aunt Noi-noi's neck, while with his other hand he deftly unclasps her bra. Though short of stature, Aunt Noi-noi is magnificently endowed, and as she begins to heave and pant, her torso resembles a primordial scene, with volcanoes erupting and earthquakes ripping across the savage terrain. The roving hands of Dr. Richardson, indeed, are like nothing so much as a pair of dinosaurs, battling it out upon the steamy landscape of Aunt Noi-noi's chest. Sweat pours down her body like rivulets of lava. What splendour! I think to myself, allowing the metaphor to seize control of my imagination. But surely it is not the breadth of this poetical conceit that has caused my aubergine to firm up like a fresh-baking baguette!

All the time Aunt Noi-noi protests unceasingly: "Oh, you terrible, terrible man—you nasty, white lumbering monster—how is it that I can lower myself to permit you to touch me—what is it that you've done to me?"

"Oh, I say, what," says Dr. Richardson, whisking off his lab coat and flinging it aside. Unfortunately, the coat ends up hanging over the side of the cart, obstructing my view of the proceedings. All I can do is listen to the strange duet of their voices, the clarinet-like moaning of my aunt punctuated by the snare drum-like "what-what-what" of the doctor.

It is so frustrating that, unable to control my curiosity, I reach my hand out to the floor and attempt to steer the cart closer to centre stage. The cart zigzags and ends up very close to where they are standing. An odour of raw fish penetrates the pervasive stench of formaldehyde. I try to shift the lab coat, but I can't seem to find any openings or slits in it.

"*Eaugh,*" says Aunt Noi-noi. "*Eaugh, eaugh, eaugh!*"

I cannot quite tell whether she is *eaughing* in pain or ecstasy. The show has no video, and the audio is muffled by the lab coat. I ease the cart a little closer—

"Ouch!" says Aunt Noi-noi.

"Bloody cart needs a wheel alignment!" says Dr. Richardson, and pushes me away. I careen into the far wall. The lab coat slips. Quickly I reach out to grab it. It would be most embarrassing to be discovered now, I realize—far more embarrassing than the time I fell out of the tree into the *yentafo.* For my brief introduction to the mysteries of sex last night, confusing though it was, has taught me that these are private acts, not meant to be viewed by children in utility carts. I move the coat just far enough to form a little slit and am soon engrossed in the unfolding drama. It is hard to gaze upon so inflaming a spectacle whilst endeavouring to hold my breath, but I manage pretty well.

The two of them have doffed their clothing completely now. Aunt Noi-noi lies on her back on the laboratory table, her feet dangling from one edge, her head resting on an oscilloscope. Dr. Richardson, standing on a footstool, with his arms outstretched in a sort of crucified pose, is in the process of . . . well, suffice it to say that my previous night's hunch was not far off the mark. Something is indeed being inserted into something, and, beneath the unforgiving glare of the overhead fluorescent lighting, it is at last possible for me to discover which part of the female anatomy is involved.

So *that's* what it's for! It is a moment of awed recognition, a revelation of cosmic purpose. Stunned, I gaze on, absorbing and committing to memory every thrust, every frenzied "*eaugh*" that bursts from my aunt's lips, every grunt uttered by the good doctor. Time will gelatinize these five minutes into a slow motion replay in which I can eidetically recall every sigh and moan, every one of those fragrances so headily commingled—the raw fish, the noxious gases, the formalin, the sweat, the faint taint of carbolic acid—and freeze-frame each split second of the scene and relish every nuance as though I were once again that priggish and inquisitive child.

But now I know that it is a mere five minutes. There is a clock ticking away on the wall, and when the door flies open I chance to glance up and see how little time has elapsed. I cannot consider the metaphysical aspects of time dilation, however, because the person standing in the doorway is none other than Aunt Nit-nit, and she has no sooner taken in the spectacle than she lets out a blood-curdling scream.

The scream, too, seems to last five minutes.

Long enough, at any rate, for the lovebirds to uncouple and leap into their clothing. Nit-nit storms into the room and slaps Noi-noi resoundingly in the face.

"Good heavens," Dr. Richardson says. "I say."

"You hateful hussy!" Nit-nit shrieks.

"You horrible harridan!" Noi-noi says, weeping. "You've ruined my makeup!"

"How can you possibly think about your makeup at a time like this?"

"If you were to think about your makeup once in a while, you might have a few more men in your life!"

"You—you—" Nit-nit swoops down on Noi-noi like a vampire bat and starts to claw at her face. Noi-noi, twirling her purse like a sling, manages to get in a few good whacks on her elder sister's head. Nit-nit divests Noi-noi of a hank of her bouffant. Meanwhile both of them spit forth a barrage of alliterative abuse. In the Thai language, one cannot be inventively abusive without making constant use of alliteration, assonance and internal rhyme. I am amazed at their proficiency. Dr. Richardson, who has even less Thai than I, is so bewildered that he lights the filter end of a cigarette.

At that moment, we hear footsteps echoing from somewhere down the hall. A lot of footsteps. The entire army of relatives must be on the march. Their cacophonous jabbering is getting nearer and nearer. My two aunts look at each other long and hard, slitty-eyed, fuming.

The relatives enter all at once.

An astounding transformation takes place. I rub my eyes in disbelief. The internecine aunts have now turned into the sugar-coated aunts. Each is trying to out-smile the other. The tear stains on Noi-noi's face have magically vanished with a dab of the powder puff. The hank of her hair seems to have been dumped into a conical flask of bubbling reagent and is even now disappearing in a cloud of smoke. Dr. Richardson has figured out which end of his cigarette to light and is waving it about in order to direct the spectators' attention away from his left hand, which is energetically and erratically buttoning his fly.

Uncle Vit says, "Has anyone seen Little Frog? We've been looking for him everywhere—Nit-nit said he might be in Dr. Richardson's office."

The two Fates look at each other, then at Ning-nong, who has just come in. Their faces are perfectly composed. It is impossible to believe they were slugging it out only a moment before.

"Little Frog?" Noi-noi says. "The poor creature. I wonder if he has got lost somewhere."

"You never know with him," says Ning-nong. "He could go into one of his Homeric reveries at any moment and end up walking off a balcony!"

"We'd better find him," Noi-noi says.

All the relatives troop off in a flurry of footsteps. Dr. Richardson is left alone, looking somewhat put out. He is even more discomfited when, sitting down at the worktable and staring at the utility cart through the distorting lens of his laboratory glassware, he sees me emerge from behind the overhanging linen.

I see Dr. Richardson's face weirdly distended behind an Ehrlenmeyer flask, the lips and teeth leeringly magnified. But I am not afraid of him. No longer do I see him as an incarnation of Dr. Frankenstein or Dr. Jekyll. After all, only a few minutes before, I saw him with his trousers down about his ankles. I have seen his scrawny buttocks quiver as he hunkered over my aunt's supine and palpitating form. One can hardly retain too much respect for a person one has seen in this compromising state.

"Oh, I say!" Dr. Richardson says. "You haven't . . . I suppose . . . been there the whole time, have you, what?"

"I'm afraid so."

"And twenty-five baht, I take it, is rather too low a fee for your silence?"

"That was last time, Dr. Richardson. An introductory offer. This time I want blackmailers' union scale."

Dr. Richardson laughs. "You're incorrigible!" he says. "Would you care to see some bacteria?"

"Love to."

Dr. Richardson beckons me to sit beside him at the table. There is a microscope there. He takes a stack of Petri dishes from a shelf, tinkers with some slides, and sticks one of them into the microscope.

"Take a look, old chap," he says. "Just take a good look at those buggers."

I close one eye and apply the other to the eyepiece.

In a circle of light, I see tiny creatures wriggling. He turns up the magnification. They are beautiful—elegant, perhaps deadly. "What are they?" I say.

"I'm not quite sure yet. They're rather exotic, actually. I got them from the throat of your Aunt Nit-nit. I'm still trying to identify them."

"Do you keep bacterial mementoes of all your . . . ah . . ."

"Well, it seems a bit more scientific than locks of hair or nude photographs, doesn't it, what?"

There can be no answer to such a sentiment. I continue to gaze into the microcosm. I am moved to wonderment that there are such creatures dwelling in people's throats. I wonder if the melodious vocal cords of the fair Jessica, too, are blighted by such parasites. I wonder whether my own larynx is tainted by tiny squirming monsters. It's a delicious, shuddery thought, reminiscent of an episode of *The Outer Limits*. Dr. Richardson is not so bad.

"Look," says Dr. Richardson, "how would you like to see a real live operation?"

"You're just saying that so I won't talk."

"Well, yes, what, what, but I daresay you'd enjoy it."

I still think I ought to blackmail him for a lot of money, but perhaps I can extend him a line of credit for the time being.

17

Tragedy and Laughter

The journey back to the estate is not without its ironies. Ning-nong knows nothing; Nit-nit knows, but does not know I know; Noi-noi knows Nit-nit knows, but is at least confident that Ning-nong does not know and thinks I do not know; and none of the three Fates knows anything of Dr. Richardson's bacterial trophies.

Only I, sitting in the front seat of the Studebaker as we remain at the same traffic light for three-quarters of an hour some two kilometres from the house, am capable of imagining the good doctor sitting at his desk, nostalgically musing over his Petri dishes filled with throat cultures of the women he has loved.

I don't want to think about my great-grandmother and her suffering. I don't want to think about Jessica, for that would remind me of how, in my ignorance of the mechanics of love, I clumsily failed to take full advantage of her proffered charms last night; and I certainly don't want to think of my two rival aunts. It is more amusing to invent little scenes about Dr. Richardson and his Petri dishes.

I realize that the day-dreaming is not going very well. My thoughts have a habit of circling back round to death. The heat is oppressive, even with the air conditioning of the Studebaker going full blast. The traffic oozes like the final dollop of toothpaste from a tube squeezed to its ultimate flatness. Now and then the sisters turn in concert and, palms folded, perform a perfunctory obeisance to some roadside shrine. I know their thoughts are of death as much as mine are.

Nobody speaks. The tension is so high that if one of the aunts were to say anything it might set off another fit of screaming, scratching and hair pulling. After a long, long while, though, Ning-nong—the only one of my maiden aunts who has not, to my knowledge, had an amorous tryst with Dr. Richardson—can no longer resist popping the question that is in all their minds.

"Little Frog . . . Little Frog," she says sweetly, "did your great-grandmother happen to mention any *papers* to you?"

"Papers?" I ask. I suddenly remember my great-grandmother saying that they all wanted to know where the will was hidden. "No, Khun Aah, I don't recall any *papers* being mentioned. Not specifically, at any rate."

"Oh, don't be a tease!" Noi-noi says. "Tell us where they are at once!"

"But I don't know!" I squeal.

The three sisters settle back into silence. The traffic speeds up to a snail's pace; motorcycles swarm through the cars like locusts through paddy. Children dart in and out, selling garlands of jasmine, Chiclets and lottery tickets.

"Well," says Noi-noi, "it'll be good to take off these weeds for a while at least. Goodness knows how long we'll be in mourning when Grandmother finally goes."

"I suppose we'd better stop off at the dressmaker's first thing in the morning," says Ning-nong. "Or perhaps even right now. It's never too soon to arrange for party clothes."

"Oh, not now," says Nit-nit. "We're so close to home."

Close in space, indeed, but not in time. After another half an hour or so we begin to move, with treacle-like sloth, toward the mouth of our *soi*.

"Let's have the party right away," Noi-noi says.

"No, not right away," says Ning-nong. "We won't have time to replenish our wardrobes. And none of our friends will, either."

"Yes, I suppose you're right," says Noi-noi. "Perhaps in a fortnight."

"I daresay the old thing will hold out until then," Ning-nong says. "I think that's a very good compromise."

"Yes. A fortnight," says Aunt Nit-nit.

She sighs. I think she is the only one of the three whose mind is going through any kind of turmoil. Unlike the dour Ning-nong, who probably has no lovers at all, and Noi-noi, whose beauty makes her fickle, Nit-nit is a woman slow to love, I suspect, but once having given her heart does not lightly take it back. She is a smouldering sort of a woman, while Noi-noi sizzles and Ning-nong doesn't burn at all.

I sympathize with her. I wish there were some way I could reveal to her that I do in fact know what she is going through; that though she might have felt, in the midst of her screaming fit and her fight with her younger sister, utterly and inconsolably alone, yet she was not alone. There was also me, voyeuristic and vicarious, scrunched up among the bottled brains and throat cultures.

How can I communicate my empathy without revealing that I know all? The loss of face for her would be immeasurable. I can only sit here in the frozen traffic, tormented and elated by my secret knowledge.

I decide to seek out Virgil and Jessica when I get back home. They are not at their house. It seems that Jessica has gone off to some choir thing, presided over by Father Regenstrom—ah, happy man, to be able to spend his time gazing on her beauty!—and I find Virgil sitting in the treehouse observatory with Piak, listlessly looking at the *klong* through his telescope.

A strange fragrance hangs in the air. Though the sun is blinding just outside, here in the treehouse there are tendrils of an aromatic fog. My two companions seem a little put out to see me crawling up to the topmost level. I shake the leaves out of my hair.

What is this odour? It is akin to tobacco, yet it is not. "What's the smell?" I say. They do not answer me, but continue to take turns gazing through the telescope. Their eyes have a reddish, glassy cast to them.

"What's happening, Little Frog?" Virgil says. His voice is strangely slurred.

"I was at the hospital. Things don't look too good, I'm afraid," I say. "My great-grandmother . . . well, sometimes she seems all right, and sometimes she acts peculiar. And my relatives seem more interested in the will than in her." Then, anxious to forget all that has transpired today: "So tell me . . . what are you looking at?"

"The usual bullshit," says Virgil. "Women bathing . . . water buffaloes . . . there go a kid he peeing in that *klong*. He don't got no manners a-tall." He giggles.

I take a peek. Life on the water goes on as ever. A woman clad only in a *phaah kajom ok* pours water on herself from a huge amphora of rainwater. Children leap from *sampan* to *sampan*. Farther away, workmen are stringing up lights against the walls of a dilapidated temple. "Looks like they setting up for some kind of temple fair," I say.

"Good. One of these days we can slip away to it in the middle of the night. And call on the old shaman while we at it, too."

"I love a good *ngaan wat*," says Piak. Virgil nods knowingly, and I realize that this is another part of the world just outside my walled kingdom that I have so far failed to experience, though it seems as though everyone else has.

"What's the smell?" I say at last. Inhaling the mist seems to induce a mysterious light-headedness.

"Don't you even know?" says Virgil, laughing again.

I have the feeling I'm being left out of something.

"Maybe you'd like to join in? Do we trust him enough, Piak?" Piak shrugs.

I look from one to the other. It is as though they have drifted away toward some inner landscape that I cannot see. I am angry. It seems as though there is no one to sympathize with me, no one to understand what I have been through in the past twenty-four hours, from the exaltation of near-sex with the fair Jessica to the desolation of near-death with my great-grandmother . . . from the ethereal fantasy of my dream-encounter with Homer, with its rarefied philosophizing over sex and death, to the odoriferous reality of Dr. Richardson's laboratory, with its more down-to-earth depiction of the two subjects.

I decide that I'm just not going to have anything to do with them any more, and I start to back out down the steps to the lower level of the treehouse.

"Wait! Come back!" Virgil says. "We trust you."

I pause halfway down the trunk, with my head still peering through the gap in the floor. Virgil pulls a pack of Krong Thip cigarettes out of his pocket. "Why don't you come on back up here and try one of these?"

"I hate cigarettes," I say, for the only time I tried one before ended in my almost hawking up my small intestine.

"These things ain't cigarettes," Virgil says, "they just *disguised* as cigarettes." He lights one, and those euphoric fumes once more start coiling through the air. "We start off with regular old filter cigarettes, we takes out all the tobacco, and then we replaces it with Thai stick."

"What's that?"

"You never heard of it before? Shame on you . . . it your country's famousest national product."

Mentally I add this fact to the list of things I ought to and do not know about the world around me. If Virgil is doing it, I tell myself, it is probably bad, but have I not recently resolved to be bad? Have I not shoplifted from bookstores, cruised down the *klong* when I was supposed to be fast asleep, and spied on the illicit amours of my aunts? I climb back up into the observatory, grab the pseudo-cigarette from my friend's hands, and proceed to puff on it four or five times with all my might, inhaling every last tendril of the smoke and clenching my throat so that not one atom of it will escape my lungs.

Nothing happens.

Or does it?

Suddenly the earth-shattering events of the past few days seem funny—intolerably funny. I begin to laugh. I laugh so hard I can feel my stomach cramping up, I can feel the pressure building on my bladder, but I can't stop myself. "My great-grandmother's going to die," I manage to shriek out between spasms of laughter. Tears are streaming down my cheeks, and all I can see of my companions are blurry silhouettes, but I know that they, too, are laughing their guts out. "She's going to die!" I scream, as though it were the punch line to the world's most hilarious joke. Oh God, it hurts to laugh but I know that if I stop the pain will be much greater.

I'm not quite sure what happens after that. Everything seems to fog up. I know I am still laughing but it doesn't seem to be me somehow. I seem to have distanced myself, to be floating in the air, far above the topmost turret of our treehouse. Looking skyward, into the sun, I think I see the pavilion of my pet chameleon in the full resplendence of post-apotheosis.

"Homer—" I cry out. I seem to be reaching out for something, I don't know what. Something I'll never be able to touch. Not in this world.

A girl's voice, calling my name, brings me back to earth with a start.

"Khun Nuu," says this voice from the ground, "your aunts want to see you right away. In the *sala*. And Khun Virgil, too, I think."

I feel a stinging slap across my face. "Time to sober up, Justin!" says Virgil. "Earth to Justin . . . Earth to Justin. . . ."

The pavilion at midday: My aunts' demeanour is grim as they stand framed by the fragrant wooden support posts, against a backdrop of lotus blooms and stagnant water, gilded by the sun. The limbo device has been set up, and Chubby Checker sings faintly against the whirring of the dragonflies.

Aunt Ning-nong has a letter in her hand, and as Virgil and I remove our sandals to enter the pavilion she looks up from it. My mind is a little muddied from whatever it was I was smoking, but she does not notice.

"Bad news, I'm afraid," she says.

My mind clears very quickly. Could it be that the unthinkable has already occurred—even though I saw my great-grandmother only a few short hours ago? But no. I see that the letter is not from the hospital; it is typed on the ostentatious stationery of the Scola Britannica, with its gold border and full-colour Union Jack blazoned on the right-hand corner.

My heart sinks. I know what this letter portends. I have been dreading it for a very long time indeed.

"I'm afraid the school has come to an agreement with the Ministry of Foreign Affairs," Ning-nong says, "and its licence has been reinstated. It means that the world's longest summer holidays are over. Well, it's about time, Little Frog. Nine months is a long time to be without the company of other children."

"But I've got Virgil! And even Piak!" I say. But I know it's no use. This is the one problem that blackmailing the sisters isn't going to solve.

"Well, it could be worse," says Nit-nit. "You've still another two weeks . . . school doesn't begin until the Monday after next . . . the day after our limbo rock party."

"At least your school won't conflict with the social event of the year!" Noi-noi says, delicately sipping a tall cool glass of *nam krajieb*.

Not much of a consolation. How much badness can one squeeze into a miserable two weeks? Having frittered away my first twelve years of life, having only in the last month learned what it is like to be a real live boy with real live boyish adventures, am I now to be changed back into an academic automaton?

"Well, Little Frog," says Ning-nong, "I don't see why you should spend the rest of the day moping. Let's go and have lunch at the Sports Club, and you boys can go for a swim."

It seems an innocuous enough suggestion, but the expression that I see in Virgil's face is one I've never seen there before. It is stark terror.

"What's the matter?" I ask him.

"Um . . . I can't swim," he says.

But I know that is untrue. "Oh, come on," I tell him, "we'll have fun. Oh, come on, Virgil. After all, I did what you dared me to do."

His look of alarm is replaced by one of stony resignation. "Since you put it that way. . . ." he says.

But I know he is afraid. How is it that Virgil the intrepid is now trembling with terror? He is about to tell me something, thinks better of it, and runs back to his house to fetch a pair of swimming trunks.

18

A Day at the Club

Unable to think of any reason for Virgil's trepidation at spending an afternoon at the Sports Club, I am even more mystified when we arrive there and lunch is a remarkable success. My three aunts, freed from their obligation to mourn, have donned their brightest print dresses, and Virgil and I are decked out in garish Hawaiian shirts. Our attire is a collective aviary of toucans, parakeets, birds-of-paradise, macaws and budgerigars in cacophonous combinations of turquoise, shocking pink, baby-rice green, crimson, ultramarine and cadmium yellow.

We sweep into the club like an animated Chagall, an eye-popping contrast to the off-white walls, the white uniforms, the white tablecloths of the dining room, the elegantly colonial rattan of the veranda sun-chairs. The only thing gaudier than our eccentric assemblage is the spectacular twenty-two baht all-you-can-eat buffet that seems to stretch as far as the eye can see. There are hams, joints of beef, turkeys, pastries, assorted Siamese dishes, vegetables of every conceivable ilk, and an ice-sculpture as tall as myself in the shape of a recumbent swan. There are rock lobsters on beds of lettuce, pâtés, cheese and fruits. The muffled soundtrack of a Bugs

Bunny cartoon, being screened in some inner room to entertain the younger children while their parents are golfing, provides a kind of chamber music to accompany our repast.

There is hardly anyone in the dining room, but Virgil occasionally glances behind him as though afraid we might be attacked. I wonder what is going on in his mind but don't like to ask. He is not paranoid though, and I am beginning to suspect that there really is something afoot.

There is little conversation at lunch, but the dessert bar is so ample that one doesn't feel the need for extended philosophical discourse.

It is after lunch that Virgil's behaviour becomes truly bizarre. My three aunts lead the way to the pool area. They stake out a table next to the diving boards, order drinks, and proceed to sit around *eaughing* and more or less ignoring us. Virgil and I start walking over to the shower rooms behind the kiddie pool to get changed. The whole time, he peers over his shoulder and darts from parasol to parasol, as if trying to blend into what little shelter they afford from the blazing sunlight and the slick and chlorinated air. Could someone really be pursuing him?

I can't think of any skeletons in his closet, except perhaps the escapade with the tin of lard that sultry night . . . was it really less than twenty-four hours ago? Perhaps the Crisco people have spies to report any non-culinary use of their product to the food police? It seems far-fetched, but it's the only hypothesis that comes to mind.

There aren't many people at the wading pool either. It's a weekday, after all, and ordinary mortals have school. There are a few toddlers splashing about, some Thai, some *farang*, with their nannies in attendance; a bloated elderly man floats past on an inflated raft. As we reach the entrance to the changing room, Virgil relaxes a little.

"Virgil," I say as we change into our bathing suits, "you really must tell me what is going on. You've been acting . . . well, you know, peculiar."

"I have?" Another furtive glance around the empty room.

"Well, yes. You've been acting as if the FBI was hot on your trail. But this isn't some sort of gangster movie . . . we're only going for a swim."

"Oh." Virgil stares at the floor. It is cool in the shower room. We're standing on a patch of floor where the tropic sun streams in through slats, making zebra stripes of bright and dark and hot and cold. He won't look into my eyes, and I can't tell what he is thinking. "You really don't know, do you?" he says.

"No.

"Well, there a lot of Americans here."

"Yes." I've never thought of it, but it is true that this place is much frequented by the diplomatic set, the consular set, the industrial set, the military advisor set and so on. The percentage of *farangs* here is pretty high, but I don't see why it should unnerve my friend. "Well," I say, "you're an American, aren't you?"

Virgil laughs bitterly. "No, you really don't understand a-tall," he says. "Me and my family, we just exotic creatures to you, shit, we might as well be from Venus . . . you don't know nuthin' about the way we is . . . things is different where I come from. Let's just say that people like me just ain't allowed to set foot in places like this."

"Oh, nonsense," I say. "It's the land of the free, isn't it?"

"Yeah, yeah."

"You're right," I say. Virgil's reticence is finally starting to get on my nerves. "You *are* an exotic creature to me. I haven't the foggiest notion what you're thinking half the time. Sometimes I think you're only doing it to impress me. Mysteries of the West or something."

"Screw you," Virgil says.

"What have I done to deserve this?" I say. "I haven't insulted you, I'm just completely baffled." Frankly though, I'm becoming testier by the minute. I think I'll lose my temper soon, and I don't even know why.

"Sooner or later you all acts this way," says Virgil.

"You all? Who all? What way?"

"My mother she always be telling me, 'Learn the prestige dialect, you'll get a lot farther in life if you can get by in the language of the real world out there.' Well, you know what I think when she be tellin' me this? I thinkin', 'You want me to grow up to be a house nigger.' Well, I'm fine the way I am, and it's the way I want to be. I ain't no house nigger, and I ain't fixin' to become a house nigger, no way."

"What's a house nigger?" I say. Virgil must be from Venus after all. He speaks of worlds and viewpoints far outside my comprehension. My innocent question seems to awaken a terrible anger in him. I can't understand why. He looks like he's about to punch me in the face. I back away. All the way into a toilet stall. I slam the door.

I can hear Virgil breathing heavily. Maybe he's getting ready to ram the door and beat me up. Suddenly, though, I hear other people's voices. Kids' voices—perhaps they're a little older than Virgil and me. Laughing, making jokes as they burst into the changing room. Listening, I put my ear to the door of the stall. There are two voices. One of them sounds American, the other has a bizarre accent, a cross between English and German.

"Jesus H. Christ," says the American boy, "I come halfway across the world to find a goddamn coon lurking in my bathroom. What the hell are you doing here, boy? Get out."

Virgil doesn't say anything. I feel pressure; someone's leaning against the toilet door. I look down and see a pair of doughy white legs. How can Virgil listen to these insults and not respond? I can hear him breathing. He's scared, deathly scared, I can tell.

"Leave him alone," says the other boy, but he doesn't sound that sympathetic.

"I just want him the hell out of here. I can't get changed with a damn nigger bugging his eyes at me. I don't have nothing against them, but Jesus H. Christ, this is the bathroom here, not the street! I've a right to be with my own kind in the goddamn bathroom, don't I?"

"All right, all right, I'll leave," Virgil says.

What's wrong with this picture? I ask myself. Virgil, the stalwart jungle king, cowering in terror before some two-salueng cowboy? I'm so full of rage I can barely think straight.

"You hold him while I punch him out," the cowboy says.

I've got to do something. I unlatch the door, swing it back with a sudden movement so that the American loses his balance. Then I slam it against him as he starts to topple. It thuds against something hollow. Probably his head. When I open the door again, he's supine on the floor of the changing room, out cold.

"Oh, sorry," I say, with all the innocence I can muster.

The other boy is backing away toward the entrance. The American stirs, begins to moan; Virgil is draped over the nearest urinal, rubbing a bruised forearm. The white boys are a little bigger than we are, but I think we could have outwitted them at a pinch.

"You Americans just don't know how to handle your kaffirs," says the boy with the strange accent. He throws Virgil a five-baht note. "There, boy, go buy yourself a Coke." He lifts up his friend and they straggle out, the one leaning on the shoulder of the other.

"You saved my life," Virgil says.

"What do you mean?" I say. "Those boys were just . . . just hoodlums! They had no right to threaten you. Why did you just stand there and take it?"

"I don't want to talk about it," he says.

He stalks out of the changing room. I'm left standing there, trying to puzzle out why he has turned his animosity on me instead of those who are clearly his enemies. I can't make head or tail of it. Perhaps Mrs. O'Fleary will enlighten me. It must be something to do with Virgil's negritude, but what? I know that it's been a hundred years since the American Civil War. It's true that my aunts were scandalized when they first met Virgil, but having come to know him, they think nothing at all of his race; at most, they see it as a quirk, an eccentricity. Why should the sight of Virgil provoke such belligerence in a white American, and why should Virgil react with such uncharacteristic timidity?

I decide I've had enough of this conundrum. I march out of the changing room with a terry cloth Elvis draped over my shoulders and wend my way toward the grownup pool. Virgil is nowhere to be seen. I imagine he's sulking somewhere. Perhaps it will be better if I just let him cool off by himself.

The three Fates are gossiping with some *farang* friends of theirs. One of them is a dour-faced, white-haired woman with a hat that looks like a ziggurat with feathers. The other is a blimp-like woman whose ample buttocks and breasts are crammed into a microscopic bikini, and whose skin has been transformed by the sun into the colour of an overcooked lobster. They are all sipping iced tea from tall glasses and chattering, gesticulating, giggling with abandon.

"*Eaugh*, look, it's Little Frog," Nit-nit says, and motions me over to a nearby deckchair. "This is our nephew, the one we told you about. . . ."

"*Ja*, the one whose parents . . ." says the ziggurat woman in an ominously familiar accent. Her voice trails away, my aunts glance quickly at each other, and the subject is dropped at once. It's another fact to file away in the perennial enigma of my parents' whereabouts.

Ning-nong says, "Justin," and I see that she is using my *farang* name in order to simplify matters for their friends, "this is Mrs. van Helsing. She's from Johannesburg. I think she's going to be teaching at the Scola Britannica when it opens, so you might as well meet her now." Gingerly, I shake her hand.

"Mrs. van Helsing has invited us to a *braaivleis* at her house next month," says Aunt Nit-nit, "whatever that is!" It certainly sounds exotic, if a little forbidding.

"And this is Mrs. Andrews," says Ning-nong, indicating the monumental woman beside her, "who works for JUSMAG."

"Howdy," says Mrs. Andrews.

"Howdy," I say. I've never said that before. I like the sound of it. Her handshake reduces my hand to the same gelatinous condition as her quivering derrière.

"Your aunts tell me you're a poet, Justin," she says. "I just adore poetry. I wish you'd shove a little poetry down my son's throat. All Wilbur cares about is baseball."

I make cooing noises that I hope will give a general impression of politeness and modesty.

"There they come, the Dynamic Duo, in person," Mrs. Andrews says.

I'm getting a sinking feeling, and when I turn around it is fully justified. The Dynamic Duo are, indeed, the two boys who attacked Virgil in the changing room. They stand beside the diving board, blond, with crew cuts, blue-eyed, tall, very much alike. They're probably about thirteen. But there is no trace of evil in their faces. They look at me. I don't think they recognize me. After all, they glimpsed me for only a second, in pretty nerve-racking circumstances.

"My son, Piet," says Mrs. van Helsing.

"Bloody pleased to meet you," says Piet, vigorously shaking my hand. "You're a poet, are you?"

Wilbur, still nursing his bruises, is also introduced to me. He smiles. "How ya doin', buddy?" he says. He's got a grin full of straight white teeth, and dimples. He is charming. Sickeningly charming. I cannot reconcile this charm with the image of him badgering my friend. Maybe he has an identical twin. Or he's a multiple personality, a sort of proto-Norman Bates. Yes. That must be it. His mother certainly seems to be the domineering type.

Mrs. Andrews clumsily enfolds her son in her arms while he struggles manfully to maintain a semblance of dignity. "Oh, Wilbur," she says, "what have you done to yourself?"

"A great big kaffir tried to beat him up," says Piet to his mother. "You should have seen him! He looked to be at least six-two." I'm appalled at the ease with which he's edited the past. I'm actually a bit impressed, too. Is that disloyal to Virgil? I feel a twinge of guilt. But I'm angry at Virgil, angry because he hasn't seen fit to share his torment with me, because he seems to be blaming me for what's eating him.

"Always you are getting into trouble," says Mrs. van Helsing ruefully.

For a while, the women coo and cluck over their boys' misadventures, while the three Fates munch decorously on thin chicken sandwiches and crinkly crisps.

"You must meet Justin's friend Virgil," says Ning-nong at the first lull. "I'm sure you'll all be friends in no time. By the way, Justin, where is he?"

I panic. He's not by the sandwich stand. He's not at any of the other tables. He's not in the water—it would be easy enough to spot him, a lone black figure in a sea of white and brown. He seems to have disappeared. It is just as well. I don't think I could take another confrontation between him and these two boys. "I'll go and look for him," I say.

"We'll help," says Wilbur. "What does he look like?"

I don't answer. Quickly I walk away before they can follow. I've got to find Virgil by myself. I've got to warn him. And I've got to force him to tell me what this is all about. One way or another, I mean to understand. I *have* to understand.

Where could the boy be hiding?

19

In Quest of Virgil

Avoiding Piet and Wilbur turns out to be easy. Just when I think they're going to follow me all the way out of the swimming pool area, a bikini-clad teenage nymph, whose bosoms are fairly bursting from their scanty confinement, crosses our path. She has something of a Nordic look—one can imagine her swinging her halberd alongside the sturdiest Viking, her blonde hair streaming in the wind over the fjord—although she carries no sword, of course. Nevertheless, the way she's brandishing her tennis racket could be interpreted as a challenge to arms.

"Grimgerda!" Piet says, and Wilbur whistles.

The Amazon stops, flutters her eyelids, gestures commandingly with her racket, and suddenly the two boys are off my back and on hers, trotting behind her and sniffing the wind of her passing like a pair of bloodhounds.

I slip away from the pool area into the main building, still in my swimming trunks, a towel slung over my shoulder. It's probably against the dress code to go into the clubhouse so attired, but I am small and hard to see as I dart from shadow to shadow. I have no idea where Virgil could be. I wander along the veranda. The air is close and humid and laden with the odour of oiled rattan. No one pays any attention to me. Now and then, a uniformed waiter bearing a silver tea tray wanders by. The veranda looks out over an endless vista of meadow and hillock, with here and there the tiny figure of a golfer in the distance.

I go back to the dining room; behind it, I know, is the little playroom where children were watching cartoons earlier. Perhaps Virgil has sought refuge in its air-conditioned darkness. But the room is deserted. On the screen, Marvin Martian is pursuing Bugs Bunny, and I can hear the rattle of the projector over the thrum of the air conditioner, but there are no children here at all. Only a few half-empty bowls of popcorn. It is chilly. I leave, blinking as the afternoon sun assaults my eyes.

Where to next? I must find Virgil, must warn him that his two assailants are still at large, that they might even at this very moment be sitting under the same sunshade as the three Fates. But he's nowhere to be seen. Perhaps he has wandered off the grounds. But where? I have to find him—how will my aunts deal with the embarrassment of his disappearance otherwise? I am sure he is able to take care of himself . . . but my aunts will probably think the worst . . . they'll probably have half the Bangkok police force on a city-wide manhunt . . . only to find that he's taken the bus back to Sukhumvit. The notion fills me with exquisite dread, for I have never, of course, ridden on the public buses. I have only gazed at them from the comfort of the family Studebaker, amazed that so many people can manage to hang out of the side door without tipping the bus over.

Could Virgil really be so afraid of confronting these boors that he would willingly eschew air conditioning and brave the sun-drenched streets?

If he can do it, I think to myself, surely so can I. After all, this isn't even his country.

After contemplating it for about five minutes, though, I realize that it's probably the wrong moment to go off on a solo adventure. It is true that such a quest would rival the epic journey of Gilgamesh into the underworld in search of the soul of his dead friend Enkidu, or the voyage of the Argonauts, or the wanderings of the disconsolate Demeter. But my pockets contain a scant fifteen baht, and there is a possibility that, if I stray too far, I may not be able to afford the taxi fare back home, for I am bad at bargaining. Besides, I'd probably have to endure the ignominious impact of Aunt Ningnong's hairbrush on my buttocks.

Such are the thoughts that swirl through my mind as I, still swathed in a towel blazoned with the image of Elvis Presley, wander across the golf course. The grass is short and prickly. A centipede, curled up, dying, is being overrun by ants. The sun is unforgiving. I'm walking aimlessly. At one point, a man in jodhpurs yells at me to get out of his way, and I narrowly avoid being brained by a golf ball. I panic and start running. I don't know where to. I'm vaguely aware of the terrain changing from grass to asphalt. I don't know whether I've left the perimeter of the club.

I run smack into a thicket of banana trees that grows against a low wooden wall and stop for a breather. I look around. There is nothing familiar about this place. It is cooler in the shade. I squeeze between the trees and find myself at the edge of a *klong*. There is a breeze here; the smell it carries is a heady blend of garbage and flowers. On the other side of the *klong* are shanties and crude lean-tos built from corrugated iron. How could I have arrived here so quickly from the clean marmoreal splendour of the club?

Then I hear children laughing. And splashing sounds coming from farther up the bank of the *klong*. My feet sink into mud as I make my way toward that sound, working my hands along the top of the low wall so I won't be swept into the water, though the water is quite still; were it not for the algae, it would be mirror-still.

I pull myself along the wall. At length the wall turns a corner, and I am standing in front of a wide stretch of canal. There is a higher wall here, made of stucco and crowned with plaster elephants. Some boys are sitting on a reed mat, smoking. A covered bridge crosses the *klong* here; the bridge bears a sign in faded gold Chinese lettering. An old ice-merchant, with his bicycle-driven ice-cart parked beside the bridge, is shaving ice; tall jars of syrup are lashed to the cart. The syrup comes in rich gaudy colours, turquoise, crimson, parrot-green.

I'm soaked with sweat at this point, and I decide to get a drink. I'm still not confident of my Thai, so I accomplish my mission by pointing. The drink costs one salueng, and the merchant is unable to make change from my ten-baht banknote.

"Pay me later," he tells me, as he shaves a fistful of ice into a plastic bag, fills it with the scarlet syrup, sticks in a straw and ties it all up with a rubber band.

"But—" I begin, struggling to frame a sentence about how I may never see him again. The Thai words are on the tip of my tongue. I feel that it will only take a tiny effort to make them all come spilling out, but I am prevented from speaking by the old man's reply.

"You have a trustworthy face, young master," he says, "and I daresay that even if our paths never cross again, you will not forget the karmic transaction that has occurred today. You will repay me tenfold in another incarnation."

At least, I *think* that's what he's saying.

The drink is a blend of sugar and flower essences. It is like sucking a rose garden into one's innards on a chilly night. Its sweetness charges my veins like a bolt of lightning. So must it be on the heights of Olympus, quaffing the snow-cooled nectar of the gods at the dinner table of Zeus. But I barely manage one sip before a dark figure, swift as a whirlwind, rushes down, wresting it from my hand.

"Give us a taste, Little Frog," says Virgil.

And runs toward the bridge followed by three or four other boys, all of them slender, brown, and quite, quite naked. Virgil takes a big mouthful of the drink and tosses it back into my hands. He clambers up the bridge, climbs one of the posts that support its rickety canopy, and leaps into the *klong*, a blur of energy. Pungent water splashes my face. Disgusted, I start to wipe myself with my towel.

The cigarette-toting boys on the mat laugh at me.

I hate being laughed at. I run up to the middle of the bridge and yell down at Virgil: "What on earth do you think you're doing? Who *are* all these people?"

"Come on down!" Virgil says, doing the backstroke. "Water a lot better out here than in that fancy old club."

"I can't possibly jump into *that water*!" I shout.

He splashes me.

Then three or four other boys, shrieking with merriment, elbow me out of the way and dive into the canal. I'm soaked. From where I'm standing it's only about three feet down to the dank and odoriferous depths.

"Course you can," says Virgil, leaping out of the *klong* and clinging to the bridge post beside me. "You can do anything you want to. If you ain't chicken, that is. Of course, you has to take off them shorts first. Wouldn't want them to get all stained." He laughs.

"I can't possibly take off my swimming trunks in front of—" Wildly I look around. The ice merchant grins. All his teeth are either gold or missing. The smoking youths are smirking. "I don't even know who these people *are*."

"These people," Virgil says, "is people who don't think I'm a lower being. These people is the people who shine you shoes and wipe you ass every day, rich boy. They caddies at the Golf Club, and when they take they break, they come here to swim, 'cause they ain't allowed in no chlorinated pool with waitresses bringing them drinks."

"But Virgil," I say, "*you're* not one of these people. Nobody said you couldn't swim there. . . ." I don't want to tell Virgil that I know the identities of the boys who picked on him—that I have been quite taken with the mendacious charm of the one, and that I have been invited to a *braaivleis*—whatever that is—at the home of the other. "Virgil, those boys don't make the rules," I say. "We should ignore them. This isn't Georgia."

"Telling me."

"Well, but it isn't! Maybe you can't go to a place like that in Georgia, but that's obviously wrong, and one day someone will notice that it's immoral, and it will get changed."

I tell him this in all earnestness, but he responds by laughing in my face. "Who do you think you are, Martin Luther King?"

"I don't know who that is."

"No, I reckon you wouldn't."

Our conversation is interrupted by another spate of splashing as the boys come thudding back up the bridge and dive off. Once again I wipe myself with Elvis. I look back down at the water, which is seething with foam. Out of the maelstrom rises Virgil, shaking the wetness from his hair like a dog. He grasps the posts and hauls himself up and sits on the railing next to me. "All right," he says. "I'll come back with you on one condition."

I have a feeling I'm not going to like it. "One condition?"

"I'll swim in your club if you'll swim in mine."

"You mean—"

"Uh-huh. Bare-ass nekkid." He laughs and laughs and laughs. I fail to see the humour in the situation.

"I couldn't possibly."

"Well, then you's gone be mighty embarrassed, ain't you, when I don't show up, and your aunts start calling the police to come looking for me and they finds out you've been consorting with the lower classes—"

I squeeze my eyes tight shut. The logic of all these consequences is undeniable. "All right," I say. Wrapping my Elvis towel about my loins, I slowly wriggle out of my swimming trunks. To my horror, I am being stared at by the entire throng.

"Jump," says Virgil.

And then, spontaneously, the chorus of caddies bursts into a rhythmic chant of "Chum, chum, chum, chum!" which must be their way of pronouncing the word "jump". I climb up on the railing. Elvis still covers my nether parts, preventing anyone from witnessing that my already meagre aubergine has shrivelled into oblivion from the terror of it. Not daring to open my eyes, I whisk away the terrycloth and take the plunge.

I smack into the water. The water is warm. The water floods my nostrils. It smells of rotting mangoes and gasoline and flowers. I struggle to stay afloat. I still haven't opened my eyes. Am I drowning? Desperately I tread water. I surface. At last I take a deep breath and gaze upward into the face of the sun.

What is it I see? Is it not the golden pavilion where lies the throne of my chameleon who has been apotheosized into the ruler of the dead? Are they not *apsaras* with gilded wings, strumming on heavenly harps in accompaniment to the plangent voice of Jessica O'Fleary?

I manage to blurt out Jessica's name and then sink back under the brackish waters.

There is a timeless moment. I am in a void outside myself. Like Tantalus, I grasp for forbidden fruit perpetually beyond my reach. Then there's blackness.

The next thing I know, I am being shaken awake. I am lying on a reed mat. There's a lot of tobacco smoke in my face. My swimming trunks are being unceremoniously slid back up my legs. Virgil is kneeling beside me.

"Wake up, Justin, man," he says. "I gotta take care of my end of the bargain now."

I sit up. I am surrounded by urchins. When they see that I am recovering consciousness, they burst into spontaneous applause.

20

Thickening the Plot

The three Fates are, of course, oblivious of the momentous events that have just occurred. When we finally make it back to the pool area, having thoroughly showered away the reek and mud of the *klong*, we are relieved to discover that Virgil's enemies have departed, perhaps in the company of the Valkyrie-like Grimgerda. The rest of the afternoon passes without incident.

So, in fact, does the rest of the week. Limbo lessons continue in earnest as Virgil teaches my aunts the finer points of bending over backward. The guest list continues to grow as my aunts remember their numerous relatives, many of whom are being invited purely so they can be impressed with the magnificence of the limbo devices. Half a dozen of them have now been built; they will be scattered at intervals throughout the grounds, and flaming torches will be set on poles crudely carved to represent tiki gods. Music will pour forth from speakers concealed in the jasmine bushes and connected to a central console not unlike the bridge of a starship, which will be manned by a technician from the Hung Wing electric appliance emporium in Wang Burapha. Thank God the dry season has come upon us—the thought of the entire estate, and residences for miles around, being stricken by a rain-induced short circuit is apocalyptic.

It is an idyllic week. There are no visits to hospitals, no arguments with the Fates, and my great-grandmother is brought home amid great pomp and ceremony, carried up to the ruined house in a sedan-chair borne by the gardener and the chauffeur and followed by a procession of nurses and orderlies who will attend her round the clock. I am prevented from visiting her by a Cerberus-like matron who sits in a rattan rocking chair by the door of her suite. I can dimly make out, in the half-light, the bed, the IV dangling from the ceiling, and various beeping and flashing pieces of medical technology. Dr. Richardson attends daily and—mindful of my ability to blackmail—never forgets to give me a sizeable tip, which I spend on sweets for Virgil, Piak and me in the sweet shop at the end of the *soi*.

After the spectacle at the club, Virgil and I have arrived at a rapprochement of sorts. We don't talk about it at all. I, whose knowledge of America has so far been limited to *Leave It to Beaver*, *The Outer Limits,* and such filmic masterpieces as *Psycho* and *Them*, am beginning to understand that the land of Virgil's birth is no utopia. But the kingdom of the treehouse is still governed by the principles of freedom and equality; it is not America, but a Platonic ideal of America.

By day we dance. By night we watch the stars; we observe the preparations for the *ngaan wat* at the temple across the *klong*. Sometimes I sleep over at Virgil's house, but we have not yet repeated the strange sexual adventure of that first night, for Jessica keeps to her room, complaining of her period. I have still not figured out why women are always talking about their periods. One day I will ask Jessica to explain. I know that it makes them moody and bad-tempered.

We lie in the air-conditioned room and listen to Mrs. O'Fleary's tales of ancient Greece transplanted to the American South, and we listen to Dion and Chubby Checker. Or sometimes, back in the wooden house, to the sound of frogs and crickets, Piak, transformed once more into a servant, fans me to sleep whilst teaching me a long litany of dirty words in Thai, words I have not yet dared to utter in public. I read my Ovid and re-read my Homer, and, for variety, my ever-growing stack of DC comics. We also see *Spartacus* again, bidding Kirk and Jean farewell, knowing we will probably never savour their love and death again.

And this is how we spend our days, drifting into the hot dry season, excitedly anticipating the grand spectacle of the coming party.

On the morning of the limbo party, I awaken to find Aunt Nit-nit looking down at me curiously. It is barely dawn. Even Piak has not yet arisen to help his father with the gardening, but is snoring on the straw *sueah* at the foot of my bed.

"Come and help me feed the monks," Nit-nit says. "There's something I want to talk to you about."

I rub my eyes and slip into a dressing-gown. I grab my sandals on the way out and follow my aunt toward the gateway of the estate. It is a strange time of day. The air is only lukewarm; the sunrise tints the jasmine buds a subtle pink, and the stucco has a mysterious golden glow. I am only peripherally aware of the daily ritual of the feeding of the monks, for it is one of those things that generally happens before I awaken, like the servants cooking breakfast or sweeping out the pavilion.

A low table has been set out next to the spirit house near the front gate. The smell of incense and flower garlands pervades everything. There is a line of monks, their robes the colour of dawn itself, their begging bowls extended; Kaew and Samlee are filling each bowl with rice, curry, sautéed vegetables and crispy-fried *pomfret*. It is the first time I have been this close to Samlee in some weeks now, and when I look at her I experience all the old feelings again, and they are more intense than ever.

She looks up from a tureen of *kaeng massaman*, gazing at me through a veil of rose-coloured steam, and I seem to hear her cry out to me: "Master Little Frog, I am in anguish. The road of my karma has led me away from the place where I left my heart. Oh, I am full of pain." She wears her high-heels easily now. Her makeup is not so exaggerated, her clothes do not seem so awkward. She has adapted. Is this what it is like to follow the ways of Homer, my dead chameleon? I shudder. I do not speak to her. The two continue to fill the monks' bowls as they file past in silence. Only the sounds of distant traffic remind us that we are in the heart of a teeming metropolis.

Aunt Nit-nit does not personally feed any monks. She stands in the background, supervising. Perhaps she is making merit by a kind of osmosis. She seems too agitated to be thinking of the cycle of karma at all. "Listen here, Little Frog," she says, "I want you to do something for me. It's my last chance to . . . to . . ." She begins to weep.

"There, there now, Aunt Nit-nit, it can't be that bad."

She puts her arms around me. Dutifully, I bury my head in her capacious bosom. "I want Noi-noi to cease from ruining my life," she tells me, with a bitterness I have rarely seen in her. "It's appalling to look at her each morning and see her at the breakfast table, so beautifully proportioned, with those slender lips and liquid, limpid eyes, whilst I, I, I must suffer the torment of being a repugnant fatso! Every time a man so much as looks at me, Noi-noi has her claws out, waiting by his bedroom door! Well, this time I've a plan. I just need half an hour of your time tonight. Money is no object. You've got to help me, Little Frog, because you're the only person small enough to fit inside her closet."

"It sounds rather elaborate," I say dubiously, assuming that some kind of spying is about to be called for. "But would someone like Piak be able to do the job? He can probably be bought a lot cheaper than I can. And frankly, I don't relish the thought of spending the big party sleuthing in women's bedrooms."

"Piak can't possibly be trusted . . . what are you saying? He's a servant."

I raise an eyebrow.

"Besides," she says, "it involves technology, and you know that they can't operate electronic machinery. . . ."

I've never seen Piak have any trouble with the portable phonograph, the toaster, or any of the other appliances in the treehouse.

I wonder why my aunts persist in the delusion that there are certain things the servant classes simply don't have the brains to do. But I bite my lip and listen. Aunt Nit-nit is overwhelmed by her warring emotions. She is enlisting my aid not because she could not find others, but because she feels she needs an ally in the family, even one as junior and powerless as my wretched self.

"I have every reason to believe," says Nit-nit, "that your Aunt Noi-noi is going to slip away during the evening. Now, I have managed to conceal a tape recorder under the dirty linen in the hamper in the closet. It's all plugged in, and there's a three-inch reel of tape all ready to go. All you have to do is precede her into the bedroom by about thirty seconds, turn on the device, and—under cover of darkness, while Noi-noi is indulging her lusts—crawl away and slip out. It shouldn't take more than five or ten minutes."

"But what do you need the incriminating evidence for, Aunt Nit-nit?" I say. The monks have gone off down the *soi*, and the servants are putting away the utensils and folding up the table so they can haul it back to the kitchen.

"I want to confront her. I want to embarrass her. I want her to leave me alone!" she whispers fiercely. "Oh, Little Frog, I hate her so! It's wrong to hate one's flesh and blood, but I can't help it! Oh, why, why, why do I feel this terrible, murderous rage? Even coming out here every morning to feed the monks has not stilled the turmoil within me."

How can I refuse Aunt Nit-nit's request after all she has done for me—sticking up for Virgil, allowing herself to be blackmailed, defending me from the ire of her older sister? I am like a king in a Greek tragedy, trapped between the Scylla of obligation and the Charybdis of duty. I can tell that the Fates are impelling me ineluctably toward some grand ironic revelation that can only augur my downfall. So it was with Oedipus, Agamemnon and all those other doomed heroic figures. For I know what she does not know I know; I know that she knows that the lover of Noi-noi is none other than her own, and that the embarrassment she plans for Noi-noi can only boomerang back upon herself.

"All right, Aunt Nit-nit," I say, sighing as I extricate myself from her ample and suffocating embrace, "I'll do it. No charge."

"*Eaugh*, Little Frog!" she says, kissing me on the forehead. "You are such a dear."

As we turn to walk back to the house, the sun is already above the horizon, for dawn is fleeting. A truck laden with electric lights, marquees and folding tables and chairs has driven up. Piak has run to open the gate, and workmen are already starting to unload their equipment.

"Perhaps," says my aunt, "I'd better go and ask the spirit of the *saan phra phuum* to grant me a little inner peace before everyone starts going crazy."

Aunt Nit-nit leaves to pray at the spirit house by the gate. As I walk back, the morning silence is suddenly rent by the amplified sound of steel drums and bongos and the voice of Chubby Checker. Dance rehearsal has begun, and the music is blasting from every shrub on the estate. I glance back at my aunt as she prays, joss-sticks in her folded hands. The workmen are dollying in the marquee now, shouting orders at each other in Chinese, and the music is being turned up notch by notch so that the air seems to vibrate with the rhythms of the far Caribbean, but Aunt Nit-nit is standing in a little bubble of tranquillity; for a few minutes, it seems that she does not share our universe.

Then—as if the drumbeats have finally burst that bubble—she deposits the incense sticks in the bowl, turns to face me, and starts to dance toward the front door in an elephantine counterpoint to the music.

21

Party Time

As evening falls in our pocket universe, the grounds of the estate are ablaze with thousands upon thousands of coloured lights. They have been strung in all the mango trees in the orchard. They pepper the jasmine and the *phuttachaat* bushes. Garlands of lights adorn the canvas pavilions that have been erected—one for food, one a quiet place for the elders to squat and chew their betel nut, and several for dancing. The *sala* above the pond has been cleared of furniture and has also been designated a temple of Terpsichore.

A disc jockey has been engaged for the evening, and he is already hard at work in a little pantry that has been wired to all the loudspeakers outside. There is a rumour that the music will actually be stereophonic. If so, it will be the first time this technology has penetrated to our remote little island kingdom on Sukhumvit Road.

During the afternoon, my aunts have neglected me completely. They are trying on new clothes. At about five o'clock they send Kaew to summon me upstairs to the sitting room, a sanctum to which I am rarely admitted.

It appears that, having doffed their mourning, they cannot decide which to wear of the dozens of new dresses each has had made especially for tonight. These dresses are all over the sitting room—

draped upon sofas, coat hangers, slung over the top of the half-open doorway. Each of the three Fates is having her hair done by one of the maids, and as I enter each of them is lecturing the others on the inappropriateness of the dresses they have elected.

"Oh, there you are, Little Frog," says Aunt Ning-nong. "Now listen here. You simply *have* to settle this."

The three Fates rise at the same time and they are standing there, all expecting me to say something.

"Whatever am I to settle, Aunt Ning-nong?"

I'm afraid it's going to be the judgment of Paris all over again, but there is no golden apple, and instead of three bribes, I will probably have to choose between the least intolerable of three punishments.

"We can't decide what to wear. We've all had several dresses made, of course, so we could put off choosing until now, but now we *still* cannot make up our minds."

Indeed, the selection is bewildering. There are frilly ones with lace and bows. There are swooping ones with wing-tipped shoulder-pads and plunging necklines. There are daringly short ones and ankle-length ones. There are silks, satins, chiffons, prints, pinstripes and polka dots. There are all the hues of the rainbow and more. There are witty clothes, satirical clothes, classic clothes, ironic clothes and sumptuous clothes. And that is just the top layer. For beneath the ones spread out all over the room one can catch glimpses of other clothes, here a sleeve, there a ruff, over there a sequinned bodice.

"Isn't this overkill?" I say.

"We'll model them all for you," says Noi-noi, "and then you can write your choices down on a piece of paper, and we won't look at it until you leave the room."

"A sort of secret ballot," I say, for Virgil has been teaching me about the constitutional system of the United States.

Ning-nong simply harrumphs at my political commentary.

"But my dear, respected aunts," I say. "Let us assume that it will take you each five minutes to put on each of the dresses in this room. Scientifically speaking, the amount of time required *in toto* would increase in direct proportion to the number of dresses. If n represents the total number of dresses and t equals five, it follows that n times t equals—"

"Just give us the bottom line," Nit-nit says.

"We'll be here till next Thursday."

"Well," Noi-noi says, "you've got the brains in the family, Little Frog. Find a remedy for this Procrustean dilemma."

"Aunt Noi-noi," I protest, "Procrustes wasn't a dressmaker; he made beds. Well, I don't mean that he put bed sheets on them. He put people on them. And he cut the people to fit the beds, not the clothes to fit the—"

"Oh, don't be such an egghead," Noi-noi says. "Just pick the dresses."

"Solomon and Pericles couldn't pick the right dresses, my respected Khun Aahs. It is, in the final analysis, a matter of taste."

At length, however, a solution does occur to me. They sneer a little when I suggest it, but at length they conclude that it is the only one possible.

It is agreed upon that, rather than have to make such painful choices, each will wear several costumes during the course of the evening. Aunt Ning-nong will change her clothes every hour on the hour; Aunt Nit-nit at twenty past; Aunt Noi-noi, being the youngest, must perforce wait until twenty minutes before the next hour to display her latest couture.

Before I leave to assume my own robes of office, Nit-nit whispers in my ear: "And remember what you promised—the tape machine—the closet—the bedroom—"

Sighing, I nod and leave my aunts to their devices.

The first guests to arrive are family members. First come my cousins, Shrimp, Crab, Tadpole and Lobster, and my second cousins, Red, Green, Black and White. My aunts' cousins, Jinx, Lynx and Minx and their cousins-in-law Bong-bong and Albert. I do not, of course, know the true names of my innumerable relatives. Such secrets are not divulged to the young; we are all forced to make do with these baby-names. I rejoice, at least, that my parents have not seen fit to give me the nickname of Hockey Puck, which name belongs to an extremely corpulent cousin who is even now waddling toward me, his flesh quivering as it threatens to burst the buttons on his Hawaiian shirt, which has a design of prancing antelopes. My innumerable cousins are introduced to me, but I pay them little attention; they are mostly interchangeable.

I am waiting for the O'Flearys to show up, and indeed they do, Jessica in a pink chiffon that contrasts tellingly with her dusky complexion, Virgil in a white suit with a turquoise velvet bowtie, Mrs. O'Fleary in some kind of African thing, a muumuuesque robe of green and scarlet, with a head cloth in matching hues. Their arrival produces gasps of wonderment, for they are probably the first Negroes any of my benighted relatives have seen up close.

"Let's eat!" Virgil says. Grabbing me by the shoulder, he propels me toward the food pavilion while Jessica stands by demurely. I don't want to lose sight of her quite this soon, but Virgil is irresistible, and there's a mélange of mouth-watering odours wafting from the food tent.

Inside, the caterers have outdone themselves. The food is all on an American theme, with such exotic viands as cheeseburgers, frankfurters and apple pie; for the less adventurous, there is a wide selection of chilli sauces to spice up the burgers. Off to one side, for those unable to stomach the foreign cuisine, there are also the usual pigs roasting on spits, vast vats full of fiery curries, *satays*, *kuaitiaos* and *khnoms*.

"This food good," my friend says. He begins shovelling it in at an alarming rate. I have never seen him eat so fast and so distractedly. I don't know what can be on his mind. But the last week has been almost too picture-perfect to be true. Greek tragedy tells me that contentment is illusory. "Call no man happy until he is dead," says Euripides . . . or someone of that crowd.

"Virgil . . ." I say. But he is so absorbed in eating that he doesn't speak to me. I wander off, the task my aunt Nit-nit has set me weighing heavily on my mind. The Fates are nowhere to be seen. They are planning, I imagine, an entrance fraught with spectacle and pomp.

Because so much of the party is outdoors, special electrical mosquito-repelling devices have been hung up on the pavilion posts. They emit a blue light and a continuous *dzzzt-dzzzt*.

Some familiar people are arriving. I see Dr. Richardson at the wheel of a sports car, with the roof down, pulling in through the open gates. His wife is with him; she is an elegant woman, dark haired, with a pageboy haircut, dressed in white. Climbing out behind them is the girl of the photograph in the good doctor's laboratory—an exquisite creature with platinum blonde pigtails, dimples and a mouth full of metal.

Since Virgil is preoccupied and Jessica seems to have vanished, I go up to Dr. Richardson and greet him.

"I say, you haven't met my daughter, have you, Justin, what, what, what? This is Griselda. Griselda, Justin."

"Don't you dare make fun of my mouth. I thaw you thtaring at it." Her voice has a kind of rough music to it, reedy, like an out-of-tune oboe. "And don't critithithe my lithp, either," she adds. "I bloody well can't help it. I'm thtuck with it until I get the bloody thingth removed."

"I rather like the lisp, actually," I say. "It adds a kind of plaintive sighing to your voice. It's like lying awake listening to the wind through the mango trees in the middle of the night."

"Oh, you are abtholutely bloody well *full* of it," she says, but I get the feeling she's secretly rather flattered.

"Watch your language," her mother admonishes, but she is soon lost in the crowd, as is Dr. Richardson, who is gazing this way and that, as though anticipating another of his secret rendezvous.

At that moment, Little Eva's "Locomotion" can be heard reverberating through the mango trees.

"I thimply *love* the locomotion!" Griselda says. "Come on—you're going to have to danthe with me at onthe!"

She yanks me forward by the hand, and we make for the nearest dance floor at an earnest clip. Once there, she flings me out to centre stage and begins to perform the choo-choo hip thrusts of this, the most robotic of last year's dance steps. Her dancing has great severity, indeed, a kind of classical austerity. She keeps her features impassive and takes carefully measured little steps, preserving her dignity. I, on the other hand, dance with wild abandon, for I have no grace, and hope that sheer energy can substitute for it.

Others have ascended the dance floor too. I notice several of my younger cousins prancing around like monkeys and, a head taller than all the Thais, the lanky form of Dr. Richardson, a beaked visage bobbing up and down on the ocean of jet-black hair.

In the distance, the three Fates have appeared and are greeting the throng. They are splendidly attired. I have never seen more sequins, feathers, rhinestones and boas.

"Can you do the twitht?" Griselda says, as the music changes.

"Of course," I reply.

We charge right in. Griselda is capable of twisting all the way down to the floor in tiny increments, her incipient breasts flapping against the sheer white sweat-sluiced fabric of her blouse.

I am so astonished at this glimpse of her feminine charms that I suddenly stop twisting and stand there in the middle of the arena, gaping. Griselda is far away as she dances, utterly self-involved. She begins to twist back up from the floor, slowly raising her head to stare at me with wide cerulean eyes. God, she is beautiful, I'm thinking, and I stare back, quite motionless.

"Why don't you bloody well danthe?" she chides me. "It'th good for the thirculation. It can thtop heart ditheatheth, you know."

She is, after all, her father's daughter.

"You're an expert on diseases, are you?"

"Actually it'th jutht a thideline. Perthonally I prefer the more abthtract thienthes: nuclear phythicth, thermodynamic, higher mathematicth."

"Good heavens. But what about literature, art, music?"

"Oh, they're all very well," she says, thrusting her slender buttocks out and vibrating them, "but they're for thithieth."

"Sissies?" What, the noble outpourings of Homer, Virgil, Shakespeare and Ovid reduced to effeminate maunderings? I've half a mind to challenge her to a duel right then and there.

Just at that moment, however, I see that one of the three Fates is no longer standing with the others. She is stalking back toward the house. It is Noi-noi. It is time for espionage now.

"See you later," I tell Griselda Richardson, and start to elbow my way out of the mob of dancers.

"Heaventh!" says Griselda. "Theduthed and abandoned!"

Quickly I slip around the back of the wooden house and run up the back stairs, which are rarely frequented by the *phudiis* of the house. Only a few servants see me.

I run into Noi-noi's bedroom. I hear her stilettoed footsteps coming up the front stairs, and the ominous, heavy tread of a companion. I slide into her room—a brand new air-conditioning unit has been turned on in preparation for her advent—and, not switching on the lights, feel my way toward the walk-in closet beside the bathroom *en suite*. From the lawn outside the window, muffled by the thrum of the air conditioner, come the quasi-Caribbean strains of the "Limbo Rock".

I open the closet and settle down. I find the tape recorder easily by feel. It is, as promised, in the dirty linen hamper, and the record button is readily accessible. It takes me a moment or so to realize that there is someone in the closet with me. I can hear breathing . . . shallow breathing . . . like that of a beast of prey lying in wait in the jungle, ready to spring.

"Who is it?" I whisper.

"Oh, Justin, it only you . . . thank God. I thought I was gone get creamed."

"Virgil! What the hell are *you* doing here?"

"Same as you, I reckon . . . recordin' the proceedings for posterity."

"But who asked you to—"

"I never reveal my clients' names. Neither should you. Is you microphone on?"

"I *know* how to operate the damn thing!"

"Yeah, yeah. Quiet now. They comin'."

22

The Cavern of Desire

As Virgil shushes me, we hear the door being flung open and the creak of the inner door, with its wire mosquito-netting, as it settles into place. There are a few high-pitched giggles, then a basso profundo launches into the familiar litany of "what, what, what".

I say, "But what if there aren't any sounds? What will there be to record?"

"There will be."

The closet has a keyhole, but obviously only one of us at a time can look through. From an espionage point of view, it's a terrible design. At the moment, the aperture is completely covered by Virgil's face. I nudge him. "Let me look, too!" I whisper.

He doesn't budge. There must be something really interesting going on. "Well, at least tell me who put you up to it," I say.

"Well, all right," Virgil says. "It was your Aunt Noi-noi. She was gone hire you to do it, but she reckoned you might turn out to be a double agent."

"That doesn't make any sense," I say. "If Aunt Nit-nit wants to use the tape to blackmail Aunt Noi-noi, what possible use could the same tape be to Aunt Noi-noi?"

"Oh, she plannin' to throw it in your aunt Nit-nit's face . . . show her what it sound like when a *real* woman make love."

"So one of them wants to use the tape to embarrass the other, while the other wants to flaunt the tape to belittle the one?" I say, becoming increasingly puzzled at the complexity of my aunts' thought processes.

"If you don't shut up, Justin, we *all* gone get in trouble."

I'm quiet for a moment. There are no sounds save the air conditioning and the occasional creak of a bedspring. The lovers—if lovers they be—are speaking in such hushed tones that I am sure the microphones can pick up very little of their conversation, even though they have been planted quite close to—or possibly under—the bed, the cables to the portable tape recorders concealed by artfully discarded towels and lingerie.

"These tapes gone be useless!" Virgil says. He still doesn't budge from his keyhole. I become aware, however, of a ragged shaft of light coming in from overhead. I realize that there is enough space between the closet door and the lintel to look through, if one could only find something to stand on.

"I'm going to get on your shoulders, Virgil . . . I can look through the top there, and it's not fair that you should be the only one who gets to see what's going on!"

"Why not? I was here first."

Impeccable though that logic is, I feel that there is something unfair about it. After all, this is my house, not Virgil's. However, he doesn't object when, using the hamper as a foothold, I clamber up on to his shoulder and stand precariously, one foot on his back, the other on the hamper. My imitation of the Colossus of Rhodes is brief, though, for before I can put my eye to the crack I feel myself start to slip. I grab the first thing within reach, which happens to be a coat-hanger, and I swing back like an ape man, until I find my buttocks abutting the far wall and my knees sort of wedged against a side shelf full of sheer brassières and pantyhose.

"What was that?" It's Dr. Richardson's voice.

"Oh, nothing . . . nothing at all," says Aunt Noi-noi, and I realize that she, having arranged for Virgil's presence in the closet, is as anxious to conceal that presence as we are. "Probably just a *tukae* or some such creature."

"Oh, I say, what," says Dr. Richardson, and their voices subside into a susurrant mumbling virtually indistinguishable from the sound of the air conditioner and the distant hum of the crowd outside.

"What we need," Virgil says, "is some kind of sports commentator. Like Howard Cosell."

"And who, may I ask, is that?"

"Don't you know nuthin'?" says Virgil, as though I were the most ignorant soul on the face of the earth.

At that moment, however, I begin to have an inkling of who Howard Cosell might be. We hear Aunt Noi-noi's voice rise above the murmuring. In tones of BBC-like clarity, Noi-noi declaims: "The dragon has now escaped its clothy confines. It has reared up, and is inching its way toward the cavern of desire."

"She don't want she sister to miss nuthin'," Virgil opines.

I lean forward, extending my arms across the hanger rod and pushing my arms against the lintel whilst trying to jam my feet against the back wall. I achieve a kind of balance. My eyes are level with the crack of light above the door, my midriff is supported by the rod, and I'm sort of treading water against the back of the closet to keep from slipping. I know I cannot sustain this position for more than a few seconds, but in those seconds I manage to snatch a glimpse of a pair of scrawny white buttocks, glistening in the moonlight like the snow-clad peaks of the Himavant. My aunt's head is barely visible as it bobs up and down upon an ocean of pink satin. Before I can lose my foothold, I lower myself back down into a crouching position.

Then comes another announcement: "The dragon has now entered the cavern of desire, and is tunnelling toward the chest of jewels."

"Good heavens, what, my dear. One might suppose this were some kind of documentary sports film, and that you were providing some sort of background narration . . . somewhat in the manner of that American chap . . . Cosell, is it, what?"

This is followed by an accelerating sequence of moans, groans and whinnying noises—it sounds like nothing so much as a cavalry raid on a Cheyenne village.

Then comes a more agitated announcement: "The dragon has unlatched the chest and dislodged the pearl of infinite price!"

How on earth have I managed to get myself stuck in this closet while the party for which I've waited for weeks is going on? Aunt Nit-nit told me I should be able to slip away unnoticed during the frenetic goings-on, but this seems logistically unfeasible. I should have seen the flaw in her logic, but my sense of duty must have overcome my ability to reason.

Meanwhile, the noises off have risen in a crescendo, and, above the tumult, we hear Aunt Noi-noi's triumphant proclamation: "The dragon's head has breached the portals of the castle! The floodgates of passion have opened! The cannon are firing and the fireworks are going off over the vanquished city!"

"Oh, I say!" says Dr. Richardson. "Oh, oh, oh, oh!"

"*Eeeeeeeaugh!*" Aunt Noi-noi screams at the top of her lungs.

At that moment—

We hear another cry—a distant, collective shrieking from somewhere outside the house. And then comes the direst sound of all—footsteps pounding through the house—the unfamiliar squeal of shod foot on waxed wood. What could be so urgent that people aren't even taking off their shoes as they enter the house? In a trice comes a banging on Noi-noi's door. I hear Noi-noi screaming, and a flurry of bed sheets, and a loud thunk as someone lands on the floor and scrambles under the bed. The next voice I hear is the voice of the gardener.

"Khun Nong—oh, please excuse this brash interruption, but—"

"Get out of here at once! Can't you see that I'm changing?"

"Do you know where Dr. Richardson is, Khun Noi-noi? Please—something terrible has happened—Khun Ning-nong has a *woon sen* stuck in her throat—she's choking to death!"

I can't bear it any more. There is too much excitement in the air, and it is unjust that Virgil is getting the only decent view of the proceedings. I push him out of the way, heedless whether the noise will betray our presence. I shove my right eye against the keyhole and am treated to the astonishing spectacle of my aunt, a satin sheet modestly concealing her heaving cleavage, the gardener with his sandals and a track of dirt leading all the way out through the doorway, and the bare white feet of the good doctor poking from beneath the bed.

"*Tai haa!*" says Aunt Noi-noi. "Choking to death?" Then, cupping her lips, she looks nervously hither and thither and cries out, in accents of the utmost innocence. "Yoo hoo—Dr. Richardson—where are you?"

"If you don't mind my saying so, Khun Nong, aren't those his feet under the bed?"

"Why, so they are!" Aunt Noi-noi leaps from the bed and, still clutching the drapery to her breast, inches her way across the floor, one arm held out in a gesture of feigned opprobrium. "Come out at once, you nasty man!" she says.

Dr. Richardson emerges from beneath the bed. He is quite naked. "Come now, enough of this charade," he says. "I've a patient to see, what, what! Hippocratic oath and all that. Don't underestimate the lethal potential of a strand of *woon sen*—it is the deadliest member of the noodle family!"

Chastened, Noi-noi begins sobbing. "But my reputation . . . heavens, will she actually die? Fancy that! . . . a *woon sen*!" The screams coming from downstairs are louder now.

"Where the hell are my clothes? Can't see a damned thing." It is not that dark—the lights of the party are streaming in through the window—but in the heat of passion Dr. Richardson's clothing seems to have been scattered all over the room. To my horror, Dr.

Richardson advances toward the closet—his monstrous aubergine seems to fill the keyhole.

"No!" Noi-noi shrieks. "Not the closet! Not the closet!"

Dr. Richardson flings the door wide. Virgil and I have managed to duck behind the linen hamper and to cover ourselves and our tape recorders with a pile of colourful muumuus.

"Good heavens! Well, I've got to wear *something*," I hear him say.

The closet door slams shut once more and Virgil and I immediately jostle for the keyhole. I manage to elbow him out of the way. I look through the hole and see that Dr. Richardson has strapped a Maidenform bra around his buttocks in such a way that the two hillocks are now concealed by its cones. He has stuffed an Yves St. Laurent shawl into the strap so that it overhangs his voluminous aubergine. Above this improvisatory breechclout, his lanky body glistens with the sweat of his erstwhile amorous exertions.

I have barely had time to take in this astonishing sight when dozens of people start pouring into the room. There are cousins and uncles and there is Aunt Ning-nong, her arms flailing, being wrestled on to the bed by my burliest relatives. The lights are all turned on at once. I blink at the sudden brightness. My aunt lies on the bed now, her face a distressing shade of blue, and from her throat comes a sound like the croak of a lovelorn *ueng-aang*.

Dr. Richardson does not seem at all comical, despite his preposterous attire. Nay, rather, he radiates a calm authority as he calls for someone to run to his car to fetch his bag. The crowd stands back as he kneels by the bedside to examine his patient. Only Aunt Nitnit, wringing her hands and pacing back and forth, and Aunt Noi-noi, still cocooned in her satin sheet, do not mingle with the others but hover over the bed, their shadows dancing against the far wall's teakwood panelling with its bas-relief scenes from the *Ramayana*.

"Hey, Justin," says Virgil, who has not been able to view most of the foregoing, "this a ideal time for us to go back out there without nobody noticing."

The closet door is still a little ajar. We creep out. Indeed, we are quite inconspicuous. I seek out Aunt Nit-nit and ask her how it happened.

"Oh, Little Frog," she says, "it's the most appalling thing! One minute she was laughing at one of Uncle Vit's jokes, the next, there was a noodle stuck in her windpipe!"

At that moment I notice that Griselda Richardson and her mother have come into the room—that she has opened the closet door and is poking about inside with unbridled curiosity—and that she seems to have found one of the tape recorders!

Dr. Richardson looks up from the bed just as his black bag is brought upstairs and thrust into his hand. "I'm afraid I'm going to have to perform a tracheotomy," he says. "If any of you can't stand the sight of blood, I suggest you leave."

A gasp goes up from the assembled company, but no one makes a move to depart.

Suddenly, from the portable tape recorder, in a tinny simulacrum of Aunt Noi-noi's voice, come the words: *The dragon has now escaped its clothy confines. It has reared up, and is inching its way toward the cavern of desire.*

Aunt Nit-nit looks at Aunt Noi-noi with an expression of insensate fury. Aunt Noi-noi gazes at the floor with studied nonchalance. She attempts to shrug, but cannot do so without dropping the sheet and exposing her wanton charms to *hoi polloi*.

"Don't worry about a thing," says Dr. Richardson to Aunt Ning-nong, who continues to gag and writhe on the bed. "I know your throat like the back of my hand. I'll have that noodle out in a jiffy."

He holds his scalpel like a samurai warrior, meditating. Then, his eyes closed in an expression of rapture, jabs.

23

The Show Must Go On

"All right, all right," Dr. Richardson says. "Surgery's a private business. I suggest you all return to the party. We can't very well have thirty people crowding the bed, can we now, what, what?"

Reluctantly, one or two people leave.

"Oh, come on," says the good doctor. "A tracheotomy isn't exactly a spectator sport, you know. Do be reasonable."

"But . . . but . . ." Aunt Noi-noi says, expressing the thought that's in all our heads right now, "is it serious? I mean, will she . . . will she . . ."

"Of course she'll live," says Dr. Richardson. "She'll be fit as a fiddle, now do let me get on with my work. You might have someone send up a bottle of Mekong."

The onlookers turn to each other. One can see that they are wondering whether it is Dr. Richardson's wont to drink while he operates.

"It's to kill germs with, you silly people!" he says.

The music has been silent for the last ten minutes; but, as if on cue, the "Limbo Rock" starts to play from all the hidden speakers on the grounds. This seems to remind people that they are, after all, here to enjoy themselves, and they begin to drift away.

"Yes, yes, she'll live," says Dr. Richardson. There is a sliver of crimson against my aunt's palpitating throat. Someone lets out a little scream at this first sign of blood, and the audience quickly dissipates.

Only Virgil and I remain. We do not speak to each other as we slowly walk out of the room, leaving the doctor alone with his patient. I do not feel comfortable looking at my friend as we make our way down the stairs. I have to confess that I am angry with him. I have always been angry with him for usurping a place in the hearts of my family. I am angry with Aunt Noi-noi for confiding our innermost secrets to an outsider. I am angry with Virgil for allowing himself to play a role in the war between the Fates. Most of all, I am angry about how much Noi-noi may have paid him for spying, and I'm kicking myself that I may no longer have cornered the market in the espionage game. I'm full of rage and my rage is directed at virtually all the major figures in my life. There is so much rage knocking around inside my head, in fact, that I don't really know what to do with it. It simmers. It smoulders. It batters at the ramparts of my brain. There is nowhere for it to go, for I am, in the final analysis, a well-bred sort of child and incapable of giving full vent to my primal instincts.

On the other hand, I am not at all worried about Aunt Ning-nong. Dr. Richardson says she'll survive, and I trust him implicitly—as much as one could ever trust a man wearing a bra about his buttocks.

The limbo is in full swing when we arrive at the wooden pavilion, the smallest of the three dancing areas. Swathes of blue light crisscross the *sala*, amphibious croaking counterpoints the clang of the steel drums and ragged handclapping keeps syncopated time.

The limbo pole is on the next-to-topmost rung, and three or four of the guests are limbering up to pass beneath it. Among them is Jessica O'Fleary, and my rage is forgotten as I watch her bend backward in a poised, taut arc, her bare feet inching over glistening teakwood. Her body too is glistening. In the blue light it has acquired an alien sheen, like the ghostly Arcola of her mother's tale, risen from the dead in a distant land across the sea. She slithers under the pole with her eyes closed. She seems to be dreaming of somewhere far away.

The pole is lowered. Uncle Vit fails to make the grade. One of my cousins cheats his way through by ducking his head. And then it's Jessica's turn again, and again she bends back with closed eyes and thrusts delicately forward until she slides under the pole with her feet barely skimming the oiled wood, then, with a burst of angular momentum, snaps herself upright.

I get a lump in my throat just looking at her. But then, thinking of Dr. Richardson's scalpel, I swallow the lump as quickly as I can and go to get myself a Coke. Virgil does not come with me. He is talking animatedly with one of my female cousins, a pigtailed girl by the name of Centipede.

I do not make it to the food pavilion, however, because my path is intercepted by one of the uniformed caterers bearing a tray of drinks. I take a glass of Coke and down it in one. It doesn't taste like Coke—it has a bitter, burning quality as it pours down my throat—but I don't really think about it. Because the next thing I know, there's a hand on my hand, and I am being yanked across the lawn toward the largest of the three arenas.

"Griselda!" I say.

"Where the *hell* have you been? I've been thimply *dying* to thee you for bloody *hourth*."

"Well, I've been involved in various clandestine dealings, and then, of course, there was a medical emergency. . . ."

"Well, let'th danthe," she says, flinging me into the centre of the dance floor just as the strains of "Peppermint Twist" strike up. Tentatively, I begin to move in time to the music. Evidently my flailing efforts are not enough for Griselda, though, because she starts shoving me around the dance floor, and soon I'm reeling to and from her like a yoyo.

"You're drunk!" Griselda exclaims.

"I am?" Is that the meaning of the heat in my cheeks and the pounding in my skull? "But I've only had a Coke!"

At that moment, a waiter drifts through the scene, and I manage to reach out and get hold of another Coke. It, too, does not taste quite right. But I am beyond caring.

"Let'th thee thothe thcrawny hipth of yourth *wiggle!*" cries Griselda. She pulls me so hard I barely have time to replace the drink on the tray as the waiter waddles off toward the next pavilion.

I launch into another wild rendition of the twist. I leap. I scrunch all the way down to the floor and almost gouge the boards with my heels. I jump up and down like a kangaroo. Griselda too dances. The more bizarre my gestures become, the more restrained she gets, until she seems to be moving in sudden and discrete quanta, like sequential cells of an animated cartoon.

Presently the song comes to an end and is replaced by a reprise of the "Limbo Rock". I turn to look for something to eat or drink. When I turn back, Griselda has wandered off in the direction of the mango orchard. She is with Virgil. I start to feel my rage again, throbbing at my temples, pounding at the pit of my stomach.

I decide to march away and presently arrive at the third of the dance floors, where, to the astonishment of my relatives, my great-grandmother is actually engaged in performing the limbo rock. Almost everyone is here to observe the spectacle. Even the patriarch of the family is there, enthroned on a Louis Quinze divan that must have been brought downstairs from the fabled locked upstairs sitting room of the main house, rumoured to contain ten million bahts' worth of antique furniture stolen by the Japanese and somehow dumped in our estate when a general was billeted here during the war. The patriarch is flanked by Nit-nit and Noi-noi, who have changed into new clothes, more ornate than the last set, bejewelled and glittering.

My great-grandmother's technique is unorthodox: she is seated in her wheelchair throughout the proceedings. Piak's father, the gardener, is pushing her along, and the limbo pole is held aloft not by the special device, but by two burly caterers. My great-grandmother sort of wags her hands to and fro, pausing occasionally to propel a wad of betel-stained sputum at a passing spittoon. The gardener wheels the *khunying* all the way up to the pole and, at the moment of truth, the two bearers raise the bamboo rod all the way over their shoulders, allowing her to pass through with ease, to thunderous applause.

My great-grandmother sees me. "One more time," she says, "but this time I want Little Frog to do the pushing."

I take the handle of the wheelchair. "You're looking well tonight, Great-grandmother," I say. My great-grandmother is very elegantly dressed in what appears to be the height of 1920s fashion, shocking pink Thai silk from head to toe.

"Fancy doing the limbo rock, at my age!" she says softly. "Come on, Little Frog, push away. We're going to go through again."

I start to push. I feel a little faint.

"Bear left, you silly boy," my great-grandmother says. "You're quite, quite drunk, I'm afraid!"

"I've had two Cokes."

"Liberally laced with vodka, by the smell of them!" she says as we near the pole, taking a rather zigzag route because of my inebriation. "Well, well, well, boys will be boys, I daresay. You haven't been smoking any of that *ganja*, I trust?"

"I'm not quite sure what you're talking about, Great-grandmother," I say, though I have a sneaking suspicion it has something to do with the incident in the treehouse some days ago.

"Children today! You'll be wanting some of my betel nut next."

I spur myself forward . . . the pole vaults up . . . we pass through . . . the audience applauds once more. The music dies away. The next song is "Johnny Angel". I see the world as though through a dense and blood-tinged fog.

My great-grandmother claps her hands. "Enough of this nonsense!" she says. "Take me back to bed and fetch me my medication!" No sooner has she said this than one of the servants appears and magically whisks her off into the swirling mists. The coloured light bulbs smear across my field of vision. I blink. I wonder how many times I will see my great-grandmother again. I wonder if I will ever tell her how much she has meant to me. Perhaps I am weeping.

It is through the blur of tears, with the melody of "Johnny Angel" throbbing in the background in all its plaintive, unfulfilled longing, that I see Jessica, with her back to me and her arms around some invisible person, solemnly rocking from side to side, her feet slightly apart, her body hardly moving at all save for the serpentine undulation of her slender hips.

If the wooden pavilion was full of cold blue light, this tent of canvas burns with the fiery luminescence of a hundred crimson bulbs. Her skin glows, warm and ruddy, like a sunset. "Jessica . . ." I whisper, very softly. She seems to hear my voice above the noise, for she cranes to listen to something. She turns toward me, and it is at that moment I see that she is dancing with Piak. Piak!

It is the last straw. Furiously I charge up to them. "Jessica, stop dancing with him this minute!" I say. "Can't you see he's one of the servants?"

Piak doesn't understand what I'm saying, of course. And Jessica merely says, "Oh, Justin, don't be such a jealous fool. The slavery days been over for a hundred years."

The very reasonableness of her words drives me insane. I give Piak a shove. "What is it, Khun Nuu?"

Incoherent with rage, I merely sputter and shove again. Being addressed as Mr. Mouse only adds insult to injury.

Jessica says, in Thai: "He wants you to stop dancing with me . . . imagine that!"

Piak turns to me and says, "Now look here, Master Little Frog, I may be a servant, and you may be a big old *luuk phudii*, but servants have souls too, you know. I can see you're not like Khun Virgil. You tease me with tidbits of equality, but when push comes to shove you're just as ready to shit on my head as any of them!"

The effrontery is intolerable. I have entered the cavern of madness and found the dragon, and now it is time to slay it and rescue the dusky princess of my dreams. I start to rev myself up for a punch, but before my fist can hit home Piak lashes out in self-defence, and I suddenly find myself on the floor with birds twittering and stars dancing around my head.

When I open my eyes, I see that this incident has had unthinkable repercussions. The gardener and Piak are kneeling abjectly in front of the patriarch of the estate, and two Fates (the third being, of course, incapacitated) are standing on either side of him like the dark ravens who guard the throne of Odin, lit by the hellish crimson light.

The patriarch says, "We can't have this sort of thing—gardeners' sons beating up their *jao nais* in public—get out, right this minute, the both of you—don't you dare set foot in this house again!"

The fight is gone from Piak. With heads bowed, he and his father back away slowly from the presence of my great-uncle, the supreme judge and arbiter of our little kingdom.

Aunt Nit-nit now runs toward me with a cold compress in her hand. She kneels and begins applying the compress to my head. "*Eaugh, eaugh*, Little Frog— are you all right? Did that *awful* little boy hurt you?"

"Don't send them away," I say weakly. "It's my fault, not Piak's."

"Oh, nonsense," says Aunt Nit-nit. "We can't have this sort of thing."

It dawns on me then that there is no going back. Each action that we take leads inexorably to the next. I have had a traumatic lesson in the delectable power of karma. The responsibility of having ruined the lives of Piak and his father is impossible to bear. I begin to weep, to flail at the empty air in my frustration.

"I want them back!" I scream. "I want them back now!" But I know that the patriarch may not be countermanded.

"Oh, don't have a tantrum," says Aunt Nit-nit. "It's all for the best."

I push her arm away and throw the cold compress down. My head is awhirl with pain and confusion. I stamp my feet like a demon in a ritual dance. I bellow. I have no words to express my helplessness, my fury.

It is at that moment, thrust downward to the very nadir of my existence, that something cracks inside my mind . . . the crystal vase that holds the key to the language of the heart. I suddenly find myself able to speak Thai. Unfortunately, the first words that issue from my lips are words Piak taught me, words which no person of breeding, education or refinement could utter . . . words which now rush unbidden off my tongue with the force of a monsoon thundershower: "*Yed mae!*"

24

An Out-of-Body Experience

One might suppose that, your humble narrator having uttered those unthinkable words, all hell would break loose. That the very sky would be riven asunder, that the thunderbolts of Zeus himself would burst forth from the clouds and strike the hapless miscreant dead on the spot. One might suppose that the utterance of these scandalous words would cause so sensational a reaction that the guests would start leaving in a huff, my aunts would start advancing upon me with rods of chastisement in their hands, and the music would sputter to a stop. In truth, however, nothing of the sort occurs at all.

Instead, those in the vicinity who have been close enough to hear the offending words do an abrupt double-take, look at each other in wild alarm, come to an almost instant consensus that the matter is too embarrassing to have actually happened . . . that they must all have misheard. It is as if there has been a sudden and instantaneous rift in the fabric of space and time that has just as suddenly and instantaneously stitched itself back together again.

Aunt Nit-nit, still bending over me in concern, says to me, "Run along now, Little Frog, it's time you went to bed. I'm afraid you're going to have to go to school tomorrow."

It takes me a moment to realize that Aunt Nit-nit is now addressing me in Thai. So they *did* know what I said! But rather than reproving me, my aunts have simply refashioned the cosmos. I can understand Thai. I have always understood Thai. I have always been able to speak it. So my utterance of those words has been pretty earth-shattering after all. It has actually changed the past and irrevocably altered the present, just as in that Ray Bradbury story where this fellow goes back in time and accidentally steps on a butterfly or some such thing, and then when he comes back to the present he finds that he has made his whole world disappear and be replaced by a chilling dystopia.

Since no one is going to accept any longer the notion that I can't speak Thai, I decide I'd better make the best of it. "Yes, Aunt Nit-nit," I say, "I'll run along to bed right now."

Actually I do no such thing; the combination of rage, jealousy, remorse and vodka finally works its magic on me and I find myself drifting into oblivion. . . .

I'm not entirely sure what happens next, but it is some hours later, and I think I am in my bed. The party is not yet over. Dance music drifts in along with the cries of nocturnal creatures. The aroma of grilling hamburger meat still hangs in the air along with the scent of night-blooming jasmine.

My eyes are wide open but the room I am in is not quite my room. Ionic columns surround the entrance to the bathroom. There seems to be no ceiling. A primeval fog roils about the marble floors, and here and there stand Cupids made of stone, bows poised and eyes aflame. Is this another dream?

I get out of bed. My limbs feel curiously light, and when I hold up my hand I can see right through it. And when I glance back at the bed I see myself still fast asleep; I can hear snoring. It is clear that my *vinyaan* has taken leave of my body and that I am in the midst of some supernatural experience.

Above the columns is a marble frieze on which are portrayed in bas-relief the major incidents of my life, translated into mythic terms. I and all the other beings depicted are dressed in flowing robes; here and there winged *putti* adorn the landscape. There is the mystery-shrouded birth in a distant kingdom. There I am being torn from my parents as they embark on their quest for the Golden Fleece or some such treasure. Here is the death of the poet Homer and his metamorphosis into a heavenly chameleon, strumming on his lyre athwart some fluffy old cumulonimbus. There, seeking guidance from the oracle, is the shaman who lives down the *klong*, only here he appears as Ut-Napishtim, father of men, in his residence on the far side of the river that rides the cosmos. There I am again with my faithful dark companion, for a sidekick is an essential personage in a hero's journey. Here we stand at the gate of Inferno. Here I am, punished by almighty Zeus for the sin of hubris, crawling away from the Sacred Limbo Rock Device, desperately seeking a way to expiate my impious crimes. Oh, the horror of my lot! Pursued by the Furies, taunted by the Fates, hopelessly lusting after the Triple Goddess of Fertility in the shapes of Samlee, Griselda and Jessica, rejected by my friends, I see my marbled self take ship and flee toward distant shores . . . is it the fabled spires of Eton that I see peering from the perpetual mist of the sceptred isle? Or is it only the Scola Britannica, whose portals await me in the morning?

The frieze relates my past but does not foretell my future. I try to look past the dark scene at the midpoint, but my gaze is obscured by stone clouds and rococo draperies.

Spreading my arms wide, I float through the columned gateway, past the terrarium where Homer once lived, now tended by priests in chameleon-shaped headdresses. I pass through the walls and skim the surface of the pond. The frogs are out in force, serenading me from every lotus pad and stepping stone.

Many of the guests have departed. But in the wooden pavilion sit the two younger Fates, having changed their costumes for the fourth or fifth time that evening, leaning against triangular cushions by the railings. They are alternately paring an enormous pomelo, nibbling at the fruit, tossing the peelings into the water, watching the ripples in the artificial blue light. They are laughing. On a silver *phaan*, between them, are two reels of tape.

Weightless and invisible, I slide between them. The pomelo looks delicious. I manage to sneak some into my mouth. It is cool and sweet. After the nausea-inducing liquids I've consumed earlier, it is ambrosia. I wonder for a moment how I, a discorporate *vinyaan*, am able to eat solid food. On the other hand, the food that is left for the denizens of the spirit house by the entrance to the estate is solid enough, and is presumably consumed at some juncture by the supernatural beings who guard our land. I settle down cross-legged between the two of them and listen to their chatter. They seem curiously at peace, though they've been at each other's throats only hours before.

"Fancy us both thinking of having it taped!" Aunt Noi-noi says.

Nit-nit laughs and takes another sliver of pomelo. "You can have him for all I care," she says. "Why be so selfish, I tell myself. What's an aubergine between sisters?"

"And a *pink* aubergine at that," Noi-noi says. The two of them sigh, and throw a few more peelings into the water.

"Wasn't it hilarious when our grandmother actually did the limbo rock herself? I thought she'd have a heart attack."

"Oh, Phii Nit-nit, you really mustn't eat so much—look, the whole pomelo's disappeared! You'll turn into a hippopotamus!"

"Fancy that . . . I only had two slices."

I, of course, am the true culprit; I've devoured over half the fruit listening to their chatter.

"It makes no difference anyway," Nit-nit continues. "I shall never be thin. I bloat up if I so much as *look* at a durian or a plate of mango and sticky rice."

"Oh, you look fine as you are," says Noi-noi, staring at her own reflection in the pond. "Whereas I—"

"Oh, you are such a narcissist, my dear little sister. Even before you could talk, you always used to be fascinated with mirrors. And do you remember when you were three years old, and you were playing with our mother's lipstick, and—"

"You used to *eat* her lipstick when you were a child!"

Nit-nit looks away. "Now, it's bad of you to remind me of that," she says. But when Noi-noi pulls a long face, she starts to laugh. I have not seen the Fates this friendly toward one another for some time. Perhaps it is Aunt Ning-nong's illness that has provoked this truce. "Oh—and when Little Frog said *that word*, I thought I was going to *die!*"

I lean closer to them. Perhaps Aunt Nit-nit feels my breath on her back, because she shivers as from a sudden chill.

"So he's really been able to speak Thai all this time, hasn't he—he's been concealing it from us, the better to spy on us, the little weasel!"

"I really ought to punish him, but I was simply too taken aback."

"Quite. It wouldn't do for people like ourselves even to acknowledge such filth."

"One hears such filth often enough, dear sister, walking down the aisles of the Sunday market!"

"True, but one does not *acknowledge* the aforementioned filth, does one?"

"You're right, it's not reality that counts, it's how reality is perceived."

"With that in mind . . ."

Aunt Noi-noi takes one of the tapes from the *phaan*. She starts to unravel it. Her sister takes the other reel and begins yanking out tape. They throw it in each other's faces, drape each other with it, tie it into knots and finally fling the empty reels into the pond, giggling like schoolgirls. At last they are completely cocooned with audio tape. It dribbles from their dishevelled hair, it sticks to their dresses-like confetti, it winds round and round their arms like the wrappings of a mummy. Their laughter becomes hysterical, then it gurgles to a stop.

And, all at once, they begin to weep uncontrollably.

"How are we ever going to get ourselves decent men now that silly tape recording has been heard and all of society will know by tomorrow that we are women of ill fame?" Noi-noi says.

"We're ruined!" says Nit-nit. "Ruined!"

Feeling as though I ought to contribute something to the conversation, I say: "Maybe you can pretend nothing happened. Perhaps you can attribute the entire *faux pas* to some kind of mass hallucination, brought on by Aunt Ning-nong's sudden affliction. . . ."

They do not, of course, hear me. But Nit-nit pricks up her ears as though listening to an alien music, then she says to her sister: "Do you think they'd believe it was just all some kind of mass hallucination brought on by all the brouhaha over Phii Ning-nong's *woon sen*?"

"What a bizarre notion. It sounds like one of Little Frog's conceits."

I start to laugh out loud.

"What was that?" says Nit-nit.

"My, the frogs *are* loud tonight," says Noi-noi, who is clearly less sensitive to the presence of spirits than her older sister. But I am already fading from the scene. I feel my body call to me. I suspect it's an upset stomach or some other side effect of the alcohol and the excitement.

"We'd best be getting back to the party . . . oh, I do hope Little Frog doesn't wake up with a hangover!"

Little Frog does wake up with a hangover. At least, I think that is what it must be. It is the worst sensation I have ever felt, worse even than a jab in the posterior with a hypodermic . . . worse even than one of Dr. Richardson's enemas. It is so bad that I don't even mind spending half an hour being drenched with lukewarm water and scrubbed by some faceless person. I do not struggle as the blue-grey shorts and white shirt, embroidered with the militantly overstated Scola Britannica logo, are slid on to my person.

I don't even look twice at the elegantly prepared *khao tom kruang* that has been set out for me at the breakfast table, the hour being too early for my aunts to have risen.

To my surprise, it is not the Studebaker that awaits to take me to school, but Uncle Vit's Mercedes, and I am to be accompanied by none other than Samlee. She's very good at makeup now, and in donning her knee-length rayon business suit she seems to have shed her past. Still, she doesn't presume to sit in the back seat with me. She joins the driver in front, letting me spread myself along the leather upholstery.

"We're going to be riding together every morning now, Khun Nuu," she tells me, "because it's on the way to Uncle Vit's office on Sathorn. I'm supposed to make sure you register at the front office and go to the right room."

"All right," I say to her in Thai. If she is taken aback at my new-found ability, she doesn't seem to show it. I lie back and allow the fog to infiltrate my head once more.

The fog doesn't really clear until about midday. I register at the school. The other children are just a blur, so is the school, from the morning's half-hearted rendition of the school anthem, sung to the tune of the slow movement of Dvořák's "New World" symphony, to the queuing up and filing into a class filled with big white children all bulkier by far than myself, to the doling out of mathematics texts and slim, expurgated *Romeo and Juliets*, to the endless recitations of name, rank and serial number to any official-looking person who happens by. It will be several days before I get a clear idea of what the place looks like. My mind is on autopilot.

Around eleven o'clock, there comes a recess, and I see Virgil standing in the shade of a coconut tree at the far end of the grounds. He is alone. He has a stack of books under one arm and is staring wistfully past the wrought-iron fence that surrounds the grounds, intricately worked into mythological scenes outlined in black like shadow puppets, the monkey-god Hanuman pursuing the mermaid Maccha, the demon Ramasura chasing Mekhala, mistress of the lightning. On the other side of that fence, the Bangkok traffic races by—*samlors*, noodle vendors, ice merchants, Mercedes-Benzes, Chryslers, Studebakers, Fords and even a lost elephant crossing the street. It is a scene of chaotic pageantry and exotic beauty, but for Virgil the walls of the school are clearly prison walls. I can see that he longs to run barefoot through the mud beside the *klong*, climb mango trees, dance naked in the rain. I really feel for him. I go up to him. My only thought is to console him, for we still have the weekends, and one day, a few months from now, there must come some kind of holiday, although—what with the long-enforced closure—the holidays, too, may be long in coming.

"Virgil," I say, and I smile at my friend. My mind is starting to clear at last.

But Virgil only looks sullenly at me and says, "If you think I's ever gone talk to you again after what you done to Piak and his daddy, Justin, you got another think comin'. You ain't my friend no more."

25

More Mysteries of Sex

I start to tell Virgil that it wasn't my fault, that there was no way for me to gainsay the will of the household's supreme authority, but I can see I'm not going to get anywhere. At any rate, the bell rings—well, it doesn't *ring* exactly, for it is an electronic device that simulates the flatus of a humpback whale—and, pulling out my timetable, I see that I am now due to appear at the science class of a certain Miss Cicciolini.

I have spent the morning in a nebulous miasma. Now, for the first time, I'm able to take in the spectacle of the Scola Britannica, which is an attempt to carve out a little piece of England in the midst of all this barbaric splendour. The main building was once the house of a well-known pop singer. It is in colonial style, and its front portals look as though they are expecting the return of Somerset Maugham. In the grounds are clumps of palm trees and here and there hedges that have been clipped into the shape of such typically English animals as badgers, hedgehogs and water-voles, the better, I suppose, to remind the school's administrators of the Old Country.

In front of the school, the Thai flag and the Union Jack fly from twin flagpoles. There are a number of children in green checked uniforms—the boys in shorts, the girls in calf-length skirts. These students are, as it were, on loan from the Sacred Heart School, an English-speaking Catholic institution that the Ministry has not seen fit to allow to reopen. Father Regenstrom, too, is on loan; I have seen him stalking the corridors with a conductor's baton in his hand.

Because of the guests from the Catholic school, all the classes at the Scola Britannica are crammed to capacity, and although the rooms are air conditioned, one barely notices. I think it's because of the heat that I have managed to sweat out all the alcohol I consumed during last night's debauchery. At any rate, by the time I've scoured the corridors and run up and down the staircases looking for the right classroom, I'm feeling just about as sober as ever.

Miss Cicciolini's class isn't in the main building, but in a sort of bungalow across the back lawn. On the wall are diagrams of cell structures, periodic tables of the elements, and a big map of the solar system; against the back wall is a huge terrarium containing— it gives my heart a turn to see it—a chameleon, who, having just climbed on to a bamboo rod, is slowly dappling from baby-rice green to the yellow ochre of the wood. My heart turns a second time to see that I am seated quite close to Griselda Richardson, but the third turn is not so pleasant, for I realize that she is sandwiched between Wilbur Andrews and Piet van Helsing, Virgil's nemeses. Virgil himself is here, but he avoids my eyes and stares steadfastly at the periodic table of the elements, his gaze riveted to a point midway between the inert gases and the halogens. He also avoids the eyes of Piet and Wilbur. Between all the eyes he's avoiding, he really doesn't have anywhere to look except where he's looking.

Miss Cicciolini makes a dramatic entrance. She wears dark glasses, and her artificially blonde hair is perpetually windswept. I think she manages this by carefully positioning herself so that she is always downwind of the air conditioning unit. The first thing one notices about her face, apart from her Sophia Loren-type dark glasses with their cherry-red frames, is her lipstick, which is the crimson of fresh blood.

Miss Cicciolini is wearing a scarlet dress, so tight as to warp her legs into a state of knock-kneedness. This accentuates the undulation of her hips and distracts somewhat from the languorous gestures she employs when she speaks. After the usual "Good morning, children," "Good morning, Miss Cicciolini" she launches into an explanation of the ground rules for succeeding in our scientific studies.

"First, children," she says, "I want you to take out your notebooks and, with a *red* pencil, I want you to rule a one-inch left-hand margin on each page of the book. Then, you are to rule a top and bottom margin, also in *red*, joining up perfectly with the left-hand margin at exactly ninety degrees. Your written work must take up only the space within the *red* border circumscribed by the *red* margins that you have drawn. Any written work you produce that falls outside the *red*-bordered area will be ignored. It will not be considered to exist. Is this clear?"

Well, it's clear all right . . . Miss Cicciolini has a bizarre preoccupation with *redness* and is planning to shove this obsession down our throats by hook or by crook. Although I am not yet aware of the Freudian concept of anal-retentiveness, I shall always look back on Miss Cicciolini as its ultimate type.

For the next ten minutes, we sit around ruling these *red* borders in our notebooks, while Miss Cicciolini stalks about the room trying to find the optimum position for her windswept hair effect. Presently, she claps her hands, and we all snap to attention.

"And now, children, we shall turn to the subject of the hour: biology. I don't know what you've all studied in the past, so I'm going to ask you, one by one, what you may already know about this most interesting subject. Well, umm . . ." She consults a little plan she has of the class, showing who is occupying which seats. "Griselda—what do you know?"

"Well, Mith Cicciolini, I can name all the common varietieth of thtreptococci, thtaphylococci and pneumococci . . . can you?"

Evidently, Miss Cicciolini hasn't the faintest idea what Griselda's talking about. One can't exactly divine what she's thinking through the dark glasses, but the brows do seem to knit into something of a frown. "Very good, dear," she says, "but we won't be doing those until the advanced course. Umm, what about you, Piet?"

"Oh, it's all about birds and flowers and stuff."

"Very, very good! Yes, indeed, biology is the study of every little teeny living creature on the surface of the earth."

"What about big creatures?" says Wilbur.

"Since you didn't have your hand up, Wilbur, I'm going to ignore your question, although I suppose you do have a point of sorts. Yes, every *teensy weeny* and every great big *enormous* creature on the surface of the earth."

"But Miss Cicciolini . . ." says Virgil. "But if they don't be little *or* big? And who's to say what's big anyways? A elephant don't know he be big. If you ask me, it all sound a mite an-thro-pocentric."

I'm the only one who laughs at this. Miss Cicciolini's hands are trembling a little. Wilbur looks at me and rolls his eyes, mouthing the word "uppity". A few of the others are thinking seriously about laughing, but they have managed to conceal their smiles behind their notebooks. Miss Cicciolini seems to have the ability to teleport; one moment she's over on the other side of the room, the next she's looming over me with her hair streaming behind her. "You find this all very amusing, don't you, umm"—she consults her little diagram—"Justin."

I have managed to have my secret name inserted into the rolls this morning instead of my real name because Samlee cannot read English.

"Oh, no, Miss Cicciolini, not amusing as such."

"Well, just because that poor little boy can't quite wrap his tongue around the language of Shakespeare and Milton doesn't mean you have to snigger at his every ungrammatical outburst."

So the woman has no idea what I found so funny. She thinks I'm cruelly making fun of Virgil's accent. Thinking only to defend him, I say: "But that's just how Virgil talks. It's his dialect."

"I refuse to accept the notion that certain races are not educable. There is absolutely no reason for anyone to speak in a substandard fashion. Is that clear? Now, Justin, tell me . . . what illuminating fact of biology can *you* entertain us with?"

"Well . . ." My mind draws a blank. Science has never been my forte. What *do* I know of the mysteries of life, death and birth? Memory comes to the rescue: An image flashes through my head. It is Jessica, beckoning to me across the enormous waterbed of her brother . . . and Virgil's warning: *If you were to actually do that, why, Jessica she have to have a baby.* Surely that must be a biological fact of some importance. So, rather shyly, I tell Miss Cicciolini: "Well . . . I do know all about how babies are made."

Miss Cicciolini's face turns instantly beet-red. "How dare you!" she says.

"But I really do! I really do know how babies are made."

Miss Cicciolini slaps me smartly on the cheek. I have no idea why I have become the object of her fury.

"But Miss Cicciolini . . . I'm just trying to answer your question . . . and, all right, I admit I don't know *everything* about it, but I do know that, well, things go *into* other things, and—"

"Get out of my class this very minute, young man! Go and stand outside until the end of the period. I won't have such filth from the lips of my students. Get out, do you hear?"

There is a lot of laughter at this point. It is only at this moment in my young life that I come to understand that the act of love, which in my inchoate fashion I have viewed only as something beautiful, pleasurable and earnestly to be desired, is actually supposed by many to be rather nasty, nay, evil. It is an appalling discovery. It is my first exposure to the problem of sin, and even on this initial encounter I can see that it is an insoluble enigma.

Miss Cicciolini's slap is still reverberating through my head. She's obviously not joking, so I slink out of the room. Outside, the sunlight is blazing, and there is nowhere to sit. I end up squatting on the concrete, confused, sweating and alone. Miss Cicciolini hasn't knocked out any teeth or anything like that, but the indignity of her slap is still reverberating through my skull.

Why, why, why? Only last night, when I spoke the unspeakable word, I escaped unscathed; today, after speaking in a perfectly reasonable and polite manner, I have been brutalized and ostracized. Why? Is the slapping the karmic response to last night's uncouth utterance—a sort of delayed reaction, as though the universe were like the elastic waistband of a pair of underpants, snapping into position about the hips of reality? As I attempt to unravel this conundrum, mixing my metaphors into a goulash of clubfooted poesy, a shadow falls over me. Looking around, I see that a glumfaced Wilbur Anderson has emerged from Miss Cicciolini's classroom and is in the process of sitting down beside me.

"Boy, you sure showed that bitch a thing or two!" he says. "Gee whiz, Justin! I'd a never dared say what you said. My paw would've whupped the living shit out of me."

I am about to protest that I have no idea what it is about what I said that should have provoked such a furore, but when I see the way he gazes at me with unabashed admiration I decide that I had better just shut up and enjoy my newfound notoriety.

"So why are you out here?" I ask him.

"Oh, I shucked a spitwad at that black kid."

"Virgil?"

"That his name? How do you know?"

"He lives next door to me."

Wilbur sighs. "There goes the neighbourhood."

I'm not entirely sure what he means by that, so I do a sort of sigh of semi-agreement. Then I ask him, "Wilbur? Why aren't you going to that big American school along with all the other Americans?" I have been wondering this about Virgil, too, but I don't think it's wise to mention him at this juncture.

"I know," Wilbur says, "it sure is a pain having to wear a frigging uniform and stuff. And I hate having to *work* in school. In the States, we just sit around drawing pictures and singing songs and stuff. We don't get no algebra or biology or friggin' Latin, leastways not until high school. But my parents are into cultural diversity or something."

With his parents feeling the way they do, I am surprised that he feels this way about Negroes. I just don't understand.

"Tell you what, Justin . . . me and Piet were talking about this earlier, and boy, the way you sassed that biology teacher really convinces me you're cool . . . we want you to be our friend. Remember that *braaivleis* his mom is having? How'd you like to spend the night over at Piet's house afterward? I know he'd want you to, and we could sneak out and do wild, crazy things."

Wilbur smiles at me and his charisma is irresistible. Although I feel a twinge of distress because I know how Wilbur feels about my friend Virgil, I am also wondering whether the rift between us can ever he repaired. "I'd love to," I find myself saying. After all, didn't my great-grandmother tell me I had to make more friends my own age?

"Neat," says Wilbur "But Justin . . . There was one thing I was gonna ask you

"Fire away."

"Umm . . . well, you seem to know the answer to this, and I can't seem to get a straight answer from anyone . . . I don't wanna seem like an idiot, but . . . how *are* babies made?"

26

The Call of the Muse

"Well," I tell Wilbur, "it's all to do with aubergines and dragons entering caves of desire and that sort of thing."

"Aubergines?" Wilbur says, perplexed. "Ain't they a fancy kind of an eggplant?"

"Yes, that's right. You see, you insert your aubergine and then you sort of do a kind of dance, rather like the locomotion, actually, except that it's horizontal rather than vertical, facing your partner, and then she has a baby. At least, that's about as much as I've been able to figure out in my researches."

"But what's a dragon and a cave got to do with it?"

"Well, they're just metaphors," I say grandly.

"Oh . . . yeah . . . neat. But the thing I don't get is . . . what if you're in the mood, and there's just no eggplant handy?"

"It's always there when you're in the mood. I don't know why. It just comes popping right up."

"Oh, kind of like a boner," says Wilbur.

"Yes, that's it." I say. In intellectual discussions, it is best to bluff one's way as best one can, so as to buy a little time to figure out one's opponent's argument.

At that moment, the bell rings once again—and my classmates stream out, all chattering at once. They surround me, clap me on the back, and congratulate me on my triumphant impertinence. It is the first time anyone's treated me like a celebrity, but success is soured by Virgil's indifference. He watches me from a distance as we all amble down to the next class, which, according to my little blue schedule, is English, taught by a certain Mrs. Vajravajah.

Presumably, English is what the thin little *Romeo and Juliets* are for. They do seem very worn, with their threadbare red bindings and their faded gold-stamped lettering surrounding what appears to be the embossed image of a swan, holding, in its beak, a partially unscrolled document containing, in Gothic lettering, the legend "Service Without Levity".

This is fascinating. I am carried along by the movement of the crowd, but I walk blindly. My nose is buried in the foreword, which states: *Under the sagacious and not inconsiderate guidance of the Committee for the Furtherance of Britannic Culture in the Colonies, your humble editors have deemed it fit to remove from the hallowed text of the Swan of Avon such utterances as might appear, to the unrefined sensibilities of the less privileged races, to be uncouth, inflammatory or appealing to the baser instincts.*

The foreword is signed by one Cedric Pendleton-Smith, OBE, and further annotated *Balliol College, Michaelmas Term, Anno Domini MCMXXII*, which I am still trying to puzzle out as I find myself drifting into Mrs. Vajravajah's classroom. I am not good at Roman numerals, but I'm sure this thing is dated before my time, possibly even before Mrs. Vajravajah's.

Somehow, carried along by the press of my companions, I find that I am already seated in that lady's classroom and that she is engaged in teaching us how to pronounce her name. Although I, with my one-day-old ability to speak Thai, have no problem, the others are all twisting their tongues into crullers. The whole class sounds like a horse that is simultaneously whinnying and clearing its throat. I look up and see a slight, plumpish young woman wearing a batik dress, whose dusky complexion belies the fact that she is by far the most *eaughing* person I have yet encountered.

"*Eaugh*, all right," she tells us, "I can tell that it's simply going to be impossible for you people to pronounce my name, so let's have a contest. I'm just as new here as you are, and names, you know, are magical. Did you know that ancient people used to believe that if they could find the true names of things, they could wield power over them?"

There is a dead silence. As I look around, I realize to my astonishment that she has actually succeeded in capturing the class's collective imagination. It is the mention of magic, of secret names, of our dark and ancient past that has done this. Virgil is as spellbound as when he's listening to one of his mother's stories; even Wilbur and Piet have stopped trading notes.

"So," Mrs. Vajravajah continues, "this is what we'll do. Each one of you will try to think of an easy, pronounceable nickname—and I don't mean 'the old bag', or 'the nasty bitch', or any of those names that children customarily bestow on their teachers—I mean a practical name that we can all use, and which I'll go on using for the rest of my pedagogical career, which, I trust, will be mercifully short."

"What does your name mean, anyways?" Wilbur asks her.

"It's Sanskrit," she tells us, "and it can mean either 'Speaks like a thunderbolt' or 'The discourse of diamonds'." What a world of romance lies in a simple name! "In fact, if you turn to page twenty-three of Romeo and Juliet . . ."

We do, and come across these words:

> *O, be some other name!*
> *What's in a name? That which we call a rose*
> *By any other name would smell as sweet.*

"Isn't that interesting?" she says. "After we read this play together, we're going to find out just how powerful the magic of a name can be. Because two children—almost as young as yourselves—don't have the right names, they're going to experience the worst torment human beings can go through—a consuming passion that can only end one way—in death."

After the comedy of the previous class, the dose of pathos is almost more than some of us can bear. In fact, one of the girls—I think it is Grimgerda Nilsson, the Wagnerian Amazon—is actually wiping a tear from her eye. She is the only one in the class with lipstick and the only one whose endowments approximate those of a full-fledged woman.

"So," Mrs. Vajravajah says, "you now shall name me. Of my own free will I yield the power to you. I will never betray you."

We are all silent for a long time. We are awed. I have never felt this way, even on the rare occasions when I sat, fidgety and distracted, in front of great images of Buddha in incense-filled chapels. Gazing at Mrs. Vajravajah's face, I seem to see her suffused in a numinous radiance; something other than a teacher is speaking to me. I continue to gaze as the mood lightens and the class begin to suggest names, some playful, some irreverent, which Mrs. Vajravajah takes with a good grace. And the soft light never leaves her eyes, never, never. The love I feel for her is qualitatively different from the passion I have felt for Samlee, for Jessica, for Griselda. It is something entirely from the realm of myth.

When she speaks to me, I am tongue-tied. "What about you, Justin?" she says. "What name do *you* have for me? I've heard that you're a poet."

What appellation is grand enough for this divine visitation? It must be one of the names from the Greek myths, but which? Europa, Io, Callisto? Surely not, for these nymphs were all violated by Zeus, and Mrs. Vajravajah is surely inviolate. It must be one of the great ladies of mythology, a goddess or queen. But now, with the responsibility of selecting one of these noble names, I am faced for the first time with confusion. Names dance before my eyes, each longer than the last. I clutch at straws. A nice long straw would be best. "Clytemnestra," I manage to mumble.

"A classicist," Mrs. Vajravajah says softly. "And do you know, young friend, who Clytemnestra was?"

I know, I know, I know! But I'm drawing a blank. Finally, face to face with the Sphinx, I find myself unable to answer the riddle! "Umm . . . she was the one who always knew the future, but nobody would ever believe her," I say, knowing it's the wrong answer, knowing I am doomed to be hurled from the Theban precipice on to the rocks below. Such hubris! To think I could deem myself worthy of the poets of antiquity—yet at the moment of judgment find myself unable to tell any of them apart!

"I'm afraid not, Justin," she says. "You're thinking of Cassandra. But in any case, I don't think I'd like to be either of those women. After all, Clytemnestra killed her own husband, didn't she?"

"Yes." And then I'm on track again. "Agamemnon," I add, just to show that I didn't really forget.

"Showoff," says Piet van Helsing, and the others laugh. It seems that my tumble down the ravine has been deflected. I have been forgiven my transgression! She is no longer monstrous, but has become a Muse, holding out the laurel wreath of poesy just beyond my grasp, that Mona Lisa half-smile on her lips.

The naming continues. Piet votes for "Mrs. Truespeak", which everyone likes, but somehow seems a little silly; Grimgerda wants to call our teacher Brynhilda, after one of the nine Valkyries (she is, herself, named after one of the less distinguished ones); Griselda wants to call her Griselda, after herself.

"Why don't we just go with 'Mrs. V.'?" says Virgil. "That's easy enough to pronounce."

The entire class turns to deride Virgil for his lack of imagination, but in the end it is "Mrs. V." that prevails, simply because it's the most practical. My mythological excesses are long forgotten, and Mrs. V. finally asks us to turn to the first page of our antediluvian *Romeo and Juliet*.

"Let's start by looking at what our editor has to say about the play," says Mrs. V., and she flicks to the first page. She begins to read, and her eyes widen. "Rubbish," she says under her breath, then, turning the page, continues in a crescendo, "rubbish, rubbish, absolute rubbish! How can they expect me to teach this bowdlerized nonsense?" In a rage, she flings the book into the wastebasket. Then she turns to us, her eyes bright with passion. "I'll not have your love of English killed before it's even kindled!" she says "Cedric Pendleton-Smith indeed! Committee for the Furtherance of Britannic Culture in the Colonies! Shakespeare for wogs, is it? Shakespeare without any sex or violence . . . Shakespeare without love and death . . . intolerable! Justin, collect all these *Romeo and Juliets* and bring them to me at once!"

I do so. When they are all stacked up on her desk, she sits for a moment, glaring at them and fuming. "I shall personally send away to England for some real Shakespeare," she says at last. "But it may take some time for them to arrive."

"But what are we to thtudy in the meantime?" Griselda asks, and it seems a very reasonable request.

"I don't know . . . unless—"

The bell begins to ring. The children are all poised for takeoff, twenty-seven moon rockets waiting out the countdown.

"We'll make our *own* play!" Mrs. V. cries out in a burst of inspiration.

"But what about, Mitheth V.?" asks Griselda relentlessly.

"About—about—"

"Clytemnestra!" I yell out. Suddenly it all fits together.

"Yes . . . Clytemnestra . . . and Electra . . . and Orestes . . . and Agamemnon . . . and all those bloodthirsty, vengeance-crazed Greeks of ancient mythology . . . that's what we'll do! We'll ransack the classics, we'll run riot among the ancient stones, we'll dance through time and history—"

The children can stand the tension no more. As the bell's cetacean farting continues and the shrieks of other children sound from every side as class after class is released into the sweltering afternoon, my classmates, too, burst loose without waiting for dismissal. It is like that scene in *Spartacus* where the slaves climb up the ramparts of the gladiatorial school and run for their freedom.

I am the only one who remains. I cannot yet bring myself to leave the presence of one who so clearly has stood within the very centre of my private universe.

It slowly dawns on me that I have finally seen my Muse—I wonder whether poor Mrs. V. realizes she has served as the earthly vessel for such a divine visitation!—and I know now that though my efforts as a poet have been laughable and puerile, these things will one day change. I have seen the wreath of victory, though it has not yet been ordained that I should wear it. One glimpse is enough. I have learned of the power of words, and I know that as long as I live I shall choose no other weapon.

27

The Meaning of Life, and Other Questions

Here are the images of my bewilderment: *imprimis*, I come home from school. I wander over to the mango grove. I see the treehouse up in the mango tree. I hear familiar laughter. Sometimes I see a tendril of smoke push out through the afternoon haze. I can hear Virgil and Piak laughing above my head.

But I cannot climb that tree any more. The wooden footholds have been removed. Though the holy of holies is on my territory, it has been rendered out of reach. I have heard that there is a shrine on the Cambodian border like that; ours is the temple, but the steps to reach it are on the wrong side of the mountain.

A second image: Jessica O'Fleary at the end of the long balcony at the Scola Britannica. She avoids my eyes. I know she still thinks of me. I know she understands my remorse. I know she dare not speak to me until the war ends. It is a war between those who should be friends, a war over a woman.

I cannot sleep. I go to the Botticelli box and look over my attempt at an epic poem. It is execrable. I decide to burn the papers where I burned the body of my pet chameleon, incinerate those dreadful verses as a sacrifice to his memory.

I close the mosquito-wire door and slip past the hallway, stealing a box of matches from the drawer where the incense for the spirit-house is kept. I creep past the rows of shoes in the anteroom, unbolt the front door, and find myself at once engulfed in night. The frogs are serenading noisily in the pond. I inhale a mosquito or two with every lungful of mango-moist air. Angrily they sing as they bombard every exposed inch of my skin. I do not care about the pain, of course. Poets are supposed to suffer.

Leaving the concrete pathway and striding toward the mango orchard, I hum to myself so I won't get too scared. Appropriately, the tune is "The Wanderer". In a way, I am just like Dion in that song, the only difference being that he actually gets all his female conquests, whereas I conquer only in the imagination. It is good to sing to yourself whilst skulking about in the tropical night; it drowns out the cacophony of mating calls, and it keeps the *phii krasues* at bay. The moon is full and the night awash with light.

I teach the sacred place beneath the forbidden treehouse, which the night has transformed into the fortress of the enemy. I stop singing. But the singing does not stop. Nor is it the same song. It appears to be one of the plaintive melodies of the popular Thai tunesmith Suthep. Someone else is here with me in the dark forest—someone who is as frightened of *phii krasues* as myself, who is also singing to keep them away.

And then I see her in the light that trickles through the treetops. It is Samlee. She stands and sways from side to side with her eyes closed and her hands crossed over her heart like the hands of an Egyptian mummy. Though in the old days it was her wont to stand out in the moonlight, half-clothed, gibbering, her face caked with white powder, I have not seen her this way since she moved across to Uncle Vit's.

And she is different from how she used to be those other times. Gone is the whiteface and the soiled *panung*. She wears a hip-hugging dress that ends just below the knee, her lips are full and red as though they had been stained with betel juice, she sports stiletto heels and a Gucci clutch. And she doesn't gibber. She sees me, stops singing, and speaks to me quite cogently.

"Oh, it's you, Khun Nuu. You can't sleep either, I suppose."

"No, I can't."

"Problems on your mind?" she says. "Perhaps you're thinking of poor Piak and his father?"

"How did you know?"

"Once a servant, always a servant," she says. "Servants always know everything. A *jao nai* can hide from the tax collector and the anti-gambling squad, but he can't hide from his servants. But you're a good boy to be so worried about him. You don't *thue tua* at all."

"What do I have to *thue tua* about?" I say bitterly. "I don't feel superior to anyone any more. My friends have rejected me, and I'm a lousy poet."

"Not everything is worse than it was, Master Little Frog. After all, we couldn't even have had this conversation two weeks ago. Your tongue was hardened against the language of your heart."

That much is true, I reflect. She chuckles and adds: "And I imagine you've also learned by now that I am not actually a *phii krasue.*"

"I suppose not. But if you aren't, what was really going on that night? You know the night I mean. The funeral. The false teeth sitting in the spittoon with my dead chameleon. You were doing some kind of magic ritual on Uncle Vit, weren't you? What was all that about?"

"It is a kind of magic," she admits, "but unfortunately its effect was only temporary."

"What do you mean?"

"Well, maybe when you're a little older, I could show you." Her eyes twinkle. The half-laugh in them also holds a certain sadness.

"How much older?" I demand.

But she only smiles. "Poor Master Little Frog. How can I know the answers to your questions? I am but an ignorant *khiikhaa*, dolled up in fancy clothes and given a receptionist's desk to adorn your uncle's *baramii*. But there are those who know all the answers."

She looks into my eyes, and yet it seems she does not see me at all. I cannot see any spirits, or hear their voices, but I know she is closer to them than I.

"Who, Samlee?" I ask her.

"Why," she says, "the dead, of course."

"The dead?"

"Come with me, Khun Nuu. Have you ever visited a shaman before?"

"In a manner of speaking." I do not think she knows that I spied on her that night she made the amulet out of the hair from her pubes. I was Justin the Adventurer then, wresting the Golden Fleece from the far ends of the world-encircling *klong*. Now I am Justin the Alone. Yes, Samlee is right. My encounter with Mrs. Vajravajah has shown me that I have reached the midpoint of my hero's journey, the dark centre from which I must burst forth in splendour. I must know my shadow to find my light.

Thus it is that I travel once more up the *klong* toward the house of the *ajarn*. Thus it is that I find myself no longer hiding behind a vinyl sofa but face to face with the shaman and his gold-faced mask. The room is familiar—the rows of reagents, the dried lizards hanging by their tails, the suppliants sitting in *phabphieb* position with their palms folded in reverence, the scent of incense wafting over the odour of drifting sewage. Quickly, Samlee and I squat down among the adorers.

Only one thing has changed: There is a television set in the *ajarn's* living room. Where the antenna box should be, there is a human skull. Although the power is on, there is no image, only a hissing field of snow. I overhear some of the onlookers talking.

"It's just a new craze of his. He's acquired a sudden fondness for *Leave it to Beaver* and *I Love Lucy*, but he doesn't know how to turn the thing off when the stations go off the air. He doesn't like technology and he doesn't want to ask anyone for fear of losing face." This is a corpulent woman whispering. Her face is obscured by a cloud of smoke from the fistful of joss-sticks she's praying with.

"Oh, nonsense . . . anyone can see that the screen full of ghostly snow is an aid to his meditation . . . he stares into it and it empties his mind so that he can attain a proper state of *samadhi*," says her companion, a skinny man in a *phakomaah*.

The shaman, sitting in the lotus position, gazes raptly into the empty television screen as though he were looking at nirvana's farthest shore. When Samlee addresses him, he does not so much as turn to look at her.

"*Ajarn, ajarn*," she says, inching her way closer, "I'm frightened. The amulet and the love potion worked for a while, but I'm afraid he's seeing someone else. I don't think I can hold on to him much longer . . . I don't think I have the *vasana* for the position in life I'm aiming for . . . but somehow I can't be content with my lot. I know it's very bad of me to resent the karma that's made me into a servant, but . . ."

Suddenly the mage snaps out of his trance. "I don't do amulets on Thursdays," he says. "You know that as well as I do. Mondays, Wednesdays and Fridays are reserved for petty magics. On Thursdays we commune with the dead. Tuesdays I help people to remember their past incarnations, Saturdays I do exorcisms, Sundays I go to the movies."

"But *ajarn* . . . I *won't* return to that rickety old wooden house with those pinching, scolding young ladies . . ." Can she possibly mean the Fates? What about me—has she forgotten me? There is a hard-edged quality to her voice. When she speaks of her resentment of her karma, when she talks of her ambitions for a higher station in life, there is no softness in her voice, no compliance. I wonder how this can be the same woman who slept beside my bed for three years, who whispered ghost stories in my ear, who wept when she had to leave me for Uncle Vit's house.

"Daughter," says the shaman, "you must walk your chosen path to its end. For twenty-five satang, you can take the tram, which is confined to its tracks, and can never deviate from its predestined course. For two saluengs, you can catch the white bus to Phrakanong, which has no tracks and could duck down some unknown *soi* to avoid an accident in the road. But trams and buses are not *life*. . . ."

The entire audience cranes forward to catch the nugget of *jñana* that seems about to fall from the *ajarn's* lips.

"Ah, *life*, you see, is like a taxi. You must bargain with the driver for the fare, you must pick your own destination, and once you have set out, you're on your own, not knowing whether the driver is a madman, a kidnapper or a saint who will take you to the appointed place without giving you a heart attack along the route."

Having uttered these profound sentiments, the shaman returns to meditating on the blank television screen.

"I get it!" the corpulent lady whispers to her spouse. "The empty screen is supposed to symbolize the transience of existence."

We wait for another ten minutes or so. Then the sage rouses once more and notices me. He continues to address Samlee as though no time at all has elapsed.

"Perhaps, however, daughter, there is someone with you who *would* like to commune with the dead."

My once-beloved pushes me forward. My scalp tingles with incipient horripilation.

The *ajarn* slithers toward me, his hips swaying just above the floor planks, and I realize that he has become possessed by the spirit of Homer, my dead chameleon.

28

The Dead, the Living, and the Living Dead

There are a few screams, quickly stifled, as the sorcerer-turned-chameleon starts lurching toward me, his head bobbing from side to side like an Indian temple dancer.

"Homer?" I say softly. Panicking, I think of slipping away. I'm not comfortable with the dead, not even the friendly dead. They are unpredictable, as Samlee has frequently told me. But the lights seem to have dimmed . . . indeed, only the ghostlight from the television continues to shine, and the room seems suddenly deserted, as though the shaman's audience knows somehow that it is time for me to be alone with my visitation.

"Homer?"

He doesn't speak. He just slithers around the room. Now and then he cranes at an inhuman angle. It is Homer! It must be! No human could peer about in this reptilian fashion. And yet . . . will he speak? And if he should speak, what language will he speak? I have always assumed that Homer would speak English . . . but if he suddenly comes at me in ancient Greek? I'm not even sure what cosmology his afterlife adheres to—the cosmology of my secret world, with its Olympians and its Elysian fields, or the circles of heaven that ring the Himavant. In my dreams he inhabits a chimerical conflation of the two.

"Samlee!" I whisper. "What am I supposed to do now?" But she has melted into the shadows on either side of the cathode-ray pool of light.

How does one address chameleon men? Of course, there's Chameleon Boy from the Legion of Super-heroes who just seem to talk plain English even though they're in the thirtieth century. But this chameleon belongs firmly in the realm of fantasy, not science fiction. I decide to try the direct approach. "Homer," I say, "is that you?"

He slithers up closer. His eyes are wide and do not seem to blink. Of course not. They are the eyeholes of the shaman's mask, and behind the eyeholes are cold yellow eyes, dead eyes. I hear a voice: "Of course I'm here. Where did you think I was?"

The lips of the mask do not, of course, move. Perhaps the lips of the mage do not move either. I cannot tell.

"Oh, Homer, what am I to do?"

"Well, Little Frog, you do seem to have hit rock bottom. There's only one way to go from here and that's up."

"I see. But couldn't you be a little more specific?"

"Last week you learned a very important lesson about karma, the law of cause and effect, which rules the transient universe."

"I didn't mean to cause Piak and the gardener to be dismissed! You know that!"

"Ah, but your karma has placed you in such a position that you can, by a thoughtless act, ruin other people's lives," says the lizard man. "To rectify a thoughtless act takes much thought. Why, for example, did you take me to the funeral that night?"

"How was I to know that you would get—"

"How indeed?"

And then I seem to see it all again . . . I think I'm seeing it in ghostly colour on the television, even though I know that there is no colour television in all Thailand . . . I see the dinner table at the funeral that evening so many months ago . . . the tabletop is the boundary between two worlds, the upper world staid and respectable, the lower a dark and seething maelstrom of love and death . . . I see the high-heel plunge again and again into my hapless Homer's heart, like the knife that pierces again and again, without ever being seen to pierce the tender flesh of Janet Leigh in the film my great-grandmother and I have seen so many, many times . . . and I face, for the first time, the terrible truth that I alone killed Homer, that I alone must bear the burden of his death.

I was selfish. I wanted him with me always. I could not let go enough to keep my pet chameleon out of jeopardy. I find I am in tears. It is the first time I have really wept for Homer's death. Oh, I wept when it happened, but that was also because I thought that Samlee was a *phii krasue*, because I was afraid, because I did not want to be alone. It was me, me, me I wept for and not my fallen comrade at all.

"Tell me how I can make it up to you," I say, knowing there is nothing I can do to take back the death I have dealt.

And the voice of the chameleon says: "Don't make it up to me. You've done your duty to me. You've already sent my soul flying toward my next life, even though the funeral pyre did get a little soggy with piss! Look to the living now. You can't save me, but there are others you still can atone for."

"The living?"

The shaman doesn't answer.

We move slowly back down the *klong*. Samlee rows. This time we are not a Viking ship, and I am not in the mood for arson and rapine. This is not the fjord, this is not the River Styx. I wish it were Lethe, the river of forgetfulness, but it is not. It is impossible to fantasize. The *klong* is all too real. We drift past stilted houses. An inner tube bobs up and down. The waters are strewn with flower petals and used banana-leaf *bamii* wrappings. I sit back, still clad in the Chinese silk pyjamas, trailing the loose leaves of my turgid poem along the turgid water.

"Samlee?"

"Yes, Khun Nuu?"

"Are my parents dead?"

"I don't know, Khun Nuu. But they were good people. I remember them well. On New Year's Day your father would always give us envelopes stuffed with American dollars. I was only a girl then. I remember when he married your mother and went to *mueang nok* with her. That was the last time I ever saw them. What was *mueang nok* like?"

Mueang nok . . . the outer lands . . . is this all that the myriad countries of my imagination have been reduced to? And where are the inner lands, the ones it was promised I would discover once I started to speak the language of the heart?

I drop the poem into the water page by page. I feel nothing for the loss of all those words. Only emptiness.

Forget my parents! I tell myself. They are dead. The past is dead and irretrievable. Is it not true that at the beginning of a quest, the mythic hero tends not to know the secret of his birth? And am I not on a quest now, having doubly lost my dearest friends Homer and Virgil, searching, like Gilgamesh, for the herb that will bring them back from beyond the bourne of ultimate beyondness?

It starts to rain.

"Oh, heavens, Khun Nuu, you'll catch a terrible cold . . . you're wearing nothing but your *sueah klaam* and your *kangkaeng plaeh*! What is poor Samlee to do?"

"Can't we take shelter somewhere?"

The drizzle has become a downpour. This is the first time I realize we have finally left the hot dry season behind us and plunged into monsoon. I can't even talk without swallowing a mouthful of acrid rain. Through the wall of water I see lights from a labyrinth of shanties.

"There is a place we could go, Khun Nuu," she screams. "But I don't know if you'd want to . . ."

"Anywhere! I just want to get dry!"

I feel the boat turn, collide. I feel her hand slick against mine, pulling me up. I stagger on to a dock. My feet slip and slide. Water sluices the wood. In a flash of lightning I see the place we are in.

Buildings lean against each other like cartons, roofed with corrugated iron. Mountains of rubbish suggest the skyline of an extraterrestrial city. And high up on the mountain, silhouetted against the lightning like shadow puppets, there are naked children, dancing in the rain. The lightning fades, angry thunder drowns out the frogs, and the alien vista vanishes as suddenly as it came.

"This way!" Samlee shouts. Gripping my hand, she half drags me through mud and slush. Presently she is banging on the iron walls of one of the houses. A door opens and suddenly we are in a room. Shaking ourselves like ducks, we remove our shoes and place them by the door. The rain pelts down and the room resonates like the inside of a steel drum. The only light in the room comes from a paraffin lamp set on a wooden table. Shadows dance on the corrugated walls. A portrait of Their Majesties hangs above a bamboo bead partition, from behind which I hear whispered voices above the rain. There are other pictures on the walls, including, incredibly, a photograph of me.

"What is this place?" I ask Samlee, who has led me to a folding steel chair, the only seat in the room, and pushed me down into it, and is now methodically drying my hair with an old towel.

She says, "Perhaps you don't want to know."

But I already know. Because there is a boy my age standing across the table, his face lit eerily in the lamplight. The boy who taught me the filthy words I uttered on that fateful night. He looks at me with curiosity and with a certain wistfulness, but I don't see any anger in his face.

Look to the living, the shaman has told me in the voice of my dead chameleon. But Piak does not seem living to me. How could one live in such a world, circumscribed by four sheets of metal, with cardboard for flooring and with only the rain to bathe in? Would I not rather die than live in such a world? And is this world not a place of the living dead?

"Oh, don't stare so," Samlee says to him. "Go and fetch Khun Nuu something warm to drink. Put a kettle on the charcoal stove and make some tea."

Piak doesn't leave, so Samlee herself pads off through the partition into the other room. I am alone with him I once betrayed.

"Look at you," he says softly. "You get soaked the same as we do. Maybe more so because you don't know how to dodge the rain by sprinting from awning to awning. Without your Chinese silk pyjamas, under your uncalloused skin, you're much the same as me."

It occurs to me that it is my rash and drunken actions alone that have exiled him and his father to this slum. I don't ask him not to hate me. I know that I would hate me. I only ask him, "Are you angry with me?"

"No," he says. "How can I be? My karma isn't as good as yours, that's all."

"You know I didn't mean to—"

"Yes. I know. But something else would have happened. This is how it's always been with my father and me, drifting from one job to the next, one woman to the next. In a way, you've done him a service—you've forced him to rethink his whole nature. . . . "

"What do you mean?"

"Oh, you'll see, Master Little Frog, you'll see."

As abruptly as it began, the rain stops. That is how the rainy season is. The rain comes in explosive torrents and then it vanishes, leaving the air as hot and humid as before.

In what passes for silence in the tropical night, we hear a car moving outside. It seems to be coming in our direction, crunching tin cans and bottles in its path.

Samlee emerges from the partition with a cup of lukewarm tea. She thrusts it at me distractedly. I drink it. It is sweet and milky. Her mood has changed completely. She was solicitous before, but now she hardly notices me except to say, "We must hurry . . . before he comes."

"Who? Why must we hurry?"

Before she can answer we hear a metallic knocking.

"Hide!" Piak says urgently, pushing us through the partition.

"What's the matter?" On the other side of the bamboo curtain (on which is painted a crude image of the Royal Barge passing in front of the Temple of Dawn) I see several children lying on straw mats. There is another partition beyond, through which I can see someone moving in the glow of another paraffin lamp.

"It's the temple fair," Piak says. "He's coming to pick her up."

"Who's coming?"

"*He is*! Don't you see?" Samlee whispers urgently. "Your uncle is taking my rival to the temple fair ... that person is here ... in this very house!"

"Another woman?"

Samlee does not answer. But I can tell that she is weeping.

Then I hear the unmistakable sound of my uncle's voice: "Busaba! Busaba! I'm sorry I took so long, but it was difficult to get away, and then the rain started. . . ."

Busaba ... that must be the name of my uncle's latest obsession. I hear a voice from behind the inner partition: "I'm coming." What a melodious voice it is! And then she comes through the curtain. She is a creature of jaw-dropping beauty. She is wearing a traditional *phasin*, and her long hair has been brushed over one shoulder so that it falls over her bosom. Her face is pale—I think from make-up—and her lips blood-red. There is something strangely familiar about this woman, but I can't quite place it.

"I'm coming, Vit, dear," she says in that haunting voice of hers. She starts toward the outer partition. Then she sees me, Piak and Samlee.

"They needed shelter from the rain," Piak says.

Busaba glares at me and Samlee. Then, in a quite different voice—a deep and grating voice—she addresses Piak, refusing to look either me or my former nursemaid in the eye: "You! Make sure they get home safely. I don't want a fuss made."

"Yes, Father," Piak says softly. The woman undulates her way out through the outer partition, and I hear a door open and close.

"So that's what you meant when you said your father was re-thinking his whole nature," I say after the coast is clear, and I am once more sipping the tea and sitting on the only seat in the house.

"Yes," Piak says, as he rubs me down with an old shirt that I recognize as one I lost many months ago. "I'm afraid my father has become a transvestite. Still, there are worse things he could have become."

"You can't go on living like this," I tell him.

"What can *you* do about it?" Piak says softly.

29

Greek Tragedies

It is some days before I find an answer to Piak's question, for the following week is taken up mostly with cobbling together a pseudo-Greek tragedy at the behest of Mrs. V., avoiding the wrath of Miss C., and winning the friendship of Wilbur and Piet, since that of Virgil has been denied me.

The cobbling is a lot of fun. I look through the dusty tomes in the ruined house and bring stacks of them to school. We pore over Homer and the tragedians, copy, cut and paste, and write out the outline of the plot on ditto paper. I love to go down to the school office and operate the hand-cranked ditto machine, which smells like fresh nail polish and churns out soggy sheets of purple print that we leave out to dry until the sweet chemical scent is purged from them. Because of the itinerary of Uncle Vit's Mercedes, the driver generally cannot pick me up until an hour or two after school, but I feel no haste to return. There is the library, and there are the long discussions with Mrs. V. whilst manning the ditto, and there is also Father Regenstrom's choir, which meets after hours in a room adjacent to the library and which soothes my ears with dulcet a cappella renditions of English madrigals and Latin motets. Often I can single out Jessica's voice.

The parts in our play have been chosen by lot. Helen of Troy is to be performed by Griselda Richardson. I have drawn the relatively minor part of Calchas, the prophet. Piet van Helsing is to be Agamemnon, Wilbur is to be his cuckolded brother-in-law, Menelaus. The part of Paris, the handsome cuckolder, is to be played by Virgil.

Today, there is no air-conditioning at the Scola Britannica. Rather than shutting ourselves in and relying on the rickety ceiling fans to give us the illusion of coolness, Mrs. V. has decided that it's better to practice our makeshift drama *al fresco*.

Behind the huge colonial structure that houses the main school, behind even the bungalow where Miss Cicciolini holds court, there is a *ton kraang* or banyan tree. The main trunk is rumoured to be a century old, and there are many subsidiary trunks, so that the one tree forms a canopy that shades an area of about one *rai*. The air is just as sticky here, but a notch less hot; the slightest breeze stirs the branches overhead and makes the leaves whisper. We play out the elemental tragedy beneath this tree, whose trunks become, alternately, the ramparts of Troy, the thousand ships, the tents of the Greeks, the columns of ancient temples. The story is three thousand years old, but the words are all our own.

Today we act out the abduction of Helen. It is strange for me to see the game I have always played alone played now in common, but I trust Mrs. Vajravajah. I think she means to use this game to find out more about us, to see us as we really are.

First, there is Griselda. She passes out the dittoed sheets, which explain the story in the most skeletal terms. As the prophetic priest who will later defect to the Greeks, I am to utter a few minutes of stentorian warnings at the beginning of the play. The rest belongs to Wilbur, Griselda and Virgil.

Virgil, leaning against the central tree-trunk, is the picture of spoiled aristocratic indolence. "I am the youngest prince of Troy," he says, using what his mother calls the "prestige dialect", and I've come to Sparta to abduct Helen, the most beautiful woman in the world. You see, she was promised to me by the goddess Aphrodite as a reward for picking her to be the fairest of the goddesses. It seemed like a good agreement at the time. Unfortunately, Aphrodite neglected to tell me that the most beautiful woman in the world was already married, and I was going to have to steal her. That was in the small print, which of course I didn't read, because in those days princes were illiterate; they left the art of writing to the priests."

Eloquent though Virgil is, I dare not pay too much attention to him. I know he will glower at me. It has been weeks since our estrangement, but the rift has not even begun to be healed.

Using my dittoed sheet as a reference, I say: *"Scene two: Sparta."*

On wings of thought, we speed across the sea to Greece, where Sparta is represented by a tree-trunk right next to the school's back wall, which borders on a *klong.* The wedding of Menelaus and Helen is in progress, and Griselda and Wilbur play their parts with impressive dignity, though there is, as yet, no dialogue. The rest of the class, acting out the roles of wedding-guests, recline on the grass and sip red and green soft drinks out of plastic bags full of shaved ice.

Wilbur says: "Mrs. V., what do you want me to say when Virgil actually steals my girl?"

"Say whatever comes into your head, Wilbur."

"Sometimes what pops into my head, well, you know, ain't nice."

"My dear Wilbur," says Mrs. V. "This is 1963, not the Middle Ages. I doubt that anything you say could shock me."

Presently, Virgil comes sauntering into Sparta, whistling "I Whistle a Happy Tune". He sees Griselda and goes through an elaborate mime of being stricken, clutching at his heart, making his eyes pop out of his head, pulling his heart out of his chest and watching it pump in the palm of his hand. He elicits a lot of giggles. With feline fluidity he oozes his way into the court of King Menelaus, who happens to be carrying Helen over the threshold at the very moment. Griselda flutters her eyelashes.

"Helen!" Virgil says in his best orating voice. "Thou art the fairest creature I have ever seen. In fact, I don't reckon I'll ever see a creature lovelier than thee."

"Oh, Parith," says Griselda, "you're *theaugh* handthome!"

So far, so good.

Wilbur deposits Griselda behind the tree. He is accompanied by Piet, who, as Agamemnon the mighty but microcephalic brother-in-law, has pledged to protect and preserve Menelaus' conjugal integrity.

"Now you stay right here, honey," says Wilbur, "while I go and party with the guests for a little while longer. Why don't you slip into something comfortable while you're at it?" Assorted snickers here.

"I could use some wine," Piet says. "I mean, I deserve some consolation for not getting Helen. Her half-sister Clytemnestra's not half bad looking, but she's rather a bossy sort of woman."

"Relax, Agamemnon," Wilbur says smugly, "you can't win 'em all."

Their backs are turned, and Virgil insinuates himself from behind the tree-trunk.

"Hello, Helen," he says in that mock-*eaughing* tone of his, "I've come to take you back with me to Troy."

"Well, I hope it'th a jolly thight better than Thparta," says Griselda, smiling sweetly. She takes his hand and is just about to step back over the threshold when the two brothers show up, each bearing a deadly fountain pen in lieu of a dagger.

"Just one cotton-pickin' minute!" Wilbur says. "That coon's trying to get himself a white woman!"

All the giggling stops at once. The playfulness has turned ugly.

"You're right," says Piet. "We can't have kaffirs raiding our houses and raping our women. After him!"

"Boys! Boys!" Mrs. V. says, and attempts to interpose herself between them. Wilbur and Piet loom over this woman by half a head apiece. They ignore her.

"Let's have ourselves a lynching!" Wilbur screams. The two of them grab Virgil by the arms and drag him off, with Piet unbuckling his belt and fashioning it into a makeshift noose.

"This isn't in the script, you idiots!" I say. "He's supposed to get away with it . . . then you're supposed to go to war for ten years."

"Bullshit," says Wilbur. "I ain't fighting no ten years' war. Besides, we lost the last one."

"No, no, the Greeks won the Trojan War."

"The Trojan War's just a myth, Justin. Uppity niggers are reality." He acts as though he's explaining to a child.

They carry Virgil off by the arms and feet. Virgil doesn't resist. It's just like that time we went swimming at the club. His mind seems to have disappeared into the Twilight Zone, and his body is just marking time until the ordeal ends. They go trotting off toward the far edge of the banyan tree.

The other children are so astonished that they stand there, mouths agape, unable to speak. Except for Griselda, that is, who shouts out: "You come back with my thecret lover at onthe, d'you hear?"

"Do something, Mrs. V.!" I shriek.

Mrs. V. gives chase. The rest of us follow behind her. "Paul," she says, huffing, to one of the other boys, "run to the headmaster's office as fast as you can and bring him here!" Paul sprints away at top speed.

We pass under a natural archway formed by twin trunks. In a small clearing within the penumbra of the banyan tree, Virgil is being subjected to a mock hanging. The noose is already around his neck, and his feet are resting on the back of Piet van Helsing, who has crouched down in imitation of a footstool. Meanwhile, Wilbur is punching him in the chest. Wilbur's eyes are blazing with total, unconscionable anger, but Virgil's face is entirely untouched by emotion. I see that war they are re-enacting is as real to them as the Trojan War is to me.

It is at that moment that the headmaster, Dr. York, with mortarboard and gown draped over a Hawaiian shirt, rushes on to the scene, wielding the cane that is the traditional symbol of an English education. He lashes at the empty air.

"Better drop it, Wilbur," says Piet. "Man's got a *sjambok*."

He scurries out from under Virgil, who is almost strangulated by the tightening belt until Mrs. V. manages to free him. In a fury,

Dr. York starts flagellating wildly, but he only manages to hit Wilbur once.

"Stop!" Virgil says. "I don't need no help from you or nobody else neither. I can take care of myself."

I don't know how he can say that after his show of passivity.

Wilbur turns to the headmaster and smiles his most charismatic smile. "We were only play-acting, sir . . . weren't we, Virgil? And Mrs. V. said we were supposed to say whatever was in our minds."

Virgil looks at the ground. The leaves above our heads rustle. Perhaps it will rain soon.

Dr. York turns to Mrs. V. "My dear Mrs. Vajravajah," he says, "I was suspicious of your wanting to adopt all these avant-garde educational techniques, but really, the enactment of Freudian psychodramas wasn't what I had in mind when I hired you to teach English literature. Please have the goodness to tone down your experiments. Or I'll be forced to make you revert to the syllabus."

He stalks away, swishing his cane at the air.

I'm the only one close enough to Mrs. V. to hear her muttering to herself, "What a blithering idiot. This isn't some damned colony, you know." I see two tiny tears well up in her eyes, but she turns aside. The sky has suddenly grown much darker.

"I think," she announces, "in our next episode, we're going to have to have a less . . . improvisational script. Which means someone's going to have to write it." She looks at me. We hear distant thunder. I date my brief career as a playwright from that peal of thunder. "Come on, children, I think it might rain," she adds, and we all troop after her, back toward the main school building.

Virgil is lagging. I decide that this may be the moment to patch it up with him. I run up to him and tell him, "Virgil, Virgil . . . I've seen Piak! And I'm working on a plan to get him reinstated at the house." I'm saving the surprise for later—I mean my discovery that Piak's father seems to have metamorphosed into his mother.

Virgil turns to me with all the rage he should have unleashed on Wilbur and Piet. "Leave me alone," he says. "You got the hide of a dink, but inside you white as snow. You one of *them*."

"Oh, Virgil, let go of it. You've been angry at me for two weeks now, you know I'm not really your enemy."

"Get lost."

"The least you can do is let me back in the treehouse. I mean, it is on my land, you know."

He quickens his pace and leaves me behind.

30

They All Look Alike

Perhaps, I decide, I should turn to my great-grandmother. It was she, after all, who first caused me to meet Virgil and to see Piak in a new light, as a fellow human being. At the weekend, therefore, I excuse myself from a trip to the Sunday market with the three Fates by telling them I must write the next big scene for Mrs. V.'s drama. They leave right after the morning *khao tom*, and I immediately slip off to the ruined house to seek an audience. Her door is open, and I go straight in after a tentative knock.

My great-grandmother no longer inhabits the *Psycho*-like room with its swinging, naked bulb. A room on the ground floor has been found for her. It was once a music room. There is a grand piano with no strings; it is filled with potted plants and musty tomes. There is a shelf full of medical paraphernalia. In the background, a transistor radio has just launched into another episode of the soap opera that features the soundtrack from *Ben Hur* as its theme music.

There is a four-poster bed with a canopy of faded silk and sheer, ruffled curtains. My great-grandmother is propped up on a triangular cushion.

"Hello, Great-grandmother."

"I'm glad you've come to see me before I'm stuffed and mounted," says the *khunying*.

"Seeing you stuffed and mounted couldn't be further from my mind, actually."

"Perhaps it's my millennial wisdom you seek, then?"

"Sort of."

"Did you enjoy my performance at the limbo rock party?"

"It was wonderful, Great-grandmother. Actually, I wanted to talk to you about the party . . . a dreadful thing happened there. . . ."

I begin to tell her all about it, but presently I hear her snoring. How stupid of me to trouble her with my petty problems when she's probably at death's door! I curse myself for my lack of consideration. Then after some reflection I realize that it's better to pour out my anguish to a sleeping person than to no one at all, so I go on until I've told her everything, including Piak's dismissal, the gardener's transformation into Busaba the *katoey*, and our visits to the shaman, and Dr. Richardson's tryst with my aunts, and Virgil's near-lynching at the hands of Piet and Wilbur, and Miss Cicciolini's slap in the face, and . . . and . . . it's all very cathartic. And yet . . .

Suddenly my great-grandmother snaps out of her sleep. "I've got to piss right now!" she rasps. "Go and bang that gong by the door as loud as you can and yell for the *krathohn*!"

"The *krathohn*?" I ask her.

"Yes, yes, the chamberpot, now hurry, hurry, hurry!"

I hasten to obey. My great-grandmother's face is contorted with pain and rage. At length, Kaew runs in with an aluminium chamberpot. She is trembling in terror. She drops down on her hands and knees and begins to crawl toward the bed with her eyes lowered.

"Come here at once!" says my great-grandmother. "I don't want any ceremony, I just want to take a piss, do you hear?"

Kaew's journey to the bed seems to take forever. When she finally reaches it, it is clear that my great-grandmother can hold it no longer.

"Time and time again," my great-grandmother says, "I've given orders for someone to be on hand at all hours in case I become incontinent. I'm simply going to have to teach you servants a lesson you won't forget." The servant has finally reached the bedside and is proffering the chamberpot with quivering hands.

With astonishing agility, the *khunying* flings aside the blanket she has been covering herself with, jerks the girl toward her by the hair and proceeds to urinate on her head. The chamberpot clatters to the marble floor and rolls around for a while before it clangs against the wall.

"Remember! Remember!" my great-grandmother screeches. She seems possessed, her eyes staring, wild and hollow, her hair pointing every which way. It occurs to me that she's the only person I know with white hair and black teeth, a bizarre reverse image of a normal human being. As the maid scurries out of the room, weeping, my great-grandmother closes her eyes and takes great gasping breaths that decelerate until she seems to grow quite, quite still.

"Great-grandmother?" I whisper, hardly daring to approach.

The room smells of stale urine and hospital chemicals.

"Great-grandmother?"

And suddenly she comes to again. And she's laughing softly to herself, and in her eyes there is the glint of life. "That really was something of an exhibition, wasn't it?" she says.

"But great-grandmother—"

"There are certain advantages to being senile," she says. "At least they'll bring the piss-pot more promptly next time! They'll be talking about it for weeks down in the servants' quarters. Weeks, I assure you! And yet—"

She feels around on the bedside table for her betel nut tray. With trembling hands she folds a leaf and stuffs it in her mouth. "Sometimes," she says, "I know how senile I've become . . . when the past feels, smells, tastes truer than the present. . . . Did you know that my mother used to have slaves? Now there was a woman with *vas-*

ana. If they'd been tardy with the chamberpot in those days, their backs would have ended up with more stripes than a zebra. Or she'd have had them clapped in irons for a week without rice or water." There's a faraway look in her eyes . . . I know she's gazing back at a world that I shall never share . . . in our house, the past is not to be shared. Not like the house next door.

"Virgil's great-grandmother was a slave," I say softly.

"I daresay," she says. "And the past never quite dies, does it? Otherwise I would be so terribly afraid. Because soon I'm going to be quite, quite gone, and part of that past. . . ."

"But you said you wouldn't go . . . unless a specific thing happened. Can't you tell me what it is so that I can stop it from happening, so that you'll live forever?"

She laughs a little. Then she tells me to bring her the chamberpot, into which she spits the remnants of her betel nut. "Well, I am not going to shut the door until I am sure that another door has opened."

I decide that it's better to slip away today; I'll wait until she's feeling more lucid. I wonder if she ever will. Slowly I begin to back away toward the door. But just as I reach it, I hear her call out softly to me: "Little Frog, Little Frog . . ."

"Yes, Great-grandmother?"

"You want to know where the will is?"

I take two small steps forward. This is the information the three Fates have been trying to pry out of me for several weeks. Somehow, they are convinced that my great-grandmother has already told me the secret. "I think I'd rather not know," I say. "You see, I'll have fewer lies to tell if my three aunts try to worm it out of me."

She cackles like a stage witch. The wild laughter echoes through stone and cracked statuary, then, abruptly, it subsides. "You and I think very much alike, Norman," says my great-grandmother. "You already know the answer to the riddle, but you do not choose to know it."

"I see, Great-grandmother," I say.

"And as for our little domestic problems," she says—revealing to me that she's actually been listening the whole time I thought she was asleep—"they all look alike."

She falls asleep, and I tiptoe away.

I step out of the ruined house with its gloomy shadows and dusty air into the sunlight. *They all look alike* . . . but what had we been talking about? The dead past. The time of slavery.

It hits me all at once. I am going to have to confront them all. I am going to have to brave their silence. I am going to have to climb the tree without rungs.

It is daylight. There is nothing to fear in the mango orchard . . . no shit-eating *phii krasue*, no monstrous *prehd*. The boys in the treehouse are not my enemies. I stride toward the treehouse by the wall of the estate. I'm a seething mass of choler and adrenalin. I reach the trunk of the mango tree. I look up at the three-level tree-house, stare furiously at the top of the ladder that leans against the wrong side of the wall and grazes the barrier of broken glass. I hear the laughter of Piak and Virgil. The treehouse seems unattainable without the rungs.

I step back about ten yards, because I'll need a running start to be able to leap up to that branch. I take a deep breath and run full tilt toward the tree. I trip. I skin my knee, but I don't notice the pain. I go straight back to the starting post, kicking a few twigs and stones out of the way so that I won't trip again, take another breath and count slowly to three. I clench my teeth. I sprint forward as a *jujitsu*-type roar tears from my throat.

I find myself dangling from the branch, swinging back and forth like a vineless Tarzan. I am being pelted with unripe mangoes.

I hear voices from above. "Get him, Piak! It's an interloper!" It's Virgil speaking Thai.

"I don't have to be scared of him any more," Piak is saying. "They've already fired me—now I can do anything I want!"

A mango sails by and I manage to catch it between my feet. Mustering my last reserves of strength, I bend back my knees, swing forward and actually propel the mango upward into the treehouse. I hear a resounding plop . . . fruit against flesh.

"Shi-*it!*" says Virgil. I hear someone slump down on to the floor-boards above. I can't hold on any more, so I bring my feet up to the branch and, sloth-like, clamber toward the trunk and the next toehold. It only takes a moment to breach the fort and to find Virgil, his face covered with mango, lying on the floor moaning, with Piak looking on in consternation.

"Now look here," I say.

"I ain't talking to you no more," Virgil groans.

"Well, I ain't talking to you, neither," I say, mimicking him. "As a matter of fact, I've come here to talk to Piak. I've got a plan to get you and your father back into the house."

"Now wait a minute," says Virgil. "What right have you got to come bustin' in here like Robin Hood and telling us you gone save us from oppression? You one of them oppressors youself! I found out you plannin' to go to a barbecue at Piet's house. Some friend you turned out to be."

"So you *are* talking to me," I tell him, "even if you've nothing good to say." Virgil looks away. "You know it wasn't my fault any of those things happened. And if you don't want people to come to your aid, why don't you put up more of a fight yourself ?"

Virgil says, "How can I 'spect *you* to understand? You just a banana—yellow on the outside and white on the inside."

We hear the Studebaker's horn at the gate. The three Fates are returning from the Sunday market. "We haven't much time," I tell them. "You're going to have to help me, Virgil. We've got to shave Piak's head. And maybe you can lend him some new clothes. And get a message out to his father so that he knows what's going on. And Samlee's going to have to be in on this, so we'll have to fetch her."

"Girls ain't allowed in the treehouse," Virgil points out.

"I know, I know. We'll talk to her outside."

"But what are you going to do to me?" says Piak.

"It's very simple," I say. "They all look alike."

We hear the car moving down the driveway. We don't breathe. Virgil glares at me. He is a natural leader and doesn't like being led. But we've achieved an uneasy détente. I only hope the truce will last long enough to pull off the ruse. . . .

31

The Art of Illusion

This, then, is the plan and how it all transpires. It is early evening, and the three Fates and I have sat down to a light supper consisting of sticky rice, barbecued chicken, beef salad, braised asparagus, cheeseburgers, *woon sen* soup, lemonade, mangosteens on ice, *nam prik mangdaa*, raw shrimp in lime and fish sauce dressing, and four or five other dishes of equal drabness. We are in the teakwood dining room. My three aunts are discussing the weather. Virgil has decided to come along after all, although I don't think he really trusts me. He, too, is discussing the weather. I am appalled, sometimes, at the superiority of his social skills.

In order to be in a position to influence my aunts, I am dressed to the teeth. I've applied over half a jar of Brylcreem to my cowlicks, and I'm wearing a white shirt, white shorts and a velvet bowtie.

"To what do we owe the pleasure of seeing you so well dressed, Little Frog?" Aunt Ning-nong asks me. She still has a bandage on her throat, and she is somewhat dismayed to see a bowl of *woon sen* soup in front of her. She pushes it away discreetly, with two fingers of her left hand, for she is too much of a *phudii* to make a fuss over an item of food which, after all, only *almost* caused her death a few weeks ago.

"Been raining a lot lately, hasn't it?" Ning-nong says. She eyes the *woon sen* balefully.

"Yes, I'm afraid it has been raining, rather," says Aunt Nit-nit. She has no qualms about the noodles. In fact, she's wolfing them down. Ning-nong glares as they are slurped up into Nit-nit's mouth along the conveyor belt of her tongue. I am sure that, even as she cringes at her sister's gustatory enthusiasm, she is also seething with envy. But, as I say, she is too much of a *phudii* to express such unseemly thoughts aloud.

"I'm sure it's going to rain tomorrow, too," says Noi-noi.

"Well," says Virgil, "I'm sure glad it ain't raining now. Could you pass the *woon sen*, please?"

I don't want the three Fates to get into a snit, so I decide to proceed with the plan. "Aunt Ning-nong," I say, addressing myself to the senior Fate as custom dictates, "I've been awfully lonely since . . . you know, the gardener was sacked. I thought I'd be all right, but I'm afraid I've come to the conclusion that I'm simply too young to sleep by myself. It's . . . well . . . you know. There are . . . noises."

Noi-noi laughs. "So, our ever so contemporary young nephew is actually admitting to a bit of *klua phii*, is he?"

"I admit it," I sigh. "I actually am rather afraid of ghosts."

"I thought that that kitchen maid—whatshername—Kaew—had been sleeping in your room," said Noi-noi. "Didn't she get reassigned there after that silly man was fired?—or was that someone else?—I do get so confused sometimes."

"I know you do," says Ning-nong. "One always gets confused during the monsoon. It's an inescapable condition."

"Oh, I wish the rain were more predictable, so we could plan another outdoor extravaganza!" says Noi-noi. "I never did get to wear that last dress—you know, the pink chiffon. You were commandeering simply *all* the attention, Phii Ning-nong, with your tracheotomy; it didn't seem right to try to distract them with yet another dress. . . ."

"But honoured aunts . . ." As so often when the air is oppressive and one is not sure whether a rainstorm will burst, the conversation wanders in circles. "Couldn't we hire a new boy?"

"Out of the question," says Ning-nong. "It's because we let a slum boy share your living quarters last time that you actually went so far as to utter . . . *that word* . . . in public."

"What word might that be?" Virgil says. I try to shush him, but I can see he's trying to get back at me by embarrassing me again.

"I can't say it, of course," says Aunt Ning-nong, "but, it rhymes with . . . ah . . . *phed nae*."

"I see," Virgil says. "It too bad a word for you to say out loud, but it *rhyme* with 'it is certainly spicy'. What do you know. Must be a hell of a spicy word."

"Quite right, Virgil, and that is why, you see, we mustn't allow Little Frog's mind to be corrupted with such depravity—"

"But Justin's always reading them Greek classics," says Virgil, and they *full* of depravity. One time he be telling me all about Oedipus Rex—it by some Greek name of Sufferpleeze."

"Sophocles!" I say, horrified at his mangling of the divine name.

"Yeah, but anyways this Oedipus, he did exactly what you talking about, the thing that *rhyme* with 'it sure be spicy'. I know it's true, cause it in a book—it *poetry*."

"Good heavens!" says Noi-noi. For a moment I almost believe we're going to have our replay of the *woon sen* incident after all.

"My dear Virgil," I say with all the asperity and *hauteur* my minuscule form can muster, "the classical Greeks were most assuredly not depraved. If there are things in the ancient texts that appear to be so, it is doubtless only because of our imperfect understanding of them."

"Quite so," Ning-nong says, "classics are classics. I certainly don't remember anything depraved in the classics I did in school."

I'm too polite to point out that they didn't teach the classics at Winkfield, the finishing school in Windsor at which all three of my aunts once spent a few months perfecting their *eaughing*.

Kaew pours us all more *nam manao* as we think of what to say next. She doesn't seem to harbour any resentment of me for having witnessed my great-grandmother's bizarre attack of senility earlier today. I tap my spoon against the side of my lemonade glass twice. It's the agreed-upon signal that I'm going to broach the big proposal to my aunts, but I can tell that Virgil is still trying to think up new ways to make me look stupid. To make sure he doesn't give the game away, I give him a swift kick in the shin under the table.

"Well," I say, "I'm sorry I allowed that scurvy little fellow to corrupt me, and I quite agree that you shouldn't allow any more corruption into the house"—I'm wondering why Dr. Richardson's assignations don't seem to count as corruption—"but I was recently talking to Samlee, and she's got this nephew, you see . . . abandoned by his mother at the gates of a monastery when he was only five years old . . . brought up completely by monks . . . he's never even set foot outside consecrated ground until last week, when he was forced to come to Bangkok by catastrophic circumstance. . . ."

"*Eaugh*," cries Noi-noi. "What circumstance was that?"

"The monastery burned down," I say. "Every single person in the *kuti* was horribly killed . . . except him. He managed to survive by hiding in an *ong* full of rainwater. He's quite destitute, I'm afraid." I manage to keep a straight face, although Virgil is now returning my shin-kick five-fold.

"Heavens," says Aunt Ning-nong. The only person not entirely convinced by all this is Aunt Nit-nit, but I have a feeling she's not going to give me away. In fact, she appears to be stifling a giggle.

"As a matter of fact," I continue, "Samlee's been sheltering him in the servants' quarters for a couple of days now, ever since . . . you know . . . that terrible storm. Flesh and blood, you know. And, of course, Samlee hasn't had much to do since Uncle Vit's . . . ah . . . eye has begun roving again. . . ."

"It has, eh?" Noi-noi says. "My, you *are* observant, Little Frog." But I can see sympathy shifting toward Samlee, for two of my aunts have been jilted themselves—I cannot speak for Ning-nong.

"In any case, most revered aunts, I took the liberty of telling him that I would arrange an interview with your most compassionate selves."

"Good heavens! During dinner?" Ning-nong exclaims.

"Well . . . he's waiting outside."

I glance at the dining room door. It is flung open and there stands Piak. His head has been thoroughly shaven, and he's dressed in some of Virgil's old clothes, but I must say that he doesn't really look any different from the wild urchin who taught me all those bad words. I'm about to confess when Piak falls prostrate to the floor at Aunt Ning-nong's feet and executes a *kraab* of exquisite humility.

"Thank you so much, Khun Phuying," he says, "and may karma reward you a thousandfold in your next life for the kindnesses you have shown this abject and unworthy peon."

Laying it on a bit thick, I'm thinking, but my aunts are nothing if not amenable to flattery.

"You poor thing!" says Ning-nong. "You say your mother abandoned you on the doorstep of a temple?"

"The monks were awfully kind, your worship, and they taught me everything—meditation, the Eightfold Path, and the *dharma*. In fact, I was just getting ready to he ordained a *samanera* and prepared to devote the rest of my life to the pursuit of inner tranquillity, when . . . when. . . ."

He trails off into a passable imitation of grief.

"And you have no idea where your parents are now?" says Ning-nong.

"Well, my father . . . Samlee's second cousin . . . died when I was only two years old . . . and I don't know where my mother is. Every day of my life, until the temple . . . until . . . until. . . ." He chokes back a crocodile tear or two. "I used to stand at the temple gates in the dawn, waiting to see if my mother would come for me. . . ."

"Well, well, well," says Ning-nong.

"You wouldn't happen to know," Virgil says in Thai, "what rhymes with 'it is certainly spicy', would you?"

"Oh, don't tease the child," says Noi-noi. "It's obvious he's no knowledge of anything worldly. He's led an even more sheltered life than *we* have."

"We're simply going to have to find some position for you in this household, I suppose," says Ning-nong. "Kaew, take the boy away and feed him at once. By the way, boy, what is your name?"

"Piak," says Piak. My heart does a flip-flop. We never discussed a name. I've assumed Piak would come up with something suitable. After all, I've written the script, painstakingly taught it to him a sentence at a time, including when to pause for effect and when to appear to be choking back tears . . . you would have thought he could come up with a name all by himself.

"Nice name," says Ning-nong, as Kaew leads Piak away to the kitchen and we turn to dessert—today a modest selection of only two or three items. "You've done very well today, Little Frog. It's always good to show a little Buddhist compassion now and then. After all, we mustn't forget how much more fortunate we are than . . . well, than virtually everybody else."

"That boy looks strangely familiar," says Nit-nit.

"Well, that's the lower classes for you," says Noi-noi. "You've seen one, you've seen 'em all."

In the last ten minutes I've been on my best behaviour, terrified that something may go wrong with our plan. But now a great weight has been lifted from me. Gleefully, I kick Virgil several times in the shin. So amazed is he at the virtuosity of the performance he has just witnessed that he doesn't kick me back. I've shown him I can be just as bad as he can . . . if not worse!

32

Still More
Mysteries of Sex

You'd think that bringing Piak back into the fold would make Virgil like me again, but life never seems to be that simple. In fact, although I am once more admitted to the treehouse—the rungs reappear miraculously—and on the surface we are a happy threesome once more, there's a diffidence in our relationship. It's as though we've seen too much of each other's dark side. Or something.

There must be something that I can do to dispel the cloud. But what is it? I spend the night at Virgil's house again—several times, in fact. But it is not the same. No visions come, and though Mrs. O'Fleary tells us another story about the ancient times of slavery, there doesn't seem to be any magic in it.

And though Jessica still enchants me with her renditions of Schubert, there are no more nocturnal visits. I lie thinking of her until I fall asleep, waiting for visionary dreams to come, but my sleeps are dreamless. Doors have closed. I wonder whether this is what growing up entails—the closing of one door after another, the walling up of corridors, the barricading of alternative pathways, until there is only one road down which to journey, one odyssey per individual, one thread-thin strip of highway that runs un-swerving from the end of childhood to the end of life.

In the next few weeks I am to see a good deal more of Father Regenstrom. I have to know Latin for the entrance exam for Eton, and though I am familiar enough with Roman literature in trans-lation, I haven't really essayed the original. I am daunted by Latin, by its cadences, by its row upon row of verbal paradigms all lined up with military precision like so many maniples, cohorts and legions. It has been decided for me that I'm to spend an hour or so each day after school with the padre, since his own school is still battling the bureaucracy at the Ministry, leaving him with little to do apart from conducting our school choir.

The first time Father Regenstrom appears more than peripher-ally in my life, however, is not to do with Latin but with yet another exciting instalment of the mysteries of sex. We have gathered in Miss Cicciolini's class as usual only to discover that the priest is standing there, shifting from foot to foot and nervously fiddling with his rosary. Miss Cicciolini is in the process of separating the boys from the girls until we're in two groups on opposite sides of the room, arranged alphabetically of course, for Miss Cicciolini can do nothing without first imposing her version of order upon the chaos of the world.

"I have an announcement to make," she says. "Are we all listen-ing, now?"

"Yes, Miss Cicciolini," we intone.

"A certain young man in my classroom—we shall not name names, since this is one of the shabbier incidents of my tenure here at the Scola Britannica—boasted recently that he knew all about the . . . ah . . . the . . . the birds and the bees."

I feel the entire classroom staring at me suddenly. What birds and bees? Surely she's not referring to my offering to illuminate the mysteries of the aubergine, which has earned me nothing so far save a slapped face? Father Regenstrom is getting redder and redder in the face as Miss Cicciolini proceeds, and Piet and Wilbur are alternately pointing at me and poking each other in the ribs.

"I've therefore asked Father Regenstrom"—and here Miss Cicciolini positions herself once more in such a way that her tresses sweep dramatically across her dark glasses—"to come and give the *boys* a talk about these—ahem—matters. The *girls* and I will retire to the banyan tree outside for our own discussion of this—ahem— topic. And once this is all over, I don't want to hear anything else about it from anyone, do you hear? I'm a biology teacher, not a . . . a . . . a . . . sex therapist!" So saying, Miss Cicciolini beckons to all the girls with a wave of her arm, and she sort of swoops out of the classroom with her hair flying and her very, very *red* scarf flailing in the breeze from the air conditioner.

Father Regenstrom tells us to sit down. He then pulls out half a dozen writing implements from somewhere within his robes. He places them down and solemnly proceeds to arrange and rearrange them in various permutations along the edge of the desk. There are hundreds of possible permutations. It looks as though he's going to go through every one of these before he actually says anything, but after a dozen or so he clears his throat and addresses us in a tone of calculated bonhomie. "You may have noticed," he says, "something hanging between your legs."

You could cut the silence with a *katana*. At last, an adult was going to level with us about the function, form and *raison d'être* of the aubergine! We boys glance furtively around. It is as though the good father were about to lift up the veil of the Ark of the Covenant.

The tension is abruptly shattered when Piet says, "But Father— I've never noticed anything—do you think you could elaborate?"

"You know exactly what I mean!" Father Regenstrom snaps. "If I hear one more word out of you, young man, I shall—I shall—"

"But jeepers, Father," Wilbur chimes in, "I've never noticed anything either . . . do you think there's something wrong with me? I mean, maybe I'm deformed. I guess I could join a freak show or something, huh, Father?"

"*Schweigt!*" Father Regenstrom screams. He has turned beet-red. I've never seen him so furious. "Now listen to me and listen *gut*, do you hear?" he says. "This thing, this, ah organ, is known by a variety of barnyard names, all of which are unspeakably vulgar. But you are never to look at it—except to clean it. You must never touch it—except to clean it. In fact, it were best if you did not even *think* about it—except, of course, to clean it. If you do any of these things, without the express purpose of cleaning it, it is known as the sin of masturbation or *self-abuse*. If any of you indulges in this *mortal* sin, you will not only develop a terrible complexion, but you may even go blind or suffer the terrible pangs of *dementia praecox*."

"Even if we ain't Catholic?" says Wilbur, awed.

"Even if you're not Catholic," says Father Regenstrom.

"Holy mackerel!" says Wilbur and whistles. "I got a cousin who's a schizophrenic . . . you think that he . . . ah . . ."

"God moves in mysterious ways," says Father Regenstrom.

"Gee whiz," says Wilbur.

It is a sobering revelation. We all know what *dementia praecox* is because in those monster movies set in the nineteenth century, there's always a scene in a loony bin with a bone-chilling lecture on the various diseases of the mind from some mad professor in a frock coat.

Father Regenstrom has finally managed to get our attention. "Now, children, there is another purpose to which this . . . ah . . . organ can be put. But only, and I must reiterate *only*, within the bonds of sacred matrimony, and only for the purpose of procreation. If you're not thinking of procreation while you're doing it, you will go to hell where your flesh will be ripped from your bones with red-hot pincers by terrifying demons . . . *for all eternity*! So, remember, you *must* think of procreation whilst you're doing it—only of procreation."

But what on earth is he talking about? We boys are looking somewhat bewildered by now. Father Regenstrom's obliqueness seems designed to obfuscate rather than illuminate. At last, one of the boys dares to put up his hand. Not surprisingly, it is Virgil.

"Do *what*, Father?" he asks.

"What do you mean, Virgil? You're not following my drift?"

"Well, I'm a-trying as hard as I can to understand it. You say there's a it that we ain't supposed to do less we thinking about having a baby while we doing it."

"*Jawohl*. Precisely."

"Well, would you mind telling us what the *it* is?"

"Yeah, Father," says Wilbur. "We wanna know." His thirst for knowledge has overcome his prejudice long enough for him to agree with Virgil.

"You know exactly what I mean, children! It, it, it! What could possibly be more clear?"

By now we're all clamouring to know what it is. We're beating on our desks, and the air is rent with our plaintive cries of "C'mon, Father," and "Oh, Father, please."

"I am referring to the conjugal act!" he says. But nobody knows what that means either.

As the hubbub reaches a climax, Father Regenstrom goes through a transformation as thorough as the metamorphosis of Lon Chaney into a werewolf. His hands clench and unclench. He begins to sweat. His eyes bulge in their sockets.

We show him no mercy. After all, aren't we in school to learn? And isn't Father Regenstrom here to teach? The racket gets louder. I'm surprised the headmaster doesn't come charging in with his cane. As we cry out for an answer, the priest continues to play the pen game, although by now he must surely have exhausted all permutations. The red creeps up his cheeks and reaches the tips of his ears. It's as though there's a hideous monster within him, and he's struggling to disgorge it, like a victim of possession in the throes of exorcism. A word begins to form on his lips . . . "S . . . s . . . s . . ."

"S . . . s . . . s . . ." we all chant in an ominous, primitive unison, like a tribe of Red Indians at a war dance.

At last, Father Regenstrom shrieks out at the top of his voice: "*Shkroovink!*"

Silence falls. The priest's face is racked with terrible anguish. So must Oedipus Rex have looked when he discovered that he had slain his father, swived his mother, and fathered his sisters. We wait for him to speak. And finally he says, with murderous rage in his eyes: "All right! You made me say it. You made me say that word! Jesus, Mary and Joseph and all the Saints forgive you for causing such impurity to pass my lips!" So saying, he picks up the pile of pens, flings them at us and storms out of the classroom, slamming the door melodramatically behind him.

After a moment of silence, we turn to each other.

"Shkroovink?" says Wilbur. "What the hell is he talking about?"

"Well, I'm safe," I say. "I've never shkrooved. Have you?"

"How do I know? I don't even know what it is."

"Maybe it's just his German accent," says Piet. "Maybe he meant to say something else."

"We ain't never gone find out now," says Virgil. "He round the bend."

"Stark staring bonkers," says Alastair, a diminutive English boy.

"*Dementia praecox*," says Wilbur in hushed, mantra-like tones. "I know all about it. I told you I got a cousin who's that way. He's in the Alabama State Home for the Bewildered or something. Funny, though, I never knew you could get it from accidentally touching your dick without meaning to clean it. According to my mom, he's that way because his grandpa raped his mom."

"You think that Father Regenstrom . . ." I say.

"He must have done that . . . touched it I mean. That's why he had to warn us about it," says Wilbur. "It drove him mad but he has these moments of, umm, sanity where he tries to warn the world about his horrible secret."

"Yeah, that must be it," I say.

"Must be," everyone agrees. We also agree that Father Regenstrom's early departure, ten minutes before the class is due to end, is a godsend. Ten minutes of spitballs, paper airplanes and bad jokes leave us all exhausted and happy.

As we walk over to Mrs. Vajravajah for our next encounter with the classical past, Wilbur catches up with me. He wants to remind me that I'm spending the night over at Piet's house this weekend after the *braaivleis*, and he wants to know whether I can get a ride over or whether he should send his driver. Virgil eyes all this from the sidelines, and I can see that the problem, seething below the surface, is one that must still somehow be solved if we are all to finish the school year in one piece.

"But Justin," Wilbur says as we make our way toward the banyan tree—whence the girls, with Miss Cicciolini at their head, are already walking back to the main school building in perfect formation—where Mrs. V. is already waiting in a billowing batik caftan—"but Justin, you're smart. Can you tell me what shkroovink is?"

"I haven't the faintest idea," I say, "but after Father Regenstrom's performance today, I know it's something I never want to think about as long as I live!"

33

Shkroovink
and Other S-words

Actually, it doesn't take long to figure out the meaning of Father Regenstrom's mysterious "shkroovink". All is revealed to me that very afternoon after school, when I go into the school library to take my first private Latin lesson. The library occupies three interconnected rooms on the first floor in a side wing of the school. Enormous windows look out over an inner courtyard to the main building, beyond which can be seen the tops of palm trees. It is starting to drizzle by the time I get there with my books under my arm. Father Regenstrom is ascending a stepladder as I come in, trying to change a light bulb in the library's lofty ceiling.

"Father?" I say.

"Don't talk to me!" He's tottering, and I hasten to hold the stepladder so he won't fall off. "Can't you see I'm shkroovink in a light bulb?"

"You're shkroovink in a—"

The light bulb pops up in the comic-strip balloon of my consciousness. So that's what the good father was talking about! Yet it's clear that the simple act of screwing in a light bulb cannot be the thing that destroys souls and dispatches the reprobate to the Ninth Circle of Inferno.

240

"So—it's just a metaphor, then!" I say aloud. "Screwing . . . I see." My whole life I've heard my mysterious organ referred to as an aubergine, a thing of nature. The image of a screwdriver is colder, harsher, more mechanical; truly it is a metaphor for our technophilic times. So it's all about sex after all.

What a relief! I don't think I could stand having yet another vital topic on which to expend my adolescent angst. It's bad enough dealing with the mysteries of life and death, the problem of evil, and the meaning of the universe.

"*Ach*," says the priest, as he comes down from the ladder and flips the switch, "it's Justin, the little boy who's going to England. And you need a little help in passing the entrance exam, *nicht wahr*? Latin, in particular."

"Yes, Father."

"Well, how much Latin do you know?"

"None at all . . . but I've read Ovid, Virgil and all those people. In English, I mean."

"Well, Virgil is all very well and very noble, but I don't know about Ovid. Probably shouldn't be read by little boys like you. As for Petronius . . . Horace . . . and Catullus . . . ah, Catullus. . . ."

His eyes take on a strange faraway look. I wonder whether this is some religious transport or whether it is a more earthly passion.

"Petronius? Horace? Catullus?" I ask him.

"No. No! You are not ready to have your innocent mind corrupted by such impure thoughts, cloaked though they are in the pure severity of the Latin tongue. Shall we begin? *Amo, amas, amat*."

"Yes?"

"Repeat after me."

"But what does it mean?"

"I love . . . thou lovest . . . he loves."

So we are to begin, after all, with the art of love.

After an hour's worth of love, seated at the table amongst piles of musty textbooks designed to make Malay, Indian and Burmese schoolboys into good little artificial nineteenth-century Englishmen, with Father Regenstrom droning out the many, many, many paradigms of *amo* with the overhead fan blowing listlessly and the air conditioning set on stun, watching the summer rain lash the palm trees and rattle the battened windows of the school's main building ... after an hour of *amo, amas, amat, amaveris, amabant, amabitis, amandum, amans, amabuntur* and the like, I have come to the conclusion that the Romans must never actually have practised the *ars amatoria*. Nay, rather, they were too busy conjugating to conjugate.

I attempt to ask Father Regenstrom about this. We've taken a break from *amo* and we're both eating some *khao muu daeng* out of a refrigerator reserved for members of the staff. Every morning, a local street vendor delivers these delicious packages of rice and pork wrapped up in newspaper lined with banana leaves, so the teachers can dine in exotic splendour while we children are condemned to such classic English victuals as steak-and-kidney pie and bubble-and-squeak.

Father Regenstrom adds a soupçon of chilli sauce to his pork, and I say, "But those Romans ... didn't they have a hard time ... ah ... actually *loving* if they had to spend so much time worrying about the right ending to put on the verb?"

"It was easy for them. They were a very organized people."

"But Father, love is blind. It strikes at the oddest moment. I wouldn't have thought it was particularly susceptible to this kind of organization ... you know what I mean."

"Actually, my boy, Latin is the ideal model of the universe. Every noun, adjective, participle knows its ranking and stands proudly to attention, just as, in heaven, the cherubim, seraphim, thrones, dominations, virtues, princedoms, powers, archangels and angels all stand in perfect concentric circles about the ineffable glory of God. That is why the proper language of worship is and always will be Latin. It's the only language that doesn't offend God's ears."

"I see, Father." I don't see at all, especially since I know that Homer and Euripides didn't write in Latin. "And Greek?"

"Well, the Greeks were chatterboxes, really. Their verbs are far more disorderly and chaotic than the Romans. That explains why they fell, you see."

"But didn't the Roman Empire fall, too?"

"Yes, but that was due to, ah, sodomy."

"What's that, Father?"

"There's no need to worry your mind about such abhorrent deviations."

So that is another of those awful S-words. I am acquiring quite a collection of them, what with shkroovink, sin, self-abuse and, of course, sex itself. And Father Regenstrom utters those words with so furious an effluence of phlegm that one can imagine the very *Sssssssserpent* hissing them in the Garden of Eden. These, indeed, are words of power if they can move a man of God to such inner turmoil! "Your hour is almost up," the priest says abruptly, "so tell me the Latin for 'I shall have loved' and I'll let you go for the day." The rain has cleared and I can see the driver standing in the courtyard below.

"Father," I say with all the innocence I can muster, "there was a lot I didn't understand about your little speech today. I mean . . . I mean . . . if there are so many dire consequences to this . . . this . . . you know . . . why would anyone ever want to do it?"

"Temptation, my boy. God puts it there, you know. Free will, you see. The problem of evil."

"But Father, have *you* ever done it?"

"Done what, my son?"

"You know. It."

"It?" Father Regenstrom's pallid visage is already beginning to turn the colour of a ripe papaya. "It?"

"You know. I won't make you say it. But have you?"

"Of course not. I'm a priest."

"Then how do you know it's true? I mean, if you've never done it."

"I have sinned in my heart, my son, often enough. And that can be just as bad."

"If it is, why not just do it and get it over with? At least your curiosity will have been assuaged."

243

"If you don't stop asking those silly questions, I shall be forced to apply the rod of chastisement, so kindly be quiet, unless it is to tell me what the Latin for 'I shall have loved' might be."

I polish off the last few pieces of barbecued pork and say, "Amavero."

"You devil! You clever little monkey!" says Father Regenstrom, delighted not only at my correct answer but at the fact that I seem to have let him off the hook about those dreaded S-words.

Although I have restored Piak—disguised as another Piak—to our household, I have not yet accomplished the return of our former gardener to the fold. To do so, I must first provide for Samlee. If the gardener comes back, it will surely be in his new female guise, and Samlee will be given the boot from Uncle Vit's affections, a position she now holds precariously at best. I know that my former nursemaid doesn't want to be demoted back to working for the three Fates. The only other solution, apart from having her leave the estate altogether, is to kick her upstairs.

"Yes, Samlee," I whisper to her as we ride home from school one day, "you're going to have to get yourself a fresh supply of that nine-baht love potion. It's not enough for you to be the consort of Paris. You're going to have to seduce King Priam himself."

"What do you mean? You know I get lost when you go on about the ancient Greeks. . . ."

"Well, why fool around with Sigurd when you can aim for Odin?"

"You're losing me, Khun Nuu."

"What I meant to say was, since you're losing the battle for the affections of Arjuna, it's time you looked heavenward at the throne of Indra, his father."

"Oh." She's silent for a long time. I know she must have understood the last reference. She is a big fan of those Indian costume epics on Sunday morning television.

***

On Thursday night I contrive to go over to the big house after dinner. My ostensible purpose is to invite the family patriarch to our performance of *The Most Tragical History of the Trojan War—Abridged*, the play I have concocted, which will receive its première in two weeks.

I rarely set foot in the big house. A pilgrimage to see the patriarch is a daunting undertaking. If going to see my great-grandmother is like climbing Mount Parnassus to consult the oracle, then approaching my great-uncle is akin to scaling Olympus itself and trying to get an audience with Zeus. The big house is gloomy. From the faux Corinthian columns of the façade to the floors of gold-veined marble, from the frigid antisepsis of the foyer to the reception room with its high-backed, plush armchairs with their legs carved into the paws of mythical beasts, the folding screens of black lacquer inlaid with Vietnamese mother-of-pearl, the Sawankhalok stoneware in its glass cases, the stereophonic gramophone that pipes the late Beethoven string quartets into empty rooms, the tapestries, the lamps suspended from the outstretched hands of alabaster *kinariis* with gold-chased tail-feathers and opulent bosoms . . . these artefacts are all but lost in the overwhelming vastness and gloom . . . even the music is swallowed up in the thrum of the central air conditioning.

I loiter in the foyer—the cold air makes me shiver as if I really had arrived at the foothills of Olympus—listening for where they might be. At length I hear, as from an immeasurable height, the echoing voices of ancient men and women. They must be in the upstairs sitting room, a sanctum to which I have never been admitted. Gingerly skimming the cold banister with my left hand, I mount the sweeping staircase to the stars. I hear giggling. Or is it the cackling of witches? I cannot tell.

In the sitting room, my revered grandfather who is really my great-uncle sits on a Louis Quinze divan. It is the selfsame chair that he had brought down to the dance pavilion at that ill-fated limbo rock party. The room is everything it is rumoured to be. The rugs are soft as clouds. I waft across them. They depict, in faded

Technicolor, emperors hunting pheasant, princesses listening to nightingales, and flocks of swallows, swans, eagles, doves, hawks and peacocks. Against one wall stands the armless statue of a naked woman—not the Venus de Milo, for I know well what that looks like from the boxes of Venus brand pencils that we use in school, but some other naked woman of similar build—and on the opposite wall hangs a frayed Florentine tapestry. Most of the furniture is enveloped in plastic. Crystal chandeliers hang from the ceiling. Once more I remember the rumour that this room is full of treasure abandoned by the Japanese general billeted here during the war, who had used the house as a dumping ground for all sorts of antiques pilfered from the courts and museums of Europe.

My *khun puu* is presiding over a game of *phai tong*, which is being played by several of my grandmothers—who are all seated in a circle on the floor, leaning against triangular cushions of neon pink silk. They are giggling and cackling over the game, discarding and drawing the slender green cards with abandon.

"*Phong!*" says the senior wife, indicating that she can make three of a kind and cut the other wives out of their turn.

"I'm so sorry, Elder Sister," says the number three wife, "but that card's my *tua keng*, which means that I can go out with *thalok ha tua*, and besides, I have the *mong!*"

"On the contrary, dear *Khun Phiis*," says. a third lady whom I don't recognize—doubtless one of their friends—"I'm afraid *I've* won on that card—*paed tua.*"

"Too many jokers! That's the trouble, Kitten," my grandmother number one protests. "Next round let's not have so many wild cards. One might actually get a chance to win fair and square, the old-fashioned way."

Khun Kitten says, "That'll be—um—three thousand, four hundred and twelve baht." She gathers up a heap of poker chips.

At length the women see me. "Good heavens," says grandmother number one. "It's Little Frog . . . how extraordinary to see you here. Come and give your grandmothers all a kiss, and don't forget to *kraab* nicely to Grandma Kitten, my maternal second cousin."

I perform the requisite kisses and obeisances while the ladies *ooh* and *aah* dotingly. My grandfather looks on.

"But Grandmothers," I ask them, "isn't gambling illegal?"

"Ah, such a refined sensibility," says grandmother number three (number two has "gone to the country"—indefinitely, it seems), "to worry about the law and other such matters. Do you think he'll be a lawyer? But I hear he's a poet."

"Ah, Little Frog, that law against gambling is only for the poor," says grandmother number one. "Those unfortunate creatures would spend what little they had and squander their winnings on liquor and loose women if they were allowed to gamble! That law's not for *us*, you know."

"Not many laws are," says my grandfather, chuckling. "But there ought to be a law against husbands having to pay their wives' gambling debts. . . ."

"Khun Puu! I've brought you a copy of my play."

"Jolly good," says the patriarch in English, although he doesn't deign to look at it. "Come and sit next to me on the divan, and we'll discuss the relative merits of your grandmothers. Mother thinks the world of you, you know," he adds, referring to my bedridden oracle, as I slide into place beside him. He puts his arm around my shoulder and whispers in my ear, so that the women can't hear him, "Have you had any, young man?"

"Any what, Grandfather?" And then I manage to intuit that it is the S-word he's talking about. "I'm afraid I'm still working on it. But Father Regenstrom told me I'd go to hell."

"Bloody Catholics."

"But Grandfather . . . what about you? Wouldn't it be nice if you . . . I mean . . . something a little younger?"

"So kind of you to be concerned for me, young man! Yes, I do still occasionally get it up, you know. Frightful nuisance, really. Do you have anyone in mind?"

"Well, do you know of a woman named Samlee? She's one of the . . . ah . . . maids in this house, and—"

"Oh, Vit's plaything! I never play with my children's toys."

247

"But Grandfather, listen, listen! I'm going to have to tell this in your ear. You see, I'm not entirely sure that—"

My grandfather inclines his head, and I tell him everything I saw that awesome night, so many moons ago, under the dinner table at the funeral of that worthy whose name I never managed to discover . . . I tell him all about Uncle Vit, publicly discoursing on the wonders of the female form, whilst simultaneously enjoying secret and intimate knowledge of such a form . . . I describe the puffing of my former nursemaid's cheeks, the slithering, darting movements of her tongue—poetic licence lending many unremembered details to the telling—until I finally touch upon the set of false teeth, resting in the spittoon, the selfsame teeth with which I began this tale.

At the mention of which, my grandfather—that is to say greatuncle—begins to laugh uproariously, and to slap his hands against the cushions so vigorously that he manages to cause a rip in the fivehundred-year-old upholstery.

34

Melpomene

A few days later, I am on my way to school, and Samlee is, as usual "sitting in the front seat next to the driver. I've come to the conclusion that my hints to my great-uncle are probably to no avail, and that, as Cupid, I'm a failure. It's time to stop working for Aphrodite, goddess of love, and return once more to the service of Melpomene, the Muse of Tragedy.

After all, we're actually going to be putting on that play which I have been writing, not entirely alone as I have had ample help from the likes of Euripides, Homer, Aeschylus, Shakespeare and others, whose verses I have liberally pilfered. This morning, my nose buried in one of the thin blue notebooks blazoned with the insignia of the Scola Britannica in which I've been composing my opus, I'm not particularly disposed to listen to anyone's chatter save that of the Muse herself.

It takes me a while to notice that Samlee is trying to attract my attention, and it's only when I feel the Mercedes slowing down in order to make the hair-raising turn into the *soi* of the school that I realize she has been looking back at me and prodding my arm with a well-manicured fingernail.

"Master Little Frog, Master Little Frog—" she's saying.

But my mind is with the topless towers of Ilium.

"I was summoned to the big house last night by the *khun phra*," she tells me. "And do you know what he asked me to do?"

I think of Helen of Troy, kneeling under the banquet table at Menelaus's wedding feast, her golden tresses trailing over spittoons and spiralling mosquito incense.

"I don't know what he asked you to do, Samlee," I say, "but I'm sure you did it very well indeed."

"The thing is, I don't know how he could have known that I was able to do what I did, and I was wondering . . . well, Khun Nuu, you're small and inconspicuous, and I was just wondering whether you might have slipped under the table at that funeral banquet, you know, the one where your chameleon, well, succumbed to his karma."

We're right at the school gates now, and I realize that Samlee wants me to admit that I know all about her secret talents—that I told the familial patriarch about them in order to expedite her transfer to the big house. Should I really admit to this knowledge? All I do is smile enigmatically.

"All I can say," says Samlee, "is that if you're *not* the one who knows these things, it must be some kind of ghost, some mischievous little sprite who hides in the cracks of walls and the sills of windows and hears everything that goes on. . . ."

"That does seem to be a possibility," I say, half-in, half-out of my classical reverie.

"Perhaps it's even the ghost of that chameleon of yours," she says. "After all, it is, in its own small way, a *phii tai hong*—the spirit of someone who has died a violent death and who is doomed to stalk the earth until it is exorcised. . . ."

"I don't think that Homer is the haunting type," I say, though I know that he has troubled my dreams.

"Yet there are all these mysterious phenomena that must have supernatural explanations . . . why, for example, should I find one of your sandals, Khun Nuu, sitting on the stoop of the *ajarn* spirit doctor's house, weeks *before* I took you to see him? Wasn't that some kind of premonition?" Her expression is so inscrutable that I can't tell if she's toying with me or whether she really believes that my dead chameleon engineered an apparition of my sandal just to warn her of some impending fate.

I'm a little shocked that the sandal has come back to haunt me at this late date. Later, of course, I will come to realize that everything in the universe is connected to everything else, that all the gods are one, that every macrocosm is a microcosm of another macrocosm—and so on. But at this stage, I am merely mystified.

"Samlee," I say, "whether I or a dead reptile caused it to happen, it *was* what you wanted . . . wasn't it?"

"I don't know," she says. "Actually, I'm frightened. I don't want to become like a *dok mai fai*—a fire flower, shot into the sky with a tremendous bang, bursting into beauty for a moment, then fading into nothing. And I certainly don't want to aim beyond my *vasana*."

"Don't worry about your *vasana*, Samlee," I say. "You have no control over fate, so you might as well enjoy what it brings while you can."

"Oh, Khun Nuu, what a wise thing to say! Why, thank you. . . ."

Pearls of wisdom are, of course, the province of great poets. I've devoured many poets in the course of producing *The Trojan War*. Swallowed them whole, in fact, without bothering to chew them properly. In fact, it might even be said that I'm suffering from poetic indigestion at the moment, and any *bons mots* that escape me are but the poetical equivalent of farting.

Mrs. Vajravajah has taken over our art class as well as our literature class, and we're putting art to the service of literature by using the time to build the sets and make the costumes for the play.

The art class takes place on the front lawn, where there's a thatched pavilion with benches, that doubles as the lower forms' refectory. Mrs. V. has been teaching us how to make masks. You see, I've written in a role for the three Fates—my aunts will never realize it's in their honour—but since there are fewer than twenty children in the entire class, we can't really spare three girls. There will therefore be one girl with three masks protruding from various neck holes in a voluminous black satin robe.

To make the masks, we've prepared a clay mould, sculpted to the approximate facial measurements of Uma Bligh, the Anglo-Indian daughter of a toy mogul whose logo appears on packets of plastic Roman soldiers and rubber dinosaurs that can be purchased for five baht or so in Pratunam. Uma is a haughty girl and eminently suited to the role of all three Fates.

We have prepared a bucket full of papier mâché, made mostly from the tissue-thin international edition of *The Times*, which arrives at the school library thrice weekly from England. *The Times* has been shredded, soaked, and various other ingredients added, and the bucket has been sitting in our upstairs classroom for about a week while we made Uma's masks.

The clay mask moulds are dry now. I haven't been directly involved with making them. Somehow the sight of piles of mud being pounded and shaped by little hands doesn't appeal to me. Maybe I just don't feel that poets should get their hands dirty. Now that they are ready, I see that they don't look anything like the masks of classical tragedy. Instead, they are as eccentric as my classmates. The one created by Wilbur and Piet resembles breakfast at Virgil's—it looks like a stack of blueberry pancakes with two sunny-side-up eggs on top. Uma and Griselda have been working on one together; it looks like a cross between a Barbie doll and a stegosaurus.

The third Fate mask was made by Mrs. V. herself. I love to watch her hands fleshing out the soft clay. It is, it occurs to me now that the mould has been baked by the sun, a portrait. In fact, it's the spitting image of Jessica O'Fleary, a girl who is not, of course, in our class, since she's older than us. I realize that Mrs. V. does teach other classes, does share her time with others than ourselves. This causes me a moment of pain. It also makes me think about how Jessica seems so cool to me now. She'll talk to me, but she won't listen. After school, sitting in the library with my Ovid, I hear her voice from across the atrium, and I sigh, but that is as close as we ever get now.

Virgil and I are making the Ionic columns for our stage. Mrs. V. has carefully explained to us that the Trojan War probably occurred in about 1180 BC, when they didn't actually have Ionic columns, but she has assured us that Ionic columns are true to the spirit, if not the letter, of the time of legends.

This is how we make them: first we take four pieces of poster board, and we Sellotape them together to form a single sheet. Then we roll this mega-sheet into column shape and use staples to hold it together. We glue the column on to a base, which usually consists of a soap or beer carton. The scroll is the cleverest thing of all. It's a long strip of cardboard, which we roll up at both ends, and then we push the middle of it down the hole at the top of the column. Having constructed this, we paint the column in grey poster colour, suggesting the flutings with thin stripes of black. They don't look at all bad. Over the past week, we have constructed twenty-nine such columns. Our plan is to move them around to suggest different locations. Other children are working on the thousand ships—well, actually, there's only one: an enormous cardboard façade on one side of a long trellis table, on which the passengers will squat as they sail to Troy. The sea will be represented by crêpe paper streamers, stretched across the stage and jiggled by any actors that aren't on stage at that particular time.

Oh, and the Trojan horse—what a far cry it is from the spectacular engine of my imagination, eerie, with pupilless implacable eyes that are windows for the Grecian hordes, groaning and clanking as it is dragged up the cracked marble steps of the ruined house by thousands of citizens, ignorant of impending doom! It, too, has been reduced to a cardboard cut-out. It is crudely drawn. I think its wheels must have been the work of Piet and Wilbur, for they resemble blueberry pancakes too. Its head is as much like that of a dog, giraffe or rhinoceros as of the noble horse. Unaccountably, it has long, curly eyelashes, the work of Michiko, daughter of a Mitsubishi executive, whose style is influenced by Japanese cartoons.

"Oh, Justin and Virgil," says Mrs. V., "I do think we have enough columns now. We're not building the Parthenon."

The papier mâché, after a week of sitting in the bucket, has begun to go bad. In the heat, the sour odour just sits in the air and won't be blown away. We're all choking and retching. Only Mrs. V. appears unfazed. "Well," she says, "it does smell awfully bad, doesn't it? But after the papier mâché has been spread over the mask moulds, and it's allowed to dry out, it won't smell at all. Then we'll paint them, and lacquer them, and—"

The class backs away from her. Some move out of the shelter of the pavilion into the harsh sunlight. Others seem to he hiding behind the Trojan horse. I whirl round and see that Griselda and Virgil have managed to scoot up a tree.

And so it is that Mrs. V. turns her limpid brown eyes toward me.

"Umm," I say, "I don't really want to touch that stuff."

"Why not?" she says. "It *will* wash off. You're not going to be forced to wear that smell for the rest of your life."

"But even so, Mrs. V.—I mean, I've already written the play. Do I have to stick my hands in *that*, too?"

"Yes," says Mrs. V.

"But no one else is willing to do it!" I say, almost in tears.

"Well, but that is precisely my point," she says. "You're the one who has written the play—though I must say you've had a lot of help from the dead—and you're the one who must see it through to the bitter end. You, and only you, must soil your hands when no one else is prepared to. You above all must not shrink from the toil, the pain, the dirt of your art. You see, you can't expect your head to touch heaven if your feet aren't firmly planted in hell."

Suddenly—I don't know if it's because the sweltering sun has caused the very air to swim around us—it seems to me that inside Mrs. V., as she speaks to me so earnestly, her shapeless caftan soaked with sweat, there is a creature of pure spirit. The sunlight casts a halo about her hair. I see, at her shoulders, the shadowy outline of a pair of downy wings. Is that a clipboard in her hand, or is it a lyre? Suddenly I know who it is who has spoken these words to me, reminding me of my proper *dharma*. . . .

"Melpomene," I say softly, calling this spirit by the name of the Muse of Tragedy.

She seems to smile, seems to be about to strike a chord upon her four-stringed lyre. She is drenched in sunlight. She has become as translucent as a ghost. . . .

"Yes," Mrs. V. says dreamily, but the vision fades before I can truly know whether I have merely been dreaming, glassy-eyed, half-suffocating from the stench of putrefying papier mâché.

35

The Play's the Thing

I throw myself wholeheartedly into dirtying my hands. I dive into the stinking glop. Mrs. V. is right. To become an artist, I have to have the courage to go all the way . . . to face the inner darkness . . . even in the shape of a pail of rotting papier mâché.

It is a time of almost unbearable excitement as the première approaches. I have constructed a shrine in the ruined house where I have set up a statue of Zeus—well, it was the cover of *Every Child's Book of the Greek Myths* before I cut it up and glued it to the carton, but in any case I feel that I have outgrown any book whose titles begin with the words "Every Child's".

I pray to the shrine each evening. After all, if I am to transmit the sacred story to a new, modern audience, which does not know Homer from Agamemnon even though it can easily distinguish the mashed potato from the twist, which can argue the relative merits of Elvis and Cliff Richard while completely ignorant of the difference between Sophocles and Aeschylus, I must prove worthy of the task. In order to purify myself, taking a leaf from the holy writ of Father Regenstrom, I have therefore refrained, for the past two weeks, from touching, or even thinking about, my aubergine.

Perhaps I've gone a little too far, though, because I haven't even attempted to clean it (the one exemption in the priest's stern interdiction), and now I suspect it's starting to reek, though I have not of course (in the interest of purity) ventured to sniff it.

On the morning of the performance, however—getting up at five because, for some ungodly reason, the play has been scheduled for seven-thirty in the morning—I am so excited that, while standing in the tub and having warm water poured over me from a silver bathing-bowl, I accidentally do lean down and scrub the offending vegetable with the sponge that is handed to me.

All at once I am consumed with guilt. I fling the soapy sponge across the bathroom. At that moment, Piak comes in bearing a fresh pail of hot water from the kitchens. The sponge flies across his path, he slips, the maid who is administering the aspergation yelps as the hot water floods the bathroom and begins hopping about. Her anguished cries bring forth Aunt Nit-nit, the only one of the three Fates not too busy with her coiffure to come and see what the matter is. On such occasions—new plays, funeral dinners and so forth—it seems *de rigueur* to turn my morning ablutions into a spectator sport. "Good heavens," Aunt Nit-nit exclaims. "What on earth is going on?" She stands in the doorway, uncomprehending.

"It's appalling, Aunt Nit-nit!" I exclaim. "Isn't it time there was some respect for a man's natural modesty around here? I'm not a circus animal, you know."

"Well, I never. You've never objected to being bathed before. It's not everyone who can afford the luxury of being bathed by two or three attendants. . . ."

"I've never objected before," I say, "because it wouldn't have done any good before."

"I suppose you're right," Aunt Nit-nit says. "Well, I suppose, this being a very special occasion, we can trust you to perform your own toilet, but how are we to know, each time, if you're actually getting clean? There's got to be . . . oh, what do the Americans call it . . . a system of checks and balances."

The maid, meanwhile, is still hopping around.

"You can go now, Oi," says Aunt Nit-nit. "And Piak, I think you'd better put on some clean clothes. We shall want you along for the spectacle. Master Little Frog may need assistance carrying all of his . . . ah, Thespian paraphernalia."

"Good God, Aunt Nit-nit, I can't bring servants to school . . . it's awfully un-British."

"My dear Little Frog," says Aunt Nit-nit, "you really do have some quaint notions about the British."

"Well," I say huffily, as I drape a towel around myself, "democracy, you know. Fair play. The underdog, that sort of thing."

"Is that so? Well, let me tell you, the only reason they don't bring servants to school is that they can't afford as many as we can. When servants are cheap—and when the entire country belongs to them, as in India—they bring three or four. They even have a special servant for wiping their arses."

"Oh, nonsense, Aunt Nit-nit." How unlike her to cast aspersions upon my private land of myth! Although there are so many holes now in my myth of England that I half believe her.

In any case, the entire family—faithful retainers and all—are coming to the play whether I want them to or not. A caravan consisting of the Studebaker and a couple of Mercedes from the main house, bearing various familial elders, has already begun to line up at the gate. Only Uncle Vit is absent. Presumably he is already off at the clinic, hard at work probing the minutiae of the female anatomy. "He's promised to be by later," Aunt Nit-nit tells me, "assuming he can get away."

The Scola Britannica, as I have said before, was once the home of a prominent film star. While it does not possess a full-sized theatre, there is a large hall at one end of which is a raised inner room, perhaps a dining area. It has been relatively easy to transform this alcove into a stage, especially since it has a room off to one side (and stairs leading down to the kitchen), which can serve as a dressing room and as the entrances and exits of the performers.

The play begins with myself dressed in my robes of poesy, which are actually some old curtains stolen from a disused room of the ruined house. I have a lyre in my hand, which is actually a heart-shaped strawberry shortcake tin across which rubber bands have been stretched. I am seated on a stool and have a long white beard made of cotton wool that has been glued to a gauze pad borrowed from the school surgery.

Being Homer, I am supposed to be blind. I wear a sort of blindfold over my eyes, but the cloth is sheer enough to allow me to see pretty clearly.

I survey the audience with the *hauteur* proper to a legendary, indeed semi-divine, figure. Raising an eyebrow, I bring my plectrum down upon the first of the four rubber bands. It snaps with a resounding twang, and the entire apparatus flies across the stage and lands somewhere in the audience with a kind of *kerplunk*. A gasp arises from the assembled throng. I cannot lose my cool, for scattered among the masses of adoring parents and reproving teachers are many members of my family.

I begin to recite the following lines of workmanlike, if uninspiring, verse:

> *Ye puny mortals sitting down below,*
> *Know ye that I, blind Homer, prince of poets,*
> *Am come to relate a tale as old as time.*
> *Listen, ye mortals! Listen now, and learn*
> *Of Helen, beautifullest of womankind,*
> *Of Agamemnon, mighty general,*
> *Of proud Achilles and his friend Patroclus,*
> *Of Hector, Priam and lots of other people,*
> *Whom I shan't name for fear of running out*
> *Of envious and calumniating Time.*

I am particularly proud of this last line, coming as it does straight out of Ulysses's famous speech in *Troilus and Cressida*, which I am sure no one has read save myself.

By the time I reach the dithyrambic conclusion of my prologue, I am apoplectic with passion. This is partly because I am deeply stirred by the music of my words (and others') and partly because, in the heat of my declamation, my saliva and sweat have begun to dissolve the glue that holds my cotton beard to its frame of surgical gauze, and I have been snowing steadily on to the floorboards. Now, as I finish my speech, I fling my arms wide in a sort of crucified gesture, and the rest of the beard goes flying into the audience.

Unlike the lyre with its sordid *kerplunk*, the beard makes no noise at all. It simply vanishes.

Startled, I gaze at my public. My great-uncle is beaming. Dr. Richardson sits between Aunt Nit-nit and Aunt Noi-noi, black bag at his feet, doubtless in readiness to stanch the carnage of war. Piak, dressed in a white shirt and khaki shorts, looks like an ordinary Thai schoolboy and betrays no aura of servitude. He looks rather bored, actually; his English is not up to these lofty sentiments.

To my amazement, my great-grandmother is also there. Or is she? I think I see her, a shadowy form among the drapes of the back part of the hall. I see the glint of a wheelchair's spokes. On her shoulder, a small reptilian thing slithers back and forth. . . . Is this a vision? Or is it my imagination? I know that my great-grandmother cannot easily rise from her bed any more. . . .

Next up is the god Apollo, speaker of truth. Apollo is played by golden-haired Wilbur. Wilbur has been excluded from the role of Menelaus for fear of a repeat of the lynching scene in the banyan grove. Since no one wants to kick him and Piet off the play, they have simply been kicked upstairs to Olympus. Later, Piet will appear as Zeus.

In his vanity, Wilbur has asked to play the role of the god entirely in the nude, "like one of them ancient statues." In the interests of modesty, however, he appears in a swimsuit. He carries a bow, has a quiver slung across his back, and has oiled himself with coconut oil so that he gleams as he stands in the spotlight, flexing his incipient muscles. His hair is Brylcreemed into a state of molecular stasis, and his Elvis-like forelock never so much as quivers.

He says: "I am Apollo!"

Then he hems and haws for a long moment, until Mrs. V., sitting in the wings as prompter, murmurs, "come from high Olympus," enabling him to continue with a second prologue. I got this idea from Shaw's *Caesar* and *Cleopatra*, which embarks on an endless succession of prologues, like the seven veils of Salome, before finally disclosing the meat of the matter.

The audience fidgets. I hear a few coughs. I'm afraid that, beautiful as Wilbur is, he isn't entirely convincing as the omniscient emissary of heaven. He can't remember his lines, though his only function is to introduce the beauteous Helen of Troy, languishing loveless in the palace of Menelaus and waiting for Paris to come and abduct her.

Eventually, however, Wilbur does reach his climactic lines:

> *And here is Helen, daughter of thund'ring Zeus,*
> *Hatched from the selfsame egg from which sprang Castor,*
> *Clytemnestra and great Polydeuces,*
> *Launching a thousand ships with every glance*
> *From those fair eyes filled with insouciance.*

This is all very well, but Helen, slated to pop up between two of the flimsy Ionic columns that line the set, refuses to show up, and Apollo can't leave the stage until she does.

At length, realizing that flexing his way around the proscenium will no longer suffice to entertain the crowd, Wilbur resorts to improvisation:

> *Ah, Helen, Helen, wherefore art thou Helen?*

Like most Americans, he doesn't seem to know that the word "wherefore" doesn't mean where. Still, it's a creditable stopgap. But Griselda still doesn't appear. Watching from the wings, next to Mrs. Vajravajah's stool, I am quietly going mad. The première will be ruined!

I shall go seek the beauteous Helena.

So saying, Apollo tramps off the stage, tosses his bow and quiver into the shadows, and cries out to me, "Jeepers, Justin, where the hell do you think she is?"

The natives are getting restless. Out there, in the semi-darkness that could well be a jungle, we hear ominous whisperings of "rhubarb, rhubarb".

"You'd better get back out there, Wilbur," I say. "Silence is deadly."

Wilbur nods. He storms back out on stage. "Friends, Romans and countrymen," he says, "did you ever hear the one about—"

At that moment, we hear frantic footsteps from the stairwell outside the hall. The door is flung open and there is Griselda, her hair in a pseudo-Hellenic bouffant, her teeth gleaming with metallic architecture, her drapery cascading down her slender body in enticing disarray.

"Methinks," announces Wilbur portentously, "the beauteous one was stuck in traffic!"

Wild applause as Helen flounces on to the stage, blowing kisses to the audience and bowing. We are to be a success after all—half the audience seems to believe that the whole thing was intentional—that it's a bow to Pirandello and Brecht.

Several people have apparently been waiting outside to get in. They take advantage of the lull to try to worm their way into the auditorium. There's some slipping, apologizing and tripping going on . . . and I suddenly notice that Uncle Vit is among the latecomers. Instead of his usual untidiness, he is dressed in a spiffy suit, and he is accompanied by a ravishingly beautiful woman, dressed to the teeth in a theatregoing outfit of Thai silk, a daringly low-cut top, a chic pageboy hairdo, and a string of Mikimoto pearls. To my astonishment, I recognize Busaba, former gardener and extremely masculine father of—

"Mother!" A cry rings out across the hall.

"Piak! Is that you, my son?" Busaba says in liltingly modulated tones. "Can it really be true that my karma has caused you to be returned to me, after I callously abandoned you on the temple steps so many long years ago?"

Piak gets up and runs into her arms. Their joyous sobbing is so convincing that even I, who knows the truth, am profoundly moved. Well—I have envisaged staging a scene like this, to be sure, and I have thoroughly coached Piak on what to say when I finally introduce his father into the household, but . . . but . . . I certainly didn't intend to have the Trojan War upstaged by this maudlin display of soap-operatic emotions!

Everyone's talking at once now. Mrs. V. motions us to continue the play. The show must, of course, go on, and presently it does. But, as I peer out at the audience from behind the curtain, I see that my aunts, uncles and grandparents are only watching the performance with half an eye, so drawn are they to the drama of our family circle. . . .

36

The World
Under Piet's Bed

In some ways, the play is a tremendous success. We collect a total of 3,423 baht, which we donate to the Red Cross, appropriately enough since so many buckets of gore have been spilt during the morning's performance. All day, at school, people can talk of little else, and I gradually come to realize that the dramatic revelations about Piak, his mother and my uncle have not been quite as embarrassing as I thought they were. For one thing, not that many people at the Scola Britannica can speak Thai. For another, it is Friday, and the thoughts of all my companions are of the weekend.

As are mine. For this is the afternoon of the long-awaited *braaivleis* at the van Helsings' house. I am to spend the entire weekend there. My three aunts have decided to go to our seaside estate in Hua Hin, taking many of the household staff with them. It is my first protracted stay at a place over which my family has absolutely no influence; for even when I've stayed at Virgil's house, the land I stood on still belonged to my family. I arrive an hour early and spend an awkward thirty minutes strolling around the grounds, wondering when I shall be noticed.

Although it was half an hour's journey from our estate to this one, we have actually only traversed a few *sois*; we are still somewhere in the labyrinthine backstreets of Bangkapi. The house it-self is athwart an artificial hillock fringed with palms. Around it, a close-cut lawn stretches all the way out to a wall of conglomerate, with a watchtower by the gate. Admitted by the guard at the tower, I have been wandering the gardens. There is no one in sight, not even a gardener, although the rose bushes are perfectly trimmed, and a row of hedges, spiralling around the hill, sculpted into the shapes of *apsaras* and *garudas*, is immaculately maintained.

The day's rain was ending as I left my house. Now the afternoon air smells of the dank *klong* moisture, and the grass is slick, lapping up the emerging sun. I try to stay on the stepping stones, because I don't want to get mud on my shoes. I don't know whether these are the sort of people who wear shoes in the house. I am also carrying an overnight bag full of clothes—too many clothes—as well as an assortment of hit singles, comics and Penguin Classics. I am dressed completely in white, and the stepping stones are slippery. I am worried that even a single speck of mud will mar my sartorial splen-dour beyond redemption.

My circumambulation is almost complete when the aroma of food brings me to my senses. It appears to be wafting from a low wooden pavilion at the foot of the hill, a heady and mouth-water-ing odour of sizzling beef and charcoal. I also hear voices. Or one voice at least, the mumbling of an ancient man with a straggly white beard and matching suit, who sits in a rattan armchair behind a veil of smoke.

He squints, seems to make me out, and then yells at me: "Turn the meat over, you bloody kaffir, before I get out me *sjambok* and wallop you with it!"

"I'm afraid I don't know quite what you mean, sir," I say, ap-proaching with trepidation.

"Get a move on, boy!" he roars. "Hop to it."

I decide that probably the best thing to do is to obey. I scramble over to the barbecue, where enormous steaks are merrily blackening · in the flames. A pair of tongs hangs beside them, and I use it to flip them over. But however fast I move, I can't seem to stem the flood

265

of the old man's imprecations. Don't these people have any servants? I think. Surely they don't expect their house guests to do all the housework. . . .

Suddenly I see Piet ambling downhill from the house. "What the hell are you doing cooking steaks, Justin?" he asks me.

I jerk my hand back at the old man.

"Bloody kaffirs," he mutters.

Piet comes up to me and takes the tongs out of my hand. "Oupa," he says, "wake up. The war's over, and we're in Bangkok, not the Transvaal . . . and there aren't any kaffirs here anyway." Piet turns to me. "Blind as a bat," he whispers, "and his mind's half gone. Brain damage, you know. Hole in his head during the Boer War."

"It's quite all right," I say, wondering whether Boer was one of the disputed zones of Vietnam, but I am too polite to ask.

"You don't talk like one anyway," says Piet's grandfather. "Should've known, really. Usually I can tell a bloody *rooinek* a mile away."

"He's a Thai, Oupa, not a *rooinek*."

"Thank God. The only good *rooinek* is a dead *rooinek*."

"What's a *rooinek*?"

"It's hard to explain," Piet tells me. "It's sort of an Englishman, but it's really a South African, only it's not an Afrikaner, you see. Come on, you've got soot all over your face. Come upstairs, and I'll show you around. We don't have to hang around with old farts all afternoon, do we?"

"I'm sorry about my grandfather," says Piet as we climb the marble staircase with its gilded balustrade, "Boer War, you know. Got a silver plate over his skull. He was only seventeen."

"What's the borewore?" I ask him. We turn into his room, which is a veritable palace. A maid in a black uniform with a frilly white apron is dusting furiously. A phonograph is playing "Johnny Angel" very loudly in a corner of the room. At the same time, a radio on the dressing table is blaring out a Thai soap opera, to which the maid listens raptly as she dusts.

"What's the Boer War?" Piet says. "I don't know. Something all the *really* old people sit around reminiscing about over endless shots of booze. The English were putting us in concentration camps . . . I've no idea why . . . maybe they were trying to liberate our kaffirs."

"Oh, like the American Civil War?"

"Nothing of the sort!" Piet growls. "We built that country from nothing and they were bloody well trying to tell us what to do!"

"Why do you go to a British school if they've been so horrid to your people?" I say.

He reddens with fury, and I realize that this must be a touchy subject.

Piet's room is Napoleonic in its splendour. It has a four-poster bed, a delightfully frigid air conditioner, a magnificent wall-to-wall mirror, floors of pink-veined grey marble and many other appurtenances of luxury. An HO-scale Märklin electric steam locomotive puffs its way around the bed, now and then turning and ducking under the crooked overhang of the eiderdown.

"What a splendid train!" I say.

"Come on. I'll show you something."

We crouch down on the floor. He takes a flashlight from the ottoman, lifts up the downy covering from his bed and shines the light into the dimness beneath it. We stick our faces down there and there's a whole world under Piet's bed. There are shops, houses, curving streets, a church, a park with evergreens and a vine-draped gazebo in which stands a weathered stone statue of a Roman general. Tiny cars are parked along the alleys. There's a pub with a miniature banner depicting a boar's head. Beside the train station, there's a newsstand on which one can actually read the name's of some of the publications: *Life, Time, Newsweek* and *Health & Efficiency*, which seems to be all about nude ladies.

"It's absolutely super," I say. "Where can one buy such a . . . such a spectacle?"

"Buy?" says Piet. "I made it."

"It's . . . it's beautiful," I say. It is hard to equate this artistry with the vicious youth who ganged up with Wilbur on my friend Virgil.

"That lettering, those little spatters of weathering on the walls of the pub

"I used a toothpick," Piet says.

"What do you call it?"

"I call it the world's forgotten corner, the undiscovered country, the unknown city," Piet says. "You see, I'm creative too, you know. When it comes to my hands, that is. I can't make the words dance, the way you can."

I know my words dance, but mostly they dance to a borrowed tune.

"But why . . . why do you keep it under your bed?" I ask him as the locomotive whizzes past my eyes and makes me blink. "Wouldn't you want a thing like this to be seen by everyone?"

"Not really, Justin. I'm not a show-off, you see. I just like to lie in bed at night and think that I'm floating over the whole world that I've created."

"Oh, sort of like God," I say.

"Sort of," Piet says, "but secretly." Then, abruptly, he pulls me up. "Come on," he says, "you can help me with something I'm making."

He drags me into a back room. It's a closet actually, without windows, but with the air conditioning wafting in from the bedroom it's really very comfortable. Despite this, Piet shuts the closet door and flicks on a naked hanging light bulb. I look around. The place is as messy as the room outside is immaculate, and it takes only a few minutes to start steaming up. Nevertheless, it is fascinating. There is a desk covered with tiny figures, no taller than a knuckle. There are half-finished houses painstakingly put together from matchstick-sized pieces of balsa wood. There are plastic boxcars, a locomotive that has been dissected and splayed open like a frog in a laboratory and on the wall a photograph of Ho Chi Minh that has been used as a dartboard, the face almost obliterated by a proliferation of little black holes. There is an overwhelming smell of glue; because there's no ventilation, it's almost impossible to breathe. A row of model paint jars lines one shelf; almost every conceivable colour is there.

"Look," Piet says, "here's what I'm building at the moment. . . ." He holds up a nondescript-looking building with a glass front. Sitting just inside the window is a nude woman about an inch high. "It used to have clothes," he says, "well, a bikini, at any rate—but I scraped it off with a razor blade and painted it pink. Look! I did the nipples with a needle dipped in alizarin crimson. . . ."

"But what is it?" I say.

"It's the first building in the town's red-light district, of course— that woman is, well, you know, a *hoer*." He leers.

"I see," I say without seeing. He looks at me, and I see that he is expecting me, too, to leer and that the conversation cannot continue until I have done so. I wrinkle my face into a passable imitation of his, he nods approvingly, and we go on talking as he pulls another nude figurine out of an old pencil box. "You want to do the nipples on this one?" he says, handing me the figure, a needle and the pot of paint. It is clear that I am being bestowed an honour of the first magnitude.

Gingerly, I take the thing in my hand. I dip the needle in the paint and—with almost as much anxiety as though I were jabbing my own thumb—I pinpoint the nude woman's aureole with a fleck of dark red. He watches with the excitement of a mother hen waiting for her chick to hatch.

"Brilliant!" he says. He snatches it from me and, with a toothpick dipped in glue, moves it into place behind the first nude woman. Now there are two of them, beckoning like sirens to any luckless sailor who might chance by.

Piet then holds the toothpick to his nose and takes a deep and appreciative sniff. "Care for some?" he says, proffering the toothpick as though it were a rare champagne. We squat among old clothes and musty magazines.

"Don't mind if I do," I say, wondering whether this is some Afrikaner ritual of manhood, like becoming blood-brothers. The whiff sends me reeling. My head swims. I can't prevent a semi-strangulated *eeeeeaugh* from escaping my lips.

Piet tosses the toothpick into the wastebasket, and this time he's holding up the entire tube. "Try this," he says, and leers once more. I try it. He tries it. Soon we're passing the tube back and forth, giggling like seven-year-old girls.

"That newsstand," I'm opining between hits of glue, "is the most remarkable thing I've ever seen. *Health & Efficiency* indeed! However did you come up with such a name for a magazine?"

"I didn't," he says indignantly. "There really is a magazine called *Health & Efficiency* that's full of pictures of naked women—it's a nudist magazine."

"Prove it."

Piet fumbles under a huge stack of *Mad* magazines and pulls one out triumphantly. He thrusts it into my hands. To my amazement, I realize that the tiny thing on the newsstand in the world beneath the bed is a precise copy in miniature of what I'm holding in my hands. The contents are even more amazing, for these are no idealized goddesses like those one sees when stealing a glance at *Playboy* in the dentist's office. These are ordinary people of all sexes and ages, many of them obscenely fat, cavorting on beaches and disporting themselves in woods *au naturel* and not a single embarrassed expression among them. They exude a kind of militant blandness that is less than arousing.

"Pretty thrilling?" says Piet. "Doesn't it make you just want to take your own clothes off?"

"Well . . . not particularly."

"Tell me . . . is it true that you people have smaller *things* than we whites do?"

"I wouldn't know." My mind is a blur from the glue. "What things do you mean?"

"You know."

"I suppose I do. But you know we're not supposed to even look at—"

"Yes," says Piet, "but I'm curious. In fact, I'll be happy to show you mine if you—"

At that moment, however, the closet door bursts open, and we hear an all too familiar voice. "Boyth! boyth! I jutht had a feeling I'd find you in here . . . and ath a doctor'th daughter, I bloody well know what you're up to!"

"Griselda!" I exclaim, as the face of Griselda Richardson looms into view, the metalwork of her laughing mouth glittering with reflected sunlight.

37

War Stories

Piet seems flustered for a moment as Griselda, arms akimbo, stands in the doorway like an avenging fury. Then she starts to giggle, and we giggle with her, until finally, when she wrests the *Health & Efficiency* away from us and begins poring over the pictures, we are reduced to helpless laughter, assisted, no doubt, by the glue whose fragrance still hangs in the air. Although Griselda has made some preliminary noises about "playing doctor", the plan is abandoned. We are too busy giggling to think of anything so serious as playing a game.

"We'd better get back downthtairs," she says at last. "People will wonder about uth. Your mother thent me to get you. And Wilbur'th here, but he'th buthy thtuffing himthelf with food. . . ."

We hurry back downstairs. Griselda is tomboyishly attired today with a halter top and pigtails that bounce up and down as we trot down the marble staircase. The smell of barbecuing meat can already be detected in the foyer of the house—we have not removed our shoes to gain entry to this manse, so we are not hampered by the necessity of donning them again to get back out to the pavilion of charbroiling goodies—and this time the pavilion is full of guests. The ubiquitous Dr. Richardson is there, lowering a massive sausage into his mouth with one hand and gripping a stein of ice-cold lager with the other. Wilbur is there, as is his corpulent mother and a lanky man in military uniform who appears attached to Mrs. Andrews. The pair resemble a hippopotamus and a giraffe. Indeed, the fauna of Africa are well represented at this *braaivleis*, for Dr. Richardson is nothing if not an ostrich, Griselda a gazelle, and Wilbur has the muscled magnificence of a leopard. The servants dart back and forth like secretary birds. In the distance stand several elephants—the van Helsings—with the grizzled old Oupa a kind of albino baboon. The men are mostly wearing white safari outfits—though they seem to have left their pith helmets at home—and the cacophony that assails my ears is a hyperbolic parody of *eaughing*.

What an insensate spectacle! Mrs. van Helsing—whom I last saw at the club with her snow-white hair piled into a hat shaped like a Babylonian ziggurat—now sports an even more extravagant headpiece, so overhung with imitation fruit as to resemble a still life by some early Dutch master. She holds court in a rattan *papasan* chair. A boy is fanning her. Languorously she holds out her hand to me, and I am not quite sure whether to shake it or kiss it. "So glad you could come, Justin," she says. "We were all *most* affected by that play of yours; you certainly know your Shakespeare."

"Thank you very much, I'm sure," I say, sure as well that there must be some snide reference there to my conscious and unconscious plagiarism from the masters.

"Piet thinks you're absolutely brilliant, you know."

I have still neither kissed nor shaken her hand, but my predicament is solved when she motions toward a silver tray that is being borne by a maid in one of those black uniforms. "Have a glass of champagne. I'm sure your aunts won't object to a stimulant or two."

"I don't suppose so," I say, wondering whether one might classify glue as one of those permissible stimulants. "I've been looking at Piet's trains. Frightfully impressive," I add, trying to make conversation. But she has already lost interest. I down the champagne and deposit the glass on another tray as it glides conveniently by.

Then I go over to the grill and am helped to a plateful of barbe-cued viands.

I begin eating and walking, eating and walking. It's very hot indeed, but these people seem to mind the heat a lot less than the Thais do, for they are wearing far more clothes, on average, than even my aunts would elect to wear on such an afternoon, with the temperature well over a hundred, and the close air wringing the moisture over every inch of one's skin, and not even a hint of a breeze so that the discrete fragrances of *klong* and *phuttachaat* and citrus-blossoms hang heavy, hugging the flesh, confusing the nos-trils. Oh it's hot, and the *farangs* are sweating, for they sweat more profusely and odoriferously than the Thais; something to do with their carnivorous diet. I don't know where my friends have gone to. I eat and walk, my mind somewhere else entirely.

Presently I find a place to rest my weary legs. It's a large boul-der, conveniently in the shade of the pavilion. Just within earshot, several of the van Helsings' male guests are discoursing passionately on the subject of war. Several wars are involved: the Second World War, the Korean War—and occasionally Oupa interjects a remark about the Boer War, to which the others listen politely, murmuring at appropriate moments.

"But the war we're in now is kind of different," says a voice I recognize as the basso profundo of Wilbur's giraffe-like father. "There's no rhyme or reason in it. You can't tell who the enemy is, and you can't tell why he's your enemy. I've seen things you wouldn't believe. Uncivilized things. In the jungle, people go crazy and start re-enacting *Heart of Darkness*. Nice Southern boys go around raping native women and shoving live grenades into their . . . begging your pardon, but there are ladies present . . . still, they say it'll be over by Christmas. And not a moment too soon. It changes people, this war."

I listen intently, because although one is vaguely aware that a war is going on somewhere not far away, it is not a subject that ever rears its ugly head in Eden.

"Still," Mr. Andrews continues, "I'd rather face a hundred angry VC than be alone with Madame Nhu for five minutes. That woman's what you might call a castrating bitch. Met her at a reception once. Phew!"

"Blery Catholics!" says Oupa.

Who is Madame Nhu, I wonder? I imagine a beautiful and terrifying dragon—perhaps what my great-grandmother was like when she was younger.

"Maybe there'll be a coup," someone else says.

"Something's gotta give," says Mr. Andrews. He sighs.

More war stories are exchanged. I sit in the shadow. My eyes grow wider, for the only war I have ever studied in depth is the Trojan War. The men speak of bodies blown to bits, of entrails flying, of raping and pillage in splendidly gory detail, the kind of thing that movies only hint at.

"Another strange thing about this war," says Mr. Andrews. "It sure has opened my eyes to the problems of Negroes. I'd never really met any before, you know, except the maid, of course. But here, they're all over the place, and some of them are right educated, too. Even colonels with college degrees—O'Fleary, for instance. . . ."

To my amazement, Mr. Andrews begins narrating a story about Virgil's father, whom I have never seen since he is, presumably, involved in this nebulous war that people rarely talk about. Apparently Virgil's father is something of a war hero—bravest companion in a tight situation, nobly enjoining his men to avoid slaughtering innocents, first to charge and last to depart, a veritable Hector. Virgil must be extremely proud of his father. Mr. Andrews adds, "I never would have thought that they'd have that kind of courage. Of course, they don't get much of a chance to show it back home, but you take that for granted. . . ."

"Well, they don't feel pain like we do," says Oupa, "that's certain."

Suddenly I feel a tug at my shoulder. It's Wilbur. "Hey, c'mon, Justin," he says, "you can't just sit there listening to them old guys all day long." He drags me up to where an impressive array of pastries has been set up. The cavernous Mrs. Andrews and the stately Mrs. van Helsing are directing their deployment. There are éclairs, Napoleons and mango tarts, turnovers, puffs and *petits fours*, and huge pitchers of *nam manao* to wash it all down. Dr. Richardson, looming over the two women and simultaneously massaging both their necks, is saying, "Splendid display, what, what! Reminds me of the old days in India."

Mrs. Richardson, meanwhile, is fluttering about. In a floral cotton dress, she resembles a large butterfly. She seems nervous. She wrings her hands, and her pageboy hairdo is in disarray.

"Darn," Wilbur says, looking at his watch, "*Bat Masterson* is on." A half-eaten éclair protrudes from his mouth.

"No problem," Piet says, clapping his hands and addressing one of the servants, who runs into the house and emerges bearing a television in his arms. A lengthy extension cord snakes up into the house. Another servant carries a radio so we can hear the English-language soundtrack. We process around the pavilion while the servants—the one almost bent in two from the weight of the television—walk backward in front of us, enabling us to watch the show as we stroll.

Joyously, the four of us—Griselda and we three boys are the only children present at this *braaivleis*—serenade the startled guests with an impromptu choral rendition of:

> Now in the legend of the West,
> One name stands out among the rest—
> He wore a cane and derby hat,
> His name was Bat, Bat Masterson . . .

They respond with polite applause, but soon return to the serious business of eating and trading stories about things that do not hold our interest. The servant holding the television has become exhausted, and he sets it down next to one of the sculpted hedges. We sprawl on the grass. A momentary diversion is provided when one of the gardeners dashes past us, clubbing a cobra with a hoe. But this commonplace occurrence is not nearly as interesting as the cane-twirling antics of Gene Barry on the screen. Westerns are not really my thing. I would rather watch *The Twilight Zone* or *The Outer Limits*, but these only come on late at night. . . .

The sun is setting and trays of mosquito incense are put out. The men are imbibing enormous quantities of Black Label whisky. The women are drinking grasshoppers, white Russians, daiquiris and other weirdly coloured concoctions. We boys and Griselda are finishing off the repast with pineapple-flavoured snow cones.

I notice Mrs. Richardson being summoned to the telephone. In fact, it is brought out to her on a silver platter, its cord trailing uphill like the extension on our television. Wilbur and Piet are deeply involved in the television shootout, but I rouse Griselda with a tap on the shoulder.

"She seems awfully upset," I say. "I hope it's not bad news."

"Oh, dear," says Griselda. "Mummy'th been paying thomeone to thpy on Papa. I do hope they haven't bloody well hit paydirt. It would ruin a perfectly nithe party."

"Let's find out," I say, both because I want to see what new intrigue is afoot, and because I want to separate the fair Griselda from two potential rivals and become a conspirator with her in our own private adventure. After all, it was I who made her Helen of Troy. Surely I deserve a few moments of personal attention for that.

Indeed, trouble does seem to be afoot. Mrs. Richardson glances left and right as though she were about to cross an extremely dangerous intersection. She is, I realize, looking to see if anyone will notice, for, good Englishwoman that she is, she doesn't want to offend her hosts by any display of emotional pyrotechnics.

Satisfied that no one is watching, Mrs. Richardson begins to bear down upon the good doctor, whilst he—no longer massaging the necks of the two matriarchs—is rapidly retreating from the pavilion. He backs away on to the lawn, and then seeing that his wife—the much vaunted "bit of a nuisance"—will not stop, turns and strides off in the direction of the sculpted hedges, soon breaking into a trot as the implacable Mrs. Richardson pursues, her face purpling with rage.

The gunfight continues. The FM radio is blasting out the English soundtrack. Emboldened, I seize Griselda's hand, eliciting a half-cocked "*eaugh!*" of surprise and—I think—delight. "Let's find out what's going on," I whisper. "We can use these bushes as concealment." We set off.

The bushes border either side of a pathway that meanders through the grounds. As we recede from the well-lit and fumigated pavilion, the mosquito music saws through the air, and I feel their myriad pinpricks on my bare arms. I cannot stop. Just on the other side of the bushes, I hear footsteps, which now come to a sudden stop.

"She'th caught up with him!" Griselda whispers.

Suddenly, I notice that it is twilight.

Mrs. Richardson is saying, in carefully measured tones, "I've just had a certain tape recording played to me over the telephone."

"Oh, I say, what, what."

"You—you cad! You perfidious reptile!" says Mrs. Richardson, and we hear several resounding slaps.

"Oh, good heavens! Good for the circulation, what, what?"

"What, what indeed! Well, it may interest you to know that this tape makes reference to a certain dragon entering a certain cave of desire and that the voice of a certain British doctor is heard to say 'what, what, what' several times, and that the tape was made at the house of a certain woman, and pilfered from that house by a certain servant boy, who passed it along to me for the not inconsiderable sum of five hundred baht. . . ."

But wait a minute! Didn't I see my aunts chucking the tapes into the pond? I was there! Could it have been a dream, that out-of-body experience—and the reconciliation between the sisters a figment of a drunken imagination? Could the tapes have languished in a drawer all this time? And Piak! Could he really have perpetrated so treacherous an act? The boy has been sleeping in my room. He knows where everything is kept. He knows better than I do. . . .

Could Piak really have betrayed me for the miserable sum of five hundred baht? It suddenly occurs to me that, paltry though the sum is—it won't even buy dinner for two at a decent restaurant—it is twice his monthly salary. . . .

38

The Playing Fields of Bangkapi

With infinite care, Griselda and I part the bush to get a better view. The leaves are prickly, but we manage to insinuate ourselves among them. In fact, we find ourselves completely enclosed by the hedge—this particular one is in the shape of a giant swan—peering through little windows that we've made in the swan's verdant flank.

Dr. Richardson is seated on a granite statue of a *singha*, smoking one cigarette while holding another lit one in his hand. His wife is storming up and down the flagstones of the winding path, gesticulating and carrying on in a flamboyant, most un-English manner.

"Heavens, my dear," Dr. Richardson is saying, "you shouldn't get so excited. You know very well it's liable to cause a heat-stroke."

"I've had enough," Mrs. Richardson exclaims. "In fact, I've half a mind to go and fling myself at the nearest man. I'm tired of playing the genteel British lady whilst my husband runs around trying to bat his first century at his advanced age—"

"Heavens! I assure you, my dear, they were all maiden overs."

"I doubt that!" says Mrs. Richardson.

"What on earth is he talking about?" I whisper.

"Cricket," Griselda says. Suddenly I realize that her hand is in mine. It is clammy, but not unpleasant. She's drawing little concentric circles in my palm with a slippery finger.

"Cricket?" I say, confused.

"Yeth," says Griselda, "when my parenth argue, they alwayth uthe cricket ath a metaphor. Awfully bloody tirethome, actually. A maiden over'th when you don't thcore and—"

Griselda's hands have become more aggressive now. She has wrapped one hand around my index finger and is squeezing it rhythmically. Her other hand seems to have accidentally fallen into the general area of my lap and is rummaging around down there.

"Have you lost something?" I ask her.

"Don't be thilly!" she says, and I realize—with a mixture of horror and delight—that what she is looking for is that very appendage excoriated by Father Regenstrom in his lecture about sin—my stiffening aubergine!

"Well," Mrs. Richardson says, "this time I'm not going to take it lying down. I'm simply going to have to go back to England—and I'm going to take Griselda with me."

"Oh, I say, what!"

At this news, Griselda becomes quite upset. "Oh, Juthtin," Griselda moans, "I couldn't bear to lothe you!" At which her mouth descends upon mine like an owl on a rodent. It is a wet and mushy sensation, like eating an overripe mango, but when, with her tongue, she actually pries my lips apart and begins to probe the outer surfaces of my bicuspids, I am quite taken aback. It doesn't feel *bad* exactly, it's just not what I expected. Suddenly, my own tongue encounters the cold taste of metal. I recoil into the depths of the hedge and further away from the Richardsons' marital spat.

"Damn the bloody *thingth* in my mouth!" says Griselda furiously. "They're conthtantly getting—in the way of my amorouth activitieth."

"Well," I say, attempting to maintain propriety, and not wanting to give Griselda an inferiority complex about her oral architecture, "it's not those . . . bloody things at all . . . it's . . . well, this hedge is frightfully crowded, isn't it? And these leaves do prickle so! Not to mention the mosquitoes."

To my astonishment, Griselda begins weeping. "You jutht don't like me," she says. "I knew it all the time."

Mrs. Richardson, too, can be heard weeping beside the hedge. The bawling becomes so emotion-laden that I, also, begin to feel the tears well up in my eyes, though I don't know why I should be unhappy. I am a sounding-board, resonating with the timeless grief of jilted womankind.

After I've dried Griselda's tears with a sleeve and sopped up my own few drops, I stick my head once more into that alcove within the swan-shaped hedge that affords the best view of the Richardsons.

"Well, my dear," Dr. Richardson is saying, "I'm afraid it's a bit of a nuisance, but if you feel that strongly about it, I suppose you must have your way. . . ."

"What?" says Mrs. Richardson, reversing suddenly. "I've told you that I'm going to walk out on you, and you're simply going to say all right, what, what, and let me go?"

"Well, what can I do? It's a woman's prerogative."

"Well, it simply isn't cricket!" says Mrs. Richardson passionately.

At that very moment a small hard ball comes rolling down the garden path toward them. They leap in opposite directions. The ball comes hurtling toward the hedge.

"It'th a cricket ball!" says Griselda, astonished.

Suddenly, in hot pursuit of the ball, we see Piet, dressed in white and wearing a monstrous glove, come dashing down the pathway. The ball has lodged in the swan-shaped bush. It is, as a matter of fact, only inches from my face and would have knocked out Griselda's teeth had she not dodged in time.

"Have any of you seen a cricket ball go by?" Piet asks the Richardsons, who have frozen into attitudes of the utmost propriety.

"It went into the elephant, I believe, what," says Dr. Richardson.

"No, the swan," says Mrs. Richardson. "I think."

"Thanks a lot," Piet says, and trots over to the swan. With only seconds to spare, Griselda and I extricate ourselves from the hedge, brush off the loose leaves clinging to our clothes, and come sauntering nonchalantly round the corner, hand in hand, as though we had been out strolling and had only now chanced upon this locus.

"Mummy!" Griselda exclaims. "Oh, there you are. . . ."

"Come on, Justin!" Piet shouts to me. "We need another fielder."

"Oh, I don't know how to play," I say.

"Awfully dark for cricket, isn't it?" says Dr. Richardson.

"We've got the floodlights on," says Piet.

"But I—" I say.

"Oh, nonsense, Justin," Dr. Richardson says, patting me amiably on the shoulder and winking at his wife, it'll be good for you; I mean, the playing fields of Eton and all that. You wouldn't want to arrive in England thoroughly unprepared, would you, what? Battle of Waterloo and all that, you know, what."

Bewildered, but somewhat relieved to find an excuse for leaving this domestic upheaval, I follow Piet as he runs off.

"Oh, I say, let's go and watch the game," I hear Dr. Richardson remark as we move out of earshot.

"No thanks," says Mrs. Richardson, "I'd rather stay here and finish our quarrel."

I follow Piet round the hill—it is amazing to me that the cricket ball could have curved around it in such defiance of the Newtonian laws—and find that part of the grounds, just beyond the barbecuing pavilion, have, indeed, been floodlit and that several of the male guests are essaying a game of cricket. Well, cricket of a sort. Wilbur seems to have been up at bat for some time. Piet's grandfather is bowling—with amazing accuracy considering the fact that he has to be led by the hand to the bowling crease. The servant, bearing the television in his arms, stands a few feet from Wilbur, allowing him to continue to watch the show. As Piet throws the ball back to his Oupa, the spectators—seated and still eating—lean forward. Piet's grandfather bowls. Wilbur strikes. He begins running. The television-bearing servant runs alongside, managing to keep himself at a constant distance from Wilbur's gaze. A desultory cheer rises from the spectators. I jerk my head left and right as the ball is thrown back and forth. It's all rather mystifying, especially when, in an effort to prevent himself from being brained by the ball, the servant sidesteps, trips over the extension cord, and collides with the wicket, eliciting a rousing chorus of "Howzat?"

"Just a cotton-pickin' minute," Wilbur exclaims. "*I* didn't knock over that wicket. It was *him*."

Oupa—whose guide has abandoned him and who is now walking around in circles, flailing at the air—cries, "Would never have happened in my day! Televisions in cricket matches indeed! What will these Yanks think of next?"

Dr. Richardson and his wife—the picture of propriety—have entered the scene just in time to witness this unusual turn of events. Suddenly all eyes turn to him. He is, after all, British, and must be the final arbiter of what is or is not cricket. The television bearer, meanwhile, unsure whether he is in trouble, sits by the wicket in a *phabphieb* position, fatalistically awaiting the wrath of the white divinities. I notice that we are about to segue into an episode of *The Twilight Zone*.

It seems that Dr. Richardson is the only person deemed fit to adjudicate. "Oh, I say, what, what! In my opinion," he pontificates, as his wife smiles sweetly, "the television bearer, who was there for the sole purpose of allowing the batsman to watch the telly, must be considered inextricably linked to, and indissolubly part of, the batsman's, ah, equipment. Therefore, one would have to rule that if the television hit the wicket, so did the batsman."

There is applause. He takes a little bow. Wilbur, in a huff, says, "These limey games ain't what you'd call real sports anyway. Why can't you guys learn to play baseball?" He flings his bat away, narrowly missing the television set and stalks off toward the house.

"Well," Mrs. Richardson says, "I think it's time for us to leave now." She swoops over to Griselda and seizes her by the hand. Then she strides down the pathway toward the sculpted hedges, while the good doctor lopes after her, what-what-whating the while.

It is very late at night and all the adults and servants have gone to bed. Wilbur, Piet and I have been watching the trains thread in and out of the world beneath Piet's bed. An Everly Brothers record has been playing in the background. I'm getting tired, but my friends are quite alert. They seem to be waiting for something. . . .

"Don't you think we ought to go to bed soon?" I say. In the back of my mind I'm thinking of how Piak has betrayed me for a miserable thirty pieces of silver. I'm plotting my revenge. Perhaps I shall doctor his father's female attire so that, at some crucial and very public moment, they will fall apart. . . .

"No," Piet says, "we can't do that. Let's play another game of Monopoly."

"No way," says Wilbur. "You're the world's wickedest landlord."

"Well, what are we going to do then? We've still got an hour to kill."

"An hour till what?" I ask.

They look at each other.

I realize that some entertainment has been planned for the night—a surprise that I'm not supposed to know about. I panic for a moment, thinking of the time the two boys were trying, only half in jest, to lynch Virgil.

"Well," Piet says at last, "let's . . . let's look at some pictures."

At first I think he's going to bring out *Health & Efficiency* again, but instead he brings out an album of photographs from the closet. He opens the book. Mostly there are photographs of himself, from babyhood to the present, standing against various backgrounds, which, to me, are wildly exotic. There are also infinite grasslands, tempestuous oceans, imperious mountains. Then there are shots of a Negro boy, a ragamuffin in scruffy clothes, playing ball with Piet, wrestling with Piet, running around with Piet. "Who's that?" I ask him.

"Oh," he says, "that's Newton Mbele. He was my best friend when I was a kid. We used to do everything together."

"You were best friends with a Negro?"

"Sure," he says. "They're all right when you're just kids and don't know any better. We lived on a farm, you see. Sometimes I went to his village. They used to eat chicken feet. *Lekker!*"

"If you had a best friend who was a Negro," I ask, perplexed, "then why are the two of you always so down on Virgil?"

"That's different," Wilbur says. "I used to hang out with them, too, sometimes, but they knew better'n to piss in the same toilet or sit in the front of the bus. It ain't that I'm prejudiced or nothing, Justin, it's just, well, we don't belong together."

"Yes. As our preacher used to tell us," says Piet, "'In my Father's house there are many mansions.'"

"There are some things about the world," says Wilbur, "that are never gonna change. Maybe they oughta. But they ain't *gonna*."

And that seems to be that.

Or does it?

I feel there is a terrible wrongness in the world but that I am powerless to correct it. There is a disturbance in the *dharma* of the cosmos. Surely, oh surely I cannot be the only one to have noticed it . . . and yet I seem to be. Even Virgil, against whom these injustices have been perpetrated, accepts them as inevitable. That is why he fled from the white boys at the swimming pool, that is why he did not fight back at the mock-hanging, that is why he will do nothing to defend his right to be called human. He has been cowed. The Irish overseer's lash still stripes him even now, a hundred years later, with his great-grandmother long buried in the alien soil of Georgia, so far from the domain of King Shangó.

But what can I do, I, a fledgling playwright clothed in borrowed plumage? I am tormented by my own ineptitude.

As I sit there, agonizing to myself, an alarm clock goes off.

"All right!" Wilbur cries. "Time to vamoose!"

"Where are we going?" I say. The maunderings of self-examination seem to pale a little at the prospect of an adventure.

"You'll see!" says Piet. "Got any money?"

"Only about a hundred," I say.

"That's all right," says Piet.

"Yeah . . . I raided the cookie jar last night," says Wilbur, flashing a hefty roll of bright red hundred-baht banknotes.

"And I went through my Oupa's wallet," says Piet, pulling out a similar wad of bills. "Don't worry, Justin, you're our guest. It'll be our treat."

"Treat? What treat?"

Piet goes over to the window. "Perfect," he says. "Our taxi is pulling up . . . right . . . *now*."

39

The Fleshpots
of the Orient

Sneaking out of the van Helsings' is easy. We just tiptoe down the hall to the curving staircase, slide down the smooth marble banister and slink out through the front foyer. There is, indeed, a taxi waiting at the front gate, and the guard lets us through without a qualm. Could it be that to the staff at this manse, the actions of the *farang* masters are so inscrutable that there is no point in even attempting to fathom them?

We all pile into the back seat of the taxi.

"Aren't you going to tell him where we're going?" I ask Piet.

"Why? We have him for the whole night." He turns to the driver and, in weirdly toned Thai, says, "Go. Go."

"Okay, I go now," the driver says. We dash down the *soi* at breakneck speed. There is hardly anyone about. A renegade *samlor*, survivor from the last decade, plies up and down the *soi*, its driver huffing and puffing as he pedals the bicycle wheels. The driver honks furiously. "They ban shit *samlor* years ago," he says, "don't know he doing shit here."

We swerve into an even tinier *soi*—it's barely wide enough for the Datsun to thread its way through—to avoid some flooding in the main *soi*. Then we are suddenly through to Sukhumvit Road and whizzing in and out of traffic at the speed of light.

We dash through the neon kaleidoscope of night, breathing in the petrol fumes and the odours of decay, fending off the flower vendors that converge on us at every red light. We hurtle past flood-lit hotels and the gloomy façades of temples; past shrines, past street markets steeped in the smell of durian, shrimp paste, jasmine and peanut sauce; past a pavement shrine crammed with dancers in spangled costumes who move through the candlelight and sodium glare in strenuous strained counterpoint to the screaming traffic.

At length we reach a part of the city I have never seen before. The taxi ducks into an alley. There is an awning, which drips a steady sludge into the sewer below. Above the awning, there is a neon sign P R DISE M SSAGE C NTR.

Wilbur orders the taxi to wait at a safe distance.

"Shit I wait," says the driver.

"He must've learned English from our GIs," Wilbur says.

"Oh, a message centre," I say, looking up at the sign as we climb out.

"Precisely," says Piet.

"I'm glad you know the score," Wilbur says, and he leers.

I am perplexed, but, thinking he must be referring to the cricket match of earlier this evening, I say, "The only score I saw was a maiden over."

For some reason, my two friends think this is unbelievably funny.

There is a guard at the door, dressed in a sort of butler's costume. He barks: "No come inside! Private club!" A crudely lettered sign next to the door reads: NO CHILDREN ADMITTED.

"No children," Piet says. "That's us. Maybe we should get out of here."

"Bullshit!" says Wilbur. "Watch this!"

And, bold as brass, he strides right up to the guard and pokes him in the chest. Piet turns to me and says, "Well, Justin, you're about to see the Ugly American in action."

Assuming a commanding and masterful posture, Wilbur addresses the guard in pidgin English, enunciating as though the guard were an imbecile. "You let us in right now," he says. "My father important colonel. General! Me very important. You no let me in, you lose your job."

The guard looks dubious.

Wilbur puffs up like a frog and continues: "My father general, my uncle President John F. Kennedy, my grandfather personal friend of Field Marshal Sarit . . . you no let me in, you in trouble."

The guard looks at me. Suspecting I might be Thai, he says, in Thai, "Is any of this true? You never know with these *farangs*. They all look alike, and you can never tell if they're lying."

Piet kicks me in the shin. "You don't speak a word of Thai," he tells me.

"That's right," I say, "I don't," in the most *eaughing* accent I can manage.

"All right. Hurry up. But stay in back. No make trouble."

We follow Wilbur's lead and, in single file, follow him down a dank and musty corridor toward a dark room, full of smoke, in which a live combo is playing a version of "It's My Party and I'll Cry if I Want To".

"Try not to look surprised or nuthin'," Wilbur says urgently. "Don't do anything that'll make us look like we've never been to a place like this before."

"But I never *have* been to a place like this before," I say nervously. "Have you?"

"No," says Wilbur, "but I've heard my dad talk about them. They're R and R places. I made sure this one was safe before I picked it out."

"What are we supposed to do here?" I say.

"I'm not sure," says Wilbur, "but I can tell you it's gonna be neat."

"What's gonna be neat?" whispers Piet.

"You know."

We're standing in a line at the back of the room now, and even Wilbur seems a little intimidated. Seated at tables in the room are about a dozen male *farangs*, many in military uniforms. Mostly they are alone or in pairs. Each one has a drink in front of him, which he is ignoring. Each one has a hostess, scantily clad, who is making eyes at, massaging, or attempting to converse with him. Some of the women wear rabbit ears, others have little helmets that resemble the heads of cats. They are all heavily made up, but some are little older than ourselves.

As we stand there, drinking in the spectacle—no one seems to be offering us any other kind of drink—the feeble light dims even further, and a spotlight falls on a little arena next to the band, which continues to fumble its way through the hits of 1963. The band leader notices the change in the lighting and gives a signal. Suddenly the music changes to a sort of snake-charming theme, with the saxophonist playing an undulating melody against a bongo background.

A nude woman leaps into the spotlight. She begins to prance around, jiggling her pendulous breasts and thrusting at the air with her hips.

"Gee willikers!" says Wilbur. "She's buck naked! They sure don't have any of this shit back home. . . ."

"I bet you'd like to do it with her," Piet says.

"I sure would," says Wilbur, though I seem to recall that, not too long ago, he had been reduced to asking me what the precise nature of "it" was. I wonder if he actually knows, or whether he's just bluffing.

What happens next almost defies belief. A second woman, as naked as the first, leaps into the circle, and for a while the two simply dance. Then, producing a ping-pong ball as though by magic, the first woman throws it in the air and catches it with her . . . well, I'm not sure what it's called, but she manages to clench it quite tightly within that orifice. Then, with a powerful pelvic thrust, she sends the ping-pong ball arcing upward like a stone from a catapult. The second woman catches the ball between *her* legs, and the two of them proceed to play this unusual brand of table tennis for a while, their thrustings becoming more frenzied as the music swells to fever pitch.

The audience is transfixed. We too. I don't think any of us moves a muscle throughout the entire performance. Except our eyes, of course, which follow the ping-pong ball with the pendulum-like precision of a patient under hypnosis. We don't speak, though I am sure that my two friends are as astounded as I am at these women's athletic prowess, not to mention the shock of hair about their nether regions. . . .

The hair! It is as luxuriant as it is unexpected. No *Playboy* centrefold has conditioned us for such a sight. Not even my view of Samlee, in the half-light of the shaman's house, has prepared me.

I cast a sidelong glance at Wilbur. I see the lump in his throat. I wonder if he sees mine. I wonder if his aubergine, like mine, is straining against the confines of his underwear.

As the dance ends, a hand falls on my shoulder. I start. Turning around, I see that we have been accosted by one of the hostesses. She's an older woman—how much older I cannot guess, for she is caked in makeup. I see her through a veil of smoke and shadow. She seems attractive enough, although as older women go, she is not up to the standard of Samlee.

"Nice American boys," she says, "want massage? Want more than massage? For you, cheap. Special group rate, three hundred baht."

"Gosh, okay," says Wilbur, gulping.

"Aren't you going to bargain?" I ask him, wondering whether the ordinary rules of commerce have been suspended for the night.

Quickly, the woman says, "Okay, three hundred. Auntie Deedee don't want to argue." She puts out her hand, and Wilbur gives her a few red bills. He is so distracted that he doesn't even count them. He is bewitched.

Piet whispers in my ear: "He's going to do it with her for sure. . . ."

"Auntie Deedee show everything, do everything," says the woman, pouting. "Come with me."

"C'mon, guys," Wilbur says, feigning worldliness so well that I am almost convinced. "We don't want to keep the lady waiting."

Auntie Deedee leads us up to a dingy room. There are a couple of rattan chairs, a coffee table with an ashtray piled with old butts and a sleeping area separated from the sitting-room by a Vietnamese lacquer folding screen inlaid with mother-of-pearl elephants, butterflies and flowers.

"I'm gonna go first," Wilbur says, "'cause I was the one who paid."

Neither Piet nor I have the courage to dispute Wilbur's claim, so we sit down on the chairs and let the two of them go off behind the screen, which Auntie Deedee opens out to shield them from our gaze.

Wilbur continues to prattle on, perhaps from nervousness. Clothes are thrown over the screen, some landing in our laps. "Holy cow," says Wilbur, "I wish you guys were here with me. This is neat. I mean, she's so close I can smell her perfume and stuff."

As Auntie Deedee's brassière appears over the screen, he exclaims, "Jesus Christ! Look at the headlights on her!" and "I've never seen Mount Everests this big on a woman before," and comments of this sort.

At last comes the moment of truth.

A pair of panties is flung over the folding screen.

We hear a bloodcurdling scream from the other side of the mother-of-pearl partition. . . .

40

At the Temple Fair

"What on earth?" both Piet and I exclaim as Wilbur emerges from the screen and scrambles about the room, scooping up his clothing.

"She's insane!" he screams, hopping into his pants. "She tried to eat it!"

"Eat what?" Piet says. A very bewildered Auntie Deedee comes sauntering out in the nude, twirling her brassiere like a cheerleader's baton.

"What the matter, you no like Auntie Deedee?"

"I'm telling you, she's a goldarned cannibal," says Wilbur. "Let's get the hell out of here before we're beef stew."

"All right, all right," says Piet, miffed at being deprived of his hour of ecstasy, although judging from Wilbur's discomfiture at what I know to be merely the under-the-table-with-the-chameleon-in-the-spittoon variation on the art of lovemaking, he probably has no idea what might constitute such an hour. Well, they can't all have my advantage of having witnessed Samlee performing the aubergine-swallowing routine.

Wilbur is still buttoning his shirt as we race downstairs. Auntie Deedee is complaining bitterly in the background: "Damned *far-*

angs; can't live with them, can't live without them. Try to understand them, might as well try to understand the weather. . . ."

Downstairs, in the bar area, the music has become raucous as a buxom woman, wearing nothing but a G-string and tassels, belts her way through a bizarrely out-of-tune version of "Soldier Boy", or, in this rendition, "Sownjer Boy". The soldiers themselves, quite drunk, are staggering about. One petite young thing is being tossed from hand to hand like an American football.

Auntie Deedee comes charging down at us, screaming, in Thai, that we didn't do anything, and she doesn't feel right keeping the whole three hundred. But Wilbur is too frightened to negotiate, and when she thrusts two of the red bills under our noses, he bolts. We rush into the alley outside where the taxi driver is leaning against his battered blue Datsun, sipping an Amarit.

We cruise into the neon night. Wilbur, shattered, leans back against the seat. From the open windows comes the blare of car horns. The air that blasts our faces is hot, wet and odoriferous. I'm sitting next to him, while Piet, in the front seat, is strangely subdued.

"Wilbur, I don't quite know how to tell you this," I begin, "but—"

"Don't try to tell me anything right now!" says Wilbur. "Can't you see I've had a traumatic experience? I'm probably gonna be scarred for life now."

"No, you're not," I say.

"Gee whiz, that woman dove down on me like a barracuda chasing a minnow. I mean, she swooped down on me like an owl going after a field mouse. I mean, she was like a mountain lion springing after a—"

I can't help laughing at the variety of fauna he's managed to allude to in his agitated state.

"Don't make fun of me," Wilbur says. I think he's on the verge of crying, but he manfully strives to be a good soldier. "It ain't nice. The three hundred baht kind of sucked too . . . and you know what the worst thing of all was? I popped a boner right in front of her. I mean, gee willikers, that was embarrassing!"

"Good thing you did," said Piet after some deliberation. "Probably made her think she was going to bite off more than she could chew."

At this, I laugh so hard that my sides are literally aching. I feel the pressure on my bladder and realize that I am only seconds away from wetting my shorts.

"Ain't funny!" says Wilbur furiously.

"Is so," says Piet, who begins to laugh, too, perhaps thinking that he won't appear sophisticated if he doesn't laugh.

"Stop, stop, stop! I'm going to pee in my pants unless you stop this instant!" I say. This has the opposite effect, of course, and soon both of them are shrieking with laughter, and Wilbur has huge fat hysterical tears sluicing down his cheeks.

Sensing my dilemma, the taxi driver jams on the brakes. "Shit *klong* over there," he says. "You go pipi now."

"Good idea," says Wilbur. "I think we all need to take a whiz."

We scramble out of the car, gulping down mouthfuls of sewage-laden air. We line up at the edge of the *klong*, tallest to shortest—I, naturally, being the shortest—and proceed to unburden our bladders into the brackish water, which twinkles and glistens with the reflected light of a thousand neon advertising signs in English, Thai and Chinese. A duck glides by, receives a urinous baptism, shakes itself furiously, leaps ashore, and waddles away quacking. We laugh, and our laughter engenders more pissing, which gives birth to more laughter. We only stop laughing when the mosquitoes become intolerable.

"This is making me hungry," Wilbur says. "I wonder where we can get some food around here."

At that moment, we hear music in the distance . . . not the strains of the "Limbo Rock" . . . not the plaintive voice of Dion . . . not the music we are used to . . . but an ancient music, the high-pitched, nasal voices of women accompanied by drums, oboes and marimbas. It is the sound of a *ramwong*.

"It's coming from somewhere down the *klong*," says Piet. "Listen."

There are voices, too. Laughter. The bustle of a market. And the enticing smell of cooking food . . . of pork *satays* broiling . . . of *roti* dough being slapped against cutting boards . . . of garlic chicken being barbecued on charcoal fires. Up the *klong*, a smear of white light and against the light the silhouettes of tall pagodas against the moonlit clouds. . . .

"It's the *ngaan wat*," I say, realizing that we have somehow arrived back at a place not far from my house, just upstream from the house of the *ajarn* who was once possessed by the spirit of my dead chameleon.

"Let's go," says Piet. "There's bound to be food."

"Yeah," says Wilbur. "I could really go for some of them grey-coloured grilled meatballs on skewers, without that Texas-style chilli sauce, though."

"Right," I say, and we ask the taxi to take us right up to the temple gates. The *wat* has a dock and can also be reached by a rickety wooden bridge. The driver takes us over it—it is amazing to me that the bridge is wide enough to accommodate the Datsun—and under an archway guarded by bearded stone Chinamen, right down to the grounds themselves, which are crammed with food stalls, games of chance, a funhouse, stands selling fish mobiles, the *tukta chao wang* dolls used to populate spirit houses, handicrafts, clothes, transistor radios, used comic books, and joss-sticks. The temple dogs run rampant through the throng, barking, farting, mounting women's legs, and defecating at will.

Wilbur, waving his wad of banknotes, is already charging down toward the *satay* vendors. I wonder how many of them will be able to make change for a hundred-baht note. I'm not hungry, and there are so many distractions that I don't immediately follow Wilbur. Piet says, "I think I'll get some food, too, and then maybe we can meet up over there"—he points to a low structure with a door shaped like the gaping jaws of a demon, from which tremulous ghostly sounds, like the theremin music from *The Outer Limits*, emanate— "which seems to be some kind of haunted house thing. That ought to be fun."

I, on the other hand, am drawn to a spectacle of a different kind. Beyond the circle of drunken *ramwong* dancers, there is a makeshift stage—little bigger than a puppet theatre—on which some kind of drama is being performed. A man in classical dance costume, wearing a *khon* mask—but wearing it like a hat, rather than covering his face completely with it—is prancing around, gesticulating to a crowd, mostly children and old people, crammed together on a floor of straw mats that have been spread out over the grass. It is a *likay*.

A tinkling music underscores the actor's movements. He traipses across the stage, not with the elegance of classical dance, but with an easy informality. The children laugh. I can't hear what he's saying, and I strain to listen, but above the racket of the fair one can hear almost nothing of the play. A barker with a megaphone strolls by, bellowing: "This way! This way! For only one salueng, see the stuffed and preserved body of the notorious Si Ui, the Chinese mass murderer who ate children's livers! See the genuine eyeball of Mae Nak Phrakanong, preserved in a jar of formaldehyde! See a real-live *phii krasue*, trapped in the body of a beautiful woman! It's all in the house of fabulous horrors!" And he points onlookers in the direction of the mysterious building with the demon-jaw door. The entrance is swamped, and I see Wilbur, clutching a fistful of *muu satay*, and Piet borne by the tide of people eager for the fright of their lives. It's clear that I'm not going to be able to catch up with them, and soon my attention is drawn once more to the folk opera in the distance . . . the stage rigged up in the shadow of a stout pagoda . . . the divine creature with the headdress has gone offstage, and now the space in front of the tawdry backdrop—a garish image of a *naga*-girt pavilion—is occupied by two women wearing *chadahs* and *phah sbai chiangs*, sitting on an ornate plinth and declaiming to one another in squealing, prissy voices.

I decide to move closer, particularly since I suddenly see someone I recognize bobbing up and down in the swarm of children. It is Piak.

I begin working myself into a rage. Soon, I have completely forgotten about Wilbur and Piet and the house of horrors. I bear down on Piak, come up behind him and all but pounce on him.

"You traitor!" I scream, startling the actresses.

Piak turns and looks at me curiously. It occurs to me that I am heavily outnumbered. Here I am, an obviously wealthy kid wearing tailored clothes, surrounded by bare-chested urchins who, I have no doubt, would support Piak's position over mine, perhaps with their fists. Nevertheless, I decide to tough it out. After all, I can always take refuge in the taxi, parked in the middle distance with the motor still running and the driver on his fourth Amarit of the evening.

"Oh, hello, Master Little Frog," says Piak. "Khun Virgil's over at the house of horrors—he doesn't much care for *likay.*"

"You perfidious cockroach! You . . . you . . . sea-monster!"

"What are you talking about?" Piak says. If he's not confused, he's putting on a good bluff. "How could I possibly betray the omniscient and compassionate *khun nuu,* who saved me and my family from our plight?"

"Yes, but the tape! The tape!"

The *likay* band has struck up. The two weeping women get up and after a perfunctory ambulation around the stage in the *sodsoi mala* style, rotating their arms as though weaving an immense garland about their persons, they make their exit.

"Oh, you want protection money," Piak says with a knowing wink to some of his companions. "You rich people are all alike, always after a piece of the action. Would ten per cent be sufficient?"

"What do you mean, ten per cent? It wasn't even your tape . . . and now Mrs. Richardson's in a pee with her husband, and she's going to yank Griselda out of the Scola Britannica and ship them both off to England, and—and—"

"Oh, come on, Khun Nuu. A Thai male can always find other women. But my father—I mean my mother—and I, we're desperate. We're saving up to send my father to Singapore, you know."

"Whatever for?"

"Well . . . he can't get the operation in Bangkok. The specialists are all in Singapore, you see . . . and your uncle, well, he's . . . he's being rather choosy about . . . you know . . . certain body parts."

"What do you mean? Is your father dying of some disease?" I ask him, a little ashamed to be nitpicking over five hundred baht if that is indeed the case. "How much money does he need?"

"No, he's not ill," Piak says, "unless you're referring to his capacity for reason. And it's a *very* pricey operation, and your Uncle Vit says it's not his responsibility. . . ."

"But if he's not sick, what is the operation supposed to do? Turn him into a woman?"

"You said it," says Piak.

The idea of the former gardener being surgically transformed into a woman is so disturbing that I can't look Piak in the eye. How much could such a miracle of science cost, I wonder?

I turn away from Piak, my fury forgotten, and concentrate on the drama before me. The god Indra has come to Bangkok in the guise of a humble taxi driver, who, escorting a *farang* to a sleazy bar, discovers that the bar's proprietress is really the misplaced daughter of a millionaire shipping magnate, kidnapped from the hospital at birth and brought up in the slums of Klong Toey by a Catholic priest, who happens to be her uncle, captured as a boy by *farang* pirates, converted and set ashore only to be rescued by a talking monkey who turns out to be. . . .

It's entirely magical, and in a moment or two I am no longer aware of the ripped backdrop sealed with masking tape, the mingled odours of barbecue, sewage, booze and sweat, the botched makeup and patched costumes of the actors, the giggles and interjections of the audience . . . all these things vanish.

What I seem to see is the ideal drama, of which this bumbling rendition is but a pallid shadow. For even in this crowded place, I am within a hair's breadth of the other country, the secret kingdom of my fantasies.

41

Inferno

Well, the plot of the *likay* is so labyrinthine, so baroque, so glee-fully absurd, that watching it is not so much like watching a movie as like staring into a kaleidoscope and finding oneself slowly sucked into its idiosyncratic interior logic . . . utterly losing one's hold on the real world.

Presently, however, I begin to realize that, convoluted as it is, the story of this *likay* is firmly anchored in reality. For example: Here's the god Indra, disguised as a taxi driver, gliding through the scene wearing a foot-long cardboard cut-out of a taxi on his waist. He's complaining about how things have gone downhill since he became king of the universe.

But every wisecrack he utters makes the audience howl with laughter . . . he talks about the betting on the boxing at Lumpini stadium . . . about the sourness of the *kuaitiao* broth at the vendor on the corner of Soi Aree . . . the price of a decent massage from a blind *ajarn*. These are all real things, things known to the audience, and because they are real they also make real his preposterous god-head. And then there are the orphaned babies swapped at birth, the women of noble blood accidentally brought up by peasants, the dashing young prince searching through the slums of the city for his long-lost beloved . . . oh, these are the tropes of myth all right . . . I recognize them from my dusty books about Greeks and Romans and Sumerians and Egyptians . . . yes, the same stories, but oh, how greedily these unlettered children are devouring them . . . because they see in the mock-heroic figures echoes of themselves.

Thus it is that I find myself simultaneously laughing and weeping into my bottle of Green Spot. I am horrified at how moved I am. Why is it that I cannot move my audience as profoundly as a six-salueng sideshow? Disheartened, I drown my sorrows in my orange drink and toss the empty bottle away without bothering to collect the fifty-satang deposit.

"Piak," I say. But he is too entranced to listen to me. The fury I have suppressed before comes back now. I've never begrudged Shakespeare or Euripides their brilliance, but I am livid with jealousy at this three-penny opera. Maybe it's because Shakespeare *et al.* are dead and immutable. But this tawdry production is very much alive . . . I mean, the actors are actually improvising a lot of their lines . . . and when they go off stage they are to be seen in the sidelines, giggling, quaffing Mekong, and slurping huge bowls of *bamii nam*.

Oh, now we're in a battle scene. The god-cum-taxi-driver is taking on an evil slumlord who is insisting on making the princess-cum-ragamuffin pay the rent even though her adoptive mother is coughing her lungs out with consumption. Indra hurls bolts of invisible magic at the slumlord, accompanying each with the mystical incantation of "*Ohm phiang!*"

"Stuff and nonsense," I cry out. "Enough, enough!" No one pays the least attention to this disenfranchised dramatist, a lone classicist crying in the wilderness.

Except for Piak, who turns to me and says, "Shut up, Khun Nuu, this is an exciting part . . . it turns out that the princess has this magic emerald, see, and she can use it to summon the monsoon."

It's even more galling that Piak should be familiar with the plot of this twaddle—as is all too apparent when the princess in question does, indeed, whip out and brandish the bumptious bijou, causing the audience to break out in spontaneous applause.

I know that if I start shoving Piak around it will occasion the same kind of débâcle as the one at the limbo rock party. I swallow my anger. On stage, the magic jewel summons the monsoon, represented in this case by a clashing of cymbals. The nasty slumlord staggers back. Indra suddenly reveals himself in his transcendent shape, whipping off his cloak to reveal the costume of a god underneath. The children shrink back in amazement as if the miracle were real. I strive to remain unimpressed.

But impressed I am despite myself. Comedy, I think, base, lowly slapstick, has led this gullible audience through the entire spectrum of emotion. What am I doing wrong?

I don't want to think about all this any more. I tell Piak, "I've had enough of this rubbish. I'm going to go to the house of horrors."

"Good," says Piak. "I'm sure Khun Virgil will be glad to see you. He always complains about not seeing enough of you any more."

If he does miss me that much, why has he never said anything to me about it? Could he really be that stiff-necked? I don't want to admit that it might be I who am guilty of overweening pride, so instead, puffed up with nameless rage, I stalk off in the direction of the house of horrors, pausing only to purchase, and devour, three *roti sai mais*.

After I pay the requisite two saluengs (it is true that the barker announced that it was only one, but for some reason the price doubled as soon as they saw me coming) I am ushered into a sort of antechamber lined with black-velvet drapery. There aren't many people in the room. On a table, in tall formaldehyde-filled jars, are various deformed creatures—an unborn baby with two monstrous heads—a staring eyeball—that sort of thing. The labels are in Thai, so I can barely puzzle them out, for my literacy in my native language has not kept pace with my acquisition of its vulgar vocabularies. The eyeball claims to be that of Mae Nak Phrakanong, the long-tongued female monster who once lived by the *klong* somewhat farther down Sukhumvit Road from us. The promised mummified body of Si Ui, the notorious child killer, is in a glass cabinet and looks suspiciously as though it has been slapped together from papier mâché and mud. The only light is a naked bulb suspended from the ceiling. Outside, loudspeakers are blaring out *ramwong* music, and with every thud of the drum the bare bulb flickers.

Following my nose, I reach a cage, which, according to the sign, contains a giant rat—the world's largest. It is, indeed, extremely large, and wears its rodent prosthesis with conviction, but now and then it has a tendency to oink.

A flap of canvas provides the way into an inner area. A man stands at the door demanding an extra fifty satang before he will lift the flap.

"What's behind there?" I ask him.

"It's what you came for," he says. And puts a finger to his lips. "Listen."

I hear screams . . . some recorded . . . some alarmingly real. I hear crashes, thuds and echoes. There are flashing lights, too. It is one of those haunted houses that one reads about in Ray Bradbury stories . . . except they're usually in Ohio or some other bucolic Arcadia. In such stories, invariably set in a "sizzling" summer, a twelve-year-old boy goes to a carnival, enters a house of horror . . . and, five thousand words later, experiences some epiphany after which he will never be the same again.

A scream. My heart pounds. A creepy, low-pitched laugh, and the back of my neck begins to prickle . . . this canvas portal is far more nerve-racking than a dozen jars of pickled foetuses.

"How can you pass this up?" he says. "Hell itself is beyond this door. Walk through it if you dare. Just two saluengs, and you'll get a taste of the most frightening features of the afterlife—"

And then I hear a lone voice above the hubbub: "Stop! Just leave me alone! I ain't done nothing to you—" Virgil's voice.

Quickly I hand the attendant a shiny blue one-baht banknote and charge through the curtain.

The first thing I encounter is a narrow passageway. The walls, painted in lurid, glow-in-the-dark colours, show a grisly assortment of *prehds*, *pisaats* and *phiis*—the creatures of the night. The passage gives way to a bamboo bridge. I clutch the ropes at its sides. The fall is only a few feet, but through a miracle of forced perspective it looks like an immense vista of the underworld. Mists swirl about me. Keenings and ghastly screams play continuously in the background—the *ramwong* music, from outside, forms a surreal counterpoint at the threshold of hearing. Out of bubbling pools of lava pop demons with tridents, ripping out the tongues of the damned, cutting off their heads, poking them, prodding them, swinging them by their hair. The god Yama is seated on a throne, wearing a necklace of human skulls, filling the chamber with cavernous guffaws.

The bridge curves and now I'm in a labyrinth of mirrors and Plexiglas walls. The mirror panels and the clear walls are mounted on servos and rotate randomly, forming a new labyrinth each time I think I can see the way out. I try to go straight, bump into myself, turn, see myself reflected tenfold, turn again, slip through a side passageway, glance behind, see, in a mirror, an image of Virgil.

Virgil wide-eyed with terror in a strobing red light being menaced by demons who seem to be—

"Virgil!"

I only hear my own voice echoing. I look again and cannot find the mirror.

"Virgil!" I scream.

The mirrors turn once more with a grinding noise that hurts my ears. I squeeze between two panes. There is the scene again. It's down there in the representation of inferno, under the rope and bamboo bridge. I turn a corner and suddenly find myself on a ledge overlooking the hellish pageant. Below me, I see Virgil, Piet and Wilbur. The two white boys have Virgil backed against a vat of fuming pseudo-brimstone. A two-headed demon pops out of the vat, a squirming human soul in his mouth, its legs twitching. As I watch, Wilbur pounces on Virgil and has him in a head-lock, while Piet calmly proceeds to kick him in the face.

Without thinking, I leap down from the ledge. The forced perspective makes it look like a twenty-foot drop, but it is not nearly that far. I land almost instantly. It's a hard metal floor, strewn with scenic rocks. A sharp pain tears through my gluteus maximus.

"Get off him," I say.

"Oh, Justin," says Wilbur, "you finally made it here." He tightens his grip around Virgil's neck.

"Let him go," I say.

"Don't be such a sissie," says Wilbur.

"Stay out of this," says Virgil. "I can handle it."

"What do you mean, you can handle it?" I scream, too furious to pay attention to my agonized arse, "you *can't* handle it! Whenever they start doing this to you, you end up curling up like a *king-kue*! What the hell's the matter with you anyway?"

"Go to hell, Justin! You don't understand," Virgil says miserably.

"He knows his place, that's what," says Piet. "Come and help us, Justin. You're almost English yourself, you know, and *Boer en Brit moet saamstaan*—you and me have to stick together."

"*Almost English*?"

Although I'm not entirely sure at what or at whom I'm feeling this unbounded fury, I'm so enraged that I can barely see straight, and this time it's not vodka. I charge the two boys with every ounce of strength in my eighty-eight pound frame, my fists flailing, shrilling a bloodcurdling war paean at the top of my lungs.

42

The Way Out of Inferno

Wilbur and Piet are so astonished at the ferocity of my attack that at first they do nothing. I am able to punch Piet in the stomach while simultaneously kicking Wilbur's shin so that he collapses in a heap on top of Virgil. The laws of conservation of momentum, however, decree that, having charged the foe with x amount of energy, I now require an equivalent amount of energy to bring me to a stop. Unfortunately, since I meet no resistance, I have no alternative but to trip over the writhing pile of Wilbur, Piet and Virgil, and the next few minutes are spent punching at anything that moves whilst attempting to extricate myself from the tangle.

Someone's foot is hooked around my neck. I shove and find myself with my legs locked around Wilbur's shoulders. He thrashes about and finally dislodges me, and I fly into the air for an ignominious landing in the glop that passes for the fiery lake of brimstone. The mechanical demon pops up, and I find myself climbing up its arm, drenched in cochineal-dyed syrup which tastes like a mixture of petroleum and honey.

"Come back here, you dadburned coward," Wilbur screams. "I'm gonna kick your nigger-loving ass all the way to the dark side of the moon. Get it? *Dark* side of the moon? Ha, ha, ha."

I'm clinging to the demon's arm, and the arm is moving inexorably toward the creature's mouth, and in its mouth there are the legs of its mechanical victim, scissoring the air and surely preparing to decapitate me if I can't disengage myself. The demon's eyes glow red, and the head turns this way and that with a ratchet-ratchet-ratchet sound, like a human skull being pulverized under a millstone. The eyes dart to and fro in time to the grinding noises, and now and then there's a muffled shriek from the victim. Even though I realize that it's all motors and plaster and flashing lights, I am so terrified that I can barely pucker up my rectum to stem the floodgates of my colon.

I'm completely covered with the sticky goo, and the more I struggle the more stuck I get to the arm. I can't really pay attention to Wilbur's abuse. I unbutton my shorts and wriggle out of my shirt, and, clad in only my underwear, leap to freedom, landing a foot or so away from where Virgil is once more being set upon by the other two.

I'm too exhausted to fight. A failure in peace, a failure in war! I sink back on the stony metal floor, ready to faint, knowing full well that when I awaken Virgil will have been reduced to a quivering jelly, and I will have done nothing to prevent it.

At that moment, however, we hear a voice from the rope bridge over our heads. "You let go of him at once, you hear?"

I look up. It is Jessica, resplendent in a white pants suit, with Piak standing by her side.

Wilbur and Piet laugh.

"Quick, Piak," says Jessica. "Plan M."

Piak holds on to the ropes as, extracting a penknife from her bosom, Jessica cuts them. She and Piak swing down in Tarzan-like fashion, grab Wilbur and Piet between their knees, and lift them bodily into the air, depositing them in the very ooze with which I have so lately been baptized. They scream in ear-splitting stereophonic harmony before their voices are drowned in the hellish lake.

Then the two heroic figures land on the ground. Jessica, still brandishing the penknife, stalks about, her eyes flashing like a vengeful Fury's. Piak hastens to Virgil's side. His nose appears to be bleeding. I hear Jessica calling out, "Virgil . . . Justin . . . is you all right?"

So overwhelmed am I by the barbaric splendour of this battle scene that I swoon away completely. . . .

***

I awaken to gentle rocking. It is a boat, and we are gliding down the *klong* toward home. I have been wrapped in a Chinese silk blanket, which drains the heat from my fevered limbs. Virgil is lying next to me. He aches all over and moans as he shifts from side to side. It is his movements that cause the boat to yaw against the still waters of the canal. Piak is rowing, and Jessica is seated at the stern. The breeze toys with her hair and the moon highlights her sweat-slick cheeks with a soft blue glow. She looks down at her brother and me, and I see that she has been weeping. The billowing blouse of her white suit is now stained with blood and dirt. I gaze at her through crusted eyes. She continues to speak, very softly, to Piak in Thai, afraid, perhaps, that she will wake us up.

"That was some fight," says Piak. "Do you think those two boys'll manage to make it home?"

"Sure," Jessica says. "They had a taxi waiting for them, and anyway, we didn't rough them up *that* badly. Cuts and bruises, that's all, and they deserved it."

"What a day! And Master Little Frog's all annoyed at me because I'm trying to save up money for my father's sex-change operation. He doesn't seem to realize it's our only ticket out of the ghetto."

"Well, I realize it," says Jessica. "I know about ghettos."

"Look . . . Khun Nuu's awake," Piak says, in response to a moan.

"But I'm supposed to be spending the night at Piet's house," I say. "Whatever am I to do? I don't even have any clothes . . . and I think I've crapped in my underpants."

"Don't worry, Justin, honey," says Jessica, and she touches my hand, looking down at me with an expression of the utmost gravity. "Everything gone be just fine."

Then Virgil stirs. And he says, "It sure embarrassing to get rescued by my older sister. I wish you'da kept out of it."

"Be reasonable, Virgil," I say. "She saved our lives."

"Be reasonable? What you know about it, banana? And you didn't have no business butting in yourself."

"No business?" I sit bolt upright, and the boat shakes and Jessica is in danger of falling into the water. We bump into the dock of the *ajarn's* house. We can smell the incense and the votive wreaths and hear soft mantras drifting down from the shaman's audience chamber. "No business?" Piak shoves against the dock with his oar, and we go hydroplaning toward the other shore. He paddles wildly to correct our course. Two naked youths, on a midnight swim, leap over us, twin dolphins, larboard to starboard, splashing as they crash. "How can you say I had no business trying to save you from two racist bullies?"

"Yeah, I can say that. Because it not your fight."

"Well, it bloody well ought to be."

"Shut up."

"No, you shut up!" I say. "You're fighting a war on two fronts, and one of those fronts is inside your own head, because half of you *believes* what those boys are saying about Negroes, half of you *knows* that somehow you deserve what you're getting . . . that's what's wrong with you."

Jessica says, softly, "It about time somebody told him that."

"You *all* against me, ain't you?" Virgil says bitterly. And sinks back into slumber.

It must be at least three in the morning by the time we reach Virgil's house. Virgil and I are lying on couches, and I find myself suffering the ignominious fate of having my underwear removed, and my nether parts sponged off by Mrs. O'Fleary. I find the O'Fleary living room strangely comforting. The great big drum, the assegai, the African masks, the hot chocolate that Jessica is painstakingly trying to get me to swallow. A plate of cookies sits on the coffee table, and even from where I am lying I can tell that they are still soft and warm, for their sugary aroma wafts toward me.

Mrs. O'Fleary sighs. "If only your Daddy was here," she says to Jessica. "Every night I worry myself sick he gone get killed, and meanwhile at home my kids are getting theyselfs killed without no help from that VC."

Jessica says, "I thought we left all that behind us when we come here . . . this is as far from Georgia as you can get . . . and we *still* niggers."

"Don't use that word, honey," says Mrs. O'Fleary.

"We done baked a apple pie this afternoon," Jessica says. "Would you like a slice? Maybe with some of that Foremost ice cream?"

"I'm not sure I could, actually," I say.

"Apple pie?" Virgil moans in his sleep.

"It won't take a moment to heat it up," says Jessica and disappears into the distant gloom.

I take another gulp of the hot chocolate. It feels good. I gobble up a couple of chocolate chip cookies and say to Mrs. O'Fleary, "Those boys who beat up Virgil weren't bad people. They were kind to me. They shared their secrets with me. Piet's very creative, you know, he does wonderful things in miniature, he's built a whole city under his bed . . . and Wilbur's wild and funny and a little bit innocent, I guess . . . like Virgil. But suddenly, all at once, they become evil . . . split personality or something, I don't know. I don't understand why it is, but I want to know why. I want to so much it makes me shake all over."

Mrs. O'Fleary—switching automatically into standard English—says, "Why, Justin, that's a very special gift."

"What do you mean, Mrs. O'Fleary?"

"A lot of people, Justin, they'd rather not know things. They'd rather just go on the way they've always gone on. Wanting to know so hard that it aches inside you, that's a gift. Could be it won't give you much happiness in your life, but it's a gift all the same."

"I don't think I want a gift like that," I say. "I mean, if it's not going to make me happy."

"Don't ever say that, Justin, honey," she says. "If Adam hadn't eaten the apple of knowledge, there wouldn't be any history. We'd all be stuck in Paradise for ever."

"But wouldn't that have been better?"

"Maybe for some people. But a walled utopia, even if it takes care of your every need, is still a prison. Someone has to say, 'There's a whole world out there . . . and I'm willing to pay the price to find out about it.' Someone has to take the first step . . . out of Eden . . . into the real world. That takes courage."

This is a hard thing to swallow. In only a few months I, too, will be exiled from the walled kingdom. I can no longer believe that this will be an entirely good thing.

"Jessica," Mrs. O'Fleary says as her daughter emerges from the kitchen, "you go upstairs and bring down the portable tape recorder. There's something I want Justin to hear."

Jessica leaves and presently returns with the machine and a four-inch reel of tape. "Last month," says Mrs. O'Fleary, "a man marched on Washington at the head of a quarter of a million people. He was a Negro man. But I don't think that what he said was just for Negro people. I think it is for you, too."

She plugs in the recorder and presently I hear a voice issuing from its tinny speaker. Even through the crackle of static it is a mighty voice, with ringing cadences, and the speech has the intensity of a sermon:

. . . I have a dream that one day on the red hills of Georgia the sons of former slaves and the sons of former slave owners will be able to sit down together at the table of brotherhood . . .

. . . I have a dream that my four little children will one day live in a nation where they will not be judged by the colour of their skin . . .

. . . Let freedom ring . . . let it ring from every village and every hamlet . . . to speed up that day when all of God's children, black men and white men, Jews and Gentiles, Protestants and Catholics, will be able to join hands and sing in the words of the old Negro spiritual, "Free at last, Free at last, thank God Almighty we are Free at last!"

How is it that the words of a black man in a foreign country can shake the very foundations of my secret kingdom? Oh, they are beautiful words. But they have not lifted the bruises from Virgil's face, nor have they solved the dichotomy of how I feel about my friends and foes, Wilbur and Piet. I do not know if words alone can heal those wounds or unravel the twisted conundrum of my life. I am still wandering in the labyrinth of mirrors. I am still a poet without a purpose, a quest without a vision.

Are these the words I must heed? Is this the dream that will show me the way out of Inferno? As the tape runs out and the reel spins empty, I sniff the air and realize that I'm getting an irresistible craving for apple pie.

43

Justin the Healer

The next day is a very strange day because I spend it at home, in bed, and there is no need to explain to anyone why I am not at the van Helsings' house because the three Fates, of course, are still in Hua Hin. I spend Sunday in a kind of stupor. I do not even dream, which is strange, because so much has happened in the previous twenty-four hours: the glue-sniffing, the Richardsons' spat, the cricket match, the house of ill repute, the *likay*, the war in the house of horrors, the rescue by Tarzan and Jane, and the reverberant rhetoric of Martin Luther King.

Sunday evening, the Fates return from the beach and the household is as bustling as ever. But as I sit down at dinner, listening to their gossip, I find I am less interested than before. My mind is full of tremendous ideas. The trouble is that they are also rather vague. A grand concept is about to be born but gives me no inkling as to its nature.

Monday, however, is even more strange.

The first class of the day is Mrs. V.'s. When we file in, we see a large pile of thin blue books on her desk. "Would you mind giving these out, Griselda?" says Mrs. Vajravajah.

The books turn out to be *Romeo and Juliet*—the Pelican edition. Unbowdlerized, uncontaminated by the well-meaning hand of Cedric Pendleton-Smith, OBE. As my copy lands on my desk, I flip through it. The creamy-smooth paper and the way the lines dance across the page almost make me forget the torments of the weekend. A woodcut of the bard himself gazes serenely at me from the cover.

"All right, children," says Mrs. V., "this is the real thing . . . what we've been waiting for these long months. So, if you don't mind, let's turn to the very beginning of *The Most Excellent and Lamentable Tragedy of Romeo and Juliet* and plunge straight into the prologue."

And we do. For the next forty-five minutes we bask in the opulence of Shakespeare's language, are appalled at the gang violence in sixteenth-century Verona, and thrill to the erotic drumbeat of iambic pentameter, for Mrs. V. does not shrink from telling us that the word "die" in Shakespearean English also means to experience an orgasm; and those of us who aren't quite sure what an orgasm is are nevertheless titillated by the shocked gasps of those who are in the know, or think they are.

Virgil, Wilbur and I sit staring at our textbooks. None of us dares look at either of the others in the eye. Piet is not present, his mother having apparently phoned in to say that he is indisposed.

But later, between classes, finding myself by chance at the adjacent urinal to Wilbur and seeing that we are alone together, I give him my coldest stare.

And Wilbur says—without a trace of the easy charm that is his most characteristic trait—"I'm sorry, Justin."

I don't want to forgive him, and I just stand there, baleful and unbending.

"But Virgil's right . . . it wasn't your fight," Wilbur says, and he steps away from the urinal, turns his back to me and drops his shorts all the way to the floor. His buttocks are completely covered with livid stripes. Here and there, a deep puncture shows the impact of a belt buckle.

"Oh, my God," I say.

Matter-of-factly he pulls his shorts back up and fastens them. "My dad can be pretty mean sometimes," he says.

"He did that to you for fighting?"

"No," he says, "for losing."

"Losing?"

"To a nigger," he says. He shrugs. "Hey. Can't win 'em all."

I am incredulous. "That's not possible," I say. "When we were at Piet's house, I heard your father talk about Virgil's father . . . about his bravery in the battlefield . . . about how it made him think quite differently about Negroes."

"But Justin, that's the war. You can't always keep the same values you grew up with, not when you're being attacked by hordes of slopes. But it'll be over soon. General Harkins says the military advisors will be home by Christmas and home, now, things're different. Don't worry about me, Justin. I'm used to it. Shit happens."

At first I can't believe my eyes and ears. I had been ready to give him the cold shoulder for the rest of the school year, but now I see that he, too, is the victim of a self-perpetuating cycle of injustice. It's not him. It's not Piet, it's not Virgil. It's the whole forsaken universe, locked in a maze without doors, all of us, each one of us an island, each one of us alone.

"Are you crying, Justin?"

"No. Something in my eye." I turn away so that he won't have to see me.

"Don't feel sorry for me. I took it like a man."

"Yeah." But I know he is anxious not to lose the last vestige of my respect.

"Hey, it was worth it. It was neat to prowl through Bangkok in the middle of the night. The lights—the sleazy bars—the wild women—even that bitch who tried to bite off my dick—it was *real* neat. I'd do it again tonight, if I could. But I'm grounded for a month."

I'm hardly listening to him because my mind is racing faster than I can keep up. I'm thinking of the *likay* and the rapt attention of its audience—the inspired commingling of the divine and the mundane. I'm thinking of the world of the high Olympians, the world of absolutes. I'm thinking of the bedtime story that Mrs. O'Fleary told us, that night, so many moons ago, about Orpheus and Eurydice and an African king named Shangó and Abraham Lincoln. And finally, all these disparate visions are beginning to coalesce into a great concept waiting to be born.

Look to the living, as my dead chameleon has told me through the miming of a shaman. Yet I can't single-handedly bring about the dream that moved more than two hundred thousand people to march on Washington. I can't abolish apartheid. I can't even force my feuding friends to acknowledge each other's common humanity. I feel so helpless it hardly seems worth taking even one step towards healing the world's dark pain.

And yet there *is* one tiny thing that I can do, is there not?

After school, between the final bell and my daily dose of Father Regenstrom, I go to Mrs V.'s classroom. She is sitting at her desk, marking tests with a red pen and tossing them on to a pile. She looks up and sees me and smiles.

"Justin," she says, "you must be pleased that we're actually working on Shakespeare now. I know you've already read *Romeo and Juliet*, so it will be smooth sailing for you at least until Christmas."

"Actually, I'm not here about Shakespeare . . . I'm here about the possibility of doing another play."

"Well, perhaps we could mount a production of *Romeo*. You'd love to play someone like Mercutio, wouldn't you? Full of wit and anger and bitter irony."

"Actually, I'm thinking of writing another play . . . a much better one. A play about . . . about something real."

"Social realism, eh?" says Mrs. V. "I thought you were more of a classics sort of person."

"Well, you see, I want to do Orpheus and Eurydice, but I want to move the setting to the American Civil War . . . and I want to put in a lot of contemporary references . . . and I want to sort of combine

317

all these things together so that it'll actually *mean* something to . . .
I mean . . . to the other children. In your class. You know." I am barely
capable of expressing myself, because, you see, the huge idea is only
now beginning to gel in my mind. . . . "Well, you see, I saw this *likay*
the other night at the *ngaan wat*, and I got to thinking . . . well, here's
something that's got gods and goddesses and mythological beings
in it, but somehow it's all *real* to the audience, you know, it's not
like they were up there on Mount Olympus hurling down the odd
thunderbolt to alleviate their boredom, I mean . . . well, Mrs.
O'Fleary told me this bedtime story, you see, and . . . well, you
remember, that day out under the banyan tree, the lynching? Well,
you see—okay, I'll put it another way. My friends are all hurting. I
want to bring them all together in this one big *thing* that'll make
them understand one another, and I know I'm not really saying this
right but you see, it's because I know that they *could* understand
each other if only they would see each other through each other's
eyes, and, oh, my thoughts are getting so convoluted that I can't even
remember where the beginning of this sentence was, but I . . . well,
I heard this tape of Martin Luther King, and . . . oh, Mrs. V, it's all
rushing together, rolling up into a great round ball and trying to
force its way out like . . . like . . . a monstrous huge massive . . . I don't
know, *turd*! I can't explain it . . . it hurts in my belly . . . I. . . ."

"Well," says Mrs. V, laughing a little, but not unkindly, "it has
been said that giving birth is very much like shitting a watermelon."

Well. With that homely simile, she's popped the balloon of my
pretension. I can't help laughing. In fact, I laugh until it hurts so
much that I end up having to make a quick run to the bathroom,
where, as it happens, Virgil has just finished.

"I'm sorry, Justin," Virgil says softly. "Guess I shoulda stood on
my own two feet."

I race past him in my haste to urinate. He stands in the doorway a moment. I say, "Why are the two of you apologizing to *me*
all the time? I mean, couldn't you just apologize to each other?"

"Don't work that way," says Virgil, closing the lavatory door. It
occurs to me that each of them might be using me, in some way,

as a conduit to the other, since their code of conduct forbids them to address one another directly.

When I creep back to Mrs. Vajravajah's room to finish our conversation, I hear voices. I stand just outside the door. I am sweaty and the air conditioning feels good. A man is speaking, and I realize that it is Dr. York, the headmaster, whose *eaughing* out-*eaughs* even the transcendent *eaughing* of Dr. Richardson.

"So, my dear Mrs. Vajravajah," he is saying, "whatever are we to do with that wayward young playwright of ours? Miss Cicciolini almost committed suicide last week when he handed in his biology notebook with the margins drawn in green instead of *red*"—I note that he automatically emphasizes the word "red" in deference to Miss Cicciolini—"and Father Regenstrom has been popping barbiturates before confronting the boy at his daily Latin lessons— he *will* ask those embarrassing questions about Petronius and Ovid, for heaven's sake! Oh, I know he's intelligent, and so on, but he's so damned disruptive, I've half a mind to expel him just to avoid the aggravation! Why, today I heard from Mrs. van Helsing that the boy went over to spend a weekend at their house and the next thing she knows is that her boy is lying in a ditch somewhere, with Justin nowhere in sight! The boy's a menace!"

This latter story ought to strain credulity. I remember how Piet once told his mother—after his attempted bullying of Virgil at the club—that he and Wilbur had been attacked by a "great big kaffir". But the headmaster doesn't seem to doubt the mother's word at all. It's this way grownups have of always supporting each other's positions, no matter how preposterous. "And now, you say, he wants to put on another play?" he continues. "I suppose you'll do what you want anyway—you're as stubborn as he is, in a way—but I can't say I really think that all these goings-on are conducive to decent education. . . ."

"Well, headmaster," says Mrs. V., "I think we're on the verge of an important breakthrough here. It's true that the boy is . . . well . . . distracted at times. But he has a certain vision. He sees past people's masks. He has compassion, you know. He wants to redeem the whole world, starting with his closest friends. I think that his play could make it happen. I want to try."

"Well, I've given you a lot of leeway . . . I've little choice in the matter, since your uncle at the Ministry of Foreign Affairs has the power to dissolve the school all over again with a stroke of his pen . . . but if this is another of your well-meaning fiascos, I'm simply going to have to call a halt to all this newfangled experimental education."

So there is more riding on this than I imagined. It's not just that I have the chance to heal the rift between my friends. It's not only going to be a chance to prove that I *can* bridge the mythic and the down-to-earth. Mrs. Vajravajah's career is also on trial, and my own tenure at the Scola Britannica is apt to be abbreviated if my plan falls short.

I don't dare go back inside to face the headmaster. The task I am about to undertake is Promethean. I am torn by self-doubt. How could I possibly hope to accomplish all these things? Yet I, too, have a dream, though it is not of millions of blacks and whites walking hand in hand into some rose-tinted sunset. It is merely a dream of me and Wilbur and Piet and Virgil and Piak all sitting together in the treehouse . . . the branches groaning under our weight, the treehouse ready to tumble, plank by plank, on to the grass strewn with deliquescing mangoes . . . but we don't care because this is a magic moment, we are all laughing at the same bad jokes, curious about the same forbidden things, sharing our common strengths and frailties.

This time, the play *will* be the thing.

But so daunting is the responsibility of it all, and the grandeur of it that I can't face Mrs. V. or Dr. York right now. I slink away to the library. For once in my life I am looking forward to an hour of Father Regenstrom's Latin conjugations.

44

The Trojan Horse

Some weeks have now passed since the weekend at the van Helsings'. I have been hard at work on this grand synthesis of East and West, which, I have no doubt, will revolutionize the course of literature—nay, indeed, all art.

I work on the play day and night, so I haven't really paid any attention to the world at large. I have noticed dimly that Griselda is moodier than usual; that Wilbur, Piet and Virgil appear to have reached a mutual détente, though they are not quite cordial to one another in school; that Samlee is spending more and more time over at the main house and that her attire has become rather less flashy, less, dare I say it, *nouveau-riche*; that Aunt Ning-nong is much less dour than she used to be; that the ex-gardener, having managed to parlay his way into my uncle's affections, has become considerably more outré in his choice of feminine attire.

I spend my afternoons at the ruined house, dragging old tomes off their shelves and poring over them, raising dust each time I turn one of those brittle foxed pages. Evenings, sometimes, I visit the O'Fleary's and listen to Virgil's mother tell more tales of Great-uncle Orpie and doomed Arcola. Before I go to bed, I look in on my great-grandmother, who lies in her bed, speechless and expressionless, wondering whether she will turn and blink at me. An image of the Four-faced Brahma has been placed in the foyer outside her room. Each night, the servants light votive candles. Perhaps it is the Brahma that has kept my great-grandmother still among us, though she wavers between the worlds of life and death.

One evening, we're all dining at Uncle Vit's house. Busaba the transvestite has been taking a cooking course at the Alliance Française, at my uncle's expense, and tonight is her début. Two of the Fates—the eldest has been unaccountably delayed—and even my grandfather and a couple of my grandmothers are present. Samlee is there, too, having made a fairly convincing exterior transformation to *phudii*hood. The O'Flearys are there—except for the colonel, who is off in the jungle as usual and whom I have yet to meet, and Jessica, who is at a rehearsal of some choir or other.

Given the increasingly anomalous position of Piak in the household, it is unclear whether he should actually join the *phudiis* at the table or eat in the servants' quarters. The solution is a compromise; he dines in solitude, at a card table at the far end of the dining room from which vantage point he can see through the open doorway clear to the scullery whence he so lately came.

The décor in my uncle's dining room includes an art deco jukebox, which does not work, and a battered Victrola, which does. It is even now filling the room with scratchy, squeaky music of the Mantovani variety. In honour of the dinner's European theme, we have even been asked—nay, commanded—to wear shoes into the dining room. The entire floor has been covered with a clear plastic sheet to protect its polished marble surface from the assault of footgear.

While it is true that it was years before I actually allowed a morsel of Thai food to pass my lips, and then only by accident, it is also a fact that after becoming used to the idea that this food wasn't going to kill me, I have enjoyed it ever since. French food, however, is still quite alien to me. The pinching of my brand-new patent leather shoes adds to its piquancy. The first course is a potage in which decapitated fish stare up at me from a sea of unpeeled crustacean and bizarre molluscs. It takes me a long time to unhinge the shellfish, crack open the prawns, and reposition the fish heads so they are no longer making eyes at me. By the time I have finished rearranging the food so I can safely ingest it without regurgitating, it is time for the second course, which consists of snails.

The spectacle of the solicitous Busaba, whose five-o'clock shadow is clearly visible to those in the know beneath the mask of pancake makeup, is purest tragicomedy. Piak's father seems to have mastered the gestures and movements of the opposite sex, but I am always aware that I am witnessing a simulacrum of femininity rather than the *verum corpus*. He is wearing a Bardot-like blonde wig and a gown that would flatter Venus. Our dinner conversation is limited to the weather, everybody's health and of course the artistry of the cuisine. As Uncle Vit rhapsodizes about Busaba's skills, Samlee is sensuously feeding my grandfather a baguette—an interesting case of role reversal to those acquainted with Samlee's special abilities.

"You're a gynaecologist, aren't you?" Mrs. O'Fleary asks Uncle Vit.

"I love my work," he says, "and I hope one day to have the honour of seeing you on my stirrups. I must confess that female pudenda are the most beautiful sight in the world. One wishes sometimes," he adds, glaring at Busaba, "that more people had them."

I almost choke on an escargot.

"Jolly good snails," says my grandfather.

"The next course is coming up," says Busaba, sailing in from the pantry. "It's veal medallions in a bordelaise sauce—"

Suddenly, the dinner is interrupted by the appearance of Aunt Ning-nong and Dr. Richardson. My aunt, dressed to the teeth, appears unwontedly distraught. Dr. Richardson is his usual self— more than that—his *"what-what-what"* is positively manic tonight. At the sight of Aunt Ning-nong and Dr. Richardson, the other two Fates glare grimly and only pick at their food.

Two chairs are quickly moved in. They do not eat. I am about to ask whether our rude fare might be too meagre for them but stop myself in time.

"Ahem," said Aunt Ning-nong. "I've a rather momentous announcement to make. For the past few months, I'm afraid there have been a number of, ah, surreptitious goings-on. I'm sorry that I have concealed the details from you, my friends and relatives, but I couldn't really say anything until I was absolutely certain that I wouldn't make a fool of myself."

"Well, don't keep us in suspense all night," my grandfather/ great-uncle says between being fed spoonfuls of veal. "I'm an old man. At this rate, I'll expire before the big revelation."

"Well, it's very simple really, you see," says Ning-nong, though it is clearly nothing of the kind. "It seems that I am to become . . . after a few minor inconveniences are taken care of . . . the new Mrs. Theodore Richardson."

"Oh, I say, what, what," says Dr. Richardson. Seizing Aunt Nit-nit's wineglass from the table, he swigs its contents in a single gulp.

The silence is so profound one might have heard a cockroach farting.

What could be racing through the minds of Aunt Ning-nong's two sisters, each of whom has been the objects of Dr. Richardson's lust? Their faces run the gamut of emotions: anger, disbelief, shock, relief, envy, sibling-resentment, wounded pride, affronted dignity, dismissive *hauteur* and feigned indifference. Aunt Ning-nong does not appear especially radiant at being the bearer of such auspicious tidings. Why? I wonder. What on earth could have possessed her to do it, if it's not going to change her in any way?

I am sure the whole thing is a way for Ning-nong to out-trump her younger siblings. Perhaps she is doing it to save her younger sisters from themselves. Perhaps, beneath her old-maid exterior, she has been plotting this coup all along. It is, of course, not much of a coup, and Dr. Richardson not much of a catch; the "few minor inconveniences" she has mentioned must surely include such complex proceedings as divorce.

My feelings, too, are complex, for they include Griselda. If the divorce and wedding do in fact take place, would not Griselda become some kind of cousin of mine? And would not the passionate, metallic kiss that she bestowed on me in the swan-shaped hedge at the van Helsings then constitute incest? And if it is, is it retroactive? Do I now, like Oedipus, have to pluck out my eyes and wander the earth to expiate a heinous sin I never knew I committed? More to the point, what about the sins of the future? I wonder if Father Regenstrom sells plenary indulgences.

I find myself becoming furious. "I think it's a terrible idea," I say, crossing my arms and glowering.

"Nobody asked you," says Aunt Ning-nong.

"Dr. Richardson," I say, "this has gone too far. You've already indulged your lusts with two of my aunts"—at this point my grandmothers look at each other and sigh—"and I know you keep a collection of the throat cultures of all your paramours in Petri dishes in your laboratory—and you seem to think nothing of ruining people's lives—like Mrs. Richardson's—and Aunt Nit-nit's—and Aunt Noi-noi's—not to mention Griselda's. You're an absolute cad, and it's very wicked of you to ask Aunt Ning-nong to marry you, and if it's the money you're after, you ought to know that my great-grandmother's will is going to surprise every last one of you. . . ."

"The will!" says Noi-noi excitedly. "So she *did* tell you where she hid it!"

I am, of course, bluffing, for I have been unable to figure out the clue my great-grandmother gave me.

"Wait a minute," says Dr. Richardson, "I didn't ask her to marry me; *she* asked *me*, what, what."

"Well," says my grandfather, "why not? After all, Phra Law, one of the greatest heroes of Thai literature, married two sisters at the same time. By all means, take the bloody lot of them. You're a foreigner and all that, but we're a modern family, and we shan't hold it against you."

"Grandfather, how could you!" I say. I can't explain the panic I'm feeling. The idea of introducing Dr. Richardson into our family circle is shattering to me. "Dr. Richardson's going to spoil every-thing . . . he's like . . . like a Trojan horse!"

"Why, I do believe the child is jealous!" says Aunt Ning-nong. "How flattering!"

"Jealous?" I scream. The thought had not occurred to me, but the fact that it contains a kernel of truth only serves to exacerbate my rage. "Jealous? Jealous?" I sputter several more times before becoming incoherent.

"Justin! Get a grip on youself!" Virgil whispers, as his mother looks about uncomfortably.

I bite my lip. The three Fates are the most ill at ease of the com-pany. It occurs to me that this is the first time their common inti-macy with Dr. Richardson has been openly discussed. I've put my foot in my mouth in more ways than one. The silence goes on and on and on, and sometime during the course of that silence we all become aware of the smell of burning.

I see the others one by one glancing furtively toward the kitch-ens. Has Busaba botched the soufflé? She's nowhere to be seen. The smell grows stronger. In fact there's a certain cloudiness in the air. It is smoke, and it is drifting in from outside.

Suddenly Busaba rushes into the dining room, so distracted that she forgets to speak in falsetto. "The ruined house! It's on fire!"

The votive candles!

Suddenly I realize that my great-grandmother is lying in the ruined house—that the flames may already have—

For a moment, everyone is frozen in position, like a living tableau. A strange emotion flickers across Aunt Ning-nong's coun-tenance—is it because her bombshell has been so thoroughly out-gunned? One more moment . . . then another . . . then, all at once, everyone leaps into action.

"Oh, heavens, someone ring the fire department!" Uncle Vit cries, waiting for some lackey to pick up the phone, which is no more than three feet away from the hands he is wringing. "We've got to have someone put the fire out."

"Don't be crazy!" says my grandfather. "It'll take them an hour to get here in the traffic. We're going to have to put it out ourselves."

At which point everyone gets up and scrambles for the front door. We race to the ruined house. About twenty people are already standing on the lawn. Flames leap from the windows. The wood is old and rotten and cracks as the fire darts along the walls. Dr. Richardson *has* been a Trojan horse after all! And Troy is falling before my very eyes . . . hundred-gated, gold-rich Troy where I have fought a thousand battles fantastical. Smoke billows out of the front door and pours down the porch steps, its acrid scent mingling with the sickly-sweetness of ripe mangoes and *phuttachaat* flowers. The crowd in front of the ruined house begins to swell. Why won't someone *do* something? They're all talking at once.

"Let's put this thing out," Uncle Vit is saying. "Could some of the servants go and get some water-buckets or something? Perhaps a hose? There is a water spigot and a coiled hose right in front of him, but apparently it's beneath his notice. My aunts are indulging in some very competitive screaming.

"For God's sake!" I shout. "Don't any of you realize that great-grandmother's probably still in there?"

No one is listening. A porch-column snaps and the crowd takes a few steps backward, then continues to jabber and scream as before. Busaba appears to be trying to get Uncle Vit to pick up the hose, but he merely looks at it in confusion. At length, the ex-gardener can't stand it any more.

"All right!" she shrieks. "I'll put out the damn thing." She grabs the hose, turns on the water, and runs toward the building. As the heat waves pound her, she rips off her blouse and casts it aside. Her bra comes off too, and we see that it is stuffed with wadded newspaper. Busaba's Bardot wig is now askew, and her once busty figure has become the ripplingly muscled torso of a man.

The women scream.

"Dad! You're blowing your cover!" Piak yells at him.

"I don't care," says Busaba. "The *khunying* was very good to me. I just can't stay to see all these rich people standing around wringing their hands."

I'm horrified at the realization that she must be in there somewhere. Doesn't anyone care? Are they so paralyzed with terror that they can't think of an aged woman?

I'm not thinking about smoke inhalation and self-immolation. Only of the topless towers of Ilium going up in flames in the midst of the Phrygian plain . . . of countless books tumbling from their shelves . . . of the clank of bronze on the cobblestones . . . of men in flames plummeting from Cyclopean walls . . . of my great-grandmother, lying in her bed and unable to move, waiting for death. . . .

"I'm going to get her out!" I shout, and I begin running toward burning Troy, heedless of the fumes that scour my nostrils and abrade my lungs. Everyone is screaming at me to stay back, but they sound infinitely far away. As I run toward the ruined house I am also running back in time, running toward history.

45

Out of the Burning City

I leap on to the front porch. I sprint into the foyer. On a niche above the entrance to my great-grandmother's room sits the golden image of the Four-faced Brahma. I was right. It was the votive candles that started the fire. A circle of flames surrounds the god, but he himself sits serene, untouched. Smoke billows around me, but I'm not afraid. The ruined house is still my secret kingdom. I cannot be harmed. Already the great balustrade has become the battlements of Troy. Already the fire's breath is the wind that sweeps over the Phrygian plain and carries the stench of death toward the sea. In the citadel, King Priam clasps the altar of the gods and waits for death, but he is already doomed.

The door to my great-grandmother's room is open. It is a dark rectangle. The fire has not yet reached it. I am like Aeneas who must bear his ancient father on his back and flee the burning city to found a new one on the shores of Italy. The screams of my relatives from the lawn echo in the distance like the death-shrieks of the Trojan women. The fire roars. The smoke spirals.

Awakened from sleep by the clamour of slaughter, I have barely had time to put on my armour. My bronze blade has splintered. But there is someone I must rescue. The gods will shield me from the flames. I look up and see the god and think I see him smile. No matter that it is Brahma. I know now that they are all the same. My dead chameleon dwells both in the Elysian Fields and in Kailasa, abode of the eastern gods. The two worlds are merging. As I murmur a prayer to my father Zeus, I also pray to the four-armed one who sits above the flames. I pray to him for the first time in my divided life . . . for I sense that this awful fire is welding the sundered pieces of my soul.

I have fought my way to the citadel. I have ripped down the veil and entered the sanctum of the goddess. She is lying on the bed just as I last saw her, her eyes closed.

"Great-grandmother." I creep over to her bedside, tug lightly at her arm.

She opens her eyes. "Oh, there you are, Norman," she says. "Very good of you to come. You're just in time for the shower scene."

"We've got to go, Great-grandmother! No more scenes from *Psycho*. The house is burning down." Where is the wheelchair? I don't see it anywhere in the room. There's sweat in my eyes, and I can't seem to blink it away, and it smarts.

"Burning down?" she says. Slowly . . . agonizingly slowly she sits up in the bed. "Why, so it is." Her eyes are far away. It is as though she were gazing right through me, through the wall of smoke, to another country that is closed to me.

"Great-grandmother, where do they keep the wheelchair? We've got to get you out of here."

"Don't worry, my son," she says. I don't know if she realizes she is talking to me, or whether she thinks that my great-uncle is beside her rather than out panicking on the lawn. She smiles. "We are protected. Because of my vow. I cannot die yet. Have you figured out the puzzle about where I put the will?"

"No, Great-grandmother."

"It's strange . . . I don't see so clearly any more. When I look at you I see something very spiritual . . . perhaps an angel . . . standing in a shaft of light."

"That's not a shaft of light, Great-grandmother. That's . . . that's the fire through the doorway. We've got to go." She starts to cough. The smoke is working its way into the room now. It's forking up between cracks in the floor. I, too, am coughing now. "Come on, Great-grandmother." I start to pull off the bed sheets. She is frail, almost a skeleton, shrouded in a stained nightgown. I put my arms around her and try to lift her . . . she is so light that I pull too hard and she cries out . . . the pain jolts her into awareness of the world and she whispers, "Gently, gently, Little Frog."

"The wheelchair. . . ."

"There's no wheelchair, Little Frog. They took it away to mend a broken spoke. But it doesn't matter. Hold my hand, and I'll follow. My soul will leave my body. I am light as air."

I try to carry her in my arms. I stumble. The smoke roils at ground level and tears blind me. We're both on the floor now, and I'm dragging her . . . inch by inch . . . toward the entrance.

"Towels . . . the water-jug. . . ." she says.

Looking up, I see towels draped across the nightstand. There is a half-empty carafe of water. I get up and stagger over. I slosh the water over the towels. I crouch back down and wrap our faces in the towels. Then, propping up my great-grandmother against my shoulder, I head for the doorway, almost falling with every step.

The ancient hero in me speaks: "Don't be afraid. We'll soon be free of this place. The city may be razed, but they can't touch our hearts. Soon we'll go across the sea and found a new kingdom, more shining and more grand."

"Across the sea?" my great-grandmother murmurs. "We'll be lucky if we reach the front door. . . ."

We're through the door of her room now, and we're crawling across the marble-faced floor of the foyer. Somewhere behind us comes the *crack* of a falling beam. The tall celadon vase that once stood by the landing has rolled down the steps and shattered. The marble floor has heated up so that its touch scorches our hands and knees.

"Just a few more feet, Great-grandmother!" I tell her. "A few more feet, that's all—"

The exterior wall collapses. We're on an island of marble in a sea of flame. The far shore is the lawn, and it's jammed with people now. Men in uniforms—firefighters perhaps—are hosing us with water. The fire roars and hisses where the water strikes it and gives off clouds of thick black smoke. "We're saved!" I say. "The firemen finally made it through the traffic. . . ." It is beginning to dawn on me that this is no epic fantasy . . . my secret kingdom is really being destroyed . . . there is no turning back. Someone dashes across the steps with blankets, throws them over us. I turn back, gaze up the stairs to the first floor . . . the cobwebbed rooms full of moth-eaten clothes and ancient porcelain . . . the library. Not the library! Not all those dog-eared tomes of poesy! Shakespeare, Euripides, Aristotle . . . those million million words that have rung in my ears since I first found the chamber of dust and books . . . I'm going to lose all the books! The firefighter puts his arms around me and steers me toward a patch of grass. Safety is only a step away. Already my great-grandmother is being eased into a wheelchair brought over from the main house, and Kaew is fanning her and holding a bottle of *ya dom* to her nostrils so that she won't pass out.

I think of Euripides, and I go crazy. "Let me go!" I shriek. "I've got to get the books!" And I twist away and sprint across the marble that sears my tender feet, up the burning stairway toward the library . . . The wet towel has gone. I'm gulping down smoke with every breath. There's no more fantasy here.

I enter the room of books. Smoke twirls through the stacks. One bookcase is already unsalvageable, the tomes charred beyond recognition, books I have never yet had a chance to open, worlds lost before I even discovered them. But there is still Shakespeare. I lug the big leatherbound edition off the shelf. I march up to the window, smash it open and toss the book out into the jasmine bushes. I run back and grab another armful: Keats, Euripides, Wilde, Grace Metalious—classics and bestsellers mixed up together—I throw them down into the garden. I go back.

Aristotle! Snoopy! Nabokov! Sir Thomas Browne! Indiscriminately now, unable even to read the spines, I grab, dash, throw, dash, grab, dash, throw.

I'm sweating, and I'm coughing and I go back and forth, though the fire is creeping closer and closer to me—

My briny eyes see almost nothing now. The flames are being doused, and I'm completely encircled by steam and fumes. I can barely make my way toward the books, but still I move, unthinking, an automaton. Each book feels heavier in my arms, until I feel I am carrying all the learning of the world, I am snatching the fire of knowledge from the fire of the sun and, like Prometheus, casting it down into the mortal cosmos.

I am exhausted. My blood has been racing, but now it feels sluggish and cold. The smoke is finally affecting me. Everything swims.

I think I see the shadow of a giant chameleon in the mist. . . .

"Save us, Homer," I whisper softly. Homer the poet is still there somewhere amid the shelves of unrescued books. Perhaps he has already burned.

There comes, as though in response to my prayer, a monsoon thundershower. Great blinding sheets of water sluice over the flames. The roof of the ruined house gives way and crumbles around me. I do not know how I avoid being crushed to death. Is it perhaps the shadow of the chameleon that seems to hang in the air like a thundercloud, blotting out the dying flames, blocking the burning debris.

Three figures emerge from the wall of smoke and water.

"Virgil?" I say softly. I don't know if he can hear me above the thunder.

"What the hell you doing in here?" he says.

"The books."

"Let them burn," he says.

Behind him stands Wilbur Andrews, and behind Wilbur, Piet. "How—why did you come?" I ask.

"I telephoned Piet's house," Virgil says, "and Wilbur was spending the night there, so he came too."

"You telephoned Piet's house? But . . . I thought . . . after the night at the *ngaan wat* . . . I thought. . . ."

Virgil says: "Somebody gots to make the first move."

"Is my great-grandmother—"

"She's fine," Wilbur says. "She's resting over at the main house. She doesn't even have to go to the hospital." Wilbur and Piet stand apart from Virgil; they don't trust each other yet. But the rain won't let up, and we end up huddling closer, under a piece of ceiling that yet overhangs the library like a jagged parasol.

Piet says, "We were talking. The three of us. We were thinking—"

"This country that we're in," says Wilbur, "it ain't home. There's a lot of garbage we're carrying around that doesn't make sense. So we've kind of agreed to, you know, leave it behind from now on."

"Yeah," says Virgil.

The fire and my endangerment have done what nothing else could do—forged a détente among my warring friends. My play is going to work. We will move the audience because the pain and the healing of the characters will have been distilled from the pain and healing of real people.

Chameleon-shaped, the last thundercloud drifts away from the face of the moon, and the charred, slicked, shattered walls of the library glow with a strange liquid radiance. I shall never again stand in this room, I'm thinking. The loss is too big for tears. A deep and nameless emotion grips me and makes me shake all over, as though from a fever. I can't understand it but I am sure the others are feeling it too, for as the rain begins to subside I can see it clearly in their eyes, this quality of awe.

"We'd best get inside," Virgil says.

"Yes," I say. "Inside."

46

The Passion
of Aunt Ning-nong

It is not to be surmised that, after the cataclysm at the ruined house and the tentative steps my friends are now making toward rapprochement, I am immediately transformed from a plagiarizing poetaster to an embryonic Shakespeare. Such metamorphoses belong to the realm of myth and it is only now that I begin to see that there is between the real world and the dream world a clearly demarcated boundary.

Yet there is still magic to be wrung from the last months of childhood. There is still the play to come, and I have yet to take the entrance examination for Eton, which my relatives are all assuming will not be a problem yet which causes me almost daily nightmares in which I see Father Regenstrom pounding me into the ground with an unabridged *Cassell's Latin Dictionary*.

Of the three aunts who live in the wooden house with me, Aunt Ning-nong has always been the hardest to comprehend. Her decision to marry Dr. Richardson is the most inconstruable thing she has ever done. Indeed, the very idea that she might have a love life at all seems far-fetched, never more so than at the dinner-party where she announced her impending matrimony. The two did not act like lovebirds, and nothing has occurred since that day to suggest that they are in love with each other.

Over the next week or so I become convinced that if I understand Aunt Ning-nong, I will indeed have solved the final mystery of the universe. For she has become stranger and stranger of late. Some mornings she appears brightly attired, like a bird of paradise, wearing about a pound of makeup; on other occasions she dresses sombrely, as though we were still mourning for the unknown kinsman who died almost a year ago. I think she is trying on new selves. She hasn't found one that fits. She seems to be getting desperate. She seems to think that a personality is something that can be acquired, like a language, or the ability to play the piano.

Then, on the Sunday after the fire, we are thrown together. The other Fates have gone to Sampheng to shop, and all my friends are otherwise engaged. We are having lunch in the pavilion, just the two of us. Aunt Ning-nong has opted for ringlets. They must have taken all morning to do. Her dress is a subdued grey after the flamboyant, parakeet-festooned muumuu of yesterday.

We eat in silence for a while. Finally, she says, "Little Frog, Little Frog, I need to talk to you." She turns to one of the maids and asks her to bring down something from her bedroom. "Yes . . . the large brown envelope . . . the one tied up with string."

We continue to eat in silence. The meal is a simple *khao man kai*, bland and unobjectionable. My aunt does not even bother to make scathing comments, as she usually does, about the way I put Maggi seasoning on my chicken instead of the traditional fiery sauce that the adults insist on. At length, since she was the one who brought it up, I ask Aunt Ning-nong, "What is it you want to talk about?"

"Well, well, Little Frog, it's . . . we received news yesterday. From"—and she lowers her voice to a melodramatic stage whisper—"your parents."

"My parents?" Of all the things she could have said, this is the furthest from my mind. "How are they?" I ask her, trying to keep my voice level.

"Well . . . they've finally agreed to let me tell you a little bit. She scrutinizes me, wondering perhaps if she can trust me. "But you must solemnly swear that you won't reveal a thing I tell you, not even to your friends in the treehouse."

Perhaps I am a changeling of some kind. Perhaps, like Oedipus, I was abandoned on the steps of this estate in infancy because of some doom-laden prophecy. Aren't I a little old for solemn oaths and secret promises? Not really, I tell myself.

"I swear," I say.

"It's the war, you see. It's not going to be over by Christmas the way the Americans think it is. In fact, it's not going to be over at all. In fact, there's going to be a coup."

"What do you mean, a coup? You mean, tanks rolling down the streets? Perhaps we'll have a few weeks off school again. . . ."

"No, no, not here, silly. In . . . you know. There. The place where they're having the war."

It is, I think, the first time the war has ever been mentioned by any of the three Fates. "They're in the war? But we're not in the war, are we? I thought only Americans were in the war."

"Well, even *they* aren't officially in it, you know."

"Are my parents *spies*?"

"They're doing very important work. Very secret work. I don't know much about it. They've had to be in disguise most of the time. This is the first news we've had for a long time. But it will be over soon, and they will be coming back. That's why they said I could tell you. And they wanted you to have"—at this point the brown envelope tied up in string appears, and Aunt Ning-nong hands it to me gingerly, as though it contains a live cobra—"this."

I open the envelope. Some photographs fall out.

One—a frail young woman standing in front of a clump of banana trees. She's wearing the costume of a hill tribe woman. I don't recognize her at first. Then I remember the eyes of the woman in the photograph framed in Vietnamese mother-of-pearl lacquerware that sits on the dresser in my bedroom. Her eyes, my eyes. There's another picture that is clearly my father, wearing some kind of evening dress, shaking hands with a man whose face is somewhat out of focus but who reminds me of someone I've seen frequently—on magazine covers and newsreels, things like that—oh yes, President Kennedy. That's who it is.

And there's a note.

Dear Little Frog:

We're going to come back to Thailand for the premiere of your new play. Break a leg—or whatever it is they say.

Love,
Mummy and Daddy.

"Aunt Ning-nong . . . you've always known where my parents are, haven't you? And you haven't told a soul. Not even . . ."

"Your other aunts have no idea, really. They think your parents are in America or something. I've had to keep it secret, you see. I promised. Oh, Little Frog, it's been difficult!"

"I see." In every myth, there is a moment when the hero learns that he is really the son of King Aegeus or some other august personage, that his obscure upbringing has all been a sham. The epiphany is supposed to crystallize the inchoate feelings of destiny that have been churning in the hero's mind, and then he sets off on a quest and so on. But mythology has ill prepared me for the discovery that my parents are really working for the CIA. This should be the moment when I deluge my aunt with questions, but instead, it is so hard for me to grasp the enormity of it all that I simply change the subject. "So why are you marrying Dr. Richardson?" I ask her. I am appalled by my own tactlessness, but it's too late.

"I see," says my aunt dryly, "it's truth or consequences."

"Well . . ." I say. "He's hardly what you might call a catch. Or is there something about him I don't know?"

"You know more than anyone else," says Aunt Ning-nong, "with all your tape recordings, hiding under hospital utility carts, and falling out of treetops."

This is getting rather embarrassing. "How do you—"

I, too, have my sources," says Aunt Ning-nong primly. "After all, I am, nominally at least, in charge of your upbringing for the time being. I would be somewhat remiss if I had absolutely no idea what goes on under my own roof." The image of Aunt Ning-nong as a tight-lipped repository of family secrets will take some getting used to. "But since you seem to want to know the truth . . . you know very well that I've *got* to get married. I am the eldest, and doubtless, in the eyes of most of the available men, the least desirable of the lot. But unless I marry, the other two will be unable to do so, and they will continue with their unseemly trysts. For the sake of the family, it seemed advisable to kill two birds with one stone—to remove an obstacle to my sisters' placement in the marriage market and to eliminate the chief source of temptation from their grasp. Besides, thanks to certain sordid revelations from certain reels of tape, Dr. Richardson is soon to be without a wife. It's a very convenient arrangement under the circumstances." The Ning-nong who tells me these things is more like the Ning-nong I have always known. She is truly the eldest of the Fates, coolly weighing the alternatives, tempering her sisters' passions with pragmatism.

"I see, Aunt Ning-nong. But, if you don't mind my saying so, you make it all sound so very . . . so very calculated. I mean, what about *love*?"

"What indeed, Little Frog?" she says. "Why do you think I have been suffering the pangs of hell for the past few weeks? God, I think I'm going through puberty, adolescence and menopause all at once. Love is a terrible thing, and I've always been thankful to be too old for such rubbish. But now that I've gone and made all the arrangements for this match, I suddenly feel . . . well . . . oh, how can I expect you to understand?"

"Oh, but I do understand, Aunt Ning-nong. You've completely submerged yourself in the welfare of this family. And now you're afraid you may have lost track of your own true self." I can see now that the severe and austere Aunt Ning-nong I have known all these years is an assumed persona, but one which has somehow frozen hard around her and immured the soul within. Inside this self-made martyr is a creature of tormented longings and imprisoned passions.

As I consider these revelations, the dishes are silently whisked away. Dessert, a fruit salad of papaya and mangosteen floating in a sweet-salt syrup, comes and goes. Aunt Ning-nong downs a demitasse of coffee afterward, while I continue to sip my Green Spot orange drink. We don't talk to each other. Aunt Ning-nong, I think, already regrets her outburst of emotion. She probably won't have another one for years.

At last, Aunt Ning-nong says, "Shall we go and have a look at the demolition?"

I get up and follow her to where the ruined house once stood. The bulldozers have come and gone. A group of workmen are hard at work with hoes. A couple of gardeners are packing the ground with squares of turf. It is really and truly gone, that house wherein lived all the gods and heroes of the ancient world. The chambers of horrors and the towering parapets and the ancient piles of laundry are all, all gone.

"I know the place meant a lot to you," Aunt Ning-nong says. "But what shall we put there instead? Perhaps we will build a new house on it . . . for when your parents come home. They won't want to occupy the big house. It's such a daunting place, and the old people will drive them crazy. But if you like you can join us when we call in the architect, and you can help pick the design for the house."

She's no longer talking to me as though I'm a child. I think that our conversation in the pavilion has changed things permanently between us. Truth always has consequences.

I wonder what kind of house we'll build on the hallowed ground where my imagination lies buried. Something with towering spires and ornate columns? Hardly. It no longer matters. My parents are coming home. The husk of the ruined house has been removed with the efficiency of servants changing the dishes between courses. Reality has outstripped imagination.

47

Twilight of the Gods

But, of course, imagination has not passed at all. In a sense, imagination has merely thrown away its crutches, taken wing, left its nest, flown, soared, hovered, alighted, found a fresh roosting-place in the treehouse of my soul.

At six-thirty in the morning, the mist still clinging to the boughs of the banyan tree, we meet to rehearse *Orpheus*. We meet before the start of school because the headmaster has decreed that *Orpheus* will be an extracurricular activity and cannot be allowed to impinge on our proper education.

I doubt that the play is much of an improvement over my tragical history of the fall of Troy. But there is something new about it. It doesn't posture as much. It has sincerity. It has commitment. Not just from me, but from the others.

There is a sense that we are building an acropolis on sand, and that the tide of time will soon sweep us away toward our separate destinies. There is a sense of urgency. We all know that Griselda is going back to England after Christmas, and that I'm probably leaving myself, assuming that I pass those entrance examinations. We also have a feeling that the Americans are all going to disappear soon. Everyone says the war's going to end by Christmas. I am the only one who seems to think otherwise and only because of Aunt Ning-nong's revelations about my parents. There's been a kind of coup in Vietnam, just as she said there would be. That leads me to believe that the other things she said might be true too. But I am sworn to secrecy and cannot speak of these things.

Nobody seems to mind coming to school early. We're relishing these final days together. The actors mouth my lines with genuine feeling and lend even my most wrenching turns of poesy a kind of grace.

Many of us are turning or have turned thirteen. Indeed, the première of the play has been scheduled for the day after my own birthday, not long before Christmas. Thirteen, I think, is when the slide show ends. Already I am starting to see the world in terms of act and consequence and further consequence. And so to the rehearsal. . . .

Mrs. O'Fleary's bedtime story was, of course, the myth of Orpheus and Eurydice, superimposed on the landscape of the antebellum South. Since it's already a Greek myth, it has not been difficult to readapt the tale to the format of a Greek tragedy. My big innovation is that Wilbur Andrews will play the role of the Negro slave who journeys to the fantastical Yoruba kingdom to try to wrest his dead lover from the clutches of King Shangó, who is to be played by Piet van Helsing. In the best Euripidean manner, I have tacked on a *deus ex machina* to the finale—Virgil will play the role of Abraham Lincoln, who will descend from heaven at the end of the play to free the slaves, fix everyone's problems, and redeem the universe. The wicked overseer will be played by Jessica in a virtuoso *travesti* performance, and the unfortunate Arcola by Griselda. That is the essence of the grand scheme that I've propounded to Mrs. V.—that the white people will play Negroes and the Negroes white people—that each will achieve an understanding of the other by acting out the other's role. None of the parents is to be told. They will find out only at the première. Perhaps they, too, will be forced to face their prejudices.

This is the theory of it. I am compelling my friends to take part in an audacious experiment in civil rights. The Scola Britannica has become an improbable intersection of disparate universes. Only at this moment, at the tall end of 1963, with these particular children thrown together in these particular circumstances, does this experiment even begin to make sense.

I believe it will be my last and most spectacular feat of magic.

At the moment, however, the magic isn't working very well. We are reading through the prologue, which, as in Euripides, is the purview of the gods—in this case two of them—Abraham Lincoln and King Shangó According to the script, they will both appear in traditional Greek costume, except that, to help the audience identify them, Lincoln will wear a top hat and false beard, and Shangó will sport an assegai and a necklace of human skulls. They are not dressed that way at the moment of course. I've handed out the acetone-smelling purple dittoed copies of the script—I typed up the masters myself, two-fingeredly, on the Hermes portable—and Virgil and Piet are each standing under one of the banyan tree's trunks, waiting to begin.

Here are the opening lines.

```
ABRAHAM ~~LINCONN LINNCOLN~~ LINCULM:
O noble humans of the distant future,
I, too, was once a ~~myetle~~ mortal. But since then
Much more than fourscore and seven years have passed
And I have been translated into god ~~hood~~ head,
Joining the company of High Olympus,
Along with Zeus and all them other ~~guys~~ folks.
```

"And that," says Virgil, "is the dumbest shit that ever done passed my lips."

"Yeah," Wilbur says, "You can't have Abraham Lincoln talking like, you know, some redneck."

"But he's an American!" I say. "And every American I've ever met has talked like—"

"Yeah, well, it's okay for *me* to talk like that, but it just ain't right for the President of the United States to sound like white trash."

Piet, meanwhile, is tapping his feet, waiting to utter his own deathless lines. This is appalling! I mean, I'm perfectly aware that I haven't yet achieved the loftiness of Shakespeare, but how dare these philistines criticize my creation! After all, no one said anything about the Trojan War play, and I know that there were plenty of linguistic gaffes in that. . . . I look from one American to the other. Then I turn to appeal to Mrs. V., who is sitting on a blanket at the edge of the tree's shade, marking our test papers.

"Mrs. V., they're complaining about the script!"

Mrs. Vajravajah merely shrugs.

"But no one said anything about the terrible poetry in the Trojan War play—"

"Because," says Virgil, "they was ancient Greeks, and no one knows how they used to talk back then. But if you want to have someone sounding like Abraham Lincoln, he can't be spoutin' no fake Shakespeare mixed with hillbilly. Have you ever read any of his speeches?"

"Of course I have," I say indignantly. "Didn't I put in the four-score and seven part?"

Piet says, "I don't see why he's in it at all, frankly. I mean, obviously *my* character has to be in it, because the god of the underworld is in the original myth, *and* in Mrs. O'Fleary's story . . . but why Abraham Lincoln? What's the motivation for him being there at all?"

"Well, he's a *deus ex machina*," I say. "It's a rule. You have to have a *deus ex machina* in a Greek tragedy."

"But do you have to have one in a *Southern* Greek tragedy?" asks Wilbur.

Bewildered, Griselda looks up from her script and says, "Ith it the thouth of Greeth or the thouth of America?"

"Oh, you are a lot of uncultured savages," I say.

"Maybe you thouldn't have him thay anything at all," says Griselda. "At leatht, not at firtht."

"How can you have a prologue with no dialogue?" But actually, an idea is coming to mind even as I stand there temporizing. I recall that in *Hamlet*, in the scene where they put on the play in front of the king and he has the fit of conscience that convinces Hamlet that he probably did kill the other king, and you'd think it'd be the end of it except that Hamlet's simply too much of a wet to make up his mind for another two more hours after that, well, in that scene, the actors put on this "dumb show" thing before they actually start acting. "A dumb show!" I say excitedly. "That's what we'll have!"

"You're telling me!" says Wilbur.

"No, no, I mean like a mime, like, you know, charades. We'll have Abraham Lincoln come on . . . maybe even show his assassination . . . and then we can have someone tell the audience that the entire play is kind of a dream vision that he experiences in the moments before his death."

"Bravo!" says Mrs. V., suddenly putting down her test papers and clapping her hands. "I believe Justin has independently discovered the *Verfremdungseffekt*."

"The *what*?" everyone says at once.

"Oh, it's something invented by the playwright Bertolt Brecht, and it's most awfully avant garde. It's to do with shattering the illusion of theatre, the convention that what happens on the stage is somehow 'real', by deliberately violating theatrical realism and invoking things outside the perceptual universe of the characters on stage. . . ."

We are all baffled by this explanation until Jessica says, "Oh . . . you mean like when someone steps out of his role and addresses the audience directly?"

"I get to be the assassin," says Wilbur, and he's got one of those evil-villain glints in his eye.

"You can't play the assassin," I say, "you're already playing the slave."

"*I'll* be the assassin!" says Piet. "I know what I'm going to say."

"No, no, it's all going to be in mime at first." As I quickly rethink the structure of the play, encasing it in a framing device somewhat like that of *The Taming of the Shrew*, I'm scribbling frantically on a notepad. "We will open with Abraham Lincoln settling down in the theatre to watch the play. We'll have sort of a musical overture as he sits there reacting to the play—which will actually be the audience, you see, there's one of those verfremderwhatchamacallits, reversing the roles of the audience and the actors—think you can do that, Virgil?—and then—the music is suddenly cut short by the squeal of a bullet. Virgil clutches his chest and falls to the ground."

Virgil immediately does so and expires dramatically for about five minutes to much laughter. I hold my hand up for silence. I'm starting to get fired up now—this is obviously *much* more effective than what I'd planned originally. "As he dies"—Virgil rolls about again, but no one's watching him much any more—"he suddenly sees a vision of the mythical African King Shangó. Lincoln is racked by agony and doubt." I'm reading now from my scrawled lines of dialogue. "'Was it worth it?' he asks the death-god. 'Was it all for naught, my country's anguish and mine own untimely death? Tell me, O god of darkness!' To which the death-god answers, 'Judge for thyself, O President of the United States. I will show thee a vision from the days of slavery, and thou shalt see for thyself what manner of magic thou hast wrought over the lives of the defenceless and the downtrodden. Thou shalt see Orpie, the bard, the beauteous Arcola, and O'Fleary, the villainous overseer, who will act out a timeless drama, plucked from the mists of myth and transplanted to thine own time.' And then we're back to the original text, you see, and Lincoln doesn't have to talk like white trash at all—whatever that is, Wilbur—he can sound perfectly elevated throughout."

I have described this portentous prologue with such conviction that I think I've talked my friends into buying it for the time being. Or perhaps I have merely talked so much that I've simply blandished them into submission. At any rate, they decide to give it a try.

346

A low branch of the banyan tree becomes a box at the Ford Theatre. Virgil clambers up and sits there, his hands folded across his lap, his lips pursed, the very picture of presidential dignity.

"Okay," I say, "the curtain is rising now."

Freeze. Virgil endeavours to retain his expression of *hauteur*. Everyone looks up at him. Presently he says, "So when you gone kill me?"

"I suppose there's going to have to be some kind of aural clue—a sound effect or something," I say.

"I'll do it! I'll do it!" says Wilbur.

"Oh, all right."

"Bang! Bang! Eat lead, nigger-lover!"

"No dialogue, Wilbur, just the sound effect of—"

But Virgil has already fallen out of the tree and launched enthusiastically into his death throes, thrashing, kicking and clutching his heart. We're all enjoying his death scene immensely, and I hold Piet back from his entry for a few minutes so that we can squeeze in a bit more agony. Finally, I wave at Piet to make his grand entrance as the African king.

At that moment, we hear an authoritative throat-clearing. The headmaster of our school has appeared. He has crept into our midst with such unwonted timidity that no one has noticed his approach. He appears to have materialized out of thin air—to be, indeed, the very *deus ex machina* of whose dramaturgical appositeness I have so far failed to convince my classmates.

Dr. York says . . . very quietly . . . "Children, could you be silent for a moment, please?"

Virgil continues to twitch. Dr. York looks at him bemusedly, then decides to pretend he's not there. "In view of the assassination of the president," he says, "I don't think anybody feels like having school today, so I've decided to let everyone go home."

"Dr. York, sir?" I saw, rather amazed, that Virgil's thespian talents have managed to get us all a free holiday. "We really appreciate your endorsement of our theatrical skills, but would it be all right if we assassinated him a few more times first? We haven't quite got it right yet."

Dr. York looks from me to the still-undead Virgil. Then back to me. Then at Wilbur. Then at Piet, who leans against a tree-trunk brandishing a rolled-up copy of my script. He says, "I see. You all came early for the play rehearsal, didn't you? You missed the morning papers. None of you knows anything about it yet. It's not your play I'm talking about. It's President Kennedy."

48

Hiding Places

It takes a few more moments for Dr. York's information to sink in. Slowly, Virgil stops writhing and sits up. We all look uncomfortably at one another, unsure what to do. Even Mrs. Vajravajah, who can usually be relied on to take charge in a crisis, is silent. To most of us, half a world away, President Kennedy has never been seen as exactly human. He has occasionally served as a *deus ex machina* in our affairs. He lives and moves in a distant kingdom known to me only through science fiction and television sitcoms. It is not so much grief that I feel as unease. The mock-assassination of Virgil as Abraham Lincoln was a bad omen. Somehow, I think, we all feel we have caused it by some kind of sympathetic magic gone haywire . . . like sorcerer's apprentices who have conjured up dark demons we cannot control. The three Americans are so stunned they seem to register no emotion at all.

"The school office is ringing your parents to send their drivers," says Dr. York. "You can all wait at the front gate."

"I don't have a driver," Virgil and Wilbur say at the same time.

"I'll drop them off," I say. "They live close to my house."

We end up in the Studebaker instead of the Mercedes, which is over at the clinic with my uncle.

We are turning into the *soi* that leads to Wilbur's house when he suddenly says, "Hey, don't drop me off. I'm . . . I kind of don't want to go home right now. Sometimes when bad things happen, I mean, my dad gets kind of drunk and, I mean . . ."

"It's okay, Wilbur," I say. "You can stay for lunch at my house if you like." I can't quite believe that Wilbur, Virgil and Jessica are all sitting in the back seat of the Studebaker without precipitating World War Three.

"Maybe we imaginin' it," Virgil says. "Maybe it just a April Fool's joke or somethin'." But that is wishful thinking. Beside me, on the front seat, is a Thai newspaper. I can't read it, but the front page has a black border around it and a photograph of the American president. I peer at the Thai letters and wish I knew what was going on. I'll be able to find out from the *Bangkok Post* when I get home.

I tell the driver to take us straight to the house, and he reverses in the middle of the *soi* and backs out all the way to Sukhumvit at top speed. But even the rollercoaster ride can't make anybody smile. We race down more alleys, bridge a *klong* or two, and then, before we know it, we're gliding into the main driveway of the estate.

We all climb out of the car, and we all turn at the same time to look at the place where the ruined house once stood. The bulldozers have gone, and the land is flat and fragrant with wet, churned-up soil. Behind us is where the mango orchard begins.

"Virgil," I say, "do you think we could—"

"I don't know," he says, reading my mind. "We ain't never had a honky up there before. I just don't know."

"What are you talking about?" Wilbur says.

And Jessica, realizing we're all going to go up into the treehouse, turns up her nose just a little and says, "Well, I'm going to go on over to the house and call Griselda. You boys have a good time now." And she slips away. Virgil may, after all, decide to admit a white person into the holy of holies, but a woman would be going too far.

I pause to admire the way Jessica walks, stately but delicate. She stops at the gate and gives me the merest shadow of a smile. I watch her unlatch the side gate and disappear. The other boys have already raced each other to the treehouse. Slowly I follow.

Now I spring up from branch to branch, sure-footed, knowing the tree as well as I knew the rooms of the ruined house. I overtake Virgil and Wilbur and swing into the mezzanine level to find Piak methodically counting up stack after stack of blue one-baht notes and putting rubber bands around them. "Hello, Khun Nuu," he says. "I've saved up quite a lot for my father's operation now. Did you hear about Kennedy?"

"Yes," I say, although I still know little about what has happened.

The Thai newspaper is spread out over the floor. Piak is using it to wrap up his money. There's the front page, with the portrait of the president and the black border. There's a picture of Jackie Kennedy, too, distraught and weeping. "They say he was shot by communists," says Piak. "One of my uncles was, too. Way upcountry, I mean. I didn't know the communists had got all the way to America. It's a terrible thing, the King of America getting shot like that. No one'd ever dare do a thing like that here. We have too much respect for our *jao nais*. Thank God we're civilized. The Americans have great music, but they don't have any *bhakti* to speak of."

He stops talking when Wilbur and Virgil reach the level. He carefully stuffs his packets of money into an aluminium cracker box and presses the lid tight shut. Wilbur whistles at the poster of Marilyn Monroe, but it's the toaster that stops him dead. "Gee whiz," he says, "you got electricity up here."

"Sure we do," says Virgil.

"Hey, my grandpa in West Virginia doesn't even have electricity in his *house*."

"Show him the observatory," I say to Virgil, still not quite believing how friendly the two of them seem to be. Virgil and Wilbur hoist themselves up to the topmost level and I can hear, from Wilbur's many interjections, that he is very impressed indeed. And

I can hear Virgil telling our guest about how, at night, you can see the moons of Jupiter sometimes, and zero in on the craters of the moon. And Wilbur's laughing hysterically at some bad joke.

After a few minutes, though, they come back down again. They settle down on the planks, stretching themselves out along the branches that are sticky with mango juice. They are no longer smiling. Grief has finally caught up with them. I realize now that the gaiety of the last few minutes had a kind of desperation to it.

"I guess we'll never go to the moon now," Virgil says at last.

"Not the moon," Wilbur says tonelessly. "They can't take the moon away from us, too. I was gonna be an astronaut when I grew up."

"Holy shit," says Virgil, "you were?"

There's not a trace of mockery in Virgil's voice. Because Virgil and Wilbur come from a country where for a child to dream of going to the moon is not necessarily asking the impossible . . . a country of tract houses with huge backyards in cul-de-sacs with perfect mothers and fathers who know best . . . a land where Dion wanders and where teenagers twist briskly as they rollerskate their way to schools where the only tests are multiple-choice . . . a crystal paradise that an assassin's bullet has shattered in a single moment. The world turns on such moments.

"I was gonna go into orbit. I was gonna go to Mars," Wilbur says. "Now it's never gonna happen."

"White people was going to Mars," Virgil says bitterly.

"Nuh-uh," says Wilbur firmly. "Anyone coulda gone. We coulda left all that behind us, but now we're gonna stay on earth and live with the same old garbage that we had before."

I say, "Maybe I should take that assassination scene out of the play."

We don't talk for a long time. Finally Piak says, "Will Kennedy's son be the new king now? But he's young."

Wilbur doesn't understand him, and Virgil ignores him. I realize that this is the first time those two have ever had something to share. And I can never share what they are feeling, because I don't share their history, their past, not even their past enmity. I'm envious of their grief, and I have to confess that I'm angry at the way the assassination has pre-empted my own plans for making peace between my two friends. What did John F. Kennedy ever do to merit coming between me and my closest friends? Oh, I'm seething inside, but I know I can never show them this rage. I know it is unseemly, and the guilt I feel almost overwhelms my fury.

Presently we feel someone shaking the base of the tree. Wilbur looks down. "It's Piet," he says. "Do we allow him up, or what?"

Virgil says, "Hmm. Two honkies in one day . . . I don't know. A klansman and a Boer. Shi-it." He smiles. "Come on up," he hollers down to the ground, "if you dare."

The floorboards bounce and quiver as Piet makes his way up to our level. "Catch this," he says as his face appears, wreathed in mango leaves, and he throws me a length of string. "Now pull," he says, easing himself up to the mezzanine, which is getting pretty crowded. "Ah!" he says, seeing the toaster. "I was hoping you'd have electricity." I start tugging on the string and presently an enormous gift-wrapped box comes up the trunk. It gets stuck on a fork, and I slither out to disentangle it.

"It's your birthday present," Piet says. "I know it's not for a few weeks yet, but we're all having such a bad day I thought I'd give it to you now, and we can all play with it, you see."

The parcel, when opened, comes in two parts. One is a regulation train set—a Bachmann—with a little red engine and two cars. "It's Central Pacific," says Piet, "from the 1860s." The engine has the word JUPITER written across it; I know that's why Piet has chosen it for me. I am too stunned to say anything at all. "Open the other side now," he says. "That's the important part." As I do so I see that there are five model buildings. "I had to do a lot of kit-bashing to make these," says Piet, obviously proud of his creation, "but it was worth it. Look. . . ." I hold them up one by one. "It's the start of a village or a town, you see. One building for each of us. This is me . . . a sober little Calvinist church. But not too sober, see . . . there's graffiti on one of the walls. This is Wilbur's building—

it's a diner. I did those fountain drinks in the window with a tooth-pick . . . a root beer float . . . a black and white shake. His favourites. I don't really know Piak, so I guess this is for him . . . it's the railway station. This is yours, of course, Justin. . . ."

With a flourish he unwraps a wad of tissue and unveils an ancient temple with Doric columns. The word IVPPITER appears between the cornice and the architrave. I'm bursting with delight. I hold the temple in my cupped palms, peer into its depths, imagine that I see the gold-chased visage of Capitoline Jove within.

Then Piet says, "Oh, and there's something else, too." He doesn't look into Virgil's eyes, but he hands him something. It's a news-stand, just like the one I saw under his bed. *Health & Efficiency* is there in all its unclad splendour. There is also a *Time* magazine whose cover is a postage-stamp-sized image of Martin Luther King. "You're not angry, are you, Virgil?" he says, still looking away.

I put down the temple. I look at Virgil. I think about the first time I saw him, when I cloaked him with misconceptions about Darkest Africa drawn from *Tarzan* and *King Solomon's Mines*. I think about the Virgil I know now, still too stubborn to speak the language of white people, still scarred by a war that ended a hundred years ago.

"I ain't angry," says Virgil softly.

Piet says, "I'm sorry about your president." His words embrace both Virgil and Wilbur, and my momentary anger at having been upstaged by John F. Kennedy's death is subsumed in a kind of bitter joy.

And that is how we spend the rest of the day. While others are glued to televisions and radios, we unplug the toaster, set up the village, lay down the train tracks so that they snake all around us, and then we make the C.P.R.R. run in and out of the cluster of five buildings. This artificial village is home to all of us in a way that no place in the real world ever can be. The morning wears on . . . lunch is five packages of *bamii haeng*, ordered from a street vendor, the steaming pork and noodles wrapped in banana leaf and news-paper and tied up with twine and pulleyed up to our private king-dom in a basket.

It is from the noodle wrappings—which, as it happens, are the *Bangkok Post* and *World*—that I begin to glean, fragment by fragment, the full picture of that day of spectacle and bloodshed in Dallas. These images will soon become part of the world's mythology, but that day each one is new: the procession that will become a funeral cortège, the despairing cries of Jacqueline Kennedy, the sniper in the rooftops of the city. By nightfall, when my friends have all gone home, I have re-enacted the murder a hundred times over in the theatre of my mind.

It haunts me even after I've gone to sleep. I dream I'm riding in a long black limousine drifting over a crowd so vast that its roaring surges and shatters like the sea. The limousine is like a whale, and across the great wide ocean a temple rises from the waters, its marble stained in chryselephantine hues by the sunset, its frieze bearing the legend IVPPITER OPTIMVS MAXIMVS. I float, buoyed by the crowd. There is someone sitting beside me. I know it is someone important, but this person is cloaked in shadow and seems to have no face. It is not my name that the crowd cries out, but I am content to bask in the radiance of this other, this dark one. The eye of the world is upon us.

A shot rings out.

The dark personage turns to me and croaks out, "Norman . . . Norman. . . ."

"Great-grandmother!" I scream, and I wake up sweating.

I've woken up Piak, too, who rubs his eyes and reaches over to switch on the electric fan. "What's the matter, Khun Nuu?" he says.

"Nothing. Nothing."

I close my eyes, and I seem to hear my great-grandmother's voice: *Do you want to know where the will is? You already know the answer to that question . . . you've been the keeper all along.*

"Great-grandmother," I whisper. A beam of moonlight breaks through the leaf-mottled mosquito netting of the window. I see the photograph of my parents and the box of blue Italian marble in which I used to store my epic poem about my parents, the one I have strewn over the waters of Lethe. It is still there, untouched since I abandoned the poem that has become irrelevant in any case because now they are coming home. "Piak, go and get me a glass of water," I say. Because I have to be alone.

As he slips away I touch the box. The marble sucks the last warmth from my fingertips. I open it, running my fingers along the bas-relief figure of Venus rising from the foam. The inside of the lid is lined with velvet, but now, as I touch the soft material, I can feel paper folded up underneath it. There is something sewn into the lining; it comes away easily, as though the seam has frequently been ripped and resewn. Yes. The paper slides out just as Piak returns.

"Khun Nuu," he says, "you weren't supposed to see that."

"I'm not so sure about that," I say, noticing with relief that the text is written in English. I begin to read my great-grandmother's will.

49

The Cabinet
of Dr. Richardson

After leafing through it, I discover that only the first page is in English after all. It is written in longhand, in a spidery, almost indecipherable script; the rest is typed in Thai. I don't dare turn on the light because I know I should not really be up this late, but the moon is bright. I drink the cold Polaris water that Piak has brought me and tell him to go back to sleep. He curls up on the straw mat next to the bed, and I read.

Dear Little Frog, the document begins, *the will is an ongoing thing, and frequently I pay the boy to steal it from the box so I can make a few small changes, and have it sewn in by the time you get back from school. It's strange, isn't it, but there are so many warring factions in the family that it has become necessary for me to resort to such cloak-and-dagger tactics—doubtless your parents would approve—in order to keep their greedy fingers away from this little document. Oh, what a nuisance these endless nephews and grandnieces of mine have proved to be!*

The time is drawing close, Little Frog. I feel it now. I told you once that I was waiting for the next door to open before I let myself out through this one—and now I see that it is ajar, and I see a brilliant white light through the crack, and I know that the time has come for me to be reborn in some other body. The next step, as always, is up to you. I've a fancy to stay with our family a little longer, you see. I want to watch you grow to manhood. The future holds so many wonders. We're going to the moon, if that American president fellow is to be believed, and even though his life has been cut short I think that his ideas have a life of their own. I am writing this from an upper room in the main house, and I can see the mango orchard, and I know that you and your friends have finally come together, have found a place where you need only be yourselves, not what your disparate worlds have made you.

My mind wanders. I am indescribably old now, Little Frog. You must see to it that I am properly reborn. I await that moment, hanging on to life by a tenuous thread, waiting by the door.

Oh, by the way, I know you won't be able to read the will since it's in Thai, but you should know that everyone's being taken care of. I've even put in a small bequest to that gardener . . . you know, the one who's going around masquerading as a woman. You can tell Piak to tell his father to go and order his passport so he can go to Singapore for that operation, though frankly it amazes me why someone like him would turn out to be a katoey. *Who would ever have thought it? It is just another of those surprises. You think you've got a handle on things, but the world is always slipping from your fingers. Even as I am easing away from life. But I bear no rancour. We will probably not speak again. I feel that I'm slipping into a grey area between life and death. You've seen me there before . . . in those strange poetical visions you sometimes have of the worlds beyond our world . . . the difference is, you still have the power to come back . . . not I, not I.*

I fold the papers up and place them back into the velvet lining. "Piak, are you awake?" I say. He stirs, mumbles something. "It's good news, Piak. Your father can become a woman now." It seems that magic has returned to the world after all. But Piak is snoring.

But how is it that I must see to it my great-grandmother is properly reborn? I return to sleep perplexed and restless.

A few days later, I am finally vouchsafed the comprehensive tour of Dr. Richardson's laboratory, promised to me so many moons ago in exchange for my silence. I have, of course, already seen part of it, but that was while sharing a utility cart with a pickled brain. This time it's to be a state visit, and I am to wear my best clothes. I am to come alone, for it would be unseemly for the *sanctum sanctorum* to be invaded by hordes of boisterous boys.

I meet Dr. Richardson in the familiar room where I once witnessed his tryst with Aunt Noi-noi and peered at his collection of streptococci through a microscope. The Petri dishes containing the mementoes of his amours have grown a little in number, forming a neatly labelled stack inside a refrigerator, from which he extracts a bottle of Mirinda orange drink to refresh me with. I sit on a little stool and stare at an array of electronic devices, bubbling flasks, retorts and reagents—all the props of the Hollywood mad scientist.

"And this is my skeleton, Krishna," says Dr. Richardson. "Say hello to Justin, now," he adds, and proffers its bony hand. "Or perhaps you would rather have it *wai*, Justin." He puts the skeleton's palms together. It rattles.

"Why is he called Krishna?" I ask him.

"What, what? Oh, I see. Well, we get a lot of skeletons from India, you see. Famine, you know. Life is cheap, that sort of thing. Though to tell you the truth this skeleton oughtn't to be called Krishna at all. As a matter of fact, you see, it's a woman, what. But the poor old dear's dead, you see, so compared to being dead, the indignity of a sex change is scarcely noticeable."

"That's true," I say, surveying Krishna's immovable leer with some discomfort, "but it is possible to change one's sex when one is alive, isn't it?"

"Oh, I see they've let you in on the Busaba dilemma. Well, yes, it *is* possible, but I wouldn't if I were you . . . you see, it involves . . . ah . . . slicing it off, you see, and reshaping it into the . . . ah . . . you see what I mean."

"Slicing it off? Good heavens."

"Yes, I'm afraid so, rather as one might sever a link of sausage from its companions."

I gulp. "Why would anyone willingly have such a thing done to them?"

"Well," says Dr. Richardson, "it is simply one of those things. There is no end to the mysteries of the human condition, you see, what. Anyone who tries to say that there is an answer for every question is a fool."

"I thought that all adults believed there's an answer for every question," I say, and it is curious to me how Dr. Richardson has managed to retain his awe, his sense of wonder. "Don't *you* believe that?"

"Well, actually, being a doctor, I'm always having to assume the mask of omnipotence, what. Otherwise the patients, thinking their physician doesn't know what he's doing, would run off to the nearest shaman for a two-baht bottle of some elixir."

"I think it's gone up to about nine baht since you last asked," I say, laughing.

But seriously," he says, "have you ever seen a dead person?"

"Well, only Krishna here."

"Ah, we must remedy that, you see. Got to face the source of all fear, then you'll understand everything, including the reason I spend so much time . . . ah . . . browsing over the nether regions of the female anatomy."

"You're going to show me a corpse?" I say. My heart begins pounding. "What kind of corpse?"

"Well, that depends on what's available, doesn't it?" he says.

"I've seen corpses," I say with attempted nonchalance, for did the *ngaan wat* not boast the mummified body of Si Ui, the notorious child killer? Yet that was behind glass, and there was something inhuman about it. Besides, judging from the hokiness of the rest of the show, there was a good chance that it, too, was part of the make-believe.

"Be that as it may," says Dr. Richardson, "would you care to see one now?" It is obviously a challenge, one I can't say no to without looking like an idiot. Dr. Richardson is a veritable Mephistopheles.

"Why not?" I tell him.

"All right then," he says, and fishes out a lab coat from a cabinet. "Throw this on, and try to act as though you know what you're doing."

"But . . . I don't think I'll pass for a . . ." The sleeves are far too long for me, and the lab coat drags on the floor like the train of a wedding dress.

"Oh, nonsense, no one will even look twice," he says, and soon I find myself following him to the hall lift, which takes us down and down and down, past the ground floor, down to some dungeon level that smells faintly of decay, though the corridors are immaculately scrubbed and the floors well waxed, and the overhead fluorescent lights are as bright as any other level in the hospital. But there are no windows. The air feels heavier here, as though the air conditioning can't quite blow away the odour of death.

Presently Dr. Richardson opens a door and motions me inside. The room is spartan, the light cold and antiseptic. It's so cold that I start shivering. I feel as though I'm standing inside an enormous grey fridge.

The wall is lined with long metal drawers. There is a table with an overhead lamp, and there are metal basins full of baroquely shaped surgical tools. The good doctor goes over to the drawers and begins reading their labels.

"Oh, I say, here's a good one," he says, and pulls the drawer open, waving me over and perching me on a stool so I can peer inside. "Heart attack," he says ruefully. I look down and see, as Dr. Richardson peels back the sheet, a man. His eyes are closed, and he is quite, quite still, and his skin has a bluish cast to it. "You can touch him if you like," says Dr. Richardson. "Go on. It's quite all right."

I jab the dead man's face. I expect it to be either hard as rock or slimy as a slug, but no. It has the firmness of a medium-rare rump roast.

"Rather outlandish, isn't it?" he says. "Entropy, you know. We all end up this way. Doesn't matter what we dream about. Doesn't matter whether we're politicians or dustmen, poets or torturers. You see, Justin, it's not a nice thing to know that one day you're going to end up as the Diet of Worms." He chuckles, but I don't get the joke. "That's why, you see, we all have to, oh, how does that poet put it, 'rage against the dying of the light'. In other words, if you're a poetical kind of man, be a poet. If you're a venal kind of man, be venal, I suppose, within reason. Ergo, what, what, the three aunts. Beautiful creatures, are they not?"

"At times, I suppose," I say, wondering by what stretch of the imagination the dour Aunt Ning-nong and the chubby Aunt Nit-nit could be considered beautiful.

"All I'm saying, Justin, is that, before one dies, one might as well live, eh, what? Think of those gorgeous aunts of yours as my insurance against the encroachment of eternity."

"Why, Dr. Richardson, I do believe you're asking me to . . . forgive you or something." I stare at the dead man's face, finding it hard to believe that this chill, rubbery simulacrum of a human being was once alive, once had a name, was once imbued with a soul. Dr. Richardson is telling me that this is how it all ends. He's proffering it to me as a kind of excuse for his profligate promiscuity. I wonder why he needs to make excuses to me. Surely he does not dream that he will end up, decades later, lampooned in the memoirs of an ageing fat man.

He slams the drawer back into the cabinet. With a clang, the corpse disappears from sight. "Well, as a matter of fact, what, I suppose you are right, in a sense," he says. "Yes. But also I want to say that you should seize life by the throat and shake it up and down until the change falls out of its pockets."

I'm beginning to see the attraction Dr. Richardson exerts on my wayward aunts. He does have a certain charisma in spite of—or even because of—his rakishness. He doesn't believe in the eternal cycle of rebirth, as Buddhists do, nor does he seem to think, as does Father Regenstrom, that he need only refrain from "shkroovink" to enjoy the transcendental joys of paradise—the sort of "pay now, fly later" view of the world. But this lack of faith has not driven him to any kind of existential angst; far from it. It has merely given him an excuse to make love wherever, and to whomever, he can get away with it. Unaccountably, I find myself laughing. The laughter's echo is metallic, tinged with cold. My breath hangs in the air. "But Dr. Richardson," I ask at last, "why aren't they all pregnant?"

"*Eaugh*! Good question," says Dr. Richardson. "I don't suppose Father Regenstrom covered that particular angle, did he?" I am astonished that he's heard of Father Regenstrom's little talk at all, but perhaps the news has filtered through to Griselda, and thence to him. "Well, I'll just have to complete your education for you myself."

He looks furtively around for a moment. Then he fumbles in the pocket of his lab coat and hands me a little packet. "Here," he says, "you'd better keep this in your wallet. You're almost thirteen, aren't you, what? I'm afraid you're going to need it soon. In case of fire, break glass, if you get my drift, what."

I examine the thing. The packet bears only the legend "Durex", and there's something flat, circular and squishy inside it. Not knowing how to respond to this curious gift, I slip it into my pocket and change the subject to something I know that Dr. Richardson, as an Englishman, will feel comfortable discussing. "Awfully nice weather we're having, aren't we?" I say.

He looks at me funnily, then, chuckling, responds in a conspiratorial tone, "Yes. I say. Ra-*ther*."

50

The Judgment of Paris

Dr. Richardson's gift remains with me, unused, until the day of my birthday party, the eve of the première of my *Orpheus*. It is not a gathering of socialites like the three Fates' limbo party was; it starts in the afternoon with an extravagant English-style tea, and it will end with a group of my friends spending the night . . . maybe we'll run through the play one final time before we present it in the morning.

The tea portion of the proceedings is one of the most *eaughing* gatherings I've suffered. Every relative I've ever had, and many I never dreamed I had, seem to be there, and by sunset the pile of presents has become a Kilimanjaro of expectation. In our family we are not so Westernized as to allow the public opening of presents, so I am forced to wait until nightfall, after most people have left, to see what I've received. I try to console myself during the day by telling myself that they are probably nothing but an endless succession of matching pen-and-pencil sets, neckties, and other supplies that I will presumably need at Eton, assuming, that is, that I get in.

Mrs. V. shows up briefly at the tea. Even Miss Cicciolini stops by, wearing a stunning scarlet ensemble and presenting me with a crimson-wrapped package, which, by its feel, *must* be a matching pen-and-pencil set. She tells me that I am really a very good boy, and I see a tear form in the corner of one eye as she flutters away, her hair streaming, toward a waiting beau in a Lancia. Father Regenstrom drops in, and he accompanies Jessica on the guitar as she sings "*Plaisir d' amour*". My various grandparents make godlike appearances and bedeck me with gold watches, an ancient Buddha image on a chain, and envelopes full of cash which I am too well brought up to open in their presence, though I'm itching to know how much I've managed to rake in. The three Fates primp and preen and fuss and do not quarrel any more; Aunt Ning-nong's sacrifice has ended their rivalry.

Only my great-grandmother is absent; she is in hospital. I have told no one of the will yet. It is entirely possible that there will come a revised version, sewn into the lining of the Italian box sometime when I'm not around.

Occasionally there is talk of death. Field Marshal Sarit, too, is in the hospital. Sometimes one can hear, amid the small talk, the grownups' dire predictions about the future of the country should he pass away. Such talk passes right through me, and that is strange. Perhaps the assassination of the American president has somehow numbed me; now I know that all the leaders of the world are mortal. And moreover, I have touched a corpse's flesh, I have been a hair's breadth from the bourne of that dark country. I wonder where Dr. Richardson is. It is strange he has not chosen to share the day with us, since he is now practically family.

In the evening, I sit in the pavilion with Virgil, Jessica, Piet and Wilbur, ripping open package after package, while the train Piet gave me runs round and round us. Piak unobtrusively gathers the scrunched-up wrapping papers and throws them in a wastepaper basket. The presents are more or less what I expected, but the loot surpasses all my expectations.

"What you gone do, Justin, buy a *house*?" Virgil says after another wad of red bills emerges from an envelope.

"Gee whiz, we could go back to, you know, that place . . . with Auntie Deedee I mean," says Wilbur. "I think I could handle it now."

"You're not afraid of having it bitten off any more?" says Piet, laughing.

"Fugghead," says Wilbur, and they start wrestling, and presently we all join in, except for Jessica, who sits by the edge of the pond, her slender body swathed in mosquito incense.

***

Much later, the boys are all snoring in my room, sleeping every which way on rubber mattresses. I can't sleep. There's a great big something inside me that's swelling up and getting ready to explode. I lie on my bed, floating on a sea of snores. This great big something sits on my chest like a *phii am*. What is this feeling? I can hardly breathe. With a Herculean effort I jerk myself into a sitting position. The snoring of my friends blends into the night-music of frog, *ueng-aang* and mosquito. I get up, and I step over them one by one. I'm not sure why, but I slip back into my clothes and walk out into the hallway.

"Don't scream!" A hand reaches over my mouth. I am held fast. I mumble something and the hand releases me. It is Griselda.

"I didn't recognize your voice!" I say. "You didn't lisp."

"Look again."

She stands in a slant of moonlight that has bounced off the waxed teak floor on to her face. She is smiling. But there's no silvery glint in her mouth. "They're bloody well gone," she says. "Removed for good. My teeth are going to be *beautiful*. Oh, to smile again without feeling like a twit!" She laughs, then hushes herself. "Mustn't wake up anybody."

"What are you doing here? I thought you and your father weren't coming."

"Oh, first I had to get these things removed from my mouth, and then we had to take Mother to the airport. But I'm spending the night over at Jessica's. She sent me to get you. Come on!"

I can't resist her because she's already tugging at my hand, and to struggle would be to awaken the servants or, worse still, the Fates.

I follow her through the mango orchard to where a stepladder has been conveniently placed by the wall. So this is no impromptu romp in the night. It's all been planned, and I'm the only one who's been kept in the dark.

"Be careful," Griselda says, "hop over the broken glass . . . there's a ladder on the other side."

She lets me into the O'Flearys' house. The living room is in shadow except for a dim light that plays over the assegai and the African drums. Griselda half pulls, half pushes me up the stairs. "Come on, come on," she whispers. "We need to ask you something."

And now we're in Jessica's bedroom with the closet that connects to Virgil's. Music plays from the portable phonograph: soft songs about surfers and beaches and sunlight. I've never set foot in Jessica's room before. Jessica is nowhere to be seen. The room smells faintly of an orangey spice. Griselda doesn't turn on the light, but the room is suffused with moonlight. The air conditioning is not turned on, but a breeze, still moist from the afternoon's rain, blows through the mosquito netting with all the *klong's* mingled fragrances. Griselda stands close to me and doesn't pull away. Her breath is fruity, like well-chewed bubblegum.

"Where's Jessica?" I ask her.

"Oh, never mind her," she says. "Justin, I'm leaving for England soon, I'll probably never get to be alone with you again. My parents are such a bloody nuisance. Do you think I'm beautiful?" I start to reply but she puts a finger to my lips and says, "Don't answer that." Then she brushes her lips against my lips and her hand grazes the tip of my swelling aubergine. She utters a sharp little "*eaugh!*" and pulls back her hand. Then she steps back from me and, with a kind of coy deliberation, begins to unzip her dress, wriggling herself free from its confines like a banana from its peel. "Do you think I'm beautiful?" she says again, and now she takes my hand and firmly places it between her unripe breasts. "Tell me, Justin, tell me."

"I—"

"No," she says, "don't tell me."

"Are we going to have sex now?" I ask her.

She begins laughing. I feel my cheeks flush. My fingertips are sizzling against the cool flesh. "I'm serious," I say, "because, if we are, your father told me I have to use . . . uh . . ." I snatch my hand from the source of passion and scrounge in my pockets for Dr. Richardson's mysterious packet. "Except I'm not quite sure what it is. It's encased in plastic and . . . well, it seems to be round, so I suppose it's some kind of . . . *pill*." The *pill* is a subject I've heard mentioned once in a while, always in hushed and reverential tones. "Perhaps you could fetch a glass of water? The problem is, your father didn't tell me who was supposed to *take* the pill, you or me."

She takes the packet from me, feels it curiously with her hand for a moment and then . . . abruptly . . . begins to giggle. "Oh, Justin, you silly goose," she says, "it's a rubber johnny!"

At which there comes another peal of laughter from behind the closet door, which now flings open to reveal, resplendent in her dusky nakedness, the second woman I have loved, black Aphrodite herself. "Jessica," I say.

"Yes," she says, "now you got to decide which one of us is more beautiful. It either me or Griselda."

And I am thinking that this is like the judgment of Paris . . . that I'm a mortal trapped into having to answer a divine riddle . . . but where is the third of the three goddesses? How can I decide between the two of them, the ivory and the ebony, sandwiched as I am between them. "You can't expect me to answer that," I say. "Whichever I choose, the other one would eat me alive."

"Catch!" says Griselda, and throws her father's gift to Jessica.

"I know you was smart," says Jessica, "but I'd a never thought you'd come prepared for *this* birthday present." And she smiles wryly, and the two girls advance toward me, and I feel this nameless thing welling up inside me again, and the two girls wrap themselves around me and begin methodically to unbutton my clothes. And presently they teach me the true nature of Dr. Richardson's gift, and, as a gentle rain begins to patter against the battens, I begin to probe the final mysteries of sex. Oh, they dance, the two girls, or rather their fingers dance all over me, and their tongues flick at my ears like the tongues of serpents, until presently a kind of machine-gun-like release explodes from me . . . like the jolt of lightning that galvanizes Dr. Frankenstein's monster . . . a little earlier than I had hoped . . . oh, why so soon? . . . and then there's a kind of stickiness against the walls of Dr. Richardson's balloon . . . and I glance fearfully around, hoping they haven't noticed that my aubergine has somehow been visited by a fit of uncontrollable sneezing . . . but of course they notice, and then they start giggling, and giggling again, and the three of us are giggling now, giggling against the persistent drizzle of rain on the sill and the pit-a-pat of geckos' feet on the mosquito meshing and oh, the bright moon, which soon begins to vanish behind the rainclouds. But when it's over there comes a sadness, swooping down like the monsoon over the jungle treetops, and I see how tears and laughter always come together, intermingled, like *galonga* and coconut milk, like death and love. But we're still giggling. And crying. And giggling. And crying.

"But, but," Griselda says, "we mustn't cry." She looks out of the window and perhaps she is thinking of England . . . the far country for which I too must soon depart.

"Is this all there is to it?" I say, and then I wonder if I shouldn't have said that, if I've somehow hurt their feelings, because I also meant to say that that great lightning bolt that has just ripped through my whole body was the biggest, grandest, most monumental thing I have ever felt. Surely I will never feel such a thing again. I hardly dare remember it, though it is only five minutes old.

"Oh, you are so insufferably silly at times, Justin," Griselda says. "It takes practice to be able to sustain it; that's what Daddy always says." But Jessica only smiles enigmatically, as if to say, "We must be alone sometime."

And so it is that I limp back to the ladder and vault over into the mango orchard. The rain has cleared, and my shirt buttons are all mismatched, and Dr. Richardson's prophylactic is somewhat the worse for wear, caking up in the back pocket of my shorts. The moon is back out now and the scent of jasmine clings to the particulate moisture in the air.

In a shaft of light I see Samlee, kneeling, with her hands folded over a small votive object. This is not the chic new Samlee but the old one, clad in an old *panung*, her face whitened with antique beauty lotion. I stand just outside the luminous circle, afraid that my shadow will fall on her and betray that I am spying on her. Presently she rises and reaches up into the branches of the tree, which, I realize, is the very tree that contains our secret clubhouse. She attaches the fetish to the lowest limb with a ribbon. Curiosity overcomes me, and I move closer. The fetish is in the shape of a little aubergine . . . the human kind that is . . . rampant, with two wooden grapes at its base . . . a cunningly wrought miniature sculpture whose source is surely the magic shop of the *ajarn* down the *klong*. I must have stepped on a twig because Samlee whirls round and sees me, and it's too late for me to abscond into the shadows. "Why," she says, "Master Little Frog; what a curious thing . . . considering the nature of my prayers tonight."

"What on earth is that?" I say, pointing to the fetish. "You haven't put a curse on the treehouse, have you?" For I well remember that I have always believed Samlee to be on intimate terms with the dark forces of the night.

"You've been seeing the *ajarn* again, haven't you?" I say.

"No . . . that charlatan! . . . he promised so many things . . . no, I've gone back to a far more ancient magic . . . a fetish from my uncle in Isaan. I'm sure this will work a lot better; it's been in my family for two hundred years."

"But what is it you want?" I ask her. Seeing her like this, ghostly in the moonlight, I don't feel thirteen anymore; I'm weak-kneed, not only from unease, but also from lust, for she exudes that heady odour of *nam pla* mixed with a cloying perfume. "Didn't I talk to grandfather on your behalf?"

She smiles sadly. "Women like me, Khun Nuu, we have one or two meagre talents, and we must somehow struggle to survive with the few skills our karma has given us. But sometimes they just aren't enough for a poor upcountry girl like me. . . ."

"Doesn't my grandfather like you any more?"

"It's not that, Khun Nuu, it's just that he's always thinking of the succession and the inheritance. . . ."

Abruptly, it begins to rain once more. This time it's a downpour, not a drizzle. The water sluices over us and gouges the white from Samlee's face. It batters me, and when I close my eyes it pounds against my eyelids. "Quick!" I say. "Up the tree! Into the treehouse!" Without thinking, I begin to climb, reaching down to help her as she hugs the slick bark and slides against the toeholds.

As we crawl through to the mezzanine level I suddenly realize I have broken Virgil's inviolable rule: *No Girls Allowed.* Treehouses are the final bastion of boyhood against the female world. Does the arrival of Samlee portend disaster? Is it like bringing a woman on board a man-of-war? Too late now. She sits there, soaked, tantalizingly close to me. Tonight there are no rules, I tell myself. I am thirteen now. Traditions will break and empires be ground into dust. I move closer to her. I dare to profane her bedraggled tresses with the hands that have just caressed two other goddesses . . . knowing now that this is the third goddess, that tonight is truly the night when I shall re-enact the judgment of Paris.

And I ask her, with a boldness I cannot quite myself believe: "Samlee, Samlee, that thing that you do with your false teeth removed . . . how exactly does it feel?"

"Little master," she says with a coy laugh, "you really *are* getting older. Do you think that I am beautiful?"

"Beautiful?" I say. "Of course you are beautiful. You are the most beautiful of all."

"But you've seen so many high society ladies . . . and you've seen the *farang* women with their golden hair, and sapphire eyes . . . oh, and you've seen a girl who is black as night with eyes like opals, white and full of fire. How can you say that Samlee is more beautiful than any of these?"

And now I know that the nameless thing that has kept me sleepless through many full moon nights is about to happen. I fish out the rubber johnny from my pocket. She takes it from me and tosses it aside. "No, Khun Nuu!" she says. "Not now. Not tonight. Tonight you're not Master Little Frog at all. You've come to me as an answer from the gods I've been praying to. Khun Nuu, you have to understand, I need a child inside me, I need the seed of a *phudii* to grow in my womb, or else I'll be a servant until I'm old and haggard and fit only to sweep the dogshit from the driveway . . . oh, Master Little Frog . . . you must help me, you must." And so saying she throws her arms around me, and I breathe in the heady odours of my first love, she surrounds me, she engulfs me . . . and oh, I feel greater than myself, I feel a cosmic wind stir in me, I feel like god. She is not like the other two were. I did not become one with Jessica or Griselda. My passion has not grown from a full year of fantasy and frustration. She circles me as Oceanus circles the world. I ride as a dolphin rides the sea, and all the while the rain lashes at the tree and bends it and splashes on to our bodies, until at last I feel the very floorboards, built for the patter of children's feet and not for the mating of titans, heave and buckle, my foot flies out and smashes through one wall, the roof planks tumble one by one and I know that I have doomed Virgil's Eden by introducing the serpent into it . . . but I don't care. Oh, oh, I dive, I plunge, I darkly sound the profoundest mystery of this woman. No matter that the treehouse is crashing to the ground around us. No matter that the rain is bursting from the sky. I leap. I soar. And then, after the moment of shuddering release, there comes the grief again, pouncing like a bird of night. "Samlee, Samlee," I murmur, "I think that someone has died."

"I think," she answers softly, "that someone will be born."

51

A Piece of Paradise

It is morning, and I still cannot rid myself of this melancholy. When I wake, my friends are no longer lying all around my bed. I hear their chattering from the pavilion outside. I rise and go to join them. It is not yet six o'clock, but the world première of *Orpheus* will occur in only about four hours, and four hours is also about how much sleep I've had last night after tussling with three goddesses, running back to the house in the rain, diving fully clothed into sudden and blissful oblivion.

I get up and perform my ablutions with deliberation. Nothing has changed, yet everything has. Gradually the sense of loss lifts from me, and I am left with a residue of sweetness. But the details of the previous night elude me. They flit about my memory like fireflies. By the time I reach the breakfast table, my script under my arm, it is as though I am grasping at a dream. And yet I know it happened. Because the three goddesses are all seated at the table, not talking, not eating, but seemingly all bathed in an ethereal light, like a fragment of that dream that has somehow leaked into the world.

Seeing me, Samlee rises and says, "Master Little Frog!" She gives me a quick *wai* as befits my station. I search her face for a reminder of last night. At first I detect nothing at all. It's not like the other two girls, who, as I approach, nudge each other and giggle, and smile at me, and say, "Justin, Justin, come and sit with us." Then there's a twinkle in Samlee's eye, but only for a split second. Last night, I know, was a special treasure, for it can never be repeated; it will live only in remembrance, never spoken of, ever living.

A television has been moved to the pavilion. I suppose many feel it a civic duty to follow the regular bulletins about the health of Field Marshal Sarit. At the moment one cannot tell if he will live or die. In fact, though, it is only the servants who glance respectfully at the television as they glide past with trays of juices and bowls of *khao tom*.

The boys are sitting in a row by the railing, gobbling down misshapen flapjacks from a communal platter. "Me and Virgil made these," says Wilbur, his mouth caked with syrup. Virgil looks at me quizzically. Does he know? Surely he knows! Surely they can all see, written all over me, the evidence of last night's conquests! I don't say anything at all to them . . . I just sidle along, sneak a flapjack off the dish, wander over to the far corner to chew on it without benefit of bacon or syrup. God, I hope they don't notice that the treehouse has been destroyed by the temptations of Eve. At least, not before this afternoon. Not before the play is over and done with.

Oh, and the three Fates are there too. They too are quite oblivious of the momentous goings-on of the previous night. They're chattering away. Dr. Richardson is in their midst. The pavilion has never been so crowded, and I am beset by an irrational fear that it, too, will collapse into the pond, and we'll all be attacked by mobs of furious amphibians.

"Little Frog!" says Aunt Ning-nong. "Someone very special is here to see you today."

It is only then, after gulping down the rest of the flapjack in one strangulating swallow, that I look across to the low rattan sofa that has been moved into the pavilion and see my parents. I am not sure at first. They seem to resolve out of the twisty texture of the rattan until they're really there, in the flesh, bearing little resemblance to those elegant figures in front of the snowbank in the photograph in my bedroom. My father's wearing a kind of a homespun peasant costume, and my mother, her hair cut short, wears a plain *panung*. They are clearly still in disguise. But surely no one would follow them here, to the inner sanctuary of our family. Surely this place is still inviolate. I look at them for a long time, unable to speak, bursting with pride and joy. And then, very slowly, brushing the crumbs from my school uniform on to the polished teakwood floor, I move toward them.

"Sornsunthorn," my father says, which is only the second time my real name has been uttered aloud in the last twelve months.

"Little Frog," my mother says.

I'm unable to speak. I know they've been doing really important things, they've been out there saving the universe or whatever it is great undercover heroes do. I do feel this burning pride inside me, but the words that finally come out are only, "Why did you have to leave me for so long?" And I start to cry, bitterly and noisily, so that everyone looks away in embarrassment.

Aunt Ning-nong interrupts my display with, "Now, Little Frog, what a terrible exhibition to make of yourself . . . don't you realize that they've travelled all this way in order to—"

"Oh, be quiet, Ning-nong," my father says. "Let him cry."

A remarkable change comes over the Fate who has ruled my life for the past few years. She suddenly becomes meek; and, proffering a quick *wai* of apology to my father, says, "Well, Khun Phii, I suppose you know best."

"It's all right, Little Frog," my father says. "I, too, have often felt like weeping. Sometimes we can't choose who we are."

"But you'll go away again soon. And you're sending me to England where I'll be completely alone." And for the first time I face that part of me that fears the coldness of the far north, which doesn't want to go adventuring except within imagined kingdoms. "I'm totally, unspeakably *furious* about this . . . can't you see that?" And I'm stamping my feet and having a tantrum of the most childish kind and looking like an idiot, but I can't help myself. The guilt I feel at losing my temper only fuels my rage, and I cannot tell if it's me or them I'm incensed about. And instead of getting angry, the others are simply looking away uncomfortably or sitting with the frozen smile of *kreng jai* on their faces . . . until Piak comes to me, crawling slowly toward me to avoid having his head higher than those of the high-level persons present, holding up a Kleenex to my clenched fist. I take it and begin to dab at my eyes. Everyone waits, with excruciating politeness, until I finish crying.

At last, my mother says to me, "Yes, Little Frog, it is a terrible thing we did, in many ways. But it wasn't all pain and grief, now, was it? Have the last three years been as miserable as all that?"

So many things flash through my mind: the smoke of the dead chameleon rising to the sky . . . the shaman . . . the false inferno at the temple fair, the real inferno in the ruined house . . . Miss Cicciolini flaunting her Sophia Loren-like smile . . . children in flowing robes playing at being ancient gods and heroes . . . no, I have not been miserable. "Not miserable at all," I say softly. "Not miserable, but beautiful . . . yes, even the bad things had a kind of beauty."

My mother smiles. "I'm glad, Little Frog," she says. And at that I go up to her and deliver a dry kiss to her left cheek. And suddenly the three of us are embracing, hard, and we are all in tears again.

After the storm has passed, we are all still seated in the pavilion. On television, there is another bulletin about the Field Marshal, who seems to be clinging to life. Coffee is being served, and, in honour of my newly attained teenagerhood, I am vouchsafed a cup myself. I sit quietly at my parents' feet. My friends are running wild, acting out scenes from the play and putting in silly words instead of my deathless dialogue. My parents make small talk with our other relatives. Slowly it dawns on me that their coming has changed things, has eased this tiny gnawing pain I have always felt these past few years, heartache so chronic I could not know of its existence until it went away.

"You don't have to go to England if you don't want to," my mother tells me at last.

"It's not that I don't want to. It's just that—" How can I explain that the England of my fantasies, the England of noble poets and white-maned gods, of spires seen through diaphanous mists and crenellated castle walls, that this England perished in the flames of the ruined house, and I do not know the England I am going to?

My father says, "I don't blame him for not wanting to leave. I mean, just look around you. This place we're in now is a piece of paradise. The world is in turmoil. A war is brewing next door. But in this tiny Eden, there is no hint of the change that will sweep the world. We're not really of this earth, and that's the truth of it; but it can't last." He looks me directly in the eye in a way that makes me realize that somehow he must know that something has transpired in my life that has triggered the slow relinquishment of childhood. "But Sornsunthorn, you see, the thing about all paradises is that we *must* leave them. If we don't have the courage to eat the apple of knowledge and accept the consequences, then we're not really people yet, you see, we're sort of pre-persons, unformed, with the wet clay still clinging to our ears."

"I see," I tell him, though frankly I really don't. But the fact that he has once again used my real name, the fact that he's speaking with such seriousness, lends his words an air of truth. What truth there is in them is a difficult truth, one I will probably not be able to accept for some time yet. I sense that there was a time in his life when he was unaware of this truth, and that he has struggled to understand it and come to terms with it. And so I say, "I've had glimpses of what goes on outside, Father. There's a lot of pain." I'm thinking of Virgil, Piet and Wilbur, and the war that was not of their making. I'm thinking of Father Regenstrom, agonizing over the horrors of shkroovink, of the colonial committee in England altruistically trying to shield us natives from an unpredigested version of Shakespeare. Yes, there is so much unnecessary pain. "But I've been working on opening people's eyes, Father. And my own. That's what my play is about, you know."

"Poor Little Frog," my mother says, "did this place seem like a prison to you? We sought only to shield you. Not to cage you in."

"Only sometimes," I say, "because I was afraid you might be dead, or worse, that you might not love me."

"Oh, Little Frog," my mother says, and strokes my hair, sighing softly.

My friends have all gone. My aunts have slipped away. I am alone with my parents. Fiercely I say, "But now I know that's not true."

Suddenly we hear Virgil shouting from clear across the mango orchard. "The treehouse! It's been flattened by the storm!"

I suppose that my face clouds. It is I, after all, who broke the rule about girls and who invoked the curse of the God of Little Boys and wrought the treehouse's destruction. I glance out, wondering whether I should go and take the blame for it all. I start to get up but my father stays me with his hand.

"You'll build another," my father says. And he smiles at me. "In time."

52

I Have a Dream

The slide show is about to end and the curtain about to rise. The train is finally pulling away from the platform, and it's not a model train. I cannot pull the plug from its socket. I cannot stop the wheels with a finger on the tracks. I cannot, I cannot.

The curtain is a new development, a gift to the school from some foundation for the furtherance of Britannic culture. It's a gorgeous red velvet thing, so much grander than our paltry proscenium that it makes the proceedings faintly ridiculous.

I'm standing behind the curtain and peering out at the audience . . . just as I have been standing all my life, just behind the bourne of my secret kingdom, gazing at the world beyond. I see my parents deep in conversation with Dr. York. Soon the curtain will rise and the slide show will end.

Which is not to say that there are not other slides to come, single images that hold still against the onrush of time. There will come the funeral of my great-grandmother, held with great pomp and magnificence, with feasts of many courses and monks chanting and our entire clan gathering by hundreds to pay their respects. At the funeral with which this story began, I did not know the honoured dead, and there was a nagging guilt about not feeling any grief. But here, honouring the passing of a woman I loved and who loved me deeply, there will also be little grief. Because my great-grandmother, arch-manipulator that she is, has even managed to control the Fates—the real Fates—themselves. She has engineered her own reincarnation back into the family she loves so much. Soon I will suspect it; later I will come to believe it.

As I peep through the crack in the curtain I do not know that she is already dead. Nobody knows that my great-grandmother has slipped away in the night, in the hospital, alone. They will not tell me until I come home from school. They will allow me to bask in my triumph. I will walk into the house, where the table will have been set for an afternoon snack, and I will stare at the mournful faces of my three aunts for a long moment before divining what must have happened in the night. No one will want to tell me, but I will know. Because of what Samlee said to me as the treehouse crashed about us: *I think someone will be born.*

Chanting, the monks will tell us life is illusion, life is brief, it is suffering, it is transient. And I will know that it is true, for I will have seen the turning of the wheel.

The theatre is filling up now. I don't know what they are expecting. I hear the chattering from the makeshift dressing room.

Griselda, costumed as a slave girl, with cardboard manacles, comes traipsing across the scene. She giggles and disappears behind the Southern plantation mansion whose façade is not dissimilar to that of my grandfather's house, faux Corinthian columns and all. The columns are made of construction paper and the house itself is a painted backdrop.

"Justin!" a voice whispers. It's Virgil, strutting across the stage with his robes and his top hat. We will have the assassination scene after all, but not the *thees* and *thous* of the second speech I wrote for him. "What you doin' out here? Ain't you gone get ready?"

"I want to look at the audience."

He creeps up next to me. We part the curtain just another hair, and he looks out. "Look at Miss Cicciolini," he says. "She's making eyes at Father Regenstrom." She's wearing a scarlet, hip-hugging suit, and she's contrived to sit right next to an air conditioner so as to tousle her hair convincingly.

"Only because she knows he can't do anything about it," I say.

Dr. York, sweating away in an immensely *eaughing* three-piece suit, sits on a kind of throne, with his nose in the air. My parents aren't talking to him any more, but are glancing at the curtain. I wonder if they know I'm watching them.

I know they'll go away again. In fact, they will stay only until after my great-grandmother's funeral. They won't be there for the gloriously demented triple wedding that we celebrate on the eve of my departure to England. Busaba will be radiant in her manufactured femininity, having stepped off the plane from Singapore the previous day. The other bride, Samlee, not yet obviously *enceinte*, in traditional Thai *phasin*, deliriously happy to have been elevated to the position of a concubine in my grandfather's household. Aunt Ning-nong in virginal white . . . the only one of the three brides who might qualify for that colour. The wedding will take place all over the estate, with an eclectic mixture of ceremonies from different religions. The three couples will make an incongruous mélange in their official portrait, taken by a society photographer and appearing on the cover of a prominent women's magazine.

In the photograph, Dr. Richardson wears morning dress, top hat and all, and must be soaked in sweat under all those layers of British clothing. Aunt Ning-nong, flanked by her two sisters in matching white outfits, is attempting not to stumble over her own bridal train.

My grandfather wears the traditional uniform, medals and all, that he once wore at court—seemingly centuries ago—and behind him stand all his wives, even Number Two, who has magically returned from retirement upcountry to help us celebrate the miracle of my grandfather's amazing fertility. (My grandfather will be so astonished to have impregnated Samlee that he will distribute a case of Black Label to every male member of the family, including me . . . little knowing how much I deserve the reward. A couple of years later, in a moment of candour—or perhaps of wandering mind—

he will confess to me that he's not entirely sure how the trick was achieved, since, to his knowledge, their lovemaking had been confined to Samlee's dentureless speciality.) News of my grandfather's virility will have spread far and wide. He will be the medical toast of Bangkok. Indeed, a certain *ajarn* who lives down the *klong* will soon call on him to discuss the use of some of the Great One's bodily fluids in the preparation of a new fertility formula—with royalties, of course. To which he will graciously consent, though, with characteristic generosity, he will waive the royalty requirement. Why not? Has he not been made the guardian of his mother's estate, the bulk of which will pass, according to the will hidden in the marble box in my bedroom, to the "next child of his loins"? What a superb joker my great-grandmother has been—to engineer her own rebirth, and leave herself all her money!

Everyone will agree that no bride could be more beautiful than Busaba. She will be a triumph of the cosmetic surgeon's art. Everyone will have conveniently forgotten the spectacle of the gardener shovelling compost by the rose-beds and sweating as he drags the limbo rock device on to the pavilion. Uncle Vit is the only person who does not come to the wedding dressed to the teeth. His mismatched socks and his spectacle frames patched with Sellotape only serve to remind us that he is, after all, a genius, even if he didn't quite make it through medical school.

Oh, what a wedding it will be!

Except that many of my friends will not be with me. They will have moved on: Griselda with her mother, Piet back to South Africa, Wilbur and Virgil because of the war.

"Holy shit!" says Virgil. "It's Wilbur's momma talkin' to mine."

"No."

"Yeah, take a look! Over there!"

It is true. What are they saying, I wonder? But they do not seem to be enemies. They are smiling at each other. Wilbur's father has not come, but perhaps it is too late to change him. The play hasn't even begun yet but already its magic is beginning to work.

I, too, have had a dream, you see.

Not the kind of dream that transforms the earth, not the Martin Luther King sort of dream about universal brotherhood and love of all mankind. Only a little dream . . . that the five of us, Piak, Wilbur, Piet, Virgil and I, would sit in our little treehouse, sheltered against the chaos of societies we did not make, just being together. Not masters and servants, and not members of different races and cultures, but just ourselves, together.

And my dream came true. It came true . . . for one brief afternoon before the collapse of Eden . . . it came true!

Soon the curtain will rise and the story will end. The play itself is no longer important. It's only a confirmation that once, on a steaming afternoon in a mango tree in a house of planks, that dream came true.

The war is not going to end by Christmas. A wrenching transformation is going to sweep the world. When my American friends come of age, the war will still not have ended. Perhaps it will even kill them. But now, waiting for the curtain to rise and for my life to begin, I cannot know this. I cannot know all the agony to come, nor should I know these things, because to know the future is to cease to live. I will watch the war from the cold shores of England.

(It will be February and bitterly cold when I step off the BOAC jet at Heathrow. I will be met by a stern-faced man in a long grey woollen coat and grey scarf. After the preliminary greetings, he will say to me, "Now then, what is the Latin for 'I shall have used'?" Unfortunately, this is not one of the verbs that Father Regenstrom taught me. I will stand in the snow, just as in the portrait of my parents in the lacquer frame in my bedroom, but somehow it won't be quite the mythic moment I had anticipated.)

The audience is murmuring now. It is impatient. At length, Mrs. Vajravajah gets up to give a brief speech introducing the play.

She says: "This play is a kind of farewell for many of us. Justin, our playwright, will soon be off to the playing fields of Eton, and many of our actors are also leaving. I, too, alas, will not be with the Scola Britannica after next term." We all gasp. We realize that she has had her differences with Dr. York, but it is hard to believe it has come to this. "The play you are about to watch has many elements. It is based on an ancient legend, it is based on a bedtime story that has been handed down for three generations in the family of one of my pupils. It is, like all art, a story of love and death, but it is also an attempt by an idealistic young boy to solve some of the problems of the world."

Perhaps all this is true, but that still doesn't make the play any good, of course. Moments before the curtain rises I realize that once more my verses are hackneyed, my sentiments cliché-ridden, and all my good lines are stolen from the classics. The play doesn't matter.

Only the dream matters.

I'm only thirteen years old, and I have known love, death, joy, grief and loss, and all these things are shiny and spanking-fresh to me, feelings to be tried on like brand new shirts that come fresh from the box, the collars still stiff with plastic. Oh, God, I don't want the feelings to become old and worn down.

Though the treehouse is shattered, I know I have to cling to the shards of the dream. We all do. Though the ruined house has been ploughed into the soil, in my dreams it is still there, and the Trojan War is still being fought along its passageways and balustrades. My great-grandmother and Homer the chameleon still look down from the clouds. Oh, I'm terrified that the curtain will rise, terrified that reality will smash the dream into pieces too small to hold on to. But it must rise.

The slide show must end.

Great-grandmother! Homer! Oh, all you ancient gods and goddesses on your towering, cloud-girt thrones! Don't leave me! Must I walk away from paradise? Must you turn your backs on me? Must you now become mere fantasy? The curtain rises and the slide show must end. The curtain rising is the final slide.

Rising. I'm scurrying out of the way so that I don't obstruct the audience's view of the backdrop. Scattered applause, rising in a crescendo. The curtain's rising. Not so fast! I'm not ready yet! Slowly! Slowly! One more moment . . .

Rising.

A Glossary
of Siamese Words

The Thai or Siamese language is a tonal one, rich in bizarre vowels but relatively poor in consonants. Much of its "learned" vocabulary is borrowed from Sanskrit, but the words are subject to such wrenching mispronunciation as to render them hard even for Sanskritologists to figure out. Most transliteration systems either follow the Sanskrit orthography, giving no idea of how words should be pronounced, or approximate the pronunciation, giving no clue as to etymology.

In this book I've used an unabashedly, idiosyncratic method of transliteration that agrees with no other system. Long vowels are either doubled (ii) or followed by a silent *h* (*ah*). Little attempt has been made to find equivalents for the tongue-twisting diphthongs and triphthongs, and no attempt whatsoever has been made to indicate which of the five tones belongs to each syllable. Generally speaking, though, vowels have the continental values, not the English ones. Sanskrit-derived words familiar to English-speaking people, like *karma* and *dharma*, have been spelt the way they are in English even though, in Thai, they are pronounced *kam* and *tham*.

As for Consonants:

th, ph, kh and *ch* should be strongly aspirated, like English "t", "p", "k" and "ch" as in *church*, respectively; *t, p* and *k* should be unaspirated, as in French or Spanish; *ng*, even when it begins a word, should be pronounced as in "singing", not as in "finger".

ajarn—a term of respect: "professor"; Sanskrit
apsaras—celestial women
baht—in 1963, approximately 4d.
bamii—egg noodles
bamii haeng—egg noodles served without broth
bamii nam—egg noodles in broth
baramii—the state of possessing the ten transcendent virtues
bhakti—religious devotion
bhasa khon—the speech of human beings
buoi khem—an extremely sour and salty confection made from dried plums
chadah—a pagoda-like hat worn by dancers; a royal crown
dharma—the eternal principles of nature; the law of the Lord Buddha
dok mai fai—fireworks
farang—a slightly pejorative term for a white person
ganja—marijuana; from the Sanskrit
garuda—half-man, half-bird; the winged messenger of the gods
jao nai—lord and master; the upper classes
jingjok—a small lizard often found in houses
jñana—a Sanskrit word denoting knowledge
jongkabaen—a complex, formal brocaded trouser-like garment
kaeng massaman—a curry made from meat and potatoes that originated in the south of Thailand
kamadeva—Cupid
kangkaeng plaeh—Chinese silk pyjamas, tied around the waist by hand
kaolao—a clear soup

katoey—a transvestite or male homosexual of the passive variety

khao chae—dishes served with rice in crushed ice

khao man kai—chicken with a special rice cooked in stock from the boiling chicken

khao muu daeng—rice with barbecued pork

khao tom—rice soup

khao tom kruang—rice soup topped with various goodies

khiikhaa—a pejorative term for a slave or servant

khnom—sweets or candy

khon—traditional Thai masked drama depicting episodes from the *Ramayana*

khun—a respectful title: "your grace"

khun aah—"younger sibling of my father"—respectful language

khun mae—a respectful title for one's mother

khun nong—"respected younger sibling"

khun nuu—Mr. Mouse, a term of respect for children

khun phii—"honoured older sibling (or cousin)"

khun phra—a title of nobility

khun phuchai—the master of the house

khun phuying—the mistress of the house

khun puu—"father of my father"; also any male sibling or cousin of one's paternal grandfather

khun yaah—respectful title: "mother of my father"

khunying—a minor title of female nobility

kinarii—a composite mythological creature, half-woman, half-bird

kingkue—a large millipede

klong—one of Bangkok's former vast network of canals

klua phii—to have a phobia about ghosts

kluai buat chii—a dessert made from bananas and coconut milk

kraab—a form of prostration to one's elders

krathohn—chamberpot

kreng jai—the idea of always seeing one's actions from the point of view of others

kuaitiao—noodle soup

kuti—the monks' residences in a temple

likay—a folk opera

luuk phudii—a person of breeding; an aristocrat

Mae Nak Phrakanong—a baleful, succubus-like spirit, also a patroness of childbearing women

mong—a special joker in phai tong, which is coloured in by hand

mueang nok—foreign countries; the outer lands

muu satay—satay (q.v.) made with pork

naga—a mythical serpent

nam krajieb—a sweet fruit drink

nam manao—a kind of limeade made with sugar and salt

nam pla—a fish sauce used instead of salt in much Thai cooking

nam pla prik—fish sauce with diced chilies

nam prik mangdaa—a spicy sauce made from chilies and the crushed wings of a cockroach-like insect

ngaan wat—a temple fair

ohm phiang!—a pious exclamation often used when wishing for something

oliang—Thai iced coffee, containing much sugar and caffeine

ong—a huge earthenware jar for catching rainwater

paed tua—as *thalok ha tua* (q.v.), but with an eight-card set; only possible with a lot of wild cards

panung—a large piece of cloth wrapped about the hips

phaah kajom ok—cloth wrapped around the breasts while bathing

phaan—a presentation platter, usually of precious metal

phabphieb—a way of sitting considered elegant and refined

phah sbai chiang—an archaic feminine form of dress, a sash wrapped crosswise around the upper torso

phai tong—a card game played with 120 narrow cards

phakomaah—a homespun cloth wrapped about the legs

phasin—a traditional Thai skirt, often made of richly embroidered silk

phed nae—"It is certainly spicy"

phii—any sort of spirit, often malevolent; also used as a shortened version of *khun phii* (q.v.)

388

phii am—a squatting sort of evil spirit

phii krasue—a shit-eating, malignant spirit

phii tai hong—a particularly malevolent spirit, usually a person who died violently

phin—a kind of harp

phnom mue—a humble gesture of reverence

phong—to obtain three of a kind in *phai tong*

phudii—a member of the upper classes

phuttachaat—the plant *Jasminum auriculatum*

pi—a kind of oboe

piphaat—a traditional Thai orchestra

pisaat—a malevolent spirit

prehd—a malevolent spirit

rai—a measure of area, equivalent to 400 *wah* or 1,600 sq. m.

ramwong—a folk dance

ranaat—a kind of xylophone

roti—a doughy dessert of Indian origin

roti sai mai—a roti stuffed with stranded sugar

ruesii—a holy man or *rishi*

saan phra phuum—a spirit house, built to house the displaced spirits of the land

sala—a pavilion

salueng—25 *satang*; in 1963, about ld.

samadhi—a state of profound meditative concentration

samanera—a novice monk

samlor—a pedicab; a cross between a bicycle and a rickshaw (obsolete in 1963)

satang—the smallest unit of Thai currency; in 1963, about six to the farthing

satay—skewered meats in peanut sauce

singha—a mythical lion

sodsoi mala—a traditional gesture in Siamese court dance: "weaving a garland"

soi—a narrow alley leading off a large main road

sueah—a straw mat

sueah klaam—a sleeveless undershirt

thalok ha tua—to win in *phai tong* by drawing a card that completes a five-card set

thaokae—a term of respect for a Chinese businessman

thue tua—to carry oneself with hauteur and disdain toward those of humbler birth

thun hua—a term of affection for young people or lovers

toh chiin—a Chinese banquet consisting of at least ten courses

ton kraang—a banyan tree

tua keng—a high-points winning card in *phai tong*, different for each player; a favoured card

tukae—a large gecko or barking lizard

tukta chao wang—miniature figurines of courtiers, used to adorn a *saan phra phuum* (q.v.)

ueng-aang—an amphibious creature with a distinctive cry

vasana—fate or destiny

vinyaan—soul or spirit

wai—a respectful gesture, folding the palms together

wat—a temple

woay!—a "rudeness particle" expressing contempt

woon sen—bean thread; a transparent sort of noodle

ya dom—smelling salts

yaah saneh—a love potion

yaksha—a demon (from the *Ramayana*)

yed mae—"fuck your mother"; an unspeakable obscenity

yentafo—noodles in a vinegary, bright-red soup stock

About the Author

Called by the *International Herald Tribune* "the most well-known expatriate Thai in the world," Somtow Sucharitkul (S. P. Somtow) is a composer, author, and media personality whose talents have entertained fans the world over.

Born in Thailand, Somtow grew up in several European countries and was educated at Eton and Cambridge. His first career was in music. In the 1970s, Somtow established himself as a prominent Southeast Asian avant-garde composer, causing considerable controversy in his native country as artistic director of the Asian Composers Expo 78. He founded the Thai Composers Association, and was the permanent representative of Thailand to the International Music Council of UNESCO.

A severe case of musical burnout caused Somtow to turn to writing in the early 1980s, and he soon produced a succession of over forty books in several genres under the pen name S. P. Somtow, winning numerous awards for such novels as *Vampire Junction* (Gollancz), today considered a classic of gothic literature and taught in "gothic lit" courses around the USA. His semi-autobiographical memoir *Jasmine Nights*, published by Hamish Hamilton, prompted George Axelrod, Oscar-winning writer of *Breakfast at Tiffany's*, to refer to him as "the J. D. Salinger of Siam."

Somtow has just finished a stint as president of the Horror Writers' Association. His most recent books are *Tagging the Moon*: *Fairy Tales of Los Angeles*, and *Dragon's Fin Soup*. His novels have been translated into about a dozen languages. He has also dabbled in filmmaking, directing a couple of low-budget films during his years in Los Angeles.

In the 1990s, Somtow began to turn back to music, rejecting his previous embrace of the musical fashions of the 60s and 70s and reinventing himself as a neo-Romantic composer. His recent works include the ballet "Kaki" and the "Mahajanaka Symphony" composed for the King of Thailand's 72nd birthday. In 1999, he was commissioned to compose what turned out to be the first opera by a Thai composer ever to be premiered, "Madana", inspired by a fairytale-like play written by King Rama VI of Siam and dedicated to his wife, Queen Indrasaksachi, who was also the composer's great-aunt.

S. P. Somtow lives in Bangkok and Los Angeles.

More Great Reading . . .

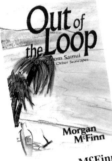

by Morgan McFinn

Ever Felt Like Cashing in Your Chips and Moving to a Tropical Island Paradise? Well, Our Man McFinn Did Just That . . . .

In dread of waking up one morning twenty years on, with nothing to show for himself "other than one busted marriage, two unpublished manuscripts, three career changes, a four-bedroom house, a five handicap at golf, and a six-figure income," McFinn decides to go on the bum and scratch his itch for authorship . . .

And so, slipping out of the Chicago Loop, our hero retreats to the idyllic tropical shores of Koh Samui, making his new home a rustic seaside bungalow. *Out of the Loop* chronicles McFinn's humorous adventures and misadventures as he ponders the world from his verandah, encountering assorted bums, bores, boors, and beautiful women (with varying degrees of romantic success and disaster) along the way.

From boxers, business tycoons, bargirls, and bodysnatchers to street vendors, slum-dwellers, socialites, and singers, *Bangkok People* takes the reader into the daily lives of city denizens— both Thai and expat, and from the filthy rich to the just plain filthy.

Penned by one of Thailand's best-known writers, this fascinating, funny, sometimes serious, and occasionally odd collection plunges right into the heart of the myriad masses who make this mad metropolis tick.

by James Eckardt

S. Tsow—linguist, theologian, philosopher, and sage-in-residence of the City of Angels—writes authoritatively and eloquently on the burning issues of our time: the scourge of cellphones, the escalating price of noodles, the inanity of political correctness, and the bad gramer and speling ov the yooth ov tooday . . . not to mention beer drinking, bad medicine, backpacking in the old days, and the boisterous bedlam of Bangkok.

S. Tsow is one of the most underrated writers in Bangkok today — and with good reason."
Fardley Nerdwell, literary critic.

by S. Tsow

"As his writing reveals, S. Tsow has managed to make the difficult transition from adolescence to senility without passing through an intervening stage of maturity."
Turk Grogan, philosopher.

by Roger Beaumont

Factually sweetened, slightly surreal, occasionally critical, but always biting and hilarious, these finely-crafted stories are guaranteed to make you laugh out loud. Take a trip inside for further enlightenment on life in Bangkok and life in general...

"A rich feast of humour . . . ambushing the reader with a full arsenal of language and irony."
- Christopher G. Moore, novelist.

"Roger Beaumont . . . takes delight at the absurd things in life and shares them with us in his unique style. A thoroughly entertaining read."
- Roger Crutchley, *Bangkok Post.*

. . . from ASIA BOOKS

The ASIA BOOKS Collection
Covering Thailand and Southeast Asia

FICTION

Kicking Dogs by Collin Piprell ISBN 974-8303-44-6

Bangkok Knights by Collin Piprell ISBN 974-8303-45-4

Yawn: A Thriller by Collin Piprell ISBN 974-8303-43-8

The Occidentals by Caron Eastgate James ISBN 974-8237-34-6

The Big Mango by Jake Needham ISBN 974-8237-36-2

Tea Money by Jake Needham ISBN 974-8303-46-2

Unusual Wealth by Gregory Bracken ISBN 974-8303-35-7

HUMOUR AND NON-FICTION

What's Your Name I'm Fine Thank You by Roger Beaumont ISBN 974-8237-11-7

Out of the Loop by Morgan McFinn ISBN 974-8303-40-3

Thai Lite by S. Tsow ISBN 974-8303-38-1

Mai Pen Rai Means Never Mind by Carol Hollinger ISBN 974-8303-35-7

The Year of Living Stupidly by James Eckardt ISBN 974-8303-48-9

Bangkok People by James Eckardt ISBN 974-8237-35-4

Off the Rails in Phnom Penh by Amit Gilboa ISBN 974-8303-34-9

The Ravens by Christopher Robbins ISBN 974-8303-41-1

Tragedy in Paradise by Charles Weldon MD ISBN 974-8237-38-9

Healthy Living in Thailand by The Thai Red Cross Society ISBN 974-8303-49-7

If you would like to order any of the above books, visit any Asia Books
store or other leading bookstores, or contact Asia Books'
customer service department on 02 715-9000 ext. 3202-3204